We hope you enjoy this book. Please return or renew it by the due date.

You can renew it at www.norfolk.gov.uk/libraries or by using our free library app.

Otherwise you can phone 0344 800 8020 - please have your library card and PIN ready.

You can sign up for email reminders too.

7/12/19		

D1350086

Also by Jodi Picoult

Songs of the Humpback Whale
Harvesting the Heart
Picture Perfect
Mercy
The Pact
Keeping Faith
Plain Truth
Salem Falls
Perfect Match
My Sister's Keeper
Vanishing Acts
The Tenth Circle
Nineteen Minutes
Change of Heart
Handle with Care
House Rules
Sing You Home
Lone Wolf
The Storyteller
Leaving Time
Small Great Things

Jodi Picoult and Samantha van Leer

Between the Lines
Off the Page

About the Author

Jodi Picoult is the author of twenty-four internationally bestselling novels, including *My Sister's Keeper*, *House Rules* and *Small Great Things*, and has also co-written two YA books with her daughter Samantha van Leer, *Between the Lines* and *Off the Page*. She lives in New Hampshire with her husband and children. Jodi's UK website is www.jodipicoult.co.uk and she can be found on Facebook and Twitter at facebook.com/JodiPicoultUK and @JodiPicoult.

SECOND GLANCE

Jodi Picoult

HODDER

First published in the United States of America in 2003 by Atria
A division of Simon & Schuster, Inc.
First published in Great Britain in 2005 by Hodder & Stoughton
An Hachette UK company

This paperback edition published in 2018

6

A CIP catalogue record for this title is available from the British Library

Paperback ISBN 978 1 444 75444 5

Typeset in Berkeley Book by Palimpsest Book Production Limited,
Falkirk, Stirlingshire

Printed and bound by
CPI Group (UK) Ltd, Croydon CR0 4YY

Hodder & Stoughton policy is to use papers that are natural, renewable
and recyclable products and made from wood grown in sustainable forests.
The logging and manufacturing processes are expected to conform to the
environmental regulations of the country of origin.

Hodder & Stoughton Ltd
Carmelite House
50 Victoria Embankment
London EC4Y 0DZ

www.hodder.co.uk

For Sammy, who is both a reader and a writer.
I love you to the moon and back.
XOXO, Mom

ACKNOWLEDGMENTS

Believing in ghosts is a bit like being pregnant – you either are, or you aren't, and there's no in between. So when I set out to create Ross Wakeman, I knew I needed to find people who not only believed, but could explain to me why. It was my good fortune to become acquainted with the Atlantic Paranormal Society – in particular, Jason Hawes and Grant Wilson, who took me out ghost hunting and convinced me that there is more to this world than meets the eye, and Andy Thompson, who explained what it's like to be a sensitive. What they taught me was so fascinating that I just may have to write another ghost story, if only so that I have a good reason to tag along again.

As promised: a nod to the Women Who Luv Books ladies who ardently helped me find my title: Lori Maurillo Thompson, Sherry Fritzsche, Sandy Langley, Joyce Doherty, Laurie Barrows, Connie Picker, Sara Reynolds, Nancy Martin, Claudia Kari, Pamela Leigh, Suzi Sabolis, Linda Shelby, Carol Pizzi, Diane Meyers, Karen Sokoloff, and MJ Marcks.

Thanks to my usual tribe of professionals: Dr Elizabeth Martin, Lisa Schiermeier, Dr David Toub, Dr Tia Horner, and two specialists – Dr Aidan Curran and Dr Daniel Collison; to my legal sources, Jennifer Sternick, Andrea Greene Goldman, Alan Williams, and Allegra Lubrano; and to my law enforcement guru, Detective-Lieutenant Frank Moran. Rhode Island State Police Detective Claire Demarais gets a special nod, for teaching me Forensics 101. Sindy Follensbee, thanks for transcribing so fast, and with a smile.

Rebecca Picoult translated French for me *très vite* and came to Mass MOCA with me; Jane Picoult, Steve Ives, and JoAnn Mapson all read drafts of this book and kept me from getting lazy. Aimee Mann put Ross's pain to music for me, and helped inspire me to translate it to fiction. To my agent, Laura Gross, I want to offer my gratitude for an entire decade of service, and hopefully a good thirty or forty years more. Thanks to Laura Mullen and Camille McDuffie, the matchmakers who take my books and find me an adoring public. And I'd like to thank everyone at Atria Books for falling in love with this book as much as I did – but I need to single out Judith Curr, Karen Mender, Sarah Branham, Shannon McKenna, Craig Herman, and Paolo Pepe. My editor at Atria, Emily Bestler, is not only incredibly gifted at making me write better than I think I can, she is also a good, true friend and the best person to have in one's corner.

And finally, thanks to Kyle, Jake, and Samantha, who share their mom's time with a lot of imaginary characters, and to my husband, Tim, who makes my life possible.

What if you slept?
And what if in your sleep, you dreamed?
And what if in your dream, you went to heaven
    and there plucked a strange and beautiful flower?
And what if, when you woke, you had the flower in your
    hand?
Ah! What then?

– Samuel Taylor Coleridge

Part One

2001

True love is like ghosts, which everybody talks about and few have seen.

– François, duc de la Rochefoucauld, Maxim 76

1

Ross Wakeman succeeded the first time he killed himself, but not the second or the third.

He fell asleep at the wheel and drove his car off a bridge into a lake – that was the second time – and was found on the shore by rescuers. When his half-sunken Honda was recovered, the doors were all locked, and the tempered glass windows were shattered like spider-webs, but still intact. No one could figure out how he'd gotten out of the car in the first place, much less survived a crash without even a scratch.

The third time, Ross was mugged in New York City. The thief took his wallet and beat him up, and then shot him in the back and left him for dead. The bullet – fired close enough to have shattered his scapula and punctured a lung – didn't. Instead it miraculously stopped at the bone, a small nugget of lead that Ross now used as a keychain.

The first time was years ago, when Ross had found himself in the middle of an electrical storm. The lightning, a beautiful blue charge, had staggered out of the sky and gone straight for his heart. The doctors told him that he had been legally dead for seven minutes. They reasoned that the current could not have struck Ross directly, because 50,000 amperes of current in his chest cavity would have boiled the moisture in his cells and quite literally made him explode. Instead, the lightning had hit nearby and created an induced current in his own body, one still strong enough to disturb his cardiac rhythm. The doctors said he was one hell of a lucky man.

They were wrong.

Now, as Ross walked up the pitched wet roof of the O'Donnells' Oswego home in the dark, he did not even bother with caution. The wind coming off Lake Ontario was cold even in August, and whipped his long hair into his eyes as he maneuvered around the gabled window. The rain bit at the back of his neck as he worked the clamps onto the flashing and positioned the waterproof video camera so that it was pointing into the attic.

His boots slipped, dislodging some of the old shingles. On the ground, beneath an umbrella, O'Donnell squinted up at him. 'Be careful,' the man called out. Ross also heard the words he did not say: *We've got enough ghosts.*

But nothing would happen to him. He would not trip; he wouldn't fall. It was why he volunteered for the riskiest tasks; why he put himself into danger again and again. It was why he'd tried bungee jumping and rock climbing and crack cocaine. He waved down to Mr O'Donnell, indicating that he'd heard. But just as Ross knew that in eight hours, the sun would come up – just as he knew that he'd have to go through the motions for another day – he also knew he couldn't die, in spite of the fact that it was what he wanted, more than anything.

The baby woke Spencer Pike, and he struggled to a sitting position. In spite of the nightlights kept in every room at the Shady Pines Nursing Home – nearly enough combined wattage, he imagined, to illuminate all of Burlington, Vermont – Spencer couldn't see past the foot of his bed. He couldn't see anything these days, thanks to the cataracts; although sometimes he'd get up to take a leak, and in the mirror, as he passed by, he would catch a glimpse of someone watching him – someone whose brow was not spotted and yellow; someone whose skin was not sighing off his bones. But then the young man Spencer had once been would disappear, leaving him to stare at the crumbs that were left of his life.

His ears, though, were sharp. Unlike the other sorry old morons in this place, Spencer had never needed a hearing aid. Hell, he heard things that he didn't even care to.

On cue, the baby cried again.

Spencer's hand scrabbled over the covers to the call button beside his bed. A moment later, the night nurse came in. 'Mr Pike,' she said. 'What's the matter?'

'The baby's crying.'

The nurse fussed behind him, turning pillows and raising the head of the bed. 'There are no babies here, Mr Pike, you know that. It was just a dream.' She patted the right angle that had once been his strong shoulder. 'Now, you need to go back to sleep. You've got a busy day tomorrow. A meeting, remember?'

Why, Spencer wondered, did she talk to him as if he were a child? And why did he react like one – sinking back beneath her gentle hands, letting her pull the covers up to his chest? A memory swelled at the base of Spencer's throat, something that he could not quite pull to the front of the fog but that brought tears to his eyes. 'Do you need some Naproxen?' the nurse asked kindly.

Spencer shook his head. He had been a scientist, after all. And no laboratory had yet crafted the drug that could ease this ache.

In person, Curtis Warburton was smaller than he seemed to be on television, but he lacked none of the magnetism that had made *Bogeyman Nights* the highest-rated show in its time slot. His black hair was shot, skunklike, with a white streak – one he'd possessed since a night nine years ago, when the ghost of his grandfather had appeared at the foot of his bed and led him into the field of paranormal investigation. His wife, Maylene, an elf of a woman whose psychic abilities were well known to the Los Angeles police, perched beside him, taking notes as Curtis posed questions to the owners of the house.

'First was the kitchen,' murmured Eve O'Donnell, and her husband nodded. A retired couple, they'd bought this home on the lake as a summer retreat, and in their three months of tenancy had experienced supernatural phenomena at least twice a week. 'About ten in the morning, I locked up all the doors, put on the alarm system, and went to the post office. When I came home, the alarm was still on . . . but inside, the kitchen cabinets were open, and every cereal box was on the table, spilled on its side. I called Harlan, thinking he'd come home and left behind a mess.'

'I was at the Elks Club the whole time,' her husband interjected. 'Never came home. No one did.'

'And there's the calliope music we heard coming from the attic at two in the morning. The minute we went upstairs, it stopped. Open the door to find a child's toy piano, missing its batteries, sitting in the middle of the floor.'

'We don't own a toy piano,' Harlan added. 'Much less a child.'

'And when we put in the batteries, it didn't even play that kind of music.' Eve hesitated. 'Mr Warburton, I hope you understand that we're not the kind of people who . . . who believe in this sort of thing. It's just . . . it's just that if it's not *this,* then I'm losing my mind.'

'Mrs O'Donnell, you're not going crazy.' Curtis touched her hand with trademark sympathy. 'By tomorrow morning we'll have a better idea of what's going on in your home.' He looked over his shoulder to make sure Ross was getting this on camera. Depending on what happened later, the O'Donnells might find themselves featured on *Bogeyman Nights,* and if so, this footage was critical. The Warburtons received over three hundred e-mails a day from people who believed their houses were haunted. Eighty-five percent of the claims turned out to be hoaxes or mice in the rafters. The rest – well, Ross had been working with them long enough to know that there were some things that simply could not be explained.

'Have you experienced any spectral visions?' Curtis asked. 'Temperature changes?'

'Our bedroom will be hot as hell one minute, and then we'll be shivering the next,' Harlan answered.

'Are there any spots in the house in particular where you feel uncomfortable?'

'The attic, definitely. The upstairs bathroom.'

Curtis's eyes swept from the hand-knotted Oriental rug to the antique vase on the mantel of the fireplace. 'I have to warn you that finding a ghost can be a costly proposition.'

As the Warburtons' field researcher, Ross had been sent to libraries and newspaper archives to locate documents about the property – and hopefully the bonus information that a murder or a suicide might have occurred there. His inquiry had turned up nothing, but that never stopped Curtis. After all, a ghost could haunt a person as well as a place. History could hover, like a faint perfume or a memory stamped on the back of one's eyelids.

'Whatever it takes,' Eve O'Donnell said. 'This isn't about money.'

'Of course not.' Curtis smiled and slapped his palms on his knees. 'Well, then. We've got some work to do.'

That was Ross's cue. During the investigation, he was responsible for setting up and monitoring the electromagnetic equipment, the digital video cameras, the infrared thermometer. He worked for minimum wage, in spite of the money that came in from the TV show and from cases like this one. Ross had begged the Warburtons for a job nine months ago after reading about them in the *L.A. Times* on Halloween. Unlike Curtis and Maylene, he had never seen a spirit – but he wanted to, badly. He was hoping that sensitivity to ghosts might be something you could catch from close contact, like chicken pox – and, like chicken pox, might be something that would mark you forever.

'I thought I'd check the attic,' Ross said.

He stood in the doorway for a moment, waiting for Eve O'Donnell to lead the way upstairs. 'I feel foolish,' she confided, although Ross had not asked. 'At my age, seeing Casper.'

Ross smiled. 'A ghost can shake you up a little, and make you think you're nuts, but it's not going to hurt you.'

'Oh, I don't think she'd hurt me.'

'She?'

Eve hesitated. 'Harlan said I shouldn't volunteer any information. That way if you see what we do, then we'd know.' She shivered, glanced up the narrow stairs. 'My little sister died when I was seven. Sometimes I wonder . . . can a ghost find you, if she wants to?'

Ross looked away. 'I don't know,' he said, wishing he could have offered her more – a concrete answer, a personal experience. His eyes lit on the small door at the top of the stairs. 'Is that it?'

She nodded, letting him pass in front of her to unlatch it. The video camera Ross had mounted outside watched them from the window, a cyclops. Eve hugged herself tightly. 'Being here gives me the chills.'

Ross moved some boxes, so that no shadows would be caught on tape that could be explained away. 'Curtis says that's how you know where to find them. You go with what your senses are telling you.' A wink on the floor caught his eye; kneeling, he picked up a handful of pennies. 'Six cents.' He smiled. 'Ironic.'

'She does that sometimes.' Eve was edging toward the door, her arms wrapped around herself. 'Leaves us change.'

'The ghost?' Ross asked, turning, but Eve had already fled down the stairs.

Taking a deep breath, he closed the door to the attic and shut the light, plunging the small room into blackness. He stepped off to the side where he would not be in range of the video camera, and activated it with a remote control. Then he fixed his attention on the darkness around him, letting it press in at his chest and the backs of his knees, as Curtis Warburton had taught him. Ross cracked open his senses until the lip of disbelief thinned, until the space around him bloomed. *Maybe this is it,* he thought. *Maybe the coming of ghosts feels like a sob at the back of your throat.*

Somewhere off to the left was the sound of a footfall, and the unmistakable chime of coins striking the floor. Switching on a flashlight, Ross swung the beam until it illuminated his boot, and the three new pennies beside it. 'Aimee?' he whispered to the empty air. 'Is that you?'

Comtosook, Vermont, was a town marked by boundaries: the dip where it slipped into Lake Champlain, the cliffs that bordered the granite quarry where half the residents worked, the invisible demarcation where the rolling Vermont countryside became, with one more step, the city of Burlington. On the Congregational church in the center of town hung a plaque from *Vermont Life* magazine, dated 1994, the year that Comtosook was lauded as the most picture-perfect hamlet in the state. And it was – there were days Eli Rochert looked at the leaves turning, rubies and amber and emeralds, and he simply had to stop for a moment and catch his breath.

But whatever Comtosook was to tourists, it was Eli's home. It had been, forever. He imagined it always would be. Of course, as one of the two full-time police officers in the town, he understood that what the tourists saw was an illusion. Eli had learned long ago that you can stare right at something and not see what lies beneath the surface.

He drove along Cemetery Road, his usual patrol haunt on nights such as this, when the moon was as beaded and yellow as a hawk's eye. Although the windows were rolled down, there wasn't much of a breeze; and Eli's short black hair was damp at the nape of his neck. Even Watson, his bloodhound, was panting in the seat beside him.

Old headstones listed like tired foot soldiers. In the left corner of the cemetery, near the beech tree, was Comtosook's oddest gravestone. WINNIE SPARKS, it read. BORN 1835. DIED 1901. DIED 1911. Legend had it that the irritable old woman's funeral procession had been en route to the cemetery when the horses reared and her coffin fell out of the wagon. As it popped open, Winnie sat up and climbed out, spitting mad. Ten years later when she died – again – her long-suffering husband hammered 150 nails to seal the lid of the coffin, just as a precaution.

Whether it was true or not didn't much matter to Eli. But the local teens seemed to think that Winnie's inability to stay dead was good enough reason to bring six-packs and pot to the cemetery. Eli unfolded his long body from the truck. 'You coming?' he said to the dog, which flopped down on the seat in response. Shaking his head, Eli slipped through the cemetery until he reached Winnie's grave, where four kids too wasted to hear his footsteps were huddled around the blue-fingered flame of a Sterno burner.

'Boo,' Eli said flatly.

'It's the cops!'

'Damn!' There was a scuffle of sneakers, the ping of bottles clinking together as the teens scrambled to get away. Eli could have had them at any moment, of course; he chose to let them off this time. He turned the beam of his flashlight onto the last of the retreating figures, then swung it down toward the mess. They left behind a faint cloud of sweet smoke and two perfectly good unopened bottles of Rolling Rock that Eli could make use of when he went off duty.

Bending down, he pulled a dandelion from the base of Winnie's headstone. As if the motion had dislodged it, a word rolled into his mind: *chibaiak* . . . ghosts. His grandmother's language, which burned on Eli's tongue like a peppermint. 'No such thing,' he said aloud, and walked back to the car to see what else this night might hold in store.

Shelby Wakeman had awakened exhausted after a full day's sleep. She'd been having that dream again, the one where Ethan was standing beside her in an airport, and then she turned around to find that he'd disappeared. Frantic, she'd run from terminal to terminal looking for him, until at last she flew out a door onto the tarmac and found her nine-year-old standing in the path of an incoming jet.

It terrified her, no matter how often Shelby told herself that this would never happen – she'd never be in an airport with Ethan in the middle of the day, much less lose sight of him. But what frightened her most was that image of her son standing with his arms outstretched, his buttermilk face lifted up to the sun.

'Earth to Mom . . . *hello?*'

'Sorry.' Shelby smiled. 'Just daydreaming.'

Ethan finished rinsing his plate and setting it into the dishwasher. 'Do you think it's still daydreaming if you do it at night?' Before she could answer, he grabbed his skateboard, as much an appendage as any of his limbs. 'Meet you out there?'

She nodded, and watched Ethan explode into the front yard. No matter how many times she told him to be quiet – at 4 A.M., most people were asleep, not racing around on skateboards – Ethan usually forgot, and Shelby usually didn't have the heart to remind him.

Ethan had XP, xeroderma pigmentosum, an incredibly rare inherited disease that left him extremely sensitive to the sun's ultraviolet rays. In the world, there were only a thousand known cases of XP. If you had it, you had it from birth, and you had it forever.

Shelby had first noticed something was wrong when Ethan was six weeks old, but it took a year of testing before he was diagnosed with XP. Ultraviolet light, the doctors explained, causes damage to human DNA. Most people can automatically repair that damage . . . but XP patients can't. Eventually the damage affects cell division, which leads to cancer. Ethan, they said, *might* live to reach his teens.

But Shelby figured if sunlight was going to kill her son, all she needed to do was to make it infinitely dark. She stayed in days. She read Ethan bedtime books by candlelight. She covered the windows of her house with towels and curtains that her husband would rip down every night when he came home from work. 'No one,' he'd said, 'is allergic to the goddamned sun.'

By the time they were divorced, Shelby had learned about light. She knew that there was more to fear than just the outdoors. Grocery stores and doctors' offices had fluorescent fixtures, which were ultraviolet. Sunblock became as common as hand cream, applied inside the house as well as out. Ethan had twenty-two hats, and he donned them with the same casual routine that other children put on their underwear.

Tonight he was wearing one that said I'M WITH STUPID. The brim was curled tight as a snail, a shape Ethan cultivated by hooking the lip of the hat beneath the adjustable band in the back. When Shelby saw the caps being stored that way, she thought of swans tucking their heads beneath a wing; of the tiny bound feet of the Chinese.

She finished cleaning up the kitchen and then settled herself with a book on the edge of the driveway. Her long, dark hair was braided into submission, thick as a fist, and she was *still* hot – how on earth could Ethan race around like that? He ran his skateboard up a homemade wooden ramp and did an Ollie kickflip. 'Mom! Mom? Did you see that? It was just like Tony Hawk.'

'I know it,' Shelby agreed.

'So don't you think that it would be totally sweet if we—'

'We are not going to build a half-pipe in the driveway, Ethan.'

'But—'

'Jeez. What*ever*.' And he was gone again in a rumble of wheels.

Inside, Shelby smiled. She loved the attitude that seemed to be creeping into Ethan's personality, like a puppeteer throwing words into his mouth. She loved the way he turned on *Late Night with Conan O'Brien* when he thought she was somewhere else in the house, to try to catch all the innuendoes. It made him . . . well, so *normal*. If not for the fact that the moon was riding shotgun overhead, and that Ethan's face was so pale the veins beneath his skin glowed like roads she knew by heart – if not for these small things, Shelby could almost believe her world was just like any other single mother's.

Ethan executed a shifty pivot, and then a Casper big spin. There was a time, Shelby realized, when she couldn't have distinguished a helipop from a G-turn. There was also a time Shelby would have looked at Ethan and herself and felt pity. But Shelby could hardly remember what her existence had been like before this illness was flung over them like a fishing net; and truth be told, any life she'd lived before Ethan could not have been much of a life at all.

He skidded to a stop in front of her. 'I'm starving.'

'You just ate!'

Ethan blinked at her, as if that were any kind of excuse. Shelby sighed. 'You can go in and have a snack if you want, but it's looking pink already.'

Ethan turned toward the sunrise, a claw hooked over the horizon. 'Let me watch from out here,' he begged. 'Just once.'

'Ethan—'

'I know.' His voice dipped down at the edges. 'Three more hardflips.'

'One.'

'Two.' Without waiting for agreement – she would concede, and they both knew it – Ethan sped off again. Shelby cracked open her novel, the words registering like cars on a freight train – a stream without any individual characteristics. She had just turned the page when she realized Ethan's skateboard was no longer moving.

He held it balanced against his leg, the graphic of the superhero Wolverine spotted white. 'Mom?' he asked. 'Is it *snowing*?'

It did, quite often, in Vermont. But not in August. A white swirl tipped toward her book and caught in the wedge of the spine; but it was not a snowflake after all. She lifted the petal to her nose, and sniffed. Roses.

Shelby had heard of strange weather patterns that caused frogs to evaporate and rain down over the seas; she'd once seen a hail-storm of locusts. But this . . . ?

The petals continued to fall, catching in her hair and Ethan's. 'Weird,' he breathed, and he sat down beside Shelby to witness a freak of nature.

'Pennies.' Curtis Warburton turned over the coin Ross had handed him. 'Anything else?'

Ross shook his head. It had been three hours, and even with a raging storm outside providing a well of energy, the paranormal activity had been minimal at best. 'I thought I saw a globule on the screen at one point, but it turned out to be a smoke alarm hung in the back of the attic.'

'Well, I haven't felt a damn thing,' Curtis sighed. 'We should have taken the case in Buffalo instead.'

Ross snapped some used film back into its canister and tucked it into his pocket. 'The wife, Eve? She mentioned a little sister who died when she was seven.'

Curtis looked at him. 'Interesting.'

The two men walked downstairs. Maylene sat on the living room couch in the dark with an infrared thermometer 'You get anything?' Curtis asked.

'No. This house is about as active as a quadriplegic.'

'How is it going?' Eve O'Donnell interrupted. She stood at the doorway of the living room, her hand clutching the collar of her robe.

'I think it's safe to say that you're not alone in this house. In fact,' Curtis held out the penny Ross had given him, 'I just found this.'

'Yes . . . sometimes there are coins lying around. I told Ross that.'

'Did you?'

Ross turned, frowning. But before he could ask Curtis why he was playing dumb, his boss started speaking again. 'Ghosts can be mischievous that way. Especially the ghost of a child, for example.'

Ross felt the charge of the air as Eve O'Donnell laid her trust at Curtis's feet. 'I have to tell you,' Curtis said. 'I'm getting some very strong sensations here. There's a presence, but it's someone you know, someone who knows you.' Curtis tipped his head to one side and furrowed his brow. 'It's a girl . . . I'm getting the sense it's a girl, and I'm feeling a number . . . *seven*. Did you by any chance have a younger sister who passed?'

Ross found himself rooted to the floor. He had been trained to consider the fact that 85 percent of the cases they investigated were hoaxes perpetrated by people who either wanted to waste their time, or get on national TV, or prove that paranormal investigation was anything but a science. He couldn't count how many times they'd found a speaker hidden in the moaning wall; fishing line wrapped around a quaking chandelier. But he'd never considered that the Warburtons might be putting on a show, too.

'It would be an additional charge, of course,' Curtis was saying, 'but I wouldn't rule out holding a séance.'

Ross's head throbbed. 'Curtis, could I speak to you privately?'

They put on their coats and went out, standing under the overhang of the garage as the rain poured down. 'This better be good,' Curtis said. 'You interrupted me as I was hooking her.'

'You don't think there's a ghost here. The only reason you know about her sister is because I told you.'

Curtis lit a cigarette; the tip glowed like a slitted eye. 'So?'

'So . . . you can't lie to that woman just to make a few bucks and get her reaction on camera.'

'All I'm doing is telling the O'Donnells what they want to hear. These people believe there's a ghost in this house. They *want* to believe there's a ghost in this house. Even if we're not getting much activity tonight, that doesn't mean a spirit isn't laying low with visitors around.'

'This isn't just a ghost,' Ross said, his voice shaking. 'This was *someone* to her.'

'I didn't peg you for such a purist. I figured after all these months, you'd know the routine.'

Ross did not consider himself to be particularly gullible. He'd seen and done enough in his life to always be on the lookout for what was real, because he so often felt like he *wasn't*. 'I know the routine. I just didn't know it was all fake.'

Curtis whipped the cigarette to the ground. 'I'm not a fake. The ghost of my grandfather appeared to me, Ross. I took a goddamned *photo* of him standing at the foot of my bed. You draw your own conclusions. Hell, remember that shot you got of a face rising out of the lake? You think I set that up? I wasn't even in the same state you were in at the time.' Curtis took a deep breath, calming himself. 'Look, I'm not taking the O'Donnells for a ride. I'm a businessman, Ross, and I know my clients.'

Ross couldn't answer. For all he knew, Curtis had managed to slip the penny he'd found beneath the tripod, too. For all he knew, the past nine months of his life had been wasted. He was no better than the O'Donnells – he'd seen only what he wanted to believe.

Maybe she *was* psychic, because at that moment Maylene stepped outside. 'Curtis? What's going on?'

'It's Ross. He's trying to decide what road to take home – I-81, or the Moral High Ground.'

Ross stepped into the driving rain and started walking. Let them think what they wanted; they'd certainly encouraged Ross to do the same. He didn't bother to return for his digital camera or his knapsack; these were things he could replace, unlike his composure, which he was fast in danger of losing. In his car he turned the heater on full blast, trying to get rid of the chill that wouldn't let go. He drove a mile before he realized that his headlights weren't on. Then he pulled off to the side of the road and took great, gulping breaths, trying to start his heart again.

Ross knew how to scientifically record paranormal phenomena and how to interpret the results. He had filmed lights zipping over graveyards; he had taped voices in empty basements; he had felt cold in spots where there could be no draft. For nine months, Ross had thought he'd found an entrance to the world where Aimee was . . . and it turned out to be a painted door drawn on a wall.

Damn it, he was running out of ideas.

Az Thompson awoke with his mouth full of stones, small and smooth as olive pits. He spat fifteen into the corrugated leather of his palm before he trusted himself to breathe without choking. He swung his legs over the side of the army cot. He tried to shake the certainty that if buried in the packed earth beneath his bare feet, these rocks would grow into some cancerous black thicket, like the ones covering the castle in that White Man's fairy tale about a girl who couldn't wake up without being kissed.

He didn't mind camping out; for as long as he could remember he'd had one foot in nature and one foot in the *yanqui* world. Az stuck his head out the flap of the tent, where some of the others had already gathered for breakfast. Their signs – placards to be worn around the neck, and picket posters tacked onto wood – lay in a heap like ventriloquist's dummies, harmless without some spirit behind them. 'Haw,' he grunted, and walked toward the small campfire, knowing that a space would be made for him.

The others treated him the way they would if Abe Lincoln got up and walked out of that tent – with humility, and no small amount of awe, to find him alive after all this time. Az wasn't as old as Abe, but he wasn't off by much. He was 102 or 103 – he'd stopped counting a while ago. Because he knew the dying language of his people, he was respected as a teacher. Still, his age alone made him a tribal elder, which would have been something, had the Abenaki been a federally recognized tribe.

Az heard the creak of every joint in his spine as he settled himself on a folding chair. He grabbed a pair of binoculars from beside the fire pit and peered at the land, a parcel located at the northwesterly intersection of Montgomery Road and Otter Creek Pass. At its crest sat the big white house, now an eyesore. It would be the first thing to go, Az knew, just like he knew everything about this property, from the surveyor's measurements to the recorded number of the deed plan. He knew the spots where the ground froze first in the winter and the section where no vegetation ever managed to grow. He knew which window in the abandoned house had been broken by kids running wild; which side of the porch had fallen first; which floorboards on the stairs were rotted through.

He also knew the license plate numbers of every vehicle the Redhook Group had parked on the perimeter. Rumor had it that Newton Redhook wanted to build himself Comtosook's first strip mall. On one of *their* burial sites.

'I'm telling you,' said Fat Charlie, 'it's El Niño.'

Winks shook his head. 'It's screwed up, is what it is. Ain't normal to rain roses. That's like a clock running backward, or well water turning to blood.'

Fat Charlie laughed. 'Winks, you gotta switch back to Letterman. Those horror flicks are getting to you, man.'

Az looked around, noticing the light dusting of flower petals all over the ground. He rolled his tongue across the cavern of his mouth, tasting those stones again. 'What do you think, Az?' Winks asked.

What he thought was that trying to explain rose petals falling from the sky was not only useless, but also futile, since the things that were going to happen had already been set into motion. What he thought was that rose petals were going to be the least of their problems. Az focused the binoculars on a bulldozer chugging slowly up the road. 'I think you can't dig in the ground,' he said aloud, 'without unearthing something.'

*   *   *

This was how Ross had met Aimee: On the corner of Broadway and 112th, in the shadow of Columbia University, he had liter-ally run into her, knocking all of her books into a murky brown puddle. She was a medical student studying for her anatomy final, and she nearly started hyperventilating at the sight of all her hard work being ruined. Sitting in the middle of the street in New York, she was also the most beautiful woman Ross had ever seen. 'I'll help you,' Ross promised, although he didn't know a fibula from a phalanx. 'Just give me a second chance.'

This was how Ross proposed to Aimee: A year later he paid a cab driver to take them past Broadway and 112th en route to dinner at a restaurant. As instructed, the man pulled to the curb, and Ross opened the door and got down on one knee on the filthy pavement. He popped open the small ring box and stared into her electric eyes. 'Marry me,' he said, and then he lost his balance and the diamond fell down a sewer grate.

Aimee's mouth fell open. 'Tell me,' she managed finally, 'that didn't just happen.'

Ross looked down the black grate, and at the empty box. He tossed it into the sewer, too. Then he pulled another ring, the real ring, from his pocket. 'Give me a second chance,' he said.

Now, in a deserted parking lot, he tipped the bottle up to drink. Sometimes Ross wanted to scratch himself out of his skin, to see what was on the other side. He wanted to jump off bridges into seas of concrete. He wanted to scream until his throat bled; to run until his soles split open. At times like this, when failure was a tidal wave, his life became a finite line – the end of which, through some cosmic joke, he could not seem to reach.

Ross contemplated suicide the way some people made out shopping lists – methodically, with great attention given to detail. There were days when he was fine. And then there were other days when he took census counts of people who seemed happy, and those who seemed in pain. There were days when it made perfect sense to drink boiling water, or suffocate in the refrigerator, or walk naked into the snow until he simply lay down to sleep.

Ross had read of suicides, fascinated by the creativity – women who looped their long hair around their own necks to form a rope, men who mainlined mayonnaise, teenagers who swallowed firecrackers. But every time he came close to testing a beam for the weight it would hold, or drew a bead of blood with an X-Acto knife, he would think of the mess he'd leave behind.

He didn't know what death held in store for him. But he knew that it wouldn't be life, and that was good enough. He had not felt anything since the day Aimee had died. The day when, like an idiot, he had chosen to play the hero, first dragging his fiancée from the wreckage and then going back to rescue the driver of the other car moments before it burst into flames. By the time he'd returned to Aimee, she was already gone. She'd died, alone, while he was off being Superman.

Some hero he had turned out to be, saving the wrong person.

He threw the empty bottle onto the floor of his Jeep and put the car into gear, tearing out of the parking lot like a teenager. There were no cops around – there never were, when you needed them – and Ross accelerated, until he was doing more than eighty down the single-lane divided highway.

He came to a stop at the railroad bridge, where the warning gate flashed as its arms lowered, slow as a ballerina. He emptied his mind of everything except inching his car forward until it broke the gate, until the Jeep sat as firm on the tracks as a sacrifice.

The train pounded. The tracks began to sing a steel symphony. Ross gave himself up to dying, catching a single word between his teeth before impact: *Finally*.

The sound was awesome, deafening. And yet it moved past him, growing Doppler-distant, until Ross raised the courage to open his eyes.

His car was smoking from the hood, but still running. It hobbled unevenly, as if one tire was low on air. And it was pointed in the opposite direction, heading back from where he'd come.

There was nothing for it: with tears in his eyes, Ross started to drive.

Rod van Vleet wasn't going home without a signed contract. In the first place, Newton Redhook had left him responsible for securing the nineteen acres that comprised the Pike property. In the second place, it had taken over six hours to get to this nursing home in Nowhere, Vermont, and Rod had no plans to return here in the immediate future.

'Mr Pike,' he said, smiling at the old man, who was plug-ugly enough to give Rod nightmares for a week. Hell, if Rod himself looked like that by age ninety-five, he was all for someone giving him a morphine nightcap and a bed six feet under. Spencer Pike's bald head was as spotted as a cantaloupe; his hands were twisted into knots; his body seemed to have taken up permanent position as a human comma. 'As you can see here, the Redhook Group is prepared to put into escrow today a check made out to you for fifty thousand dollars, as a token of good faith pending the title search.'

The old man narrowed a milky eye. 'What the hell do I care about money?'

'Well. Maybe you could take a vacation. You and a nurse.' Rod smiled at the woman standing behind Pike, her arms crossed.

'Can't travel. Doctor's orders. Liver could just . . . give out.'

Rod smiled uncomfortably, thinking that an alcoholic who'd survived nearly a hundred years should just get on a plane to Fiji and the hell with the consequences. 'Well.'

'You already said that. You senile?'

'No, sir.' Rod cleared his throat. 'I understand this land was in your wife's family for several generations?'

'Yes.'

'It's our belief, Mr Pike, that the Redhook Group can contribute to the growth of Comtosook by developing your acreage in a way that boosts the town economy.'

'You want to build stores there.'

'Yes, sir, we do.'

'You gonna build a bagel shop?'

Rod blinked, nonplussed. 'I don't believe Mr Redhook knows yet.'

'Build it. I like bagels.'

Rod pushed the check across the table again, this time with the contract. 'I won't be able to build anything, Mr Pike, until I get your signature here.'

Pike stared at him for a long moment, then reached out for a pen. Rod let out the breath he'd been holding. 'The title is in your wife's name? Cecelia Pike?'

'It was Cissy's.'

'And this . . . claim the Abenaki are championing . . . is there any validity to that?'

Pike's knuckles went white from the pressure. 'There's no Indian burial ground on that property.' He glanced up at Rod. 'I don't like you.'

'I'm getting that sense, sir.'

'The only reason I'm going to sign this is because I'd rather give that land up than watch it go to the State.'

Rod rolled up the signed contract and rapped it against the table. 'Well!' he said again, and Pike raised one eyebrow. 'We'll be doing our due diligence, and hopefully we'll finish this deal as soon as we can.'

'Before I die, you mean,' Pike said dryly as Rod shrugged into his coat. 'You don't want to stay for Charades? Or lunch . . . I hear we're having orange Jell-O.' He laughed, the sound like a saw at Rod's back. 'Mr van Vleet . . . what will you do with the house?'

Rod knew this was a touchy subject; it always was for the Redhook Group, which usually razed whatever existing properties existed on the land before building their own modern commercial facilities. 'It's actually not in the best shape,' Rod said carefully. 'We may have to . . . make some adjustments. More room, you know, for your pizza place.'

'Bagels.' Pike frowned. 'So you're going to tear it down.'

'Unfortunately, yes.'

'Better that way,' the old man said. 'Too many ghosts.'

The only gas station in Comtosook was attached to the general store. Two pumps from the 1950s sat in the parking lot, and it took Rod a good five minutes to realize there simply *was* no credit card slot. He stuck the nozzle of the pump into his gas tank and pulled out his cell phone, hitting a preprogrammed number. 'Angel Quarry,' answered a female voice.

Rod held the phone away from his ear and cut off the call. He must have dialed wrong; he had been trying to reach the home office to let Newton Redhook know the first hurdle had been cleared. Frowning, he punched the buttons on the keypad again.

'Angel Quarry. May I help you?'

Rod shook his head. 'I'm trying to reach 617-569—'

'Well, you got the wrong number.' *Click.*

Flummoxed, he stuffed the phone in his pocket and squeezed another gallon into his tank. Reaching for his wallet, he started toward the store to pay.

A middle-aged man with carrot-red hair stood on the porch, sweeping what seemed to be rose petals from the floorboards. Rod glanced up at the sign on the building – ABE'S GAS & GROCERY – and then back at the shopkeeper. 'You must be Abe?'

'You guessed that right.'

'Is there a pay phone around here?'

Abe pointed to the corner of the porch, where a phone booth tilted against the railing, right beside an old drunk who seemed disinclined to move aside. Rod dialed his calling card number, feeling the shopkeeper's eyes on him the whole time. 'Angel Quarry,' he heard, a moment later.

He slammed down the receiver and stared at it. Abe swept once, twice, three times, clearing a path between Rod and himself. 'Problem?' he asked.

'Must be something screwed up in the phone lines.' Rod dug a twenty out of his wallet for the gas.

'Must be. Or maybe what those Indians are saying's true – that if they don't get their land back, the whole town'll be cursed.'

Rod rolled his eyes. He was halfway back to the car by the time he recalled Spencer Pike's comment about ghosts. He turned around to ask Abe about that, but the man was gone. His broom rested against the splintered porch rail; with each breeze, the neat pile of flower petals scattered like wishes.

Suddenly a car pulled up on the opposite side of the gas pumps. A man with shoulder-length brown hair and unsettling sea green eyes stepped out and stretched until his back popped. 'Excuse me,' he asked, 'do you know the way to Shelby Wakeman's house?'

Rod shook his head. 'I'm not from around here.'

He didn't know what made him look in the rearview mirror after he got into the car. The man was still standing there, as if he did not understand what should happen next. Suddenly Rod's cell phone began to ring. He dug in his breast pocket, flipped it open. 'Van Vleet.'

'Angel Quarry,' said the woman at the other end, as if he'd been the one to call; as if that made any sense at all.

'Yeah, I'm coming,' Shelby muttered, as the raps on her front door grew louder. It was only 11 A.M. If this moron woke Ethan . . . She knotted her hair into a ponytail holder, tugged her pajamas to rights, and squinted against the sun as she opened the door. For a moment, backlit by the daylight, she didn't recognize him.

'Shel?'

It had been two years since she'd seen Ross. They still looked alike – the same rangy build, the same intense pale gaze that people found it hard to break away from. But Ross had lost weight and let his hair grow long. And oh, the circles under his eyes – they were even darker than her own.

'I woke you up,' he apologized. 'I could . . .'

'Come here,' Shelby finished, and she folded her baby brother into an embrace.

'Go back to sleep,' Ross urged, after Shelby had spent the better part of an hour fussing over him. 'Ethan's going to need you.'

'Ethan's going to need *you*,' Shelby corrected. 'Once he finds out you're here, you might as well forget about getting any rest.' She set a stack of towels on the end of the guest room bed and hugged him. 'It goes without saying that you stay as long as you like.' He buried his face in the curve of her shoulder and closed his eyes. Shelby smelled like his childhood.

Suddenly she drew back. 'Oh, Ross,' she murmured, and slipped her hand beneath the collar of his shirt, pulling out the long chain that he kept hidden underneath. At the end hung a diamond solitaire, a falling star. Shelby's fist closed around it.

Ross jerked away, and the chain snapped. He grabbed Shelby's wrist and shook until she let go of the ring, until it was safe in his hand. 'Don't,' he warned, setting his jaw.

'It's been—'

'Don't you think I know how long it's been? Don't you think I know *exactly*?' Ross turned away. Why was it no one spoke of how kindness can cut just as clean as a knife?

When Shelby touched his arm, Ross didn't respond. She didn't force the issue. Just that one small contact, and then she backed her way out of the room.

Shelby was right – he ought to sleep – but he also knew that wouldn't happen. Ross had grown used to insomnia; for years it had crawled under the covers with him, pressed the length of his body with just enough restless indecision to keep him watching the digital display of a clock until the numbers justified getting out of bed.

He lay down on the bed and stared at the ceiling. He held the ring so tightly in his hand that he could feel the prongs of the setting cutting into his skin. He would have to get something – string, a leather cord – so that he could wear it again. Wide awake, he focused his attention on the clock. He watched the numbers bleed into each other: 12:04; 12:05; 12:06. He counted the roses on the comforter cover. He tried to remember the words to 'Waltzing Matilda.'

When he startled awake at 5:58, Ross could not believe it. He blinked, feeling better than he had in months. He swung his feet over the side of the bed and stood up, wondering if Shelby might have a spare toothbrush.

It was the absence of the slight weight against his chest that reminded him of the ring. Ross opened his fist and panicked. The diamond he'd fallen asleep clutching was nowhere in sight – not under the covers, not on the carpet, not even behind the bed, which Ross moved with frantic haste. *I've lost her,* Ross thought, staring blankly at what he'd awakened holding instead: a 1932 penny – smooth as a secret; still warm from the heat of his hand.

2

For an eight-year-old, Lucy Oliver knew quite a lot. She could list all the state capitals; she could explain how a thundercloud formed; she could spell *RHYTHM* forward *and* backward. She knew other things too, more important, non-school things. For example, she knew that her great-grandma had come home from the doctor a month ago with little white pills that she hid in the toe of an orthopedic sneaker in her closet. She knew that when grown-ups lowered their voices it meant you had to listen harder. She knew that even the smartest person in the world could be scared by what he or she didn't understand.

Lucy also knew, with staunch conviction, that it was only a matter of time before one of *them* got her.

They changed form, from night to night. Sometimes they were the shifting shape of the patterns on her curtains. Sometimes they were the cold spot on the floor as Lucy raced across the wide wooden boards into bed. Sometimes they were a smell that made Lucy dream of leaves and dark and carcasses.

Tonight she was pretending that she was a turtle. Nothing could get into that hard shell; nothing at all. Not even the thing she was certain was breathing at this very second inside her closet. But even with her eyes wide open, Lucy could see the night changing. In some spots it got more pointed; in others it drew back . . . until she was staring into the see-through face of a woman so sad it made Lucy's stomach hurt.

I will find you, the lady said, right inside Lucy's own head.

She stifled a scream, because that would wake up her great-grandmother, and whipped the covers over her head. Her thin chest pumped like a piston; her breathing went damp. If this woman *could* find her, anywhere, then where would Lucy hide? Would her mother know she'd been snatched, just by the dent Lucy's body left behind on the mattress?

She snaked one hand out far enough to grab the phone she'd placed on her nightstand and stamped the button that automatically dialed her mother's lab. Lucy imagined an invisible line connecting her from this phone to the one her mother was holding, a wireless umbilicus, and was so grateful for the picture in her head that she couldn't squeeze any words around it.

'Oh, Lucy,' her mother sighed into the silence. 'What's the matter now?'

'It's the air,' Lucy whispered, hating her voice. It came out tiny and frantic, like the scramble of mice. 'It's too heavy.'

'Did you take your inhaler?'

Lucy had. She was old enough to know what to do when her asthma flared. But it wasn't *that* kind of heavy. 'It's going to crush me.' There, it had gotten even worse. Lucy lay down beneath the weight of the night, trying to breathe in small puffs, so that the oxygen in the room would last longer.

'Honey.' Her mother spoke in a tone that made Lucy think of cold glass vials and mile-long white countertops. 'You know air can't change its weight, not inside your bedroom. This is all your imagination.'

'But . . .' Lucy hunched away from the closet, because she could feel the lady watching. 'Mom, I'm not making it up.'

There was a beat that lasted the exact amount of time it took her mother to lose her temper. 'Lucy. There are no such things as ghosts, or goblins, or demons, or . . . or air-crushing invisible beasts. *Go to bed.*'

Lucy held the receiver after the line went dead. When the metallic voice of the operator came on, asking her to hang up if she wanted to make another call, she buried the phone beneath her pillow. Her mother was right; she knew on some rational plane that nothing in her room was out to get her; that monsters didn't hide in closets or under beds, that crying ladies didn't appear out of nowhere. If the air was becoming as thick as pea soup, there was a perfectly logical explanation, one that could be explained by physics and chemistry.

But all the same, when Meredith Oliver came home hours later, she found her daughter sleeping in a tub lined with pillows and blankets; the bathroom lit bright as midday.

Ross watched his nephew defy gravity one more time, the skate-board rising on the air beneath his balanced feet. 'That's a fifty/fifty,' Ethan informed him, his cheeks flushed with exertion; his hair-line damp beneath the scrolled brim of his baseball cap.

He pretended to try to lift up Ethan's ankle. 'You sure you haven't got these tied on with fishing line?'

Ethan grinned and started for his ramp again, then turned around and rolled back. 'Uncle Ross?' he said. 'Having you here is totally the bomb.'

On the blanket beside Ross, Shelby plucked at the grass. 'That's about the highest endorsement you could receive.'

'I figured.' Ross lay back, resting his head on his hands. A shooting star streaked across his field of vision, painting with its silver tail. 'He's great, Shel.'

Her eyes followed Ethan. 'I know.'

Ethan rattled down the wooden ramp. 'Great enough to go ghost hunting with you?' he called over his shoulder.

'Who told you I go ghost hunting?'

'I have my sources.' Ethan spun the board, leaping off it at the same time, so that it seemed to rise into his hand. 'I'm fast, see? *And* I don't get tired at night . . . and I can be so quiet you wouldn't even believe it . . .'

'I'm sure I wouldn't,' Ross laughed.

'No, I mean, really, Uncle Ross, why *wouldn't* you take me?'

'Let's see. Because your mother would skin me alive; and because I'm retired.'

'Retired?' The boy ran his tongue over the word. 'Does that mean you're, like, worn out from it?'

'I guess, in a way.'

Ethan seemed stunned by this. 'Well, that totally *sucks*.'

'*Ethan*.' Shelby shook her head, a warning.

'Now you're just like some normal relative,' the boy muttered. Ross watched him skate off. 'Was that an insult?'

Shelby ignored him, eyeing Ross carefully instead. 'So you're all right?'

'Fine.' He smiled at her. '*Totally*.'

'It's just that I get worried, you know, when you don't call. For six months.'

Ross shrugged. 'I've been moving around a lot, with the Warburtons.'

'I didn't know you'd stopped doing paranormal investigation.'

'I didn't either, until I said it. But I'm sick of not seeing what I want to see.'

'There's a difference between being a paleontologist and not finding what you're after, and being a ghost hunter and not finding what you're after,' Shelby said. 'I mean, there are dinosaur bones out there, even if you aren't lucky enough to dig them up. But ghosts . . . well, if they're all over the place, how come no one's proved it by now?'

'I've been in a room where the temperature drops by twenty degrees within a few seconds. I've taped church choirs singing in empty, locked rooms. I've seen faucets turn themselves on. But I've never seen a spirit appear in front of my eyes. Hell, for all I know any of those things could be explained away. Maybe it's God, maybe it's elves, maybe it's some technical genius three miles away making it happen by remote control.'

Shelby grinned. 'Is this the same kid who believed in Santa until he was fifteen?'

'I was ten,' Ross corrected. 'And you weren't the one who set the trap on the roof and got proof.'

'You got a *shingle*.'

'With a hoof print on it.' Ross reached in his pocket for a cigarette, then looked at Ethan and changed his mind. 'I should have quit a long time ago.'

'Smoking?'

'Ghost hunting.'

'Why didn't you?'

Ross thought of Curtis Warburton: *Half this business is telling people what they want to hear*. He thought of Aimee's lost engagement ring, which had vanished overnight, although he'd torn his room apart trying to find it. 'Because things happened that I didn't understand . . . and I thought that if I looked hard enough, I might be able to figure out why.'

'Maybe you should have gone into physics, then.'

Ross shrugged. 'Science can't explain everything.'

'You mean, like God?'

'Nothing that profound. What makes you walk past thirty thousand people without a second glance, and then you look at the thirty-thousandth-and-first person and know you'll never take your eyes off her again?'

'Love may not be rational, Ross, but it isn't paranormal.'

Says who? Ross thought. 'That's not the point. It's that even when you can't see something right before your eyes, you can still feel it. And you're willing to trust your senses in one case, so why not the other?' Getting to his feet, he brushed off his jeans. 'You know, I'd go into these houses . . . and all I'd have to do is be willing to listen, and these people would just talk. Not just psychos, Shel . . . professors with Ph.D.s, and *Fortune 500* CEOs. It's like once you've seen a ghost, you're part of the club, and you can't wait to find someone else who doesn't think you're insane for admitting that what your parents told you wasn't true.'

It's what Ross had wanted to believe. He had met some psychics who claimed that they could barely turn around without crashing into a spirit. That ghosts were constantly trying to catch their attention. But now, he had his doubts. Now, he was starting to think that once you died, that was that.

'Even Ph.D.s and CEOs can be liars. Or crazy,' Shelby said.

'How about four-year-olds?' Ross turned to his sister. 'What about the kid who comes up to his mom in the middle of the night and says there's an old man in his bedroom who told him they have to leave the workshop so he can make a table? And then you go to the library and find out the house is built on a carpentry studio from two hundred years back?'

'That . . . happened?'

The four-year-old boy had eventually started hitting himself in the head to stop hearing the ghost's voice; he'd scratched at his eyes so that he wouldn't see it. 'Well. I guess kids can go crazy, too. Point is, I'm through with it.' But Ross wondered whether he was trying to convince his sister, or himself.

Shelby patted his shoulder. 'For what it's worth, Ross, if anyone was going to be able to find concrete evidence of a ghost, I have no doubt it would have been you.'

Hesitating, he looked at her, then dug into his pocket. He extracted his wallet and pulled a photo from the liner.

'You're going to tell me that looks like a mouth, and eyes.' She squinted. 'And a hand.'

'I didn't tell you anything. *You* told *me*.'

'So what is it?'

'Curtis Warburton would call it ectoplasm. When I took this picture, there was nothing on that lake . . . no fog, no breath, nothing. But this is what made it onto the negative. Film is sensitive enough to pick up light, heat, and magnetic energy . . . which are the same sources of energy spirits use to materialize.' Ross slipped the photo back into his wallet. 'Then again, it could have been some crap they spilled at the photo lab.'

He did not say that at the time he took the photograph, the

air suddenly grew so cold that all the hair on his arms and legs stood up. He did not say that for the rest of that day, his hands shook and his eyes could not seem to focus.

'There was no mist there when you took the picture?' Shelby clarified.

'Nope.'

She frowned. 'If I saw that in some newspaper, I'd think it was doctored. But—'

'—but I'm your brother, so you have to trust me?'

Ethan roared to a stop in front of them. 'There's this rock quarry in town where a guy got murdered a really long time ago. Everyone says it's haunted. We could go and—'

'*No,*' said Ross and Shelby, simultaneously.

'Jesus H.,' Ethan muttered, loping away again.

Ross looked over the horizon, the blue night starting to bleed. 'Isn't it time to go in?'

Shelby nodded and began to gather the remains of their picnic. 'So what will you do now?'

'Track UFOs.' He looked at her. '*Kidding.*'

'You could baby-sit for me while I work. Although taking care of Ethan might be even scarier than your last gig.'

'Ghosts aren't scary,' Ross said before he could remember to speak hypothetically. 'They're just people. Well, they used to be.'

Shelby paused in the middle of folding the blanket. 'But you've never seen one.'

'No.'

'Even though you wanted to.'

Ross forced a smile. 'Hey, I've never seen a ten-thousand-dollar bill, but I've always wanted to see one of those too.'

Retirement made sense. It was simply a matter of convincing himself. The truth was, in nine months, he had not found what he was looking for. He had not witnessed an apparition because there was nothing there.

But then again, he had a mind-boggling photograph burning

a hole in his back pocket; a spirit that might have taken strength from heat or from light or even his camera batteries, so it could project itself and be seen. To Ross, that was perfectly logical. After all, Aimee had been the one who energized him. Without her, he was no better than a ghost himself, slipping through his own life, unseen.

'I ain't bulldozing over him!' shouted the foreman on the job, his face shiny and florid as a plum. He glared down at Eli from the vantage point of the truck's cab, arms crossed over the shelf of his belly.

'Mr Champigny—'

'Winks.' The guy lying supine on the ground smiled gamely at Eli. 'That's what everyone calls me.'

Eli's dog bounded out of nowhere and planted his front paws on Winks's chest. 'Down, Watson,' Eli ordered. 'Mr Champigny, I'm going to have to ask you to get up. The Redhook company has contractual permission to perform due diligence on this land.'

'He speakin' English?' Winks called out to a group of picketers nearby.

'Can't you arrest them?' Rod van Vleet asked.

'They haven't made any trouble yet. This is civil disobedience, is all.' At least that's what Eli's orders were from Chief Follensbee, who didn't want to stir up what could quickly escalate into an angry racial disagreement. Eli knew that the Abenaki wouldn't press the issue, if they weren't pressed themselves. All the same, he wasn't much in the mood for this. He'd had to pick up Abbott Thule, the town drunk, from the Gas & Grocery and set him in a lockup to dry out. He needed to get Watson something to eat. He did not want to be screwing around now with a bunch of Indians with enough hubris between them to fill the bowl of Lake Champlain.

He rubbed the back of his neck. Times like this, he wondered why he hadn't moved to Florida after his mother passed. He was thirty-six, and working way too hard. Hell, he could be out with his dad now, playing a round of golf. He could be sitting under a palm tree. At his side, Watson grinned up at him.

'There are human remains on this land,' Winks insisted.

'That true?' Eli asked.

Rod's face darkened. 'There haven't been any found. Just a tin locket, some pottery shards, and a 1932 penny.'

'An arrowhead,' Az Thompson called out, although Eli would have thought the old man was too far away to hear their conversation. 'Don't forget the arrowhead.'

The developer rolled his eyes. 'Yes, all right, they found an arrowhead. Which is proof of absolutely nothing, except that some kid played Cowboys and Indians here.'

Az Thompson came toward them. 'We don't care about arrowheads, either. Just our ancestors. Didn't you see *Poltergeist*? You dig up their resting place, it stands to reason that whatever you build on here isn't going to be at peace.'

Eli wondered where the old man's attachment to the property came from. As far as he knew, Az had moved to Comtosook from somewhere out west. Granted, he'd lived in town nearly as long as Eli had, but it wasn't like Az had any special connection to this spot. Apparently his grievance with the development wasn't personal as much as it was principle.

'That's a threat,' Rod said to Eli. 'You heard him.'

Az laughed. 'What did I threaten you with?'

'A curse. Some . . . hex.'

The old Indian cupped his hands around a pipe and lit the leaves in the bowl. 'Gotta believe in that kind of stuff before it can do its work on you.' He inhaled, his words slipping out on the smoke. 'You believe in that kind of stuff, Mr van Vleet?'

'Look,' Eli sighed. 'I know how you all feel about this development company, Az. But if you have a grievance, your best bet is to go through the courts.'

'The last time the legal system said it knew what was best for the Abenaki, it did a damn good job of nearly wiping us out,' Az replied. 'No, Detective Rochert, I don't think we'll go to your courts.'

'*His* courts?' Winks, standing now, snorted as he dusted off his jeans. 'Eli, who went and told you that fancy blue uniform of yours makes your skin look less red?'

Eli didn't think, he just lunged for Winks, grabbing the smaller man by the lapels and slamming him up against the side of the bulldozer. Watson was a moment behind, teeth bared. Eli heard the satisfying crack of Winks's head against the metal frame, and then reason settled over him. He could feel Az Thompson watching; could feel the air caught in the bellows of his own lungs.

As he turned away and called off his dog, Eli remembered going with his mother's relatives to fish for a summer month along the banks of the lake. The kids, brown and barefoot, played so much tag they had flattened the tall grasses for nearly a mile square. Eli had been ten before he realized that the lake he knew as *Pitawbagw* – the water that lies between – was marked on a map as Lake Champlain.

Nodding to the driver of the bulldozer, Eli gave the okay to start digging. Purposefully turning away from the Indians, he steeled himself to keep the peace.

A week after his arrival in Comtosook, Ross wandered along the edge of the lake, ignoring the scratch of pebbles beneath the arches of his bare feet. The water was cold – too cold, for August – but this he did not mind. Feeling anything, even discomfort, was a nice change.

Lake Champlain was so long that you could not see it from end to end, although the Adirondacks loomed like distant soldiers on the opposite shore. Aimee had been born on that other side, in upstate New York. They had been driving to her parents' home the day the sky fell down.

Once, at the bookstore in Manhattan where Ross had worked, an author came in to give a speech about death rituals. In Tibetan burials, a monk stripped the flesh from the bone of a corpse and cut the body into pieces, so vultures could devour the remains. In Bali, a body was buried during the years it took to plan the spectacular cremation ceremony. But before the interment, the deceased was spun and splashed and shaken in a colorful bamboo tower, so that the spirit couldn't find its way back.

Ross had been working that night, which meant setting up the chairs for the audience, arranging the books to be signed on a small table, getting the author bottled water at the podium. It was a good crowd – academic sociologists rubbing tweedy elbows with spiky-haired Goths in black overcoats. As the lecture went on, Ross stood in the back, amazed at how many ways there were to say good-bye.

Aimee had stumbled in sometime in the middle. She was still wearing her scrubs, and Ross's first thought was that she must be cold; she was always cold when she wore them as pajamas, yet here she was running through the streets of the city in December.

His second thought was that something was terribly wrong.

'Hey.' Ross caught her as she almost wandered past him into the stacks of the store.

She threw herself into his arms and started sobbing. Several members of the audience turned around; the speaker himself glanced up, distracted.

Ross pulled Aimee by the hand into the gardening section, where nobody in New York City ever bothered to browse. He framed her face in his hands, his heart pounding: she had cancer; she was pregnant; she did not love him anymore.

'Martin died,' she choked out.

Ross held her, trying to place the name. In fits and starts the story came out – Martin Birenbaum, fifty-three, had been the victim of a fire at a chemical plant. Third-degree burns covered

85 percent of his body. It had fallen to Aimee, as a third-year medical student in the ER, to try to make him as comfortable as possible by debriding his wounds, keeping them clean, and administering Silvadine. When he asked if he was going to die, she had looked him in the eye and said yes.

He was the first patient she had ever lost, and because of this his face was scarred into her mind. 'I stayed with him because I knew I couldn't help,' Aimee confessed. 'Maybe it gets easier, you know, every time it happens. But maybe it doesn't, Ross. Maybe I shouldn't be in medicine.' She suddenly stared at him. 'When I die, you have to be there. Like I was, today.'

'You're not dying—'

'Ross, Jesus Christ, I just had a profoundly upsetting experience . . . can't you promise me this?'

'No,' he said flatly. 'Because I'm going first.'

She was silent for a moment, and then a tiny laugh escaped. 'Did you already book your ticket?'

'*Guei*, or hungry ghosts,' the lecturer said just then, 'are the souls of the Chinese who passed on unnaturally . . . as a result, they wander the earth making trouble for the living.'

At that, Aimee looked up. 'What the *hell* are we listening to, Ross?'

'Yes,' he'd answered. 'That's close enough.'

Afterward, they never spoke of Martin Birenbaum. Ross had accompanied Aimee to the funeral. Over the course of her residency, more patients died in her care. But he could not remember her ever breaking down over it. Eventually, like most doctors, she came to understand that death was just the tail end of life.

He skipped a stone into Lake Champlain, which sank before the second rock he threw even skimmed the surface. Aimee had been cremated. Her ashes were somewhere on the other side of this lake, with her parents. He did not know what they had done with them; after the first three years he had stopped returning their phone calls and letters, simply because it hurt too much.

Ross picked up his shoes, intent on heading back to his car. As he slid into the driver's seat he remembered one more story from the speaker at the bookstore. The Mexicans believed that for one day every year, the veil was lifted, and old souls could journey home to visit people they'd left behind.

When I die, you have to be there.

But he hadn't been. Yet now, he couldn't seem to leave.

Meredith Oliver's office at Generra Institute had a Washington, D.C., zipcode, and if you looked closely from the window, you could see the Jefferson Memorial. She found it fairly ironic, since most of the scientists at her place of business flouted the very concept of all men being created equal – in their opinion, only the strongest survived.

Sitting across from her, nervously wringing each other's hands, were Mr and Mrs De la Corria. 'Good news,' Meredith said with a smile. In the decade she'd been doing preimplantation genetic diagnosis, she'd learned that the only thing more stressful for a couple than in vitro fertilization was waiting for the results of the tests that led up to it. 'There are three viable embryos.'

Carlos De la Corria was a hemophiliac. Terrified to pass the disease on through his offspring, he and his wife had opted for assisted reproduction, in which embryos were created from their own sperm and eggs and then genetically screened by Meredith. Before the embryo was put into the mother's uterus, she would know that her baby did not possess the gene for hemophilia.

'How many are boys?' asked Carlos.

'Two.' Meredith looked him in the eye. The gene for hemophilia was carried on the X chromosome. That meant a male child born to the De la Corrias would not be able to pass on his father's illness. In effect, if they had only boys, they'd stamp out hemophilia in future generations of their family.

Carlos lifted his wife from the chair and whirled her around Meredith's small office. All those ethicists who were terrified of what might come of gene modification – well, they need only witness a moment like this. Meredith kept two pictures on her desk – one of Lucy, and another of her first patient, a beaming woman with cystic fibrosis holding her son, who – thanks to Meredith – had been born without the disease.

Mrs De la Corria sank down in her chair again, still breathless. 'The girl?' she asked softly.

'The third embryo tested is, in fact, a carrier. I'm sorry,' Meredith replied.

Carlos squeezed his wife's hand. 'Well, then,' he said optimistically. 'It looks like we'll be having twin boys.'

There were plenty of obstacles still to overcome, and there was every chance that the embryos wouldn't succeed – but Meredith had done her part of the job. From here, other doctors at Generra took over with the implantation. Meredith accepted the De la Corrias' gratitude and then scanned her appointment sheet. Two more consultations, and then she had the afternoon to work in her lab.

She slipped on her reading glasses – she kept them in a pocket, too vain for overt display – and pulled the pen that anchored her curls into some semblance of a knot. Her honey-gold hair tumbled around her shoulders in a tangle, the mess it always was, as if it were God's joke to give Meredith Oliver, the control freak, hair that had seemed to have a mind of its own. She scrubbed her hands down her face, rubbed bloodshot brown eyes. 'Tonight,' she told herself out loud, 'I will not let myself work. I will go home, and take a hot bath, and read Lucy something other than an article from the *Journal of Theriogenology*.'

She wondered if saying it, instead of just thinking it, made it any more likely to happen.

'Dr Oliver?' A knock on the door, followed by her secretary. 'The De la Corrias signed this release.'

Without looking, Meredith knew what it was – permission for Generra to discard their third, female embryo. 'They should wait until after implantation. There's a chance that the in vitro won't take, and then . . .'

Her voice drifted off. And then, it would make no difference. The De La Corrias would rather be childless than utilize this damaged embryo. The baby would not be hemophiliac herself . . . in all likelihood she'd be a perfectly healthy girl with her mother's shining hair and her father's chestnut eyes. But she had the potential to pass the illness to her own male children one day, and given that, her parents would rather she never be born.

Meredith signed off on the release and set it to one side of her desk. 'The Albertsons are here,' said the secretary.

'Give me a minute.'

As soon as the door closed, Meredith picked up the phone and dialed home. She imagined her daughter sitting at the kitchen table, two braids curling down her back like replicas of the human genome, as she practiced her *U*s and *V*s for handwriting home-work. *Ula unrolled uneven umbrellas.* Lucy lifted the receiver. 'Hello?'

'Hey, Noodle.'

'Mom! Where are you?'

'On Jupiter. Where are you?'

'In the Calamari Desert.'

Meredith smiled. 'That might be Kalahari.'

'When are you coming home?'

'Soon.'

There was a beat of silence. 'Before it gets dark?'

Meredith closed her eyes. 'I'll be back for dinner,' she prom-ised. 'Tell Granny Ruby. And no more Oreos until I get home.'

Lucy sucked in a breath. 'How did you know I was—'

'Because I'm the mom. Love you.' Meredith hung up, then twisted her hair onto the top of her head. She scrabbled through her drawer for a rubber band, but could only come up with a few paper clips, which worked about as well as bobby pins. Her glance fell on the release the De la Corrias had signed. On impulse,

Meredith slipped the form into the lower drawer of her desk. She would lose it, temporarily. Just in case.

She pushed the button of her intercom and a moment later the door swung open, revealing the Albertsons. They looked beaten and drained, like most of the other couples who came through her office for the first time. Meredith held out her hand. 'I'm Dr Oliver. I've reviewed your case. And,' she said briskly, 'I can help.'

Az knew that if push came to shove, he wouldn't be able to chase a squirrel out of Angel Quarry, much less give full pursuit to an armed intruder. The owners kept him on as a security guard out of kindness, or pity, or maybe because he only bothered to pick up half his paychecks, not having much use for them in the long run. Luckily, there was only one access road into the quarry, not that Az paid much attention to it. He sat in the small illuminated booth at the quarry office, where three closed-circuit televisions monitored activity at different locations, and kept his eye instead on the fourth monitor, tuned to the Red Sox.

'Ha,' Az snorted at the batter. 'They pay you eleven million bucks a year for *that*?'

The quarry was one of Vermont's granite mines, veins of rock etched into the cliffs like the deep lines of Az's face. A long time ago, they'd drilled the charges by hand, blasted, and milled the stone for export. These days, it was mostly computerized. Working alone at night, he never saw another soul . . . for all he knew, it was like that at peak hours too. Az sometimes wondered if he was the only human employed there.

In the thirty years he'd been working at the quarry, he had filed only two security reports. One involved an electrical storm that set off an explosion intended to detonate the following day. The second was about a suicidal man, who scaled the protective wall and tried to jump off one of the cliffs into the jagged rubble at the base. The fool broke both legs, recovered, and started a dot-com business.

Az liked working at night, and he liked working alone. If he was quiet when he made his rounds, he could hear buds burst; he could smell the turn of the seasons. On occasion he would lie on his back, his hands propping up his head, and watch the stars reconfigure themselves into the constellations of his life – an angry bull of frustration, the imbalanced scales of justice, the twin loves he'd lost ages ago.

He wondered what was going on at Otter Creek Pass. In the week Rod van Vleet had been on the site, the Abenaki protest had intensified, and the public had noticed. It helped that Thule Abbott, the town drunk, had awakened one morning with all his straight hair gone curly, and he'd spent a day in the church getting a dose of Jesus and blaming the ghosts for his misfortune. Rumors flew through Comtosook like the occasional dusting of rose petals, which fell like pollen on the cars parked at the Dairy Twirl and clogged the drains in the outdoor showers at the town pool.

If Rod van Vleet had half a brain, he'd roll his construction equipment in during the night, when most of the Indians were snoring in their tents a distance away. Good thing the frontman for the Redhook Group was a fool. Given the habitual disorganization of the Abenaki protest, it put them on equal footing.

A small firefly winked past Az's left eye. Then he realized it wasn't a June bug at all, but a small bobbing light on the pitch-dark screen of one of the satellite TVs, the one that viewed the mine's northern wall and most active stripping site. A flush of heat ran down between Az's shoulders – it took a moment for him to recognize excitement for what it was. Jamming his hat on his head, he struck off toward the spot where the light had been. The years fell away with each footstep, until he was once again straight and strong as an oak that punched the sky, until he was needed.

* * *

Ross didn't know whom he blamed more: Ethan, for planting this seed in his mind; or himself, for bothering to listen. *Angel Quarry is haunted,* his nephew had said, *everyone says so.* He walked softly along the narrow path until he felt the hair on the back of his neck prickle. This, then, was where he would set up. He didn't dare use his flashlight yet – something he'd learned early from the Warburtons. Authorities usually left ghost hunters alone, but trespassing was trespassing. If you were exploring a graveyard, you learned to back in with your headlights off, so that you could make a quick escape. Likewise, if you were creeping through private property in the middle of the night, you did everything possible to keep from calling attention to yourself.

Thinking of Aimee this afternoon had made him want to try, one last time, no matter that he'd told Shelby he'd hung up his paranormal shingle. So from Lake Champlain he'd gone to Burlington, to a discount electronics store, where he bought a new infrared video camera. When Shelby put dinner on the table, he told her he had a date that night.

'Really?' She'd smiled so brightly it hurt Ross just to look. 'Who is it?'

'None of your business.'

'Ross,' Shelby answered, 'this is exactly what you need.'

He hated that he'd lied to his sister. He hated the way she had reached into the window of his car before he left to straighten the collar of his shirt, how she told him the door would be open whenever he got home.

Now, while his sister wondered which eligible female he was meeting, Ross balanced his flashlight on an outcropping of rock, so that he could set up the tripod for the video camera. 'I am not going to see anything,' Ross murmured as he peered through the viewfinder. He hesitated, then swore.

He was retired.

He didn't believe in ghosts, not anymore.

But what if this was the time that *something* materialized? What if he walked away now, without finding out for sure? If Ethan was right – if someone had been murdered at the quarry – there was an excellent chance that a restless spirit was hanging around. The ones who didn't go on to heaven or whatever came next were the ones who had unfinished business left – people who had died violently, or committed suicide without communicating a message. Sometimes they stayed because they didn't want to leave someone they loved.

Ross knew that if luck was on his side when he ran the camera, he might get some zipping lights, maybe a globule or two. He might catch some EVPs – electronic voice phenomena. And if there was any evidence at all that something paranormal existed in this quarry, there was a chance Aimee was somewhere, too.

Going by his senses, Ross pointed the video to a spot in the quarry that his eyes kept coming back to, although he had no idea if in fact that was where a murder had occurred. He loaded a fresh tape and checked the battery, then sat back to wait.

Suddenly he was blinded by a beacon. 'I can explain,' he began.

Whatever Ross was going to say, however, died on his lips as he found himself face-to-face with an ancient man wearing a vintage security guard's uniform; a man who held so much of the world in his eyes that Ross was certain he was looking at a ghost.

'Who *are* you?' the man whispered to Az. He was gawking like he'd never seen anyone native before, and frankly, that pissed Az off.

'You're trespassing,' Az said.

'This used to be your land?'

Sweet Jesus, and they talked about *Indians* being hooked on peyote. Granted, Az was old, and he was rigged out in a security guard's uniform he'd owned for twenty-five years now, but *still* . . . The guy looked normal enough – maybe even had a little Abenaki blood, what with that long, dark hair. It was enough to make Az feel pity for him, anyway. 'Look, tell you what. You pack up whatever it is you're doing and get out, and I won't tell anyone I saw you.'

The man nodded, and then lunged forward in an attempt to touch him. Startled, Az drew away and pulled his billy club.

'Please! I just . . . I just want to ask you a few questions.'

Christ. Az was going to miss the whole seventh inning, at this rate.

'Do you live here?'

'No, and I don't have a teepee either, if that's next on the list.' Az grabbed his arm. 'Now shut that thing off and—'

'You can touch me . . . ?'

'I can beat the crap out of you, too, if you keep this up,' Az said. 'The Red Sox are tied with the Yankees, though, so it's going to be fast.'

The intruder – well, he faded – that was the only word for it. It was the same thing Az had seen over and over sitting at the deathbed of a friend; that light that made a person what he was, suddenly snuffing out. 'The Red Sox,' the man murmured. 'Then you're not a ghost.'

'I may be old, but I'm sure as hell not dead.'

'I thought you were . . .' He shook his head, then extended his hand. 'I'm Ross Wakeman.'

'You're crazy, is what you are.'

'That too, I guess.' Ross ran a hand through his hair. 'I'm a paranormal researcher. Well, I *was* one, anyway.'

Az shrugged. 'You ever find anything?'

Ross paused. 'Is there something here to find?'

'Never seen nothing myself. Not here, anyway.'

'But you have, other places?'

Az avoided the question. 'You can't stay. Private property.'

Ross busied himself cleaning up his equipment, taking his sweet time, from the looks of it. 'I heard there was a murder here years ago.'

'That's what they say.'

'You know anything about it?'

Az looked into the pit of the quarry. 'It happened before I was a security guard.'

'Right.' Ross lifted the camera bag and slung it over his shoulder. 'Sorry about . . . the mistaken identity thing.'

'It's nothing.' Az started to escort the younger man out. As Ross reached his car, Az curled his hand around the cast-iron gate. 'Mr Wakeman,' he called. 'Those spirits you're looking for? You aren't far off.'

He went back to the security booth, leaving Ross to wonder if that was a promise or a threat.

Over the next few weeks, the residents of Comtosook came to believe in the unexpected. Mothers would awaken with their throats so full of tears they could not call out to their children. Businessmen catching their reflections in a pane of glass were suddenly unable to recognize their own faces. Young lovers, parked at the Point and twined together like the strands of a rope, whispered desperate vows of passion only to realize their words had come out as bubbles, and burst just as quickly.

Shelby Wakeman found ladybugs swarming all the north-facing windows of her house. Rod van Vleet could drive no more than a quarter of a mile in his company car before the scent of berries burst from the air-conditioning vents, making the interior of the Taurus as cloying and thick as jam. Spencer Pike slipped his hand beneath his pillow and discovered three sky-blue robin's eggs.

Ethan, who knew better, found himself stealing glimpses of the sun.

Droves of cats escaped from their homes and walked down to the river to bathe. The level of water in Lake Champlain rose and fell twice a day, as if there were a tide. Roses burst free of their trellises to grow in wild, tangled thickets. Nothing at the dinner table tasted quite right.

And in spite of the temperate August climate, the disputed

land on Otter Creek Pass froze solid, so that excavation became
a physical impossibility as well as a philosophical one.

'What do you make of it?' Winks Smiling Fox asked, grunting as
he moved the drum a few feet to the left. Where they'd been
sitting, the ground beneath their feet was icy. Yet over here, there
were dandelions growing.

There were documented cases of ground freezes occurring
during a New England summer. In 1794, the *Old Farmer's
Almanac* predicted a frost in July as a result of a typographical
error, which then unexpectedly came true when Mount Vesu-
vius erupted and the dust it sent into the atmosphere caused a
miniature nuclear winter. Every few years, a blueberry frost
would move through Vermont, dragging temperatures below
freezing and drying the fruit on the bushes. And yet in all these
instances, the damage was done town-wide, not just on one
small patch of land.

'You remember the stories about Azeban?' Winks said. 'The
ones from when we were kids? That's what I keep thinking of.'

'Azeban?' said Fat Charlie. 'The trickster?'

'Uh-huh.' Winks nodded. 'Remember how he'd set a trap for
someone else as some big joke and get caught up in it himself?
Like when he went to stamp out the fire Fox was sleeping near,
and wound up watching his own tail get burned.'

'Wouldn't mind a little fire here, actually, now . . .'

'No, Charlie,' said Az, coming up from behind. 'Winks means
that if you set out to do bad things to others, bad things are
gonna come back to *you*.'

He watched his friends take their seats again and pick up their
drumsticks. This was how they passed the time, braiding their
voices into one long, strong cord of sound. With the exception
of the song they sang in their all-but-forgotten native tongue,
there was no other way to know that this group of men was
Abenaki. They'd learned well from the lessons of the past century,

their ancestors intermarrying in the hopes of disappearing beneath white surnames and Caucasian traits. Winks had blond hair; Fat Charlie's skin was pale as an Irishman's.

'You think there's something more to it than that?' Winks asked. 'I mean, some strange stuff's been going on.'

He did not have to explain; in addition to the frozen ground, the owner of a trucking company was using a shop vac to clear out the nooks and crannies of his excavators, which had become clogged with cicadas.

'In town, they're saying if the Indians don't drive Redhook off the land, the ghosts will,' Fat Charlie added.

'If my grave was being rolled by a bulldozer, I'd be pretty pissed off. Come back and rattle some chains, *henh.*' Winks snorted. 'You see that state archaeologist guy? He says an "Our Father" under his breath every time he thinks no one's listening. Even if there's no such thing as ghosts, it's scaring the crap out of them.'

'No such thing? The spirit of my great-great-uncle came to me during a sweat last year,' Fat Charlie said. 'You've seen 'em too, right, Az?'

'There's a difference between the spirits that have gone on, and the ones that can't leave,' Az said. He picked up a knife and began to whittle a branch to a point. 'Where I used to live, there was a girl whose parents told her she couldn't marry the boy she loved. So she hanged herself from a beech tree on top of a hill. Her boyfriend went up to the same tree after she was buried, and hanged himself too. And if an Indian gets hanged, his spirit can't go to the sky – it gets trapped behind, in the body.' He tested the point of his spear. 'After they died, two blue lights used to come over the hill at night.'

Winks leaned forward, elbows balanced on his knees. 'Anyone ever get close to them?'

The old man ran the knife down the branch again. Behind him, he could sense Rod van Vleet, doing everything in his power to pretend he was not listening. 'Nobody,' Az said, 'was stupid enough to try.'

'Ethan?'

From his vantage point beneath the blackout shades, Ethan froze at the sound of his mother's voice. He whipped his body back so that it wasn't pressed against the warm glass window-pane and slid his sunglasses between the crack where his bed met the wall. 'Hey,' he said, as she opened the bedroom door.

Her hawk's eyes took in the rumpled comforter, the hat on Ethan's head, the drawn curtains. She approached him, narrowed her gaze, and tugged down the sleeve of his shirt where a quarter-inch strip of skin showed above his wrist. 'I'm going to work,' his mother said. 'You ought to be asleep by now.'

'I'm not tired,' Ethan complained. It struck him, though, that his mother must be exhausted. To stay up with him all night, and to work part-time during the day at the library? 'Mom,' he asked, 'are *you* tired?'

'All the time,' she answered, and kissed him good-bye.

He waited until he heard her footsteps echoing on the tile floor of the kitchen. Words were traded like playing cards between his mother and Uncle Ross about how late Ethan should be allowed to stay up and what to do in case of emergency. Ethan dug along the side of his bed until he found the silver wrap-around sunglasses. He settled his cap more firmly on his brow. Then he lifted the edge of the blackout shade and curled like a kitten on the windowsill. Within minutes, burns rose beneath the chalk of his skin, small spots dotted his face, but Ethan didn't care. He'd scar, if that's what it took to prove he'd been a part of this world.

The scientists from CRREL, the Army Corps of Engineers, who had taken a van from Hanover, New Hampshire, to Comtosook and spent the day extracting soil samples with drills made to delve through ground frozen solid as stone, spoke to Rod van Vleet only peripherally. They had come out of academic curiosity and talked of the impact of thaw distribution on vehicle mobility . . . but did not explain how or why this had occurred here and now.

The fellow who arrived from the Scott Polar Research Institute said it looked like permafrost, a climate-dependent phenomenon that occurred when the ground temperature remained below freezing for two or more years – which was not the case on Otter Creek Pass. He spoke of pore ice, segregated ice, and pingos, and reminded Rod that at one point, Burlington and its environs had been glacial.

A Danish team phoned to ask if sudden freezing of the property had affected the chemistry of the atmosphere, and would Rod consider selling in the name of research?

Yet for all of the combined wisdom that these scientists brought to the table, none could explain the odd cravings they developed the moment they crossed into Comtosook – for banana chips and candied violets and the soft skin of homemade puddings. They could not comment on the way loneliness perched on the telephone lines like a crow, except to point out that this was normal in regions where cold seeped so deep it was physically impossible to reach out to anyone else.

By the time they returned to their labs and academic towers, took out their samples, and dusted away the layer of flower petals from the test tubes and Cold Paks, these quirks had been forgotten. They already knew what the residents of Comtosook were just now learning: that the world is a place where the extraordinary can sit just beside the ordinary with the thinnest of boundaries; that even in environments inhospitable to man, all sorts of entities might thrive.

The Comtosook Public Library did not get many visitors, which was a blessing given the size of the building. Tiny rooms were strung together like pearls, far more suited to a small country inn than a repository for literature. The most crowded it got was Thursday mornings, when up to thirty preschoolers would sprawl on their bellies in the two small enclaves that made up the juvenile section, for story time. The children's librarian had to run back and forth between the rooms with an open book, so that all the kids could see.

There were bookshelves at angles, bookshelves stuck in the middle of the floor, bookshelves turned on their sides if necessary – whatever it took to accommodate a large number of volumes in an inadequate run of space. The reference librarian – Shelby, on weekday mornings – needed to know the Dewey Decimal system and various computer search engines, as well as how to navigate the library to find the fruits of these labors. But for the most part, Shelby was free to do whatever she liked during her work hours, and what she liked to do was chew words.

Shelby loved them the way epicureans loved food – each syllable was something to be rolled on the tongue, swallowed, and wholly appreciated. Sometimes she would sit with the dictionary cracked open and read with all the breathless impatience another patron might save for a thriller. *Griseous: mottled. Kloof: a ravine. Nidicolous: Reared for a time in a nest.*

She imagined receiving a phone call one day – Meredith Vieira, on *Who Wants to Be a Millionaire,* or a radio disc jockey offering a fortune if she only knew the definition of one bizarre word. 'Pilose?' she would repeat, and then pretend she did not know it, for the sheer suspense. 'Covered with soft hair.'

She was smart enough, after four years of college and another two of graduate school, to know that she used language like shore dwellers used sandbags: to create a buffer zone between herself and the rest of the world. She also knew that she could learn every last word in the dictionary and still not be able to explain why her life had turned out the way it had.

She was worried about Ethan; she was worried about Ross.

She was so busy, in fact, taking care of the immediate world that it kept her from dwelling on the fact that there never seemed to be anyone around who bothered to worry about *her*.

The library was empty, a result of regular patrons being too uneasy these days to venture out into a town that changed before their very eyes. To Shelby, the recent eccentricities amounted to sweeping petals off the steps of the library; she wasn't worried about an impending Armageddon or global warming or the coming of phantoms, as conversation at the town diner suggested. To a woman who had built a home on a footing of abnormality, recent events were nothing to get excited about.

When the door creaked open, Shelby glanced up. A man she had never seen before entered, dressed in a suit too expensive to have come from any store within a fifty-mile radius. However, there was something . . . off. His tie listed to the left and his skin was nearly as white as Ethan's. He glanced from the oddly sloped floor to the jutting angles of the wall to the stacks of encyclopedias kittering up the wall. 'This is the library?'

'Yes. Can I help you?'

His gaze circled like a bird, finally coming to rest on Shelby. 'Can you even *find* anything in here?'

Rhabdomancy, Shelby thought. *Divination by wands*. 'That depends. What are you looking for?'

'Indian burial grounds. What happened to them, in the past, when someone built over them. Legal precedent. That sort of thing.'

'You must be one of the developers,' Shelby said. She led him to a spot at the rear of the library, where a microfiche was tucked behind a low shelf of cookbooks. 'There was a dispute just a year ago in Swanton. You might want to try there first.'

'You wouldn't happen to remember the outcome, would you?'

'The state bought the property.'

'Oh, great. Terrific.' He exhaled heavily and sprawled backward in the chair. 'Was that Swanton land cursed too?'

'Excuse me?'

For a moment, he seemed too frustrated to speak. 'Those Indians, what do they do . . . conjure up all their dead ancestors whenever they need them? Whatever it takes, right, to get us Massholes out of town?'

Shelby worried her nail between her teeth.

'We're just trying to build a strip mall, for God's sake. I've got the owner's signature, all nice and legal on a piece of paper. I've forked over fifty thousand dollars, to start. I do everything by the book, and in return, I've got temperatures dropping below zero for no reason whatsoever; I've got voices screaming in the middle of the night. I've got my labor force quitting. Jesus . . . this morning, I got *shoved*, and there was no one behind me!' He looked directly at Shelby. 'I am not going crazy. I'm *not.*'

'Of course you aren't,' she murmured.

The man ran a hand down his face. 'I don't know why I bothered to come here. You can't help me.'

'No, I can't,' Shelby said. 'But I think I know someone who can.'

Ross sprawled in Shelby's living room, the volume on the television cranked up as loud as he felt he could make it without waking his nephew. Wires linked his video camera to the screen, as the short tape he'd made at the quarry ran. He paused the image with the remote control, rewound it, and leaned forward to scrutinize it again. But no, the flickering at the corner of the screen was just a reflection – nothing paranormal at all.

He shut off the television and leaned back, eyes closed. 'Waste of time.'

'That bad, huh?' Shelby walked in and slung her pocketbook onto the couch.

'Ethan was fine.'

'I was talking about your date. Are you going to tell me who she was now, or is that a state secret?'

'Nobody you know.'

'How can I be sure until you tell me?' Shelby sat down. 'What's with the video camera?'

Ross set out to change the subject as quickly as possible. 'How was work?'

'Actually, I think I got you a job today.'

'Thanks, but I don't think library work is for me. I gave up alphabetizing for Lent.'

'A. It's not Lent, and B. It's not library work—'

'You're alphabetizing,' Ross pointed out, grinning.

Shelby tucked one foot beneath her. 'A man came in today, Rod van Vleet. He's working for the development company that bought a piece of land on Otter Creek Pass—'

'Where?'

'Well, it doesn't matter. What's important is that he's all freaked out because he thinks the property is haunted.' Shelby smiled, triumphant. 'Guess where you come in.'

His jaw tightened. 'Is this about money? Because if you want me to pay rent—'

'Ross, stop. I said something to him because I thought it might get you excited. You've been moping around since you got here. You've barely even left the house in weeks.'

'*You* hardly ever leave the house.'

'That's different and you know it.'

Ross got out of the chair and yanked the wires out of the TV, packing up his video camera in its padded bag. 'I didn't realize you had *expectations*,' he said bitterly. 'I didn't know that it wasn't all right to just take a breather.'

'A breather? Are you sure that's why you came here?' By now she was standing toe-to-toe with him. 'Or were you looking for someplace to stop breathing?'

Ross held her gaze for a minute. 'Shel. It was only that once, just after she died.'

Shelby's hands came up to Ross's wrists, pulled them down

between them. Her thumbs edged up the sleeves of his sweater, traced the history there. 'Once. I go to ask you if you want soup for lunch, *soup*, Ross, and you're bleeding out.'

'You should have let me,' Ross said, gently breaking away.

'Fuck you.' Tears glittered in Shelby's eyes. 'When you close the bathroom door now, I wonder if you're taking pills. When you go out driving, I wonder if you're wrapped around a tree. Did it ever occur to you that you're not the only person who's ever lost someone? Aimee died. People die. *You're* alive, and you have to start acting like it.'

His gaze was glacial. 'Will you feel that way in a few years, when it's Ethan?'

A small sound made them turn toward the doorway, but by then the boy who had heard every word had run off.

He was wearing a sweatshirt and long pants, and of course a baseball hat, but his face and his hands were uncovered. By the time Ethan reached the quarry – the highest spot in town, with cliffs that pierced the sky – his fingers were swollen like sausages, and so red they ached with every heartbeat.

Maybe a truck would hit him on the way. Maybe he would burn to a crisp, go up in flames like the pictures of that guy he saw in the *Guinness Book of World Records*. If he died now, what difference would it make?

What he knew of the town of Comtosook he had learned from maps, from the Internet. Certainly, he'd been out before – but things looked different in the daylight. He could not tear his eyes away from streets that were full of cars, from the sheer number of people on the sidewalks. He could not know that normally, this town was twice as crowded – by comparison, to Ethan, this sunny world was so busy it took his breath away.

Ethan knew he was going to die. He'd been to psychologists and doctors and social workers to help him come to terms with the prognosis of an XP patient. He might make it to fifty, but there was every chance he'd only live until fifteen. It all depended on how much damage had been done to his cells before he was diagnosed.

The way he figured it, this was one of the few things he could point to that made him just like anyone else. At some point or another, all people were going to kick the bucket. The difference was, if he wanted that day to come later rather than sooner, he wasn't really allowed to *live*.

It was only a few more blocks to the quarry; Ethan could tell because the cliffs were looming larger and larger. He did not know what he would do when he got there. Take off his shirt, maybe, until the pain got so bad he passed out. Lie on his back and stare up at the sun until his corneas burned.

He turned into the entrance of the quarry and stopped abruptly. Leaning against the hood of his battered car, arms crossed, was his Uncle Ross. 'How did you find me?'

'Find *you*? I was here first.' Ross took a look at Ethan's sunburned fingers and face but didn't comment, only handed Ethan one of his own shirts to put on, the sleeves falling down over his hands to protect them from the ultraviolet light. Then he squinted up at the sky. 'I figured a kid who had a bone to pick with the sun would try to get right in its face. This is the highest place in town.' He turned to Ethan. 'Your mother is frantic.'

'Where is she?'

'At home. In case you showed up there, first.' Standing, he opened the passenger door. 'Can we finish this conversation inside?'

After a moment, Ethan nodded. He ducked into the car, pulled off his baseball cap, and scrubbed at his scalp. 'Is it true, about you trying to kill yourself?'

'Yeah.'

Ethan felt his throat narrow. His uncle – well, he was one of the only males Ethan had any contact with, and he was certainly the coolest one. He'd done totally sketchy things, like skydiving and ice climbing. Ethan wanted to be just like him, if he ever got the chance to grow up. But he couldn't fathom how the man he idolized most in the world would not just want to live on the edge, but to die there. 'How come you did it?'

Ross reached across Ethan's body to rap hard on the glass. Then, with a flick of a finger on a console button, the window automatically rolled down; Ethan could smell the bitter fireweed that grew along the road in brilliant regiments. 'To get to the other side,' his uncle explained.

'Oh my God,' Shelby cried, and then she was running down the driveway to yank Ethan out of the car. Ross watched them hold this moment between them, the small grain of calamity now reforming itself into a pearl of relief. They tottered back toward the house, Shelby folded around her son, as if he were still an extension of her own body.

Ross leaned against the hood, thanking God he'd had the hunch to look for Ethan where he had. He didn't want to think about what might have happened, had he come home alone, or if Ethan had stayed outside too long.

He started for the front door and realized that a stranger was standing on the porch beside his sister. 'This is Rod van Vleet,' she said, in a tone that let Ross know their argument was far from resolved. 'He stopped by to speak to you.'

Ross shot his sister the blackest glance he could, given the circumstances. The man was shorter than Ross, his balding head the unfortunate shape of a peanut. He wore a fancy suit, a starched shirt, a banker's tie. 'Mr Wakeman,' he said, with a hesitant smile. 'I hear you hunt ghosts.'

3

Just this once, it was cool that everyone was staring.

Ethan was carrying the video camera, which was heavy, but he wasn't about to complain to his uncle. Anyway, Ross was hauling everything else – from the sleeping bags to the junk food (a stakeout, his uncle said, was a stakeout, even if the people you were trying to catch in the act were already dead). They walked from the car past the drummers and the bulldozer and the construction crew, and Ethan noticed that each person they passed seemed to freeze in the middle of whatever they were doing. One old Indian guy stared so hard at Ethan he thought it might leave a mark on the back of his head. But he wasn't staring at Ethan because he was a freak – just because he was curious about the man and the kid who walked across the property like they owned it.

Ethan stopped for a moment, arrested by the sight of a college kid sifting sand. The boy was stripped down to his shorts, his shoulders and back butternut brown. Ethan looked down at his own long sleeves and thick pants. He sucked in the mesh of the facemask his mother made him wear when he went out while the sun was still in the sky.

'Hey, move it,' Ross called over his shoulder, and Ethan scrambled to catch up.

The developer, Mr van Vleet, hurried over as soon as he saw them. He wore fancy businessman shoes and kept slipping on the ice that had spread over the land like frosting on a cake.

'Mr Wakeman,' he greeted quietly. 'You remember what I said about keeping this . . . discreet?'

'You remember what *I* said about letting me run my own investigation?' Ross answered, turning his back on the man. He trudged up the steps of the old house; one of which broke right in the middle while his foot was on it. 'Be careful,' he warned Ethan.

The house looked like it had been crying, black shutters hanging off their hinges like a fringe of damp eyelashes. Ethan stood back and craned his neck, so that he could see all the way to the top. It was white, or it had been, once. Most of the windows had been broken by local kids years ago. Ivy grew up and over the doorframe, a spotty handlebar mustache.

'Ethan!'

Startled by his uncle's voice, he raced up the steps. In the entryway, he froze. Plaster rained down from the ceiling, and the floorboards were thick with dirt. On the walls where patterned paper used to be there were smudged handprints and graffiti: SARI GIVES GOOD HEAD. Underneath the staircase were the remnants of a bonfire and about thirty empty beer bottles.

Ethan glanced from the broken banister to the black hole of an adjoining room, then to the ceiling. So it was creepy, he thought. So what. He squared his thin shoulders, convinced that if he played his cards right, he could get picked for *Fear Factor* or one of those other reality-TV shows. He could get Uncle Ross to take him along on every case. After all, Ethan only came out at night. Maybe it took one to know one.

He was braver than any other kid he knew . . . not that he knew many kids.

Or so Ethan was telling himself, until a touch on the back of his neck made him jump a foot.

Kerrigan Klieg was the *New York Times* reporter who did the obligatory vampire piece at Halloween, who wrote about the chemical nature of love for Valentine's Day, who interviewed the parents of the city's first millennium baby. In other words, he was a slacker. He didn't have the heart or the inclination to follow up on police corruption or political stress; his pieces were human interest, although they weren't all that interesting to Kerrigan himself. What he did like, however, was getting out and about to do the research. To Mercy Brown's grave in Rhode Island, for example, to see the undead for himself. Or to Johns Hopkins, where researchers were measuring the melatonin levels associated with lust. Kerrigan liked being reminded that there was a world outside the island of Manhattan, one where people actually walked down the streets and looked each other in the eye, instead of pretending they were somewhere or someone else.

You couldn't beat the combination of elements in this particular piece: a hundred-year-old Indian, a group of frightened townspeople, a real-estate development mogul, and a purported angry ghost. And they were only at the tip of the property – the part with the house on it. Who knew what lurked in the acres of woods behind it?

Kerrigan walked beside Az Thompson, the guy who had called the features editor in the first place, and wondered what the old man had done to stay alive this long. Did he eat yogurt, like on those Dannon commercials? Practice meditation? Inject B-12? 'People have been taking our land away forever,' Thompson said. 'But it sure is depressing to think that might keep happening to us, even after we're dead.'

Kerrigan stepped over a dog that was chewing on an old shoe. 'It's my understanding that Spencer Pike, the owner of the property, hasn't lived here for some time.'

'Not for twenty years.'

'Do you think he was aware before then that this land was an alleged burial ground?'

The old man stopped in his tracks. 'I think Spencer Pike knows a hell of a lot more than what he lets on.'

Now this was interesting. Kerrigan opened his mouth to ask

another question but was distracted by a man and a kid walking inside. 'Who are they?'

'Rumor says it's someone van Vleet hired,' Thompson said. 'To make sure there are no ghosts.' He turned to the reporter. 'What do *you* think?'

Kerrigan was used to doing the interviewing, not to being interviewed. 'That the whole thing makes for a great story,' he answered carefully.

'You ever wake up with someone else's dream on your tongue? Or slip on your boots to find them filled with snow, in August? You ever seen squash blossoms vine up through a sink drain overnight, Mr Klieg?'

'Well, no, I haven't.'

Thompson nodded. 'Stick around,' he said.

When Ross put his hand on his nephew's neck, the boy nearly leaped out of his skin. 'Ethan,' Ross said, 'you okay with this?'

Ethan was shaking in his shoes. 'Yeah. Oh, yeah, sure, I'm totally cool.'

'Because I can take you home. It's not a problem.' Ross stared soberly at Ethan. 'You can tell everyone I was the one who wouldn't let you stay.'

In response, Ethan took hold of the splintered railing on the stairs and started to climb.

With a sigh, Ross followed. Maybe Ethan wanted to be here, but *he* sure as hell didn't. When van Vleet had asked him to investigate some of the paranormal phenomena at the Pike property, he'd refused. And then he'd seen his sister watching him, waiting.

He'd set four conditions. First, Ross was in charge of the investigation, and would take orders from no one, including the head of the Redhook Group himself. Second, the only people allowed on the property during the investigation would be Ross and his assistant – Ethan, to the boy's utter surprise and delight. Third, Ross wanted no information about the history of the property until he asked for it – otherwise, the impressions he got might be tainted. Fourth, he would take no money for his services – unlike the Warburtons, who would give any client a ghost, for the right amount of cash.

In return, Ross promised to keep this investigation 'quiet.' Because the Powers That Be at the Redhook Group didn't want the entire world to know they might actually be giving credence to a belief in the supernatural.

So now, here he was, setting up for a night observation and falling back into the familiar as if it were a featherbed. Ethan waited at the top of the stairs like a zealous puppy. 'Put the camera down,' Ross instructed. 'Let's do a walkthrough and see if you get anything.'

'*Get* anything? Like what?'

Ross had to stop and think for a moment. How did you explain to a kid the sensation of splitting your mind at its seams, so that every scent and sight left an imprint? How did you describe the feeling of the air growing heavy as a blanket, settling over your ribs? 'Close your eyes,' Ross said, 'and tell me what you see.'

'But—'

'Just *do* it.'

Ethan was silent at first. 'Light . . . shooting out from the corners.'

'Okay.' Ross gently turned him in a circle, like pin-the-tail-on-the-donkey. Then he steadied Ethan's shoulders. 'Now . . . without peeking . . . where are the stairs?'

'Behind me,' Ethan said, the wonder of this sixth sense shaking through his voice.

'How do you know?'

'It . . . well, it feels like a hole in the air back there.'

Ross pivoted Ethan, then tapped him on the head hard enough to make his eyes fly open. 'Good job, Boy Wonder. That was lesson number one.'

'What's lesson number two?'

'To stop asking for lessons.'

Ross walked through the hallway. Any furniture or family relics that had been in this home were long gone, their original placement marked only by the fading of the paint or scuff marks on the filthy floor. The upstairs held three small bedrooms and a bath. A staircase led up to a tiny servant's alcove.

'Uncle Ross? When will they get here?'

'If there are ghosts, they're already here.' Ross peeked into the bathroom. The claw-footed tub was there, cracked in the middle, and an old commode with an overhead tank. 'In fact, they're probably checking us out. If they decide they like what they see, they'll try to get our attention a little later.'

When Ethan turned the faucet, a brown residue leaked out. 'Do they care that we're here?'

'They might.' Ross felt along the window, examining the seal. 'Some ghosts are desperate to get someone to notice them. But some ghosts don't know they're dead at all. They're gonna see us and wonder why we're in their house. That is,' he challenged loudly, 'if there are even any here.'

Come and get me, Ross thought.

He walked back down the stairs, examining the kitchen, the pantry, the cellar, and the living room. A small study with double doors still had a wing chair in it, a shredded hunk of leather where a family of mice had made its nest. Old newspapers littered the floor on this level, and the walls were smeared with what seemed to be axle grease.

'Uncle Ross? Is Aimee a ghost?'

He felt the hair stand up on the back of his neck, and it had nothing to do with the paranormal – only true, human shock. 'I don't know, Ethan.' He shoved aside the image of Aimee that rose to his mind, like a mermaid surfacing from the otherworld of the ocean. 'Dying . . . well, I think it's like taking a bus. Most people, they enjoy the ride and go on to whatever comes next. But some people get off before that last stop.'

'Maybe she got off to see you.'

'Maybe,' Ross said. He turned away, intent on heading up the stairs before he embarrassed himself in front of his nephew.

'Why do you think the ghost that lives here got off the bus?'

'I don't know.'

'What if—'

'Ethan,' Ross interrupted. 'Ssh.' He turned in a circle, trying to catch onto the minnow of a thought that swam through his mind, too quicksilver to show itself clearly. Trying to focus, he leaned over the railing to frown at the filth littering the base of the stairs, at the quiet twitching of rodents. He glanced at a hornet's nest in the corner.

Other organic detritus netted the hall – spider filaments and dust mites, moss and mold – the thriving scars of negligence and damp weather. Ross walked into the bedroom that looked out onto the rear of the property. There, the wooden planking was black with dirt, and strewn with broken pottery and candy bar wrappers. But the ceiling was as bare as if it had been swept clean that morning. Not a single cobweb, no fungus, no insects. In spite of the condition of the rest of the residence, no living organism had taken root in this room for some time.

Ross turned to his nephew. 'This,' he said, 'is where we'll set up.'

'I don't know what happened,' said Lucy's camp counselor, a girl so young she might have passed for a child herself. She hurried Meredith down a path toward the supply shed, inside which Lucy had locked herself forty-five minutes ago. 'One minute she was playing dodgeball, and the next minute she ran away screaming.'

One of Meredith's heels caught on a rock and nearly sent her pitching forward. Did she have Lucy's medicine? If she was scared, so scared she couldn't be coaxed out of the *dark,* she was probably having an asthma attack. 'We called home right away,' the counselor said. 'Your mother said she can't drive.'

'My grandmother,' Meredith corrected absently. In her late seventies, Ruby was smart as a tack, but she no longer felt comfortable behind a wheel. She'd called Meredith at the lab. *An emergency,* she'd said.

They had reached a small wooden building at the edge of the woods. 'Lucy?' Meredith rattled the handle. 'Lucy, you open this door right now!' She banged against it with her fist, twice. On the third strike it swung forward on its hinges, and Meredith crawled inside.

The stale heat hit first. A net bag filled with rubber kickballs to form an oversized molecule blocked her from getting to Lucy, who was wheezing hard behind a tower of orange safety cones and badminton racquets. Her daughter clutched a train of purple satin to her chest, the remnant of a costume from an old summer musical. She was crying.

'Here,' Meredith said, handing over the Albuterol, which Lucy dutifully corked into her mouth and sucked in. She had learned long ago that no matter how difficult it was to see your child struggling for air, you could not breathe for her. Her first instinct was to drag Lucy out of this musty closet, for the sake of her asthma; but something told Meredith that not attending to Lucy's fears first might be equally as damaging. So she slid an arm around her daughter's shoulders. 'How come it's even called *Dodge* ball?' she mused, as if it were perfectly normal to be holding a conversation here. 'I mean, why not Jeep ball or Lexus ball or even Chevrolet ball?'

'You're supposed to move out of the way.' This, from the side of Meredith's shoulder, where Lucy had buried herself. 'That's what the *dodge* is for.'

'Ah.' She nodded slowly. 'I probably knew that, once.'

Lucy's chest was still swelling like a bellows. 'It wasn't the game,' she confessed. 'I saw something.'

'Something?'

'Something . . . hanging. In the tree. From a rope.'

'Like a tire swing?'

Lucy shook her head. 'Like a lady.'

Meredith forced herself to stay calm. 'Will you show me?'

They stumbled outside past Lucy's counselor, past the arts-and-crafts pavilion, over the narrow bridge at the mouth of the stream to the athletic fields. A new group of campers, all older than Lucy, was playing dodgeball.

'Where?' Meredith asked. Lucy pointed to a grove of trees on her left. Firmly grasping her daughter's hand, Meredith marched to the base of the tree and glanced up. 'No rope,' she said quietly. 'Nothing.'

'It was there.' Frustration roughened Lucy's voice. 'It *was.*'

'Luce. I believe you saw something. I just think that somewhere between your retina and your cerebrum, things got a little screwed up. There's a perfectly good explanation, one that has nothing to do with a woman hanging from a tree. For example, maybe the sun got in your eyes.'

'Maybe,' Lucy repeated, without a shred of conviction.

'Maybe it was a branch that the wind moved for a second.'

Lucy shrugged.

Suddenly Meredith toed off her heels and handed her lab coat to Lucy. 'Hold this,' she said, and she started to climb the tree.

She didn't get that far – she was wearing a skirt, after all, and was in her stocking feet – but managed to reach an overhead branch, where she perched like an outsized squirrel. By now, all the campers in the field were watching, and even Lucy had a tiny smile on her face. 'Nope,' Meredith said loudly, willing to play the fool so that at lunchtime and during swimming and on the bus ride home, campers would be talking about the crazy woman in the oak tree instead of the frightened kid who'd run away screaming. 'Luce, the coast is perfectly clear . . . oh . . . oh!' With a calculated tumble that would have done Ringling Brothers proud, Meredith fell out of the tree, landing in a squat, and then rolling to the side until she came to rest a few yards away.

She was filthy and scraped and her hair had fallen out of its barrette, but Lucy put her hands on either side of Meredith's face. 'It might have been the sun in my eyes,' Lucy whispered.

Meredith folded her daughter into her arms. 'That's my brave girl,' she said, fully aware that neither of them believed a single word they'd said.

Eli Rochert did not want to wake up. He knew this as well as he knew the perfume that seemed to surround him in his dreams, a curious blend of apples and rainwater; as well as he recognized the pitch of a woman's voice, floating like a note that had never existed on any musical scale. He had only gone to bed two hours ago, having pulled a double shift to keep the Indians and the developers from coming to blows. But the telephone would not stop ringing, and finally he reached out from the cocoon of his bedclothes and snatched the receiver. 'What?' he growled.

'I'm looking for Mrs Rochert. Is she available?'

'No.'

'Can you tell me when she might return?'

Never, thought Eli, with a pang beneath his ribs that, even after all this time, surprised him. He hung up the phone without answering, then rolled onto his belly, only to find Watson hogging the pillow. 'Oh, for Christ's sake,' Eli muttered, shoving the dog's muzzle away. From within the folds of his face, Watson blinked, then snuffled right back down where he'd been.

'I should have never let you sleep on the bed,' Eli said aloud, his back pressed along the broad spine of his hound. He heard Watson begin to snore, and that was when he knew he wasn't going to be able to will himself back into his dreams. Throwing back the covers, Eli got out of bed and padded into the kitchen, where he opened the refrigerator and stared at the contents.

His doctor had told him that he should give up eating red meat, which would have been fine for most people, but devastating to Eli, who considered it one of two food groups (the other being potatoes). To this end, the insides of his refrigerator were as uninspiring as some of the vegetarian recipes he'd downloaded off the Internet – two jars of mustard, milk that smelled suspicious, a six-pack – *hallelujah,* a lunch meat that might have been turkey a week or three ago, and tofu – a food he positively did not trust, because it slid down one's throat like a rumor.

Cool air spilled over his boxers and pooled at his feet. Eli closed the refrigerator door as the telephone began to ring again. He reached for the kitchen extension. 'Hello?'

'I was hoping to speak to Mrs Rochert?'

Eli counted to ten. 'Mrs Rochert is not here. Mrs Rochert left approximately seven years and six months ago, in the company of the guy who happened to be fucking her at the time. She took all the money in our savings account, our cat, and my favorite sweatshirt. She explained to me just before she walked out the door that it wasn't about *me,* because I hadn't been around enough for her to make that sort of assessment, although in my defense all I'd been doing was working my ass off to get money to put into the bank account that she liquidated. The last I heard, she was living in New Mexico, but I'm going strictly on the grapevine here. So, no, you cannot speak to Mrs Rochert, no matter how much you're hoping to. And in fact, *should* you get the opportunity to speak to her, you might want to let her know that you're only the first in line.'

By the time Eli finished, he was breathing hard. It made up for the silence on the other end of the receiver.

'Oh,' he heard, finally, faintly.

'Maybe you could take this number off your call list,' Eli suggested, and he threw the portable phone across the room to smash against the wall.

He was sitting on the floor with his hands splayed through his hair when Watson found him. The dog dropped the telephone's battery into Eli's lap and then stood over him. Eli rubbed his hand over his face. 'If you're hoping for a snack, Watson, you're out of luck. Unless maybe bean curd tastes good with a Coors chaser.'

Eli wrapped his arm around the dog's thick neck and stared into his mournful brown eyes. It was one of the reasons Eli had picked him from the Humane Society – one look, and you knew that hound would never be happy. Which meant that Eli could not fail again.

Working for the Warburtons, Ross had learned that the witching hour was between 10 at night and 3 A.M. Most of the thumps and bumps and visions that Curtis had seen – or pretended to have seen – occurred during that time. By 10:30, Ross and Ethan had set up the bedroom in the abandoned house to his satisfaction, if not his nephew's.

'Where's all the stuff?' Ethan asked. 'You know, the *cool* equipment. Like they have on *Real Scary Stories*.' He eyed the video camera dubiously.

'Curtis says you don't want too many bells and whistles the first time you go out to investigate,' Ross answered. 'You'll wind up getting distracted by the tools, and relying on them instead of yourself. Plus, entities disturb the magnetic field. They're just as likely to make the equipment short out as they are to leave a trace.'

'Still,' Ethan muttered. 'Without tools and stuff we're as lame as Shaggy and Scooby.'

Ross laughed. 'Zoinks,' he said, then glanced at his nephew's crestfallen face. 'Look. Whenever Curtis got the feeling that something was there, he'd come back with the cool equipment to back up his senses. We can do that too. Of course, first we'll have to *buy* the cool equipment.'

The camera was pointed toward one of the bedroom walls, the junk food was within arm's distance, the sleeping bags were unrolled to form a synthetic island on the filthy floorboards. The only source of light in the room was a small Maglite set between

Ross and Ethan to form a bright puddle. Ross placed a small deck of cards in the spotlight and began to shuffle.

Ethan spoke around an enormous Bazooka bubble he'd just blown. 'Considering that you think Warburton's an asshole, you sure quote him a lot.'

'Watch your mouth. He's not an asshole, he's a liar. And even though I think he makes up half the stuff he sees, he knows his shit.'

'Watch your mouth,' Ethan parroted, then grabbed the deck. 'Uncle Ross? You think the ghost here died some horrible way?'

'I don't even know there's a ghost here yet. Are you going to deal?'

'Yeah.' The boy started to divide the cards. 'I wonder if it'll be all mad at us. If it might confuse us for whoever chopped off its head with an ax.'

'What ax?' Ross tipped his hand into the single beam of the flashlight. 'Okay, so having any member of the royal family is a good thing?'

'I can't believe you never played this. Yeah, you want to get kings and queens. And aces. But more than that you want to get cards of the same suit in a row, like two-three-four-five-six. First you have to bet something . . . you have any cash?'

'Reese's Pieces.'

'Well, whatever. A straight flush beats four of a kind, and four of a kind beats a full house. That's good enough to start, so I'm going to draw.' He looked up. 'That means pick a card.'

'Thanks,' Ross said dryly. 'I'll raise you two Reese's.'

'I won't be scared, you know, even if it comes after me.'

If put on the spot – something he had not allowed van Vleet to do – Ross would have had to say that he did not believe any entity was haunting the Pike property. In the first place, Ross had seen nothing in all his months of ghost hunting. In the second, even going on *theory*, it was crazy to think of a human spirit gathering enough energy to cause the events that had been attributed to it – from the ground freezing to rose petals raining from the clouds. Though unlikely, each of those circumstances could be explained by something natural – a latent ice floe running beneath the soil, a strange evaporation.

Then again, Ross had been wrong about things before.

At the very least, this night was good for Ethan. Ross stretched back on his elbows and watched his nephew lay out his poker hand. 'I've got a straight.'

'Three of a kind. Jacks.'

'Maybe you should play with a handicap,' Ethan suggested. He dealt a second round. 'I think I'll come back.'

'Here?'

'No, not *here* . . . just here. After I die.' He looked around the room, then at his uncle, a dare. 'I mean, I won't be done yet. You know?'

Ross had gone to homes with the Warburtons where children had died of disease, or by accident. The mothers wore hope like mantillas, framing their faces as they waited for Curtis to give them back what they'd lost. In those cases, it was not moans and thumps and strange occurrences that had led to the call, it was the lack of them.

He thought of his sister, and folded his cards.

'I'm hungry,' Ethan said. He slipped away in shadow, fumbling around and causing a loud crash.

'You all right?' Ross swung the beam of the flashlight toward the pack of junk food they'd brought, but that entire corner of the room was empty.

Ethan spoke from behind him. 'I'm here,' he said, his voice shaking. 'That, uh, that wasn't me.'

He plastered himself up against his uncle's back. 'Let's just take a look,' Ross murmured. Everything was quiet, now, and there was no evidence that anything had fallen. 'It could have been a brick outside, or a rat.' He slipped an arm around Ethan's shoulders. 'It could have been anything, Ethan.'

'Right.'

'Why don't we sit down so that I can whip your butt this time around?'

Ethan relaxed a little. 'As if,' he said, dredging up the courage to peel himself away and take a seat again.

Ross dealt the cards, but his eyes kept scanning the dark. Nothing unusual, nothing that captured his attention. Except the lens cap of the video camera, hanging down on a black cord from the side of the apparatus, which had begun to swing back and forth.

Although there was no breeze in the room.

From outside came the sound of a hollow thud – a tree falling, or a person landing on all fours. 'Did you hear that?' Ethan whispered shakily.

'Yeah.' Ross walked toward the broken window and peered out into the woods that edged the back of the property. A flash of white caught his eye – the tail of a deer, a shooting star, the eyes of a barn owl.

There was a rustle of leaves, and two distinct footfalls. A hitched wail, like the cry of an infant.

'We may just take a walk down there,' Ross murmured.

Ethan shook his head hard. 'No way. I'm staying here.'

'It's probably just a raccoon.'

'And what if it's *not?*'

Ross smiled slowly. 'What if,' he said.

Shelby was not in the habit of allowing her son to do dangerous things; it was hazard enough for him to live in this world. But Ethan had a nine-year-old's sense of adventure and wanderlust. Believing he was part of Ross's mission – well, maybe it would be good for both of them.

She walked into his room, picking up his Game Boy from the floor, as well as a few cartridges that had fallen beneath the bed. A Red Sox game schedule was on the wall, along with the textbooks Shelby used to home-school Ethan, and a haiku he'd written last year as part of a unit on Japan.

Deep in the darkness
I wake to make the night day.
How does the sun feel?

Shelby sank onto his bed. She wondered if Ross was keeping Ethan safe. She wondered if Ethan missed her, just a little.

She stared uneasily at the computer. The last time she'd decided to check up on her son, she'd hacked into his e-mail account to discover that he'd acquired six pen pals – all kids around his own age, all from different parts of the world. At first, Shelby had found this encouraging. For Ethan to have found a way to make a connection to other children seemed healthy, if not downright inspiring. But then Shelby had started to read some of the mail, and realized that Ethan had not represented himself quite accurately. To Sonya in Denmark, he was a sixth-grade preppie on the math squad. To Tony in Indianapolis, he was a star batter for a little-league farm team. To Marco in Colorado, he was an avid mountain climber who trekked every weekend with his dad.

In none of these letters did he mention his XP condition. In none of these letters did he seem any less than an average, athletic, normal American boy from a happy two-parent family.

In short, Ethan had turned himself into everything he was not.

With a sigh Shelby left Ethan's room and started down the hall. Passing Ross's door, she hesitated. She was eight years older than Ross; it seemed she had been taking care of him all her life – from diapering him as an infant to sitting by his side after his suicide attempt to worrying for his safety when he did not call her for months. Mothering had always come easily to her; when their parents had died years ago, she simply stepped into their shoes and took over.

She believed that unadulterated devotion had its share of

protective power, as if love were a steel girder the Fates could not snip through. She also believed that the moment you relaxed your guard, the moment you were anything less than ferocious in your keeping, that was the moment it all could be snatched away.

Which brought her right back to wondering when Ross would bring Ethan home.

She pushed open the door and began to clean in there, too. She made Ross's bed. She lined up his toothbrush and his hairbrush on the dresser. She put his shampoo, nail clippers, and toothpaste into his toiletry kit and zipped it shut.

The chair was piled high with her brother's rumpled clothes. With a sigh she lifted one soft shirt and creased it neatly, set it on the edge of the bed. She balled together a pair of socks. She stacked boxers and tees and finally shook out a spare pair of jeans. As she began to fold them with military precision, something fell from the pocket. Shelby leaned down to pick up what had dropped: three pennies, dated 1932, which she set on the dresser where Ross would be sure to see them.

Ross turned and waved up at Ethan in the window, then cautiously approached the spot in the woods where he'd last seen the flash of white. He had left Ethan with the Maglite, which meant Ross fully expected to plunge headfirst over an exposed root. Although he couldn't see more than a foot in front of him, he could still hear the sounds of someone – or some*thing* – scrabbling around.

Ross shivered; it was colder out here than he'd expected it to be, and he wished he'd brought his sweatshirt. He could suddenly smell wild roses, as if there were a field of them underfoot, and he knew from Curtis that this, too, was a way a ghost might make its presence known. *Show yourself,* he thought.

But any hopes he had of encountering his first apparition died as he came upon a young woman, crouching as she tried to dig into the frozen earth.

She was wearing a flowered dress, and her pale hair was wild around her face. The white flash Ross had seen was a lace collar. She was feverishly busy, intent on her task. And she was as real as the ground beneath his feet.

Clearly, she had not heard him approach, or she would have realized she'd been caught in the act of . . . well, whatever she'd been doing. Ross found himself tongue-tied – not only wasn't she the ghost he'd been hoping for, but she was young, and pretty, and uninvited. He seized on that, if only to have something to say. 'What are you doing here?'

She turned slowly, blinking, as if surprised to find herself in the middle of the forest. 'I . . . I don't know.' Glancing down at her hands, dirt caught beneath the nails, she frowned.

'Did van Vleet send you?'

'I don't know Van Fleet . . .'

'Vleet.' Ross frowned. Maybe it was only an unlikely coincidence that the night he began his investigation, an insomniac would come wandering onto the property. There *were* other homes in the vicinity, and stranger things had happened. He found himself wishing that he hadn't started this conversation on the defensive. He found himself wishing she'd glance up at him again. 'What are you looking for?' he asked, nodding toward the hole she'd been digging.

The woman blushed, which lit her from the inside. When she shook her head, he could smell that floral perfume again. 'I have no idea. The last time I sleepwalked, I wound up in a neighbor's hayloft.'

'With or without the neighbor?' Ross heard himself ask, and the woman looked so mortified that he immediately wished he could call back the words. He dug his hands into his pockets instead, trying to make amends. 'I'm Ross Wakeman,' he said.

She looked up, still discomfited. 'I have to go.'

'No, see, where I come from, the appropriate response is: Hello, I'm Susan. Or: Hey, Hannah's the name. Or: Howdy, I'm Madonna.'

'Madonna?'

Ross grinned. 'Whatever.'

A tiny smile played at the corners of her mouth. 'I'm Lia,' she said.

'Just Lia?'

She hesitated. 'Beaumont. Lia Beaumont.'

Every line of her body was poised for flight. Then again, coming across a stranger in the middle of the woods when you were sleepwalking was bound to be upsetting. If possible, she seemed even more unsure of herself around Ross than Ross felt around her. She nodded, still awkward, and started to walk off. Ross was filled with an unaccountable need to keep her from leaving, and tried to think of one thing to say that would keep her here, but all the words dammed up at the base of his throat.

Suddenly, she turned back to him. 'Were *you* sleepwalking?'

'No, actually, I'm working.' Ross wound the thread of conversation tight around himself, an anchor.

'Here? *Now?*'

'Yeah. I'm a paranormal investigator.' He could tell the term didn't ring a bell for her. 'Ghosts,' he explained. 'I look for ghosts. In fact, I came out here because I thought your collar was . . . well, anyway. You're not quite what I was expecting.'

'I'm sorry.'

'Don't be.'

She tipped her head to one side, studying him. 'You really believe people can come back after they die? Like Harry Houdini?'

'Doesn't everyone?' She wore sorrow like a hangman's hood; it shrouded her delicate features. 'Who knows?' he teased. 'We may even have company right now.'

But his words made Lia glance behind her wildly. 'If he finds me . . .'

Who? Ross wanted to say, as he realized that this woman's skittishness was not about being discovered by him, but being discovered by someone else. Before he could ask, an ear-splitting scream curled from the house. 'Uncle Ross!' Ethan shrieked. 'Uncle Ross, come *back!*'

Ross looked up at the window, where there was no longer any residual light from either the flashlight or the video camera. The blood drained from his face as he imagined what Ethan might have seen. 'I have to go,' he said to Lia, and without any further explanation, took off at a dead run.

From the *New York Times*:

THINGS THAT GO BUMP IN THE NIGHT?

by Kerrigan Klieg

Comtosook, VT – The residents of Comtosook, a small town in the northwest corner of Vermont, are eager to tell tall tales. There are stories of maple sap running in the dry summer months, of flower petals falling from rain clouds and of ground freezing solid in the middle of August, of cars that suddenly can only move in reverse. Yet the strangest part of this gossip is that it happens to be true, and these odd occurrences are just the tip of the iceberg. Experts at the nearby University of Vermont in various fields have not been able to explain the numerous events, but residents have their own ideas about what's causing the commotion: a spirit, a restless one who doesn't want to be moved.

Weeks ago, Comtosook was a bucolic Vermont town. Then the Redhook Development Group struck a deal with an elderly landowner to acquire a small tract of property. Immediately, a local band of Abenaki Indians began to protest, insisting the land was a native burial ground. Archaeological testing done by the state has not revealed any human remains, although that is incidental, says Az Thompson, a local Abenaki leader: 'I wouldn't expect some flatlander real-estate group to know where my ancestors are buried, but I sure didn't expect them to tell me I'm lying about that, either.

Who gave them the privilege to rewrite my history?' Adds Winks Smiling Fox, a fellow protester, 'Enough has happened here lately to prove that as much as Redhook wants *in*, there's something else that doesn't want *out*.'

He refers to the growing list of oddities that have begun to wear down the general public, even those who live miles away from the disputed property. Abe Huppinworth, proprietor of a local general store, has become used to sweeping rose petals off the porch. 'They fall all night long, like snow. Three, four inches deep when I come in to open up. And there isn't a rosebush within three miles of here.' Ava Morgan took her two-year-old son to Fletcher Allen Hospital in Burlington when he awakened one morning speaking Portuguese, a language with which none of his family was familiar, much less fluent. 'The doctors couldn't tell me what happened, either. They tested him forward and backward, and then one morning it all just went away, and Cole was back to saying *Mommy* and *milk*.' Not all residents are as complacent, however. Over six hundred signatures filled a petition that was given to Rod van Vleet, project manager on site for the Redhook Group. Mr van Vleet declined to be interviewed, but has previously dismissed all claims of paranormal activity on the property as preposterous.

Reports allude that van Vleet may not be as confident as he asserts. Sources say that the Redhook Group has commissioned an investigator to explore the property.

To the townspeople, however, both the hidden intents of a real-estate developer, and the angry fury of the Abenaki, are equally unimportant. 'All I know is, this is wearing me out,' says Huppinworth, at a pause in his endless sweeping of petals. 'Sooner or later, something's got to give.'

It was an established fact of the universe that Meredith was never going to meet a decent man. At work, she was too smart, and therefore too intimidating. Blind dates didn't prove any more successful. The last one she'd been on was with an actor her grandmother had met in the park, who'd arrived at the restaurant dressed as Hamlet. *To leave or not to leave,* Meredith had thought, *that was the question.* Since that debacle, her grandmother had presented her with the phone numbers of a mortician, a vet, and a chiropractor, but Meredith had conveniently lost each one. 'I want a grandchild before I die,' Ruby said, on schedule, every two to three months.

'You have one,' Meredith would remind her.

'One with a father,' Ruby would clarify.

Meredith had finally caved in, when Ruby told her that *this one* spent his free time doing volunteer work with senior citizens. So now, Meredith was sitting across from Michael DesJardins, trying to convince herself that this wasn't nearly as bad as it seemed.

He was drooling. All right, so it had to do with dental surgery he'd had that day, but it wasn't particularly appetizing for Meredith. 'So,' he slurred, 'you work in a lab? What do you do . . . feed all the mice and stuff?'

'I do PGD. Preimplantation genetic diagnosis.'

'I'm in the catering business.'

'Oh?' Meredith folded her hands in front of her, watching him butter an entire slice of bread and stuff it in his mouth. On the bright side, it did mop up his excess saliva. 'Are you a chef?'

'Yes, as a matter of fact.'

She'd always harbored the fantasy of a man whisking her to a cozy apartment, where a fabulous gourmet meal had been prepared for her enjoyment. 'I guess being in a restaurant feels like work, then.'

'This is a cut above my place, actually . . . you ever go into the Wendy's on Sixteenth Street?'

Meredith was saved from responding when the waiter approached with their entrées. Michael began to cut his entire steak into little quarter-inch cubes. It made her think of the meals they served in mental institutions.

She smoothed down her napkin and looked down at her

chipolata sausage, nestled on a bed of polenta. *The silver lining,* she told herself, *is that I'm going to get a good meal out of this.*

Michael pointed to her dinner with his knife and laughed. 'Looks like a Great Dane did his business there.' A line of drool dribbled down his chin.

I will stand up and excuse myself to go to the bathroom, Meredith thought. *And then I just won't come back.*

But if she did that, Granny Ruby would accuse her of deliberately ruining another date. So Meredith began to think of ways to make Michael want to leave of his own volition. She would ask for crayons and start to color on the fancy linens. She would sculpt with her polenta. She would lick her plate and offer to lick his. She would communicate only in mime, or Pig Latin.

'Can I ask you a personal question?' Michael said. 'Are you ovulating?'

'*Excuse me?*'

'It's just that these days, when I look in the mirror, I see *Daddy.*' He grinned and pointed to his forehead, as if the word had been tattooed there.

Meredith wished for many things in that moment: her grandmother's head on a pike, patience, lesbian tendencies. *Volunteer work with senior citizens,* she remembered. She stared at Michael's plate. 'Are you going to eat that?'

'The steak?'

'No, the bone. I wanted to bring it home to my grandmother.' Meredith leaned closer. 'She's in her seventies, practically dead, and it's cheaper than feeding her.'

Michael choked on his sip of water. Then, recovering, he raised his hand and signaled for the waiter for the check. 'You're finished, aren't you?'

Meredith folded her napkin on the table. 'Oh, yes.'

Ethan now knew what fear felt like: your forehead, being pressed in from all sides, although there was nothing around you. All the hairs on the back of your neck, rising one by one like dominoes in reverse. Your legs going to water, and shaking so hard you had to sit or fall.

'It wasn't like I was afraid,' Ethan insisted for the hundredth time since yelling out for his uncle the night before. 'I mean, it was just weird, you know? To be in the dark all of a sudden?'

Ross sat beside him in the living room, his infrared video equipment hooked into the TV. The picture was grainy and dark, the edges crackling. Plus, since it had been mounted on a tripod, it was boring as all get out. Ethan didn't know what on earth was interesting about staring at a wall for three hours of tape. In spite of the fact that this was apparently a Very Important Element of paranormal investigation, he could not keep from yawning.

That was something else Uncle Ross had taught him: When you're in the presence of ghosts, they wear you out.

His uncle was being cool, especially since – well, if he wanted to be honest, Ethan had to admit he'd freaked out when the flashlight went dead and the video camera just shut itself off. The camera, it turned out, had only run to the end of its tape. The flashlight's batteries were shot.

Now, his mom frowned at the picture on the TV. 'Am I missing something?'

'Not yet.' Ross turned to Ethan. 'You know what I think? I think it was in the room with you.'

Ethan couldn't help it; he shivered. Could a ghost hitchhike home with you? Could you catch one, like a cold or the measles? He felt his mother's arms come around him and he leaned back, lock to key. 'I . . . I thought you went outside because you saw something there.'

'No, that turned out to be *someone.*' Suddenly Ross hit the pause button on the remote. 'See those?'

'Fireflies?' Shelby said.

'When was the last time you saw so many fireflies moving around it looked like a snowstorm?' He rewound the tape and pumped up the volume, so that his voice and Ethan's could be heard again. 'This is where I leave,' Ross narrated. His footsteps, on tape, thudded lighter and lighter as he made his way downstairs. 'See? Those lights show up just after I go.'

Then the camera went black.

Ross rolled his shoulders until the bones popped. 'I think whatever it is came into the room with Ethan when I was outside. Those sparks on the tape – that was energy changing form. And that would explain why the flashlight went out. Ghosts need energy to materialize and move around; this one was using the double A's in the Maglite.' He watched Ethan stifle another yawn. 'And, apparently, whatever force keeps Ethan going.'

But Ethan had been alone in that room, and he hadn't seen anything. Or had he?

A bathtub. A foot, rising from the bubbles.

The picture rose from the still blue of his mind, then sank to the bottom before he could grab hold. Each of Ethan's eyelids, by now, easily weighed ten pounds. He heard his mother's voice, an underwater current. 'What are you going to tell the development company?'

But Ethan did not hear his uncle's answer. He was already dreaming of a beach, of sand so hot it felt sharp as a knife beneath his jitterbug feet.

Shelby knew that some librarians felt the human brain was like a microfiche file, impossibly tiny images and words on transparent leaves, arranged page by page for a person's viewing pleasure. But every time she saw those miniature dossiers, she thought that if any part of the body were similarly catalogued, it would be the heart. She imagined autopsies, the organ sliced thin. One sliver would chronicle the way you had cherished a child; one would record the feelings you had for parents and siblings. Another, scarlet, might be etched with moments of passion; angels embracing on the head of a pin. And for those who were lucky, the thinnest slice would be teeming with memories of a love so strong it turned you inside out and left you gasping, and would be an identical match to a slice stored in the heart of a soul mate.

Desiderate: to long for.

'Do you need any help?'

Shelby pushed her reading glasses up her nose and turned to the pockmarked clerk of the probate court. 'No, thanks. I can do this in my sleep.' To illustrate, she pulled out the base of the microfiche machine and deftly switched transparencies, so that she could view the next page of the will.

It was Ross who'd made the request for her investigative services – and because he so infrequently asked for help, she agreed. He had wanted her to find out how long the land had been in the Pike family, if there was any record of a Native American settlement on it. Shelby had driven to the municipal building, which housed the police station and the district court, as well as the probate department and the town offices. What she learned was that the property had only belonged to Pike since the 1930s.

There was no record of any Native American ever living there.

Shelby had taken it upon herself to discover how Spencer Pike got the deed to the land. It had not been a real-estate transaction, to her surprise, but rather an inheritance. From his deceased wife.

Shelby hadn't made a will of her own. It wasn't like she had all that much, actually – not that Ethan would be left as a tatterdemalian if she was hit by a car on her way out of the court building, but then again, she wasn't Ivana Trump either. However, the reason she hadn't bothered to go to a lawyer to have one drawn up had less to do with her assets than her benefactors. Every other parent in the universe left their worldly goods to their children. But what if you knew for a fact that you were going to outlive your son?

I, Mrs Spencer A. Pike of Comtosook, Vermont, make this my last will,
hereby revoking all previous wills and codicils made by me.

Shelby frowned at the date – it had been signed in 1931. The
lettering of her signature was delicate and spiderlike. She had
signed the will that way too – *Mrs Spencer A. Pike* – as if before
her marriage she had not existed at all. Shelby had to wade
through the legalese, but the intent was fairly straightforward:
Mrs Spencer A. Pike had left everything to her husband. Almost.

I give and devise all of my tangible personal property, including but not
limited to my furniture, furnishing, jewelry and automobiles, to my
husband, Spencer Pike. I give and devise the real property owned by
me located at the crossing of Otter Creek Pass and Montgomery Road,
in Comtosook, Chittenden County, State of Vermont, to my issue resulting
to my marriage from Spencer Pike, to be held in trust by my executor
for those issue until they each reach the age of 21. Such real property
shall be held by those issue as joint tenants. If Spencer Pike and I shall
have produced no living issue at the time of my death, I give and devise
the aforesaid real property to my husband, Spencer Pike.

There was nothing in the will about how a woman with so
little sense of self had wound up owning the property in the first
place. Nothing about how her husband had been affected by her
untimely death; whether he had ever looked at the property that
was now his and thought that he would trade every square inch
if it brought her back.

Shelby loved words, but she would be the first to tell you they
had a habit of letting you down. Most of the time, the words that
were *not* written were the ones you needed most.

She slipped the microfiche out of the machine, slid it into
its protective dust jacket, handed it to the clerk, and left the
probate office. But she had no sooner stepped off the curb
outside than a police cruiser screamed into the circular driveway

of the municipal building; coming to a stop so close that Shelby found her hand outstretched, as if that might keep the car from striking her. The cop who got out muttered an apology, but he wasn't even looking at her as he hurried into the police station.

Shelby shook the whole way to her own car. Promised herself that she would have a will drawn up by the end of the week.

Eli was late. He rushed into the lobby of the station and stuck his head into the dispatch cubicle. 'They're looking for you,' the sergeant said.

'Tell me something I don't know. Where are they?'

'In the conference room. With the chief.'

Groaning, Eli walked down the hall to find Chief Follensbee sitting with two teenage boys. 'Ah, Detective Rochert. Mr Madigan and Mr Quinn, here, said that you specifically told them to meet you here at ten-thirty to take down their statements. And yet here it is, past eleven.'

'I'm sorry, Chief,' Eli said, hanging his head. 'I got, uh, hung up.' Actually, he'd overslept. After spending most of last night awake, he'd drifted off shortly before dawn. He had been dreaming of the woman who smelled of apples, the same one he'd dreamed of before. Was it any wonder he'd ignored his alarm?

Then, he'd been driving past the Pike property and was stopped by two girls riding their bikes. There was a lady wandering around Montgomery Road, they had said, looking lost. Last year, an elderly woman with Alzheimer's had driven off in her car and had been found dead of hypothermia two days later in a supermarket parking lot – for that reason alone, Eli had backtracked to the spot the kids had indicated. But whoever they had seen was gone by then, and Eli was more than twenty minutes late.

He sat down across from Jimmy Madigan and Knott Quinn.

They lolled in their chairs in their metalhead T-shirts, torn jeans, black boots. High school dropouts, they were kids who floated on the fringe of society. For them to have willingly walked into a police station, they must have had quite a scare. 'So you boys say you saw something on the Pike property?'

'Yeah,' Jimmy said. 'Three nights ago. We went for a dare, you know, because of what people say is going on there. And that's when we saw the thing.'

'The thing?'

Jimmy looked at his friend. 'We both saw it. It was, like, taller than both of us together. And it had these fangs . . .'

'Teeth,' Knott agreed. 'All jaggedy, like a hunting knife.'

'And did this creature speak to you?'

The boys glanced at each other. 'See, that's the weird thing. It looked like it was gonna kill us, you know, but when it opened that mouth it cried like a baby.'

'Cried? Like, tears?'

Knott shook his head. 'No, it wailed. *Waa, waa.*'

'And then it just disappeared,' Jimmy added. 'Like smoke.'

'Smoke,' Eli repeated. 'Smoke. Interesting.'

'Dude, I know you think we're making this up, but we're not. Knott and I *both* saw it. I mean, that's gotta count for something.'

'Oh, I believe you saw it. Speaking of seeing things, you guys ever see these?' Eli pulled a small Ziploc bag filled with shriveled mushrooms from his breast pocket.

Knott's face went white. 'Um, truffles?'

'Yeah, truffles,' Eli said. 'Is that what you're growing at home, Knott? Because that's not what one of Jimmy's customers told me.'

'What the fuck, man? I don't know what you're talking about,' Jimmy said.

'Great.' Eli slid two pieces of paper onto the table. 'Then you won't mind when we search your rooms. Because when we find nothing, I won't be able to charge you with possession with intent to distribute.' He leaned forward, arms folded. 'Maybe there is a ghost at the Pike property, and maybe there isn't. But getting high before you go looking just might stack the odds.'

Tonight, Ross had brought equipment – not only the video camera but also one that took digital stills, as well as a thermal scanner – all ordered over the Internet on Shelby's credit card, a fact he hadn't yet broken to his sister. Ethan would have gotten a kick out of the gadgets, but he was home – Shelby's permissiveness apparently had reached its limit. It was shortly after eleven, about a half-hour before the ghost had appeared to Ethan last time. Ross hunkered down to wait. What he wanted, pure and simple, was to be as fortunate as his nephew had been.

He had set up his tools in a clearing behind the house, one that afforded him a good view of the backyard. Rod van Vleet had succeeded in razing half the house. That meant a spirit would move elsewhere – and there were nineteen acres of land to cover. The fact that Ross happened to start at the same spot where he'd met Lia Beaumont nights ago was, he told himself, just a coincidence.

For a while Ross listened to cricket sonatas and the courting of frogs. There were stars at his neck, tiny bites, and the moon pressed into the small of his back. He had no idea what time it was when he heard footsteps near the house. He glanced at his thermal scanner, but the temperature hadn't dropped enough to warrant the arrival of a spirit. Yet a moment later, as a figure stepped into his line of vision, his heart began to race.

The security guard from the quarry was not wearing his uniform, but Ross recognized him immediately; there just were not that many centegenarian Native Americans wandering around Comtosook. He was holding what seemed to be a white rose. 'You?' Az said, frowning.

Ross shrugged. 'I tend to go where the spirit takes me.'

The Indian snorted. 'So this time it took you right to working for those leeches.'

'I'm in business for myself,' Ross corrected. 'They aren't paying me a dime.'

The old man seemed to find this admirable, although he continued to scowl. 'You're looking for ghosts again?'

'Yes.'

'What would you do if you came across one?'

'A ghost? I don't know. I've never found one.'

'You think these developers have a plan?'

Ross pictured van Vleet. 'I imagine they'll want me to try to get rid of it.'

Az's mouth tightened. 'Yeah, round them all up and stick them on the Rez. You move them far enough, it's easy to believe they never existed here at all. Squatters' rights, they don't mean a damn, do they?'

Ross didn't answer. He didn't know if the old man was expecting one, and he was afraid that whatever he said, it would be the wrong response. 'You live around here?' he asked, changing the subject.

Az pointed to a campsite, barely visible across the road. 'I come here, sometimes, at night. Senior citizens don't sleep much,' he said dryly. 'Why waste time doing something I'm going to be doing forever, soon enough?' Az started to move away, then turned back at the edge of the clearing. 'If you find a ghost, you know, you won't get rid of it. No matter what Rod van Vleet wants.'

Ross lifted a shoulder. 'That's a pretty big *if*.'

'Not really. You've been surrounded by ghosts your whole life. You just don't know that's what you're seeing,' Az said. '*Adio,* Mr Wakeman.'

He disappeared around the front of the house as the wind picked up. Ross shrugged into his jacket. He swallowed repeatedly, but could not get the taste of disappointment off his tongue. He told himself it was because Az had come, when Ross was hoping for a ghost. That it had nothing to do with the fact that Az had come, when Ross was hoping for Lia.

*   *   *

'I've had it!' the nurse cried, dropping the tray of pills. 'I do not have to take this kind of treatment from a patient!'

Spencer Pike watched from his wheelchair, his hands folded in his lap. When he needed to, he could play the doddering fool well. He stared at a soap opera on the television set, feigning interest, as the supervisor approached.

She was a large woman with hair dyed the color of apricots. In his mind, Spencer called her Nurse Ratchet. 'Is there a problem, Millicent?'

'Yes, there's a problem,' the younger nurse fumed. 'Mr Pike's verbal abuse.'

Ratchet sighed. 'What did he say this time?'

Millicent's lower lip trembled. 'He said . . . he said I'm an idiot.'

'If I might interrupt, that's not what I said.' Spencer turned to Ratchet. 'I told her she came from a family of imbeciles. Not idiots. There is a difference, however subtle.'

'You see?' Millicent huffed.

'I only asked if she was related to the Cartwrights of Swanton. It's a known fact that nearly half of that family tree grew up in state homes for the feebleminded.' He did not say what he had so politely refrained from telling even Millicent Cartwright – that given the number of times she'd mistaken him for one of the other rest-home patrons, she seemed genetically wired to follow in the footsteps of her kin.

Millicent shrugged out of the cotton vest she wore as an employee of the nursing home. 'I quit,' she announced, and she walked out of the rec room, the heels of her white clogs crushing a rainbow of pills in her wake.

'Mr Pike,' Ratchet said, 'that was uncalled for.'

Spencer shrugged. People never wanted to face up to their own flaws. He ought to know.

In Dr Calloway's office, Meredith felt like a giant – too big for the tiny chairs and table, too oversized to fit in the gingerbread playhouse with the wooden slide, too awkward to fit small stubs of crayons between her fingers to color. Lucy, though, fit perfectly. Across the room and out of earshot, she lay facedown on an enormous stuffed frog, dressing one of Barbie's anorexic friends.

'An isolated visual hallucination is rare,' the psychiatrist said. 'More often, psychotic symptoms present as auditory hallucinations, or agitated behavior.' Dr Calloway glanced at Lucy, quietly playing. 'Have you seen any abrupt changes in her attitude?'

'No.'

'Violence? Acting out?' Meredith shook her head. 'What about changes in her eating or sleeping patterns?'

Lucy hardly ever ate – skinny as she was, Meredith used to joke that her daughter photosynthesized instead – and as for sleeping, well, she hadn't gone straight through a night in ages. 'Sleeping's a problem,' she admitted. 'Lucy's imagination runs away with her. She usually leaves the light on, and she gets herself so worked up about what's in her closet or under her bed that the only reason she even gets to sleep at all is because she passes out from sheer exhaustion.'

'It's possible that Lucy's suffering from the same anxieties any eight-year-old might have at bedtime,' Dr Calloway said. 'And then again, it's possible that she *is* seeing something in her closet and under her bed.'

Meredith swallowed hard. Her child couldn't be psychotic, couldn't be. Not Lucy, who would rather hop than walk; who read picture books to her stuffed animals; who had just mastered all the words to 'Miss Mary Mack.' There was a truth in the back of Meredith's head, as sharp and blue as a flame: *You didn't want her, once, and this is your punishment.*

'What do I do?' she asked.

'Just remember that eight is the age of Santa Claus and imaginary friends and make-believe. Children Lucy's age are just beginning to separate fantasy from reality – and there's a very good chance that whatever she's envisioning is part of that process.'

'But if it keeps up?'

'Then I'd recommend starting Lucy on a low dose of Risperdal, to see if it makes a difference. Let's just wait and see.'

'Okay.' Meredith watched Lucy begin to braid the doll's hair. 'Okay.'

Ross wasn't hungry, so he didn't quite understand why he'd come to the town diner – an establishment that had been around as long as Comtosook, passing like a plague through a chain of over-weight, crotchety owners who all believed that grease was a gourmet seasoning. Not that this seemed to affect business: when Ross arrived, every table and counter stool was taken. Settling against a mirrored wall to wait, he pulled out his pack of cigar-ettes. 'Sorry,' the waitress said, turning the moment he flicked on his lighter. 'We're smoke-free.'

It seemed ridiculous that an establishment whose menu catered to early heart attacks would be so hypocritical, but Ross just tucked his Merits back into his jacket. 'I'll be around back,' he told the waitress. 'Can you save me a table?'

'That depends.' She smiled. 'Will you save me a cigarette?'

Now, five minutes later, he leaned against the Dumpster behind the diner and lit up, letting the smoke curl down his throat like a question mark. He crossed his eyes a little and watched the tip glow.

He should have brought a jacket – it was easily ten degrees colder back here. Temperature fluctuations like this were becoming customary in town, and its residents seemed to have turned a corner – instead of fearing these anomalies, they unpacked their winter boots and mittens, and left them beside their beach towels and suntan lotion, because either one might be called for. The best thing about New Englanders, Ross thought, was that when they finished complaining they swallowed fate like a dose of medi-cine – unpleasant in taste, but ultimately, something you'd get through all the same and be better for it. Ross pressed his shoulders against the dark metal wall of the Dumpster, stealing the heat it had trapped. Head bent, he tossed the rest of the cigarette away.

'You didn't even finish that.'

He turned around. 'Lia.'

Ross would have known she was behind him even if she hadn't spoken; the scent of flowers was in the air. She ground out the butt with her loafer, her fingers fluttering at her sides. She was wearing her polka-dotted dress again, this time with a beaded cardigan, as if she were embarrassed to be seen in the same clothing and wanted to freshen it up.

'I've been looking for you,' Lia said.

Her words didn't match her stance; she looked ready to bolt. There was something about her – something helpless, boxed-in, that seemed familiar to Ross. 'I've been looking for you, too.' As he said it, he realized how much this was true. He had been searching for Lia in the reflection of store windows, in the cars that pulled up beside him at traffic lights, in line at the drugstore.

'Did you find your ghost yet?'

'Not *my* ghost,' Ross clarified. '*A* ghost.' He got to his feet, smiling. 'Why were you looking for me?'

Lia spoke in a rush. 'Because . . . I didn't get to tell you the other night . . . but I look for ghosts, too.'

'You do?' This was such an unprecedented, enthusiastic response that it took Ross by surprise. Most people who believed in paranormal phenomena admitted it grudgingly.

'I'm an amateur, I suppose, compared to what you do.'

'Have you found anything?' Ross asked.

She shook her head. 'Has *anyone?*'

'Sure. I mean, beyond spirit photography and mediums, there's been research from Princeton and the University of Edinburgh. Even the CIA did valid studies on ESP and telepathy.'

'The *CIA?*'

'Exactly,' Ross said. 'The *government* even concluded that people can get information without using the five senses.'

'That isn't proof of life after death.'

'No, but it suggests consciousness is more than something physical. Maybe seeing a ghost is just a different form of clairvoyance. Maybe ghosts aren't even really dead, but alive somewhere in the past, and . . .' Ross's voice trailed off. 'Sorry. It's just that . . . most people think what I do is crazy.'

'I get that a lot too.' Lia smiled a little. 'And don't apologize. I've never met a scientist who doesn't get all excited about his work.'

A *scientist*. Had Ross ever been called that? It set off fireworks of feeling inside him – pride, astonishment, fascination. Certain that anything he did was going to ruin this moment, he reached for a cigarette as a delay tactic, and offered one to Lia. Her hand rose like a hummingbird, then darted behind her back. It had hovered long enough, however, for Ross to notice the thin gold band she was wearing.

And there went his world, crashing down again.

'He won't know,' Ross said, meeting her gaze.

Lia stared at him. Then she took a cigarette from the pack and let Ross light it for her. She smoked like she was swallowing a secret – this was a treasure to be hoarded. Her eyes drifted shut; her chin rose to expose the line of her neck.

In that moment it did not matter that she was someone else's wife; that she was still looking over her shoulder; that whatever few minutes Ross had with her would only be borrowed. This might well have been the beginning of a mistake, and even that could not prevent Ross from letting her leave just yet. 'Let me buy you a cup of coffee,' he said.

She shook her head. 'I can't—'

'No one will find out.'

'Everyone comes to this diner. If he knows I was with you . . .'

'So what? Then you'll tell him the truth. We're two friends, talking about ghosts.'

Wrong answer. Lia paled visibly, and Ross saw right through to her fragility again. 'I don't have friends,' she said quietly.

No friends. And you're not allowed to have a cup of coffee, and you have to sneak out in the dead of night. Ross could not even conjure a mental image of this tyrant who dominated Lia so completely. In today's world, what husband would do such a thing? What woman would think so little of herself to let it happen? 'What if I cover your head with a paper bag and tell everyone you've got leprosy?'

She fought a smile. 'I can't drink coffee through a paper bag.'

'I'll ask for a straw.' Lia was weakening, he could see it in the sway of her knees. 'One cup,' Ross pleaded.

'All right,' she agreed. 'One cup.' She took a long drag of her cigarette, her throat contracting as her eyes pinned him. 'Have we met?'

'Two nights ago.'

'I meant before that.'

Ross shook his head. 'I don't think so,' he said, but he felt as if he'd known her forever. Or maybe he wanted to know her forever. Was there a difference?

He wanted to ask her why she was afraid of her husband. He wanted to ask her what had brought her to the diner today, at the same exact moment that Ross had come there. But he was afraid that if he said anything at all, she would disappear like the threads of smoke that hung between them.

'Do you really think there's a ghost there?' Lia asked.

'On the Pike property? Maybe. If it *is* an Indian burial ground.'

'An Indian burial ground?' Lia seemed stunned by the idea. 'I don't think so.'

'Do you know much about the area?'

'I've lived here all my life.'

'And there's never been anything to suggest that the land might have once been part of an Indian settlement?'

'Whoever told you that is making it up.'

Ross considered this. It was entirely possible.

'But this Indian . . . it isn't your first ghost,' Lia stated.

'It will be, if it ever shows up.'

'No, I meant, this isn't the one that made you want to look.' She ducked her head, her hair swinging forward to cover her face. Her part was crooked at one spot in the back, as if her hand had jumped while holding the comb. 'My mother died the day I was born. She's the one I try to find, sometimes.'

He realized then that Lia's acceptance of the paranormal was not born out of open-mindedness, but – like his – out of desperation. That what he recognized about her was, quite simply, the same pain he saw in himself.

Lia held out her forearm, pushing away the sleeve of her sweater, where a web of scars netted the flesh. 'Sometimes I have to cut myself,' she confessed, 'because I'm so sure I won't bleed.'

It had been so long since someone understood. 'My ghost,' Ross said, his voice swollen and unfamiliar. 'Her name is Aimee.'

Once he had started, he could not stop. He spoke of the things he loved about Aimee – the ordinary ones, like the wide pool of her smile; and the others, like the spot where her elbow was always rough and the way she could not pronounce the word 'drawer.' He spoke of the flash and fury of the accident, without any of the particulars that would only break him apart all over again. He spoke of what it felt like to learn that some mistakes were made in indelible ink. He spoke until his throat was raw and all his grief had been laid at Lia's feet like an offering.

By the time he finished, she was crying. 'Do you really believe that you can love someone very much, very *very* much, even though you're a world apart?'

The words were torn out of her; Ross knew better than to believe this question came from his pain alone. 'How can I *not* believe it?'

She started to back away. 'I need to go.' Ross instinctively reached for her – and just as quickly, just as automatically, Lia moved out of range.

'Lia, tell me what he's done to you.'

'He adores me,' she whispered. 'He loves a woman who doesn't really exist.'

Whatever Ross had been expecting as evidence of mistreatment, this was not it. Could you love someone so much that, even without meaning to, you hurt them?

Lia brushed the edge of his sleeve, the tears on the tips of her fingers leaving a patch of cold. 'When you find Aimee,' she said softly, 'you tell her how lucky she is.'

By the time Ross lifted his head, she was walking away. There were questions writhing inside him: What could she possibly have done that made her feel so unworthy of her husband's affection? And if Lia loved *him*, why did it seem to be breaking her heart?

Ross had not meant to upset her. He'd only wanted her to understand that she wasn't alone. 'Lia,' he called out, hurrying after her, but she only glanced over her shoulder once and began to walk faster. Her cigarette butt smoldered on the sidewalk.

'Hey.' The waitress he'd spoken with earlier stuck her head out the diner's back door. 'You still looking for a table?'

Ross followed her inside. He was ushered to a booth that hadn't been cleaned yet. As he slid into the banquette he handed her one of his cigarettes, as promised.

She laughed, tucked it into her sleeve, and wiped down the tabletop. 'You flying solo today?'

He glanced out the window. 'Yeah. I guess I am.'

The waitress scooped her tip across the table. She pocketed the bill and the quarters, snorting at the penny that was left behind. 'It always pisses me how people think I'm a piggy bank,' she muttered. 'Like I'd want this in my pocket any more than they do.'

'A hundred of them will get you a cup of coffee.'

The waitress jingled her apron. 'And a hernia.' She slid the penny toward Ross. 'Heads up. You keep it, for luck.'

As she disappeared to get him flatware and coffee, Ross picked up the coin. He flipped it in the air, caught it, spun it on its edge. It wasn't until after the penny fell, heads up once again, that he noticed it had been minted in 1932.

That afternoon Ross mentally listed what he knew about Lia:

Each time she'd run into him, she seemed painfully shy. She was fascinated by the supernatural, but was afraid of her own shadow. Freedom, for her, came at night. She was married to a man whose love kept her in a box.

And, oh, she had been broken. She hid it well, but Ross knew from personal experience that once you had put the pieces back together, even though you might look intact, you were never quite the same as you'd been before the fall.

Ross fast-forwarded through the tape he'd recorded a few nights ago, replaying the conversation he'd had with Az Thompson. The problem was, he was more interested in the mystery of Lia Beaumont than the question of whether or not this property was haunted.

He had never collected on that cup of coffee she'd agreed to have with him.

Ross scraped the edge of the remote against his stubbled chin. There wasn't a damn thing worthwhile on the tape. What would he tell Rod van Vleet?

The telephone rang, jarring him out of his reverie. He grabbed for the receiver before it woke Shelby and Ethan. 'Hello?'

There was no one on the other end, but the connection was there. Ross could hear it, couched in soft static. He cradled the receiver against his shoulder. 'Lia?' he murmured.

It was her; he would have bet everything he owned that it was her. She might not be able to meet him, but she knew where to find him. This was her way of letting him know.

Ross did not hang up. He fell asleep with the phone nestled against his ear, the first true sleep he'd had in days, thinking as he drifted off that he had not realized how very exhausted he was.

Thousands of years ago, the Abenaki had ranged from the northwest of Vermont to the southeast, as well as western Massachusetts, parts of New Hampshire, and even Quebec. They called the area *Nd'akina*, which meant Our Land. Their tribal name, *Abenaki*, meant People of the Dawn. They referred to themselves as *Alnôbak*, or human beings. At one point, they numbered forty thousand.

They relied on agriculture, and their villages had been located on the floodplains of rivers. Hunting and fishing supplemented their diets. For most of the year, they lived in scattered bands of extended families, but during the summer they would gather. They had no central authority, which meant that in times of war, the Abenaki could abandon their villages, separate into smaller groups, and resurface somewhere far away to counterattack. Often during war, they retreated into Quebec, which led many colonials in New England to think of them as Canadian Indians, and gave them an excuse to take most of their land in Maine, New Hampshire, and Vermont without compensation.

There were, in 2001, approximately 2,500 Abenaki left in Vermont.

But whether any of them had ever lived on the Pike property was still a mystery to Ross, even though he'd tried six different Internet search engines and nearly every historical reference book the Comtosook Public Library had to offer.

He laid his head on the desk, frustrated. Shelby came up behind him and began to knead his shoulders. 'Any luck?'

'You do this for a living?' Ross sighed.

'I'm going to assume that means you didn't find anything.' She sat down on the chair beside them, glancing quickly at the reference desk to make sure Ethan was still occupied with his Game Boy.

'Vermont isn't exactly known for its record-keeping precision,' she said. 'Most of the old documents are gathering mold on the floor of the town clerk's office. And even those are pretty much the story of the English who settled the area. I don't imagine that Native Americans saw the need for property deeds a thousand years ago.'

'Yeah, and look at where it got them.'

'You going to quit, then?'

'No.' He glanced at the screen, luminous and humming. 'I'm going to try to read up on some of those Brits. See if their accounts mention any Indian settlements.'

'Suit yourself. I'm going to take Ethan home.'

Ross watched his sister from a distance, chatting with the new librarian who'd come in to take over the shift, slipping the strap of her purse over her shoulder, touching the crown of Ethan's head when she spoke as if her hand had simply been drawn there, a magnet to its pole.

'Shel,' he called out, as she waved to him from the door. 'You ever hear of anyone named Beaumont?'

'Is that one of those English settlers?'

'No.' Ross found his hands moving over the keyboard as if they had a mind of their own. The search engine he opened up had nothing to do with historical documents. It was the much more mundane White Pages for the town of Comtosook.

The librarian who'd just come on duty looked at him over her bifocals. 'There's a biology library on the UVM campus named after a Beaumont. Sometimes we do book loans with them.'

'Sorry, Ross,' Shelby said, shaking her head. 'That doesn't ring a bell.'

She pushed Ethan out the door as Ross typed the name into the computer.

BEAUMONT, ABEL. 33 Castleton Rd.

BEAUMONT, C. RR 2, Box 358.

BEAUMONT, W. 569 West Oren St.

*   *   *

He had not really expected to find Lia's name listed; her husband didn't seem the type to grant a woman equal billing. There was no way of finding the Beaumont on the Rural Route, but the other two were local. He signed off the computer and gathered his things.

'Success?' the librarian asked, smiling.

Ross found himself whistling. 'You could say that.'

It frustrated Az to no end that he needed some pissant piece of paper to fish in waters that belonged to no one. Who was some game warden to tell him he needed a permit with a stamp on it in order to sit himself down on the shores of the lake and catch as many trout as he could fit into his belly for dinner?

But he had it, all the same, tucked into the pocket of his shirt just in case he attracted company at six in the morning. He sat back and threaded a shiner onto his hook, then cast toward a patch of water that seemed darker than the rest.

He left his bail open, so that the minnow could swim away. The fishing line was a neon equator, splitting the lake into two. Az closed his eyes and balanced his rod between his knees. Growing old was still a surprise to him; funny how he could not remember what he had for dinner last night but could tell you, in exquisite detail, about the constellation of speckles on the back of the first trout he ever caught. He could not always catch the name of a friend on his tongue but there were faces from the past that he knew as surely as if he'd sculpted them himself. His spine had curved in the past few years, to the point where Az wondered if he would literally come full circle before it was his time to go, but his mind was so clear he could sometimes feel its serrated edges in the moments before he let loose and sank to sleep.

Az grunted at the absolute lack of activity on his line. Patience, that's what his father had taught him, along with which shallows netted the best bait and how to cast so softly a fish heard the splash of the hook only as a memory. But Az didn't have much patience these days. Patience required time, and he was running out of that.

The sun, bloodshot eye, lit the lip of the lake. There was a sudden spray of fire overhead. Explosions rose like Roman candles, sliding the sky from night into day.

The ground trembled beneath Az as a second round of charges went off at Angel Quarry, dislodging more granite to be mined into kitchen countertops and grave markers. His fishing line began to spin out as a trout grabbed onto the shiner. Az counted once, twice, then closed the bail on the reel and began to pull in with a steady hand.

The fish thrashed into his basket, all the colors of the sunrise caught in its scales. Another detonation ripped across the lake, and this time, Az could see bass leaping in small surprised circles, desperate to escape this unplanned earthquake.

He baited his hook with another shiner. Sometimes, things just needed a little shaking up.

Meredith huddled over her microscope, examining a single cell from an embryo that had been recently conceived in a test tube. This one did not seem destined to inherit cystic fibrosis – a small miracle, given that the couple's other four attempts to conceive a healthy child had failed. She arched her back and smiled: this one would make it. This one would be a survivor. And Meredith should know.

Lucy had been one of those against-the-odds babies. Not because of a genetic disorder, but simply by circumstance. Eight years ago Meredith had broken off a fading relationship with her mentor, a biomedical engineering professor who had been too busy to accompany her to her mother's funeral in Maryland. Her mother had only been in her fifties – it had been a heart attack, unexpected and very fast. As devastated as Meredith had been, her grandmother had been even more upset, and it fell to Meredith, at twenty-six, to take care of the details of death. She could still recall the surreal trip to the funeral parlor, where she was asked to pick out the color of satin lining for her mother's coffin; to choose from a catalog of Vermont-granite headstones. She remembered the graveside service, where Granny Ruby had listed against her, the old woman's slight weight forcing Meredith to stand tall and solid.

She made the decision to go to Boston, defend her dissertation, and then come back to Silver Spring to live with Granny Ruby. But four sleepless nights had taken their toll; several hours into the journey north, she lost control of her Civic.

Meredith awakened in the hospital with a cast on her left leg, bruises on every inch of her body, and a nurse at her side who kept telling her that her baby was going to be fine. *Baby?* she had thought, or maybe said aloud. *What baby?* Answers were fed to her like pain pills – an ultrasound meant to check internal injuries had shown the eight-week pregnancy, the butterfly heartbeat.

She had not wanted to be a single mother. She hadn't wanted to be a mother, period. All she wanted was her own mother, back. So she'd made an appointment for an abortion.

One that she hadn't kept.

Meredith knew the science behind conception; she understood what parents could and could not pass along to their children. But she could not help wondering if, somehow, the intangibles bled through by osmosis. If she'd wanted a baby from the moment she'd found out – instead of wishing, in the darkest part of the night, that she'd miscarry – would Lucy have been more secure? She loved her daughter now; she could not imagine a life without her in it. But if she was going to be brutally honest with herself, eight years ago, she could have easily gone the other way.

Life was all about being in a certain place, at a certain time.

Oh, Lucy, she thought, *if I could do it over again.* She would work less, and take her daughter mountain climbing instead. She would teach her a martial art. She would admit that she did not know all the answers, and what's more, might not ever be able to find them.

With a sigh, Meredith turned back to the scope. Two days from now this embryo would be implanted in its mother's womb. The irony didn't escape her – she, who had not wanted a baby yet wound up with one, was often the last hope of parents who wanted a baby more than anything but couldn't conceive. This child would not have cystic fibrosis, but that didn't mean it might not contract meningitis. You never knew what you were going to get. Close a door, and you'd still feel a breeze through the window.

Neither Castleton Road nor West Oren Street turned out to be anywhere near the Pike property, but that didn't keep Ross from plotting the routes on a map he'd bought at the gas station and finding the houses. However, Lia Beaumont did not live at either the sleepy Victorian whose picket fence badly needed painting, or the log home guarded by the German shepherd named Armageddon. It was possible that she lived at the unlisted address, but he would ask her that the next time he saw her.

If he saw her.

Ross had eaten all his meals at the town diner, and he'd been on a vigil at the property for the past two nights, but Lia Beaumont had not materialized. He'd seen Az Thompson skulking around again, two raccoons having sex, and several times, his video equipment had picked up the most remarkable globules – large as a basketball and pearly white, streaking across the screen.

He would have liked to show these to Lia.

Ross wanted to ask her if she thought her mother would wait to be found, no matter how many years it took. He wanted to ask her if she loved her husband the way he loved Aimee. He wanted to know what differences between them could seem just as irreconcilable as death.

He was worried, too, that maybe her husband had found out that she'd met Ross at the diner, and had punished her. He didn't know what that would entail. Physical abuse? Psychological? It was possible, too, that the reason she'd disappeared was because Lia – who had admitted to cutting her arms to feel something, anything – had simply decided that the surest way to find her mother was to turn herself into a ghost.

Ross found himself reading the obituaries, and sighing with relief when she wasn't mentioned. He began to make ridiculous bargains with himself: *If I can hold my breath for three full minutes, she will come tonight. If I make this light before it turns red, she will be there.*

Some nights at the Pike property were more active than others. There were wild temperature swings and tiny flashes of blue light between the branches of trees, and the smell of hemlock occasionally seemed thick enough to choke. Twice, Ross had heard the hinged cry of an infant.

The third night, he was sitting at the edge of the clearing where he'd targeted his investigation, the night wrapped as tight as a straitjacket, when the stone fell out of the sky. It was approximately the size of a dinner plate and nearly as flat, and dropped from a high enough velocity to crack against his shin. 'Shit!' Ross yelped, jumping to his feet. Pain throbbed up his leg and a welt rose below his knee. Peering up the nearest tree with his flashlight, he could see nothing. He was in no shape to climb. So he took that same rock and slammed it hard enough against the trunk to make it shake. 'Hey!' he shouted. 'Who's there?'

He expected an animal – a bear cub, or some kind of mutant squirrel – but there was nothing. He snapped off a branch and then used it to beat at the others. He kept at this for a while, not because he really thought he was going to find anything, but because he wanted some measure of revenge. It was only when he stopped, exhausted, that he heard the digging.

It was faint, like a woodchuck scratching a hole in a garden. Ross limped toward the far side of the clearing, the sound growing stronger. His flashlight illuminated about thirty small mounds, arranged in no particular order.

Different archaeological experts and excavation teams had razed parts of the property, yet this particular spot had been intact when Ross arrived at dusk that evening. Now, enough earth had been dug out of each hole to make a small pile, although when Ross bent down and tried to dig a little deeper with a stick, the ground was just as frigid and snowy as it had been for days.

Ross had never actually seen a primitive burial ground, but he imagined it looked something like this.

He drew his digital camera from his pocket and took pictures from several angles. Then he bent to the tiny LCD display to see what the photos looked like. But in every single picture, the ground was perfectly flat, covered with a layer of undisturbed ice. Confounded, Ross shone the flashlight down on the same patch of land. There were no mounds of dirt, where minutes ago there had been many.

'I know what I saw.' Ross stomped around the small space, but there was no give to the ground; it was still frozen solid.

Had he imagined all of it? He bent down and rolled up the leg of his pants – no, the welt was even bigger now, and a vivid shade of purple. That stone had fallen. That sound had been digging. Those heaps had been there.

Another reason to miss Lia: had she come tonight, and seen this, Ross would not have thought he was crazy.

That week the Winooski River slowed its flow, leaving fish swimming in circles and washing up on the banks in confusion. Families with satellite television systems found their programming now completely in Norwegian, the mouths of the actors not quite matching up to the words, like old *Godzilla* movies. At the Comtosook IGA, all four electronic cash registers – newly purchased from an industrial catalog and recently arrived – began to add wrong, so that grapes might ring up at $45 per bunch and cantaloupes cost a penny a pound, while mousetraps and fish sticks were perfectly free. The people who dared to talk of these things found they lost their train of thought right in the middle of a sentence, and would find instead the sweet taste of sugar on their tongue, or the bitter tang of chicory, depending on what they had been about to say.

It sucked going to the dermatologist.

Not only did it remind Ethan of what a freak he was, it also meant he had to stay up all day long, because the doctor's office hours were during the time he usually slept. And after whatever procedure had been done, he had the added fun of seeing his mother's smile crack like a hard-boiled egg; she was trying that desperately to look at him as if he were perfectly normal.

Today he'd had three precancerous growths removed from his face. The doctor had taken a cotton swab and stuck it into a cup of liquid nitrogen, then held it to Ethan's forehead and nose. It stung enough to make tears come to his eyes, and it itched, now.

His mother pulled into the driveway. Uncle Ross was out – the car was gone. Ethan could have unfastened his own seat belt but he waited until his mother came around the passenger side and did it for him. 'You okay?' she asked quietly, and he nodded and got out of the car. He slipped his hand into hers as they walked up the porch, something he had not done for months, because when you have less time than everyone else it means you have to make yourself grow up faster.

In his bedroom, he pulled off his clothes like taffy. He dragged his pajamas over his head and then glanced in the mirror. The blisters hadn't formed yet – that would be tomorrow. But his face was already a globe, shifting blotchy continents where the growths had been frozen off.

Before he even realized what he was doing, he lifted his fist and smashed the mirror. Blood ran down his arm but the only thought spiking through his mind was that he didn't have to look at himself anymore.

'Ethan?' His mother's voice. *'Ethan!'* She was behind him now, wrapping his fist in a sheet yanked from the bed. 'What happened?'

'I'm sorry.' Ethan rocked back and forth. 'I'm sorry.'

'Now you're propitiating . . .'

'Pro-what?'

'It means being agreeable. Something you always are, after the fact.'

Ethan yanked his hand away. 'Then why don't you just *say* it?' he yelled. 'Why do you use these stupid words all the time no one can understand anyway? Why doesn't anyone ever just tell me, flat out, the truth?'

His mother stared at him. 'What do you want to hear, Ethan?'

He was sobbing, and his nose was running. 'That I'm a monster.' He held his splayed hands up to his face, streaking his chin and cheeks with smudges of blood. 'Look at me, Ma. *Look* at me.'

His mother forced a smile. 'Ethan, honey, you're tired. It's way past your bedtime.' Her voice kicked into soothing mode, the consistency of warm honey. It rolled over Ethan's shoulders; he had to fight to keep from giving in. He felt his mother probe his hand, lead him into the bathroom to clean the cuts.

'I don't think you'll need stitches,' she said, and she wrapped his hand with gauze. Then she took him back into his bedroom. Ethan climbed into bed and stared at the frame on his wall where the mirror used to be.

'You'll feel better after you take a nap,' his mother said, and Ethan did not know if she was talking to him or to herself. 'We'll do something really wonderful when you get up – take out the telescope, maybe, and try to find Venus . . . or watch all the *Star Wars* videos back to back . . . you've wanted to do that for a while now, haven't you?' As she spoke she crouched on the floor, picking up the shards of the mirror. He wondered if she knew she was crying.

Although he was exhausted, Ethan didn't fall asleep. His hand throbbed, and so did his face. He waited until he no longer heard his mother moving around downstairs, then crept out of bed to reach under his desk, where his mother had missed a triangle of mirror.

Ethan held it up to his face. You could only get a small spot in view – the tip of his nose, one eyebrow, a freckle. It was possible, this way, to believe that added together, the reflections might make up one very ordinary boy. It was possible, this way, to be someone altogether different.

Eli woke with a start and sat up, gasping for air. The room was redolent with the scent of apples, so strong that he looked to the side of the bed to make sure there was not a cider press nearby. He rubbed his eyes, but could not seem to shake the image that danced before his face, no matter which way he turned: it was that woman again.

He knew her voice, although he had never heard her speak. He knew that she had a scar underneath her left earlobe, that her mouth tasted of vanilla and misfortune.

His mother had believed in the power of dreams. When Eli was a child, she'd told him a story of his grandfather, a holy man who had envisioned his own demise. He had gone to sleep and seen a mountain covered with snow, and at the very top, a hawk. The hawk reached into the drifts and pulled out a snake by its neck – pulled and kept pulling – and finally attached to the end of the reptile was the empty shell of a turtle. Shaken, it made the rattle of death. Three months later, at a ceremonial rite, a freak snow-storm stranded Eli's grandfather and three other men at the top of a sacred mountain. The others found the men days afterward, frozen. Their bodies might never have been recovered, if not for the caw of a hawk who led the search party closer and closer.

'When we're awake,' Eli's mother used to say, 'we see what we need to see. When we're asleep, we see what's really there.'

He used to wonder if his mother had ever dreamed of her marriage to a white man; of the diabetes slowly killing her. He wondered if she'd known that her only son would be more likely to cut off his own arm than subscribe to the Indian belief that dreams were more than some crazy neurons firing.

The woman, the one who came to him in the dark – she had eyes the color of sea glass, a piece that Eli found once on a beach in Rhode Island, and that he kept on the windowsill of his bathroom.

He pulled the covers up to his chin and settled down on his pillows again. Most likely, he was horny. He was dreaming up beauties because he wasn't getting any honest action.

Although, he admitted, as he drifted off again, if that was the case, it made more sense to picture her in a bikini, or better yet, naked in a sauna. Not like she'd been, fully clothed and crouched on a floor, weeping as she fit together what looked like the pieces of an impossible puzzle.

The scream rang out, high and hysterical, as Meredith raced into Lucy's bedroom. *No, no, no,* she thought. *Things have been so normal.*

Her grandmother was already there, smoothing Lucy's damp hair back from her forehead and murmuring that everything was all right. 'She won't stop,' Granny Ruby said, panicked. 'It's like she can't even hear me.'

Meredith clapped her hands on both sides of her daughter's face and leaned closer. 'Lucy, you listen to me. You are fine. There is nothing here that can hurt you. Do you understand?'

Like a veil lifting, Lucy's gaze sharpened, and she fell silent. As she realized where she was and what had happened she curled up in a fetal position and skittered closer to the head of the bed. 'Can't you see her?' Lucy whispered. 'She's right *there.*'

She pointed to a spot between Meredith and Ruby, a spot where there was nothing at all. Then she burrowed underneath the covers. 'She wants me to help her look.'

'For what?' Meredith asked.

But Lucy had gone somewhere inside herself, and she didn't answer. Meredith's chest hurt; her heart might have been a stone. 'Granny,' she said, in a voice that was borrowed, 'can you watch her?'

Without waiting for an answer, Meredith walked into her own bedroom again. She picked up the telephone and the small business card she'd placed in her nightstand drawer. She waited for the appropriate series of beeps. And then she paged Dr Calloway, a surrender.

When Ross arrived at the Pike property at 11 P.M., Lia was waiting. 'Am I late?' he asked casually, as if he'd expected to see her all along. As he set up his equipment he watched her from the corner of his eye. There was something different about her – a fragile determination that Ross didn't want to jeopardize by bringing up the circumstances of how they'd last parted. So instead, he showed her the spots where the mounds had been two nights ago. He let her look at his new EMF field meter, which had arrived in the mail that afternoon. If she wanted to ghost hunt with him, then he'd let her. It was a starting point, and that was better than nothing at all.

She ran her hand lightly over the video camera on its tripod, pointed off in the distance. 'My father has a camera,' she said, 'although his is a little bigger. Bulkier.'

'This one's digital.' Ross glanced up at the clearing. He was already getting strong sensations from that spot. 'If we sit down and wait, maybe we'll get lucky.'

'I . . . can stay?'

'I figured that's why you came.'

Lia didn't answer, but settled herself beside him on the frozen ground. Her apprehension pressed between them like a chaperone.

Ross wondered what was fueling her fear – the possibility of seeing a ghost, or that her husband would come looking for her. 'You okay?' he asked.

She nodded. With the exception of a small flashlight, they were sitting in total darkness. Lia sat with her arms wrapped over her knees, her skirt smoothed to her ankles. She glanced at the EMF meter, its needle stable. 'So this compass,' she said, 'it goes off if a ghost is here?'

'Technically, it goes off when a ghost is materializing. It's the transition between states that disrupts an electromagnetic field.'

She frowned. 'I don't understand.'

'If the spirit is invisible, and then suddenly starts to look solid – or vice versa – we'll hear crackling.'

They fell into a companionable silence full of questions neither one wanted to be first to ask. At some point Ross stopped attending to potential paranormal activity and started to listen instead for the sound of Lia's breathing falling between the spaces of his own. He grew acutely aware of the distance between his shoulder and hers. If he shrugged, he would touch her. Hell, if he inhaled deeply.

It had been nearly a decade since Ross felt this – a physical awareness so intense it seemed to require all of his attention, a fleeting prayer for something beyond his control – earthquake, tsunami – that might naturally close the space between them. He had been looking for the ghost of a woman for so long, it was unsettling to find himself fascinated by one sitting right beside him. But Lia was married, and Aimee was the one he really wanted.

What if the strange tug he felt around Lia was not the need to save her, but the possibility that she might be able to save *him*? What if he was not supposed to find a ghost in Comtosook . . . but rather, this woman?

Aimee is gone. Lia is here . . .

The rogue thought stumbled into the front of his mind, upsetting him so greatly he found himself physically going in the opposite direction, scooting out of the yellow round of the flashlight and away from Lia. 'Did something happen?' she asked, breathless.

No, Ross thought, *thank God.* He got to his feet and began to walk around the clearing.

'You feel something?'

'No,' Ross answered. *Yes.*

She stood up, walking into the shadows. 'I do,' Lia murmured. 'Like everything's getting . . . sharper. Harder.'

As she moved past Ross, he could feel a breeze. The light edge of her skirt grazed his hand, and before he could stop himself, he grabbed for it, only to have it slip through his fingers like wind.

His heart was too large in his chest, and it was beating out of rhythm. Ross, who had not let his love die when his lover did, was suddenly distracted by something as mundane as the dimple on a woman's knee.

He told himself that he had built a world with Aimee; that she had known him better than anyone had in his life. But the truth was, Aimee would not recognize Ross now. Grief had changed him, from the pitch of his voice to the way he carried himself down a busy street. Aimee had understood what made Ross happy.

But Lia seemed to understand what had crushed him.

There was suddenly, quite clearly, the cry of an infant. 'Did you hear that?' Lia whispered, and she reached for Ross, her hand closing over his wrist.

He had heard it. But he realized that Lia was no longer focused on the distant sound. She picked up the flashlight, shone it square on the scars on Ross's arm. 'Oh . . .' Lia said, and the light clattered to the ground, pitching them both into darkness.

Although he could not see Lia, Ross knew she was feeling beneath her sleeves for her own old wounds. 'Why didn't you tell me?'

'You didn't ask.' Ross reached into his pocket and lit a cigarette, bringing her face back from the shadows.

'When?' she said simply.

'A while ago. Back when I didn't think there was anything left for me in this world.' He met her gaze, then took the glowing cigarette and pressed it to the flesh inside his arm, daring her to feel sorry for him. 'I still don't.'

To his surprise, Lia didn't try to stop him. She waited until he tossed away the butt, until there was an angry, blistered burn on his skin. 'I didn't come here tonight to look for a ghost,' Lia admitted. 'I came because when I'm with you, I'm not sitting at home and wondering if I should use a knife or pills or poison.' All the fine hairs on his arms stood up as she pressed her lips to his ear. 'Ross,' she whispered, 'tell me what's on the other side.'

Ross had felt like this once before – dizzy and agonized and bursting from every cell. Afterward, when he'd awakened, three doctors said he'd been struck by lightning. He brought his hand up to Lia's jaw. *If you can see me so clearly,* he thought, *then I must be real.*

A few feet away, the EMF meter began to crackle. The static came slowly at first, eventually growing so loud Ross could hear it over the blind swell of his mind. Ross had never experienced a response this strong – something significant was coming. And it made perfect sense: the spirit was using the energy that had sparked between Ross and Lia to materialize.

Ross scrambled away, grabbing for the EMF and squinting in an effort to see the readings. 'The light,' he called to Lia.

But a moment later, his shoe connected with the flashlight. The meter was already waning again, the crackles subsiding. It was the most significant proof of a spirit he'd ever witnessed, yet Ross didn't think he'd care at this moment if the ghost walked right up to him and introduced itself. He needed to find Lia, to see what was written on her face.

Ross turned on the flashlight and swung the beam, but she was gone.

It would not be the first time Ross had seen a person run away during a paranormal investigation. Yet Lia's fear had nothing to do with the coming of ghosts. What had scared her was the same thing that had scared Ross – what, even now, kept him shaking: the knowledge that for the second time in his life, he wanted someone he could not have.

4

In Comtosook, residents began adapting to a world they could no longer take for granted. Umbrellas were carried in knapsacks and purses, to ward off rain that fell red as blood and dried into a layer of fine red dust. China dishes shattered at the stroke of noon, no matter how carefully they were wrapped. Mothers woke their children, so that they could see the roses bloom at midnight.

After a while, hems on pants began to unravel and words would not stay still on the pages of books. Water never boiled. People in town found they'd wake up without a history – walking out to get the morning paper, they would trip over their own memories, unraveled like bandages across the sidewalk. Women opened their dryers to find their whites had turned to feathers. Meat spoiled in the freezer. The color blue looked completely wrong.

Some attributed the events to global warming, or personal bad luck. But when Abe Huppinworth walked into the Gas & Grocery only to find every single item balanced backward and upside down on the shelves, he wondered aloud if that Indian ghost on Otter Creek Pass didn't have something to do with it. And the three customers who had been shopping at the time told their neighbors, and before evening fell the inhabitants of Comtosook were all speculating on whether or not it might not just be best to leave that piece of land alone.

*   *   *

There was a large part of Rod van Vleet that didn't want to hear what Ross Wakeman had to say. If there was a ghost – ridiculous as it seemed – what was Rod supposed to do about it? The house had been demolished; the crews were moving the wreckage into Dumpsters. The Redhook Group was going to build, no matter how many locals' signatures and petitions crossed his desk. Maybe Rod would need to call in a priest to exorcise the damn bagel shop that was to be eventually built here, and maybe he wouldn't. The point was that the ghost was negotiable; the development was not.

And yet, Rod really wanted to know if he was displacing a spirit. If the reason his meals all tasted of sawdust, if the reason his toothbrush went missing every night, had anything to do with his current occupation.

'These things . . .' Rod pointed to the TV screen, where a grainy image of a forest at nighttime was scored by blue lines and floating balls of light. 'These things are supposed to be a ghost?' He relaxed inside. Whatever he had been expecting, this was not it. A few sparks and bubbles couldn't hurt anyone. They certainly wouldn't run off potential business.

Ross Wakeman was a charlatan; plain and simple. He'd seen an opportunity to grab a little attention for himself, and he had climbed right aboard Rod's bandwagon to do it.

'That's not a spirit in and of itself,' Wakeman explained. 'That's a spirit's effect on the equipment. I've had flashlights cut out on me on the property, and this sort of interference recording, and very strong readings on machines that measure magnetic fields.'

'Mumbo-jumbo,' Rod said. 'There's nothing concrete.'

'Just because something defies measurement doesn't mean it's not here.' Wakeman shrugged. 'Consider the difference between property value and actual worth.'

'Ah, but you *can* measure property value. It's how much people are willing to pay to acquire something.'

'You can measure a ghost, too, by what people are willing to believe.'

Suddenly the door to the construction trailer burst open. Van Vleet turned away to find three angry equipment operators storming closer, their excavators as dormant as sleeping dinosaurs.

One, the ringleader, poked Van Vleet in the chest. 'We quit.'

'You can't quit. You haven't finished the job.'

'Screw the job.' He removed his hard hat and tossed it at van Vleet, a gauntlet. 'They're driving us crazy.'

'What is?'

'The flies.' Another worker stepped forward, continuing to speak in a thick French Canadian accent. 'They come right into the ears, and they whisper.' With his hands he made small, spinning circles by the sides of his head. '*Tsee-tsee. Tsee-tsee.*'

'And when you go to bat them away,' the first worker added, 'there's nothing there.'

The third worker, still silent, crossed himself.

Ross coughed, and van Vleet glared at him. 'I'm sure it's nothing,' he assured them. 'A trick of the wind. Maybe a virus.'

'Then it's freakin' contagious, because those Abenaki out front heard it too. And the old one, he spelled the word we heard. C-H-I-J-I-S. It means *baby,* in his language.'

'Of course he's going to tell you that!' van Vleet cried. 'He wants you to leave. He wants you to be so scared you do just what you're doing now – get off your trucks and stop working.'

The men looked at each other. 'We aren't scared. But until you get rid of the ghost, you can find yourself another crew.' They nodded a farewell, then began to walk off the construction site.

'What was it you were saying?' Ross asked.

Van Vleet picked up his phone. 'I have to find another construction crew,' he said. 'I don't have time for this now.'

Ross shrugged. 'If you need me, you know where to find me,' he said, and left. Rod dialed a number and waited through a recorded message. His eyes strayed to the TV screen in his office, where static flickered. Wakeman had left his tape behind by accident. *Or,* Rod thought, watching one streak of light, *maybe not.*

The blood hit her in the face.

Meredith had no sooner walked out of the building than the liquid spattered her hair, and ran down her cheek and neck. 'How many babies did you kill today?' the protester cried.

She wiped it out of her eyes. Not real blood, but Kool-Aid, or something similar, from the sweet smell. Her employer did not get targeted quite as often as the abortion clinics in the area, but the objection was the same – part of Meredith's job included choosing which embryos got to live and which were incinerated, and the right-to-lifers couldn't accept that. 'Get back to me when you're infertile,' Meredith muttered to the small group of pick-eters, and she walked a little faster to her car.

What she wanted to say, what she did not even let herself think until she was safe inside the comfort of the driver's seat with the air-conditioning turned up high, was that she knew more about those protesters than any of them could ever know about her. Nine years ago she had walked past a line of them, all wearing the same faces they were wearing now, as if righteousness were nothing but a Halloween mask. She had canceled her genetic counseling appointments for the whole day, because even if she were feeling well enough to work during the afternoon she did not think she could sit across a desk and talk to other people about their children, not after aborting her own.

Meredith remembered that the clinic smelled like steel and mouthwash. That the chairs in the waiting area were filled with girls so young their distended bellies seemed impossible. That she had knotted the first two ties on the back of her dressing gown before she decided she could not go through with it.

What if being pregnant was not the colossal mistake she believed it was? What if the timing was not off, but terribly right – a wake-up call, a message? So what if her baby had no father. Meredith's had left at age four, when her parents divorced, and she'd seen him only a handful of times while growing up. Yet she was living proof that you could do very well with only a mother, if you had the right one. If Meredith could not bring Luxe back alive, she at least had the opportunity to show her what she'd learned from her. She would make a safe haven for her daughter; she would feed her love.

When she dressed again and got her money back and walked outside the clinic, one of the protesters had flung a bucket of fake blood at her. It was the last straw – Meredith grabbed the man by his collar and shouted right in his face that she hadn't gone through with it. She broke down sobbing in the stranger's embrace.

They gave her cookies and hot chocolate from a thermos. They let her sit on a pile of blankets. The man who had doused her offered his own dry shirt. For that whole afternoon, Meredith was a hero.

Nearly a decade later, in her rearview mirror, Meredith assessed the picketers. She wished she had the balls to walk back and ask if any of them had ever made a choice that changed their future. She wished she could take them into her lab, where so many healthy embryos sat waiting. She wished she could explain to them that there were some sorts of lives that were not worth living. That it was not cruel to be the judge of that, but humane.

Then Meredith eased the car out of the parking spot and nosed it toward home, where she would find her daughter lying on the couch, dazed and lethargic from the antipsychotic meds. She wove dangerously in and out of rush-hour traffic. She cut off trucks. She pressed her foot to the gas pedal, doing 65 through a 30-mile-per-hour zone, as if sheer recklessness might convince her that after all these years, she still had what it took to save Lucy.

Ross sat in the emergency room, searching the faces of the scarred and the sick as they came through the automatic doors. Every time it was not Lia he relaxed by degrees. He had been here for two days, long enough to make friends with the triage staff and to ascertain that no one named Lia Beaumont, or for that matter, Jane Doe, had come through the hospital. That was what he was most worried about – the thought that she might hurt herself, or be hurt by her husband, before Ross had a chance to speak to her.

He wanted to tell her that he could not remember the shape of Aimee's eyes. Maybe, at first, that didn't seem like something she'd need to hear. But for eight years now, Ross could picture this as clearly as if Aimee were just inches away – the ovals tipped up at the ends, the cinnamon at the center, the lashes that cast shadows on her cheeks when she was sleeping. Since the night that Lia had put her lips up to his cheek and whispered in his ear, he could not envision Aimee's face without it morphing into Lia's.

He changed his clothes three times a day, and still he smelled roses.

He wanted to kiss her.

He *wanted,* period.

There was no happy ending here, Ross knew that. He would not break up Lia's marriage; he would not put her in a position to choose. But he needed to know that she was all right. He needed to believe she wasn't sitting somewhere in Comtosook right now with a blade balanced over her wrist.

Suddenly a woman rushed up to the nurse's desk dragging a child behind her like a pull toy. 'I'm looking for a patient,' she demanded. 'His name is Ross Wakeman.'

Ross's head snapped up at the sound of Shelby's voice. He called her name.

Ethan turned first, then his mother. 'Ross!' She barreled toward him, face twisted in fear. Ethan, behind her, was wrapped in his daylight gear – swathed from head to toe to keep the sun from touching his skin. The parts of his face that Ross could see were mottled and raw.

Shelby glanced from Ross's face to his arms. His wrists. 'What's the matter? How long have you been here? God, Ross, why didn't you *call* me?'

Then she saw the cigarette burn he'd made on his forearm when he was with Lia. Blistered now and oozing, Shelby could not bring herself to touch it. Maybe it reminded her of Ethan. 'Shel, I'm fine.'

'You're in a hospital.'

'I know. I've been trying to find someone. I thought she might be hurt.'

'You're hurt too.'

'That's nothing. An accident.'

She didn't believe him, that much was clear. But she said, 'You're all right? You're sure?'

'Positive.'

'Excellent,' Shelby replied, and she slapped him as hard as she could across the face.

Watching Ross's head snap back, and the proof of her hand rising on his skin, was the most satisfying moment Shelby had had in forty-eight hours, which was approximately how long her brother had been missing. She'd spent that time calling around everywhere, trying to find people who had seen him. But very few residents of Comtosook even knew him, much less could identify him by sight. She'd called the police station, and was patched through to a Detective Rochert, who said a missing person's report couldn't be filed until two full days had gone by. To that end, she had taken Ethan out in broad daylight, driving slowly through town and canvassing the diner and even demanding an audience with Rod van Vleet, who had been the last person to see Ross, at ten o'clock yesterday morning.

'Jeez, Shel,' Ross said, still smarting. 'Nice to see you, too.'

'You son of a bitch.' Shelby narrowed her eyes. 'Do you have any idea where I've been? After the usual places, that is, that I would have bothered to look for my brother, who disappeared without any trace or for that matter the courtesy to leave me something like a note telling me where he was going or when he'd be back?'

'We went under the highway,' Ethan piped in. 'There was a dead seagull there. It was awesome.'

Shelby's head was red with thoughts of succussion, the satisfying concept of shaking her brother so hard it caused him damage. 'Yes, that's right. Under the highway. You know, in case you'd decided to jump off the bridge there.'

'I told you before,' he said wearily. 'I'm not going to kill myself.'

She grabbed his arm, near the burn. 'Then what's this?'

'A really inefficient way to go about committing suicide?'

Tears were coming now, and that made her even angrier. 'I'm glad you think this is so funny,' Shelby said. 'I guess I'm just an idiot, you know, to assume that the people I care about actually have some obligation to me – at least when it comes to letting me know they're not lying dead in a ditch somewhere.' She swiped at her eyes. 'I'm glad you're not killing yourself, Ross, because you're doing a goddamned good job of killing me instead.'

'The seagull?' Ethan said, tugging on Ross's sleeve. 'One of its eyes had been pecked out.'

'Stop worrying about me, will you? I never asked you to,' Ross said.

'You don't get to make that choice.'

'Then why don't you worry about someone who really needs it?'

'You don't qualify?'

'Not as much as *you* do,' Ross shot back. 'For God's sake, Shel, you're living like some kind of nocturnal animal. You've closed yourself off to everyone but Ethan. Not a single friend comes over to have coffee with you, at least not since I've been here. You haven't had a date in . . . Christ, in the past ten years the Pope's gotten more action than you have. You're forty-two and you act

like you're sixty. You're doing a really good job of killing yourself; you don't need me to do it for you.'

She was not going to break down, not in the middle of the
emergency room, not in front of Ross, especially not in front of
Ethan. Fighting for control, she pressed her fists into her lap. 'Are
you finished?' she asked tightly.

Ross took his sister's hand and waited until she looked up at
him. 'Shelby. I am not going to kill myself. I promise.'

'You promised before, Ross,' she whispered. 'And it turned out
you lied.'

Shelby had known, after Aimee's death, that her brother was
not coming back from the edge. She had seen the way he stopped
sleeping, the way his clothes began to wear him instead of the
other way around. She had seen him hold a conversation when
he was not really present. So she had been the one to give him
a psychiatrist's name, to set up an appointment. That night at
dinner, he reported that it had gone well; he'd even thanked her.
When Shelby had found Ross bleeding days later, he had mouthed
the words *I'm sorry*, before he passed out.

It turned out he'd never kept that appointment with the psychiatrist.

'You tell me,' she said, 'why I'm supposed to believe you now.'

Ross looked off into the distance, his eyes fixed on a poster
urging people to donate organs. He began to tell her a story, then,
of a woman who had disappeared. *Frightened . . . fragile . . . beautiful . . . curious*: Ross balanced adjective upon adjective to form a
friable house of cards that might collapse at any moment; and
suddenly this Lia Beaumont might have been standing between
them, shaking and unsure.

One word snagged in Shelby's mind. 'Married?' she repeated.

'She's terrified of him.'

'Ross—'

He shook his head. 'It's not like that,' he said. Shelby knew he
was lying; she just wasn't certain if Ross realized it, too. 'I'm

worried about her. She has nowhere to go. She wants out, but she can't find her way there. I think . . . I think she might try to kill herself.'

How do you like it? she thought, but before she could speak she noticed her brother's face. It was an expression she knew so well – one she had worn a thousand times, every time she looked up and saw the sun, or stared at Ethan's seasoned, sleeping face. It was an expression she had seen Ross wear, after his suicide attempt. Sometimes, when you come up against a wall of reality, there simply is not a way to get around it. *He has fallen in love with her,* Shelby thought, *and that's not going to change a thing.*

Her voice rocked him gently. 'Ross, you can't save them all.'

He reared back as if Shelby had slapped him again. 'Just once,' he said softly. 'Just once would be nice.' Staggering to his feet, he ran out of the hospital and as far away from this memory as he could.

The sun swallowed his uncle up, like the fiery breath of a dragon, the moment he raced out of the sliding-glass doors. Ethan kicked the bottom of his chair, which made the whole row shake, since they were attached. His mother sat beside him, her face buried in her hands, like she did when they watched *Friday the 13th* and she couldn't bear to see someone hacked into pieces. 'What's with Uncle Ross?' Ethan said. 'If that lady isn't in the hospital, isn't that a good thing?'

His mother blinked. 'You were listening.'

'Duh. I was, like, two feet away.'

His mother sighed, and Ethan knew she was doing the math in her head: how old he was, chronologically, multiplied by how old he was, emotionally, divided by some standard number for childhood innocence. 'One time he tried to save someone's life, and he wound up losing something very important to him.' She tightened her hold on his hand. 'You know Uncle Ross was in a car accident with the woman he was going to marry. Ross was the person who was hurt the least, and he carried Aimee out of the car to the side of the road. But the other car, the one that hit them – there was a driver still stuck in there. He left Aimee while he went to see if that person was all right.'

'And she died,' Ethan breathed, the last puzzle piece fitting snug in his mind.

'Mmm-hmm. Aimee didn't look that bad on the outside, which is why Uncle Ross thought it was okay to leave her alone for a second – but inside, her organs? They were bleeding badly. She was taken to the hospital, but the doctors couldn't do anything.'

'Like me,' Ethan said simply. His mother turned her face away.

He swung his legs a little, made the row of seats move again. 'Mom, would Aimee have gotten better if Uncle Ross had stayed with her?'

'No, honey.'

'Does he know that?'

'I think so.'

Ethan thought about this for a second. 'But her dying – it wasn't his fault.'

His mother stared at him the way she did every now and then, as if she were going to be given a pop quiz on his features. 'Sometimes that doesn't make a difference,' she said.

Lucy slept a lot. Sometimes she dreamed that she was sleeping, and she could see herself lying on the bed. Sometimes she dreamed that she was being chased, but her legs didn't move fast enough anymore. Once, she imagined that a giant had eaten her, and she curled up right in a cavity in his back molar where she slept and slept and slept.

She still screamed in her sleep, but her throat was too tired to let it out.

Every now and then a voice would slice like a knife. Her mother, begging her to get up and eat a little something. Granny Ruby, remarking on how much better Lucy looked now, couldn't everyone see the roses in her cheeks? She heard them from a distance. She had fallen down a well and was doing a backfloat, staring up at the sun.

Faces were printed on the backs of her eyelids: her mother, Granny Ruby, and the lady who came. The one who had been hanging from the tree, the one who stood by the edge of her bed and sat with her, now, on the couch, so close that Lucy's feet were freezing.

It was this woman, Lucy realized, who was supposed to be gone now. But since she'd started on the medicine, the woman was more clear than ever – the blue scan of her skin and the way sadness got stuck in the corners of her eyes, like little bits of sleep. She wasn't as scary to Lucy anymore. In fact, it was like she *knew*. She understood what it was like to stand right in front of people you loved, even though they could not see you.

It was the first time Eli could remember being called in on a reverse vandalism charge. But Rod van Vleet had called dispatch, complaining that the demolished house was being rebuilt, somehow. Overnight, the frame of the whole downstairs had been erected again. Clearly, he said, it was the Abenaki. He wanted the Comtosook police to catch them in the act.

Eli glanced over at Watson, who apparently believed that the chemicals in dog saliva might dissolve the passenger-seat window if applied liberally. They had already been to the campsite where the Abenaki were staying. With the exception of Az Thompson, everyone had been fast asleep. Yet moments later, as he and Watson stepped onto the Pike property, he could easily see why van Vleet was concerned: inside the temporary safety fencing, the demolished house seemed to be knitting itself back together.

Beside him, Watson whined and backed away. 'Scaredy-dog,' Eli murmured, and he pushed down the wire fence so that he could step over it. The reconstruction reminded him of shattered bones – support beams and roof joists healing in a way that wasn't quite right, but that managed to bear the weight all the same. More inter-esting, though, was the fact that the house had gone past the framing stage. Plaster had been haphazardly smoothed into the downstairs walls. In some places, clapboards were already hanging. It would have taken an entire building crew weeks to accomplish this; for it to have happened overnight was impossible.

Eli moved carefully over the rubble and shattered glass, and Watson, gathering courage, followed. There were no front steps yet, so he had to climb into the open doorway. Eli shone his flashlight around, assessing. Inside, patches of Sheetrock were missing and doorways were not square, but this structure was solid and standing. He could smell fresh paint.

'If the Indians did this,' Eli said softly to Watson, 'I'll eat my hat. Which, come to think of it, would taste better than most of the stuff in our fridge.' He crept carefully into each room, unsure if the splintered floors would hold him. When he rattled the banister on the stairs, it tumbled to the ground. Steps shifted beneath his boots; Eli bent down to see that they had not yet been nailed into permanence.

The second floor of the old Pike house was less complete. One whole wall opened out onto the night; the roof was a blanket of stars. Only two rooms seemed to be finished – a large bedroom off at the end of the hall, and the bathroom beside it. Eli's feet crushed tufts of plaster and glass as he walked, and he glanced at Watson, worried for the dog's safety.

The sound of running water drew his attention, and Eli turned toward the bathroom. He thought back to last night's dream. His woman, again. This time she was opening a door. She wore a white bathrobe and had a blue towel twisted over her hair, as if she'd just gotten out of the shower. She had been looking at him like he had all the answers.

Watson hunkered down on his belly and began to whimper. Then he turned tail and flew down the stairs, loose boards scattering in his wake. 'Some K-9 unit you are,' Eli murmured, edging his way into the bathroom. The rush of water grew louder, although a sweep with his flashlight revealed no fixtures and no pipes. When the beam reflected into his eyes, Eli squinted, then moved closer to find a mirror mounted on the wall. It was a miracle that something this fragile had survived the wrecking ball, given that so much glass was ground up in the soles of his shoes. The surface was foggy, and he touched it gently with his forefinger, expecting to clear a spot . . . yet nothing happened. Had he not known better, he would have thought the mirror had steamed up from the inside out.

As Eli held the flashlight a little closer to see how the mirror was attached to the wall, the haze cleared in the shape of two hands, prints rising from *behind* the glass. Eli had his gun drawn immediately, pointed – where? At the wall? The mirror? How could you beat an enemy you couldn't see?

He could taste his heart. The hands pressed harder on the reverse side of the mirror. Then, right to left, backward, a finger drew letters through the steam. *H-E-L-P*.

'Holy shit,' Eli breathed, and then suddenly the mirror was wiped clear before his eyes, showing him his panic. He backed out of the bathroom, scrambling down the unsteady staircase toward Watson. With the dog at his heels, Eli jumped out of the open doorway. He had just hurdled the temporary fencing around the structure when the house suddenly lit up like a Christmas tree, so bright that Eli turned, struck by the incongruous beauty of a beacon in the middle of the woods.

All this, in a building where there had not been electricity for twenty years.

Ross could smell death. It lingered in the halls, cloaked in the scent of ammonia and bed linens and chalky pills. It peeked at him from around the corner. He wondered if the residents who came through the nursing home's door ever looked back, knowing they would not be leaving.

He had come here today, intent on throwing himself into research in the hopes that it might edge thoughts of Lia from his mind. In a week's time he had not seen her; had not heard from her. Instead, he received an endless stream of calls from Rod van Vleet. Did Ross know that the Pike house was putting itself back together? That a cop had actually filed a report saying that all the lights had turned on inside – when there were no power lines?

Ross was a firm believer that you could not force circumstance. You could buckle your seat belt, but still crash the car. You could throw yourself in front of an oncoming train, but somehow survive. You could wait for years to find a ghost, and then have one sneak up on you when you were too busy falling in love with a woman to pay attention. To that end, he made the conscious decision to stop waiting for Lia. When he least expected her, that was when she would show up.

He had come to the nursing home unannounced because he didn't know if Spencer Pike would agree to see him. And now that he sat across from the old man, Ross felt pity for him. The only animated part of Pike were his eyes, a blue that snapped smart as a flag. The rest of him was weathered, twisted like the roots of a tree forced to grow in too small a space.

'Screw the cinnamon raisin,' Spencer Pike said.

'I'm sorry?'

'It's a lousy excuse for a bagel. You ask me, not that anyone *has,* damn it, a bagel isn't supposed to be sweet. It's like a sandwich, for the love of God. Does anyone put jelly on their ham and cheese?' He leaned forward. 'You work for van Vleet; you can tell him I said so.'

'Technically I don't work for the Redhook Group,' Ross said.

'You in insurance?'

'No.'

'A lawyer?'

'No.'

'You own a bagel chain?'

'Uh, no.'

Pike shrugged. 'Well, two out of three. What do you want to know?'

'I understand that the land was originally your wife's . . . that it transferred to you upon her death, because you didn't have children.'

'That's wrong.'

Ross looked up from his notepad. 'That's the information in her will.'

'Well, it's still wrong. Cissy and I had a baby, but it was still-born.'

'I'm sorry.'

Pike smoothed his hands over the blanket on his lap. 'It was a long, long time ago.'

'The reason I'm here, Mr Pike, is to see if you know the history of the land before you acquired it.'

'It was in my wife's family. Passed down from mother to daughter for several generations.'

'Did the land ever belong to the Abenaki?'

Pike turned slowly. 'The *who?*'

'The Native Americans who've been protesting the development of the property.'

'I know who they are!' Pike's face grew red as a beet, and he began to cough. A nurse came over, gave Ross a dirty look, and spoke in low tones to Spencer Pike until his breathing had steadied. 'They can't give you any proof it's a burial ground, can they?'

'Certain . . . circumstances,' Ross said carefully, 'have led to the opinion that the property might be haunted.'

'Oh, it's haunted all right. But not by any Indians. My wife died on that property,' Pike said, the words deep and ragged.

The stillborn; the untimely death of Cissy Pike; the possibility of a restless spirit – it was coming together for Ross. 'In childbirth?'

Pike shook his head. 'She was murdered. By an Abenaki.'

*   *   *

During her lunch break Shelby took a five-minute walk from the library to the Gas & Grocery, where she usually picked up a sandwich. But these days, thanks to the *New York Times* article, the little general store was swamped by reporters trying to get their own story of the land dispute that, quite literally, would not settle. She took one look at Abe Huppinworth, nictitating at her from the porch as he swept the ever-present array of rose petals, and abruptly turned in the other direction.

She found herself walking into the municipal building before she even realized where she was headed. Lottie, the town clerk, sat at her desk with a diet book. 'I just don't get it,' she said, glancing up. 'They say eleven units, like I'm supposed to eat a condominium.'

Lottie, who had weighed well over two hundred and fifty pounds the whole time Shelby had been living in Comtosook, closed the book and picked up a celery stick. 'You know who invented vegetables, Shelby? The devil.' She took a bite. 'I ought to know better than to start a diet when I'm already in a bad mood.'

'Those reporters bugging you?'

'They're in here sniffing around for God knows what. I finally ran off photocopies of the Pike property's deed this morning, so I wouldn't have to be interrupted.' She shook her head. 'I imagine it's worse for you.'

Shelby shrugged. 'We unplug the phone.'

'I wish they would go away. I wish it would *all* go away. Myrt Clooney told me how Wally LaFleur's parrot started singing Edith Piaf ballads, just like that. The coffeemaker, here at the office? We can't get it to brew anything but lemonade.' She smiled suddenly at Shelby. 'You didn't come here to listen to a fat old lady moan. What can I do for you?'

Ten minutes later, under the pretense of finding a fact for a library patron, Shelby was sitting in the basement of the office, surrounded by boxes of town records. They were rubber-banded by year, but not in order – stacks of yellowed cards chronicling the births and deaths of Comtosook residents from 1877 to the present.

Ross had not asked for her help. Maybe that was why she was here – since their confrontation at the hospital he'd gone out of his way to avoid her, but with a politesse that felt like a knife being twisted: a note left on the counter saying he would be back between 4 and 5 A.M.; a gallon of milk set in the refrigerator to replace the one he had finished. The conversations they were *not* having had slipped under the carpeting, making it impossible to walk through the house without fear of tripping. Shelby wished she were brave enough to sit her baby brother down, to say, *Can't you see I'm only doing this out of love?* She was too afraid, though, that he might say the same thing in return.

What she wanted for him was one lucky break to turn the tide and send him swimming back to her. But since she could not find the way to tell Ross that she was sorry for doubting him, she would hand him this information, in case it might be apology enough.

The box of deaths from 1930 had survived a flood in the late fifties, and many were so faded with watermarks that Shelby could not read the names of the deceased, much less anything else about their states of affairs. The bottom of the carton was lined with an old Town Annual Report, published along with a calendar for the year 1966. 'Comtosook,' she read off the cover, 'derives from the Abenaki word *kôdtôzik,* or "what is hidden," referring no doubt to the wealth of granite found in the depths of Angel Quarry.'

No doubt, Shelby thought.

She dug a little deeper and came up with the stack of deaths from 1932. These weren't as badly stained, but the rubber band was so brittle it broke off in her hand. The cards spilled across her lap, smelling faintly of sulfur and pressed flowers. Shelby began to scan through them quickly. BERTELMAN, ADA. MONROE, RAWLENE. QUINCY, OLIVE.

Two cards were stuck together; Shelby noticed this at nearly the same time she realized that they both were labeled PIKE. The first was a death certificate for an unnamed stillborn infant, 37 weeks. *Approximate time of death: 11:32* A.M. Glued onto the back of this was another death certificate, for Mrs Spencer Pike. *Time of death: 11:32* A.M.

Shelby shivered in spite of the heat in the basement. It was not just that this woman, this Mrs Spencer Pike, who had died when she was only eighteen, had never lived to hold her baby. It was not even that this baby had never drawn a single breath. It had to do with the fixative that had cemented these cards together for so many years. Shelby was no expert, but it could only be blood.

Ruby Weber did not like to admit it, but she was getting old. She told everyone she was seventy-seven, although she was really eighty-three. Her hips moved like rusty hinges, her eyes clouded up when she least expected. Worst of all, she fell asleep in the middle of sentences sometimes, nodding off like, well, an old lady. One of these days she would just fall asleep, she supposed, and forget to wake up.

Not until Lucy was taken care of, though. Ruby knew that the medicine was helping her great-granddaughter, but at a cost – Lucy's nightmares had slinked down the hall to take up residence in Ruby's own bedroom. Now, no matter where or when Ruby dozed, she found herself reliving the phone call that had ruined her life.

It had come on a rainy Monday, eight years ago. She'd picked up the receiver, thinking it was the pharmacy saying her arthritis medicine was in; or maybe her daughter Luxe ringing from the market to let her know she'd be a few minutes late. But the voice on the other end belonged to a ghost.

She was still sitting with the phone in her hand, shaking, when Luxe came in with the groceries. 'You wouldn't believe how long it took me to get through the checkout,' Luxe said. 'You'd think people were stocking up for bomb shelters.' Then she looked more carefully at Ruby's face. 'Ma? What's the matter?'

Ruby had reached out her hand, touched Luxe's skin, smooth and warm as a stone. How did you go about telling someone you were not who they thought you were?

Now, Ruby felt hands on her shoulders, shaking her gently. 'Granny. *Granny.*'

Ruby could not answer, her mind was still full of Luxe, who had fallen down clutching her chest when Ruby told her who had called; who Luxe really was; who Ruby wasn't. She could still see Luxe's face, waxen and still, through the ER doorway as the doctor came out to say that the cardiac arrest had been fatal. How stupid Ruby had been. She'd held Luxe's heart in safekeeping all those years; to give it back, in retrospect, seemed foolish and irresponsible.

On the day her mother died, Meredith had been a graduate student in Boston. She arrived wild at the hospital, demanding a miracle. Ruby had nearly expected her to get one, for all her fury. Imagine: Luxe throwing back the sheet that covered her on the examination table, sitting up. Wonders like that, they had happened before. Ruby had seen it herself.

Ruby had never told Meredith what she'd told Luxe in the moments before her heart gave out. Now, though . . . with Lucy suffering . . . well, Meredith might understand the way love for a child could make a woman go crazy. 'Merry,' Ruby said suddenly, wanting to tell her all of it. 'Do you remember when your mother died?'

'Oh, Granny,' Meredith sighed. 'Is that what you were dreaming about?'

Her cool hand on Ruby's cheek: that was all it took for Ruby to understand she could not make the same mistake twice. She decided to put a tourniquet on the past for once and for all, until it just desiccated and disappeared. This was her life, now. Spencer

Pike had never called again, and as far as she was concerned, he could go to hell.

The dog made him nervous. It lay about four feet away from Ross's boot, a big puddle of skin completely relaxed except for its dark eyes, which had pinned Ross the moment he entered the detective's office and hadn't blinked since. 'Mr Wakeman,' said Detective Rochert. 'Put yourself in my shoes for a minute. Some guy, a *paranormal investigator,* comes in off the street and tells me to reexamine a seventy-year-old unsolved murder. Who am I supposed to get statements from – a ghost? And even if I do get a perp, chances are he's either dead or in his nineties. No prosecutor in Vermont is going to touch that case.'

Ross glanced at the dog, which bared its teeth. The detective snapped his fingers and the hound flopped onto the floor, boneless. 'I would think that, given the property dispute, you might find the case more timely than you think. All I'm saying is that there's a big difference between a woman dying in childbirth, and a woman being murdered. Maybe Spencer Pike is senile; maybe the town death records in 1932 were less than accurate. But then again, maybe that's the missing piece that explains why the Abenaki feel they have a claim to the land.'

Eli leaned forward, his dark eyes suddenly hard as flint. 'You came to me specifically because you know I'm half-Abenaki, didn't you? You think I'm going to reopen this file just because I *owe* it to them.'

Ross shook his head, surprised at this outburst. 'I came to you because you're the only detective on duty,' he said.

That shut Rochert up, but only briefly. 'Mr Wakeman, I think you and I operate a little differently. Your work is all about hunches; mine is rooted in hard evidence.'

Ross had learned long ago not to try to convert the skeptics. The fact was, there were plenty of people who believed in ghosts, and once you'd had a paranormal experience, you joined the ranks. The cynics were necessary; they limited the number of frauds. Ross wouldn't try to convince Eli Rochert that spirits existed, but he wouldn't stand here and let the man slander his investigation, either. 'Actually, my work is closer to yours than you'd think. Isn't crime-scene linkage based on the idea that people always leave a part of themselves behind?'

'Forensics can dust for fingerprints. They can't dust for . . .' His voice trailed off, and Ross watched Rochert frown, deep in thought. After a moment, he spoke again. 'Even if this murder is solved seventy years after the fact, it's not going to change anything. Pike's wife is still dead. He still legally owns the land. And he still has the right to sell it.'

'That depends,' Ross said.

'On?'

'Who actually committed a murder that night.'

It was not surprising to Eli that the Comtosook Police Department had kept the file on an unsolved homicide investigation from so long ago. This stemmed not from any particular diligence in keeping track of loose ends, but rather from absolute incompetence in record keeping. Frankly, no one had ever thought to clean out the archive closet. He brushed a cobweb out of his hair and pulled the bulky carton out of the haphazard stack.

Chief Follensbee wouldn't care what Eli did in his downtime. As he walked upstairs to his desk, he told himself that the reason he was doing this had nothing to do with what he'd experienced a few nights ago at the Pike property. Nor was it related to the nagging doubt that the woman in his recurring dreams kept coming back for a reason. He was reviewing this case because it had never been solved, and crime-scene techniques available today might be able to answer questions that had been asked and left unanswered in 1932.

Watson looked up when Eli came into the office, then decided he wasn't quite worth the trouble of getting to his feet. He watched with disinterest as Eli emptied the contents of the crate onto his cleared desk. A manila folder, a stack of crime-scene photographs, a paper lunch sack, a cigar box, and a noose.

Eli pulled a pair of rubber gloves out of his desk and picked up the rope. Nothing special about it; it looked like any industrial cable of twine you might find in the area even now. Whoever had investigated the case back then had been smart enough to leave the knot tied; after all these years it was still intact.

He picked up some of the crime-scene photos. One showed the young woman, lying down with the noose around her neck. Her chest and neck were scratched raw, not from the rope, but from the long rakes of fingernails – she'd tried to get free. Another was the porch of what seemed to be a shed. Eli squinted closer; there was a beam in the roof. Based on the puddle of what he assumed to be bodily fluids on the floorboards, that must have been where the body was hanged. A shot of the victim's bare legs, badly bruised.

In the brown paper sack was a stained nightgown and a pair of women's shoes. A small leather pouch, strung on a snapped rawhide lace, and a poplar pipe with a serpentine bowl rested in the cigar box. Eli picked the pipe up in his hands and turned it over. His grandfather had carved one like this. He sniffed, smelling the sweet tobacco he associated with his childhood.

Setting it aside, Eli opened the police investigation report.

CASE NUMBER: 32-01
INVESTIGATING OFFICER: Detective F. Olivette
VICTIM'S NAME: Cecelia Pike (aka Mrs Spencer Pike)
DATE OF BIRTH: 11-09-13
AGE: 18
ADDRESS: Otter Creek Pass, Comtosook, VT
TIME/DATE OF INCIDENT: 12AM–9AM,
September 19, 1932
LOCATION OF INCIDENT: Pike Property, Otter Creek Pass, Comtosook, VT

INCIDENT:

On September 19th, 1932, at 09:28 hrs Professor Spencer Pike (DOB 05-13-06) called the Comtosook Police Department and reported the murder of his wife, Cecelia 'Cissy' Pike. Professor Pike reported that his wife's death had occurred at their residence sometime between 12 AM–9 AM. Detective Duley Wiggs and I responded to the Pike property to investigate the incident.

Upon arrival at the residence we were met by Professor Pike. He was noticeably distraught. He directed us to the icehouse where his wife's body was found. The victim was lying on her back in front of the ice shed. I checked the victim for a pulse and found none. The body was cold to the touch. I then called for the coroner.

The victim was wearing a flowered dress and boots. A rope noose was around the victim's neck. The victim's chest and neck were scored with deep, bloody scratches. Numerous bruises were visible on the victim's lower legs. The roof to the porch was constructed using large support beams. Initial inspection suggests that the victim had been hanged from one of these beams. Photographs were taken of the body and the scene.

The area was examined for evidence. A leather pouch, strung on a length of rawhide, was found on the porch to the left rear of the body. Upon inspection it was noted that the rawhide thong was snapped. The pouch was found to contain some type of herbal matter. Underneath the porch a poplar-serpentine pipe was located. It was noted that no means by which the victim might have reached the beam herself was found at the scene.

Professor Pike reported that he married Cecelia in 1931. He confirmed his occupation as an instructor of anthropology at the University of Vermont. He stated that Mrs Pike was nine months pregnant and had gone into labor on the evening of September 18th. According to Professor Pike, his wife was assisted by their house girl, and gave birth to a stillborn female infant at 11 PM. He stated that Mrs Pike was both depressed and exhausted after giving birth. According to Professor Pike, his wife went to bed near midnight. Reportedly, this was the last time that Mrs Pike was seen alive.

Professor Pike reported that after his wife retired for the evening he went to his study and had a few drinks. He estimated that he consumed six scotch on the rocks. He reported that he fell asleep in his chair in the study and did not awaken until approximately 9 AM. Reportedly at that time Professor Pike went to check on his wife and found her bedroom empty, and the window broken. Professor Pike stated that he then canvassed the property for his wife, before locating her hanging from the beam on the porch of the ice shed. Professor Pike reported that he used a knife to cut his wife down from the beam.

The recovered pipe and pouch were shown to Professor Pike. He recognized them as the property of an Abenaki man named Gray Wolf. He stated that he had to forcibly evict Gray Wolf from his property on September 18th at noon. Professor Pike stated that he had seen Gray Wolf in the company of his wife, harassing her. Professor Pike reported that he knew the man to be an itinerant who was recently released from prison after serving time for a murder conviction in Burlington. Professor Pike stated that he confronted Gray Wolf and insisted that he leave their property. Reportedly, Gray Wolf had to be thrown off the premises.

Professor Pike also could not account for the whereabouts of his house girl, who was not present when he woke up at 9 AM. Her possessions, however, were still in the house. Her room showed no signs of struggle. Professor Pike reported that the house girl, fourteen, could not have physically been strong enough to harm his wife. He reported that her weak constitution may have caused her to run off upon finding his wife hanging, and that he was not surprised.

The coroner, Dr J. E. DuBois, arrived at 10 AM and inspected the victim's body. His initial findings suggest death by asphyxiation, consistent with hanging.

Eli leafed through several other pages. Descriptions of the house, of various items in Cissy Pike's bedroom. Signs of forced entry and struggle. The coroner's report. A set of inked prints, taken postmortem from the victim. An interview with Pike, and another with Gray Wolf, who had voluntarily come to the station for questioning. A statement by the men who served as Gray Wolf's alibi for the night. A warrant for the arrest of Gray Wolf, secured from a judge a day later, which had never been carried out because Gray Wolf had simply disappeared.

Eli glanced at the rope, at the nightgown, at the pipe. At the very least, he could send these out for DNA analysis, to see if Gray Wolf had left any record of his actions behind.

Eli absently stroked Watson's head. It was possible that Gray Wolf had left town because he knew he was going to be convicted, again, of murder. But it was also possible that Gray Wolf had never been found because he'd been on the Otter Creek Pass property the whole time, six feet under – courtesy of Spencer Pike.

Which would mean, ironically, that it *was* an Indian burial ground.

As Ross watched heat lightning connect the stars like a dot-to-dot puzzle, he thought about the first time he'd died. He really could not remember much of it, except for that instant he'd looked up at the broken sky, seen his opportunity, and had spread his arms wide in welcome. If pressed, he could recall the burning smell that was his hair; the stiffness of his limbs as the current coursed through him. He would have liked to be able to tell of crossing to the other side, of that bright white light, but if these things had happened he knew nothing of it.

The sky ripped again, a jagged tear that stayed visible for moments after the strike of lightning was gone. This time, it was followed by the tumble of thunder. On his forehead, Ross felt the first drop.

There were certain universal rules to outdoor paranormal investigation, based on temperature and weather conditions. You didn't want to find yourself taking spectral photos of what turned out to be the frost of your own breath; for the same reason, rain and falling snow were to be avoided at all costs. Ross had blatantly ignored these rules from time to time because electrical storms provided so much atmospheric energy that spirits could materialize much more easily than normal. The Warburtons had once been called down by the State of Connecticut after a lightning storm, because a municipal truck had struck a woman running across a highway. Although there had been six eyewitnesses to the accident, and a large dent remained in the fender of the truck, the lady who'd been hit had simply vanished. It was the energy in the air, Curtis had reasoned, that made this spirit so solid she could literally leave her mark.

Ross had been set up in his little clearing since suppertime, hoping that his discussions with Spencer Pike and Eli Rochert might help him conjure whatever was haunting this land, but the rain was going to thwart his plans. He whipped off his jacket and wrapped it around the video camera for protection. A wide line of lightning swaggered out of the sky and touched down just a few feet away, making the wet ground hiss.

The last thing he wanted to do was leave; it was only eight o'clock and it had been hard enough sneaking onto the land. He'd had to go through the woods, since media vans were parked along the front edge of the property. Reporters had multiplied like roaches since the *New York Times* had broken the story about the Comtosook acreage, and avoiding them was becoming more and more challenging for Ross. Packing up for the night meant hauling his equipment back the way he had come, this time in the middle of a deluge.

Ross strapped his camera bag over his shoulder and tucked his flashlight into the pocket of his cargo shorts, then ducked his head and began to walk into the woods. The frozen ground, now wet, slipped beneath his feet. When he crashed into a person hurrying just as hard into the woods as he was hurrying out of it, Ross swore under his breath. He didn't have to give up his cover. He'd say he was a reporter too; who would know, with his camera?

He raised his face, an excuse on his lips, and found himself staring at Lia.

What Eli had noticed, lately, was that certain dog food smelled like meat. Even though it wasn't – he knew, because he'd read the ingredients on the can – they processed it in such a way that all you had to do was stick your face close like a feed horse and you conjured up images of chops and steaks, roasts and flame-broiled burgers. Watson looked happy enough, eating so greedily his ears kept falling into the bowl. Maybe Eli could call up Blue Seal and find out what kind of gravy they used. Maybe he could pour it over his damn tofu.

The phone rang, and he reached for the receiver. 'Eli,' said a female voice. 'What are you doing home on a Saturday night?'

He smiled. 'What are you doing at work, Frankie?'

Frankie Martine was a DNA researcher, and an old friend. He'd met her at a Twin States Forensics Conference, where she'd beat him playing Quarters. She lived in Maine, now, and although Eli had said numerous times he was going to visit her, he hadn't actually done it until two days ago, when he'd personally brought her the evidence from the Pike murder. It was his only option, really – his own boss would never condone spending taxpayer money on DNA tests that were going to go nowhere, and Frankie had agreed to do it as a personal favor.

'The reason I'm at work is because my so-called friends keep me chained to my lab,' she said. 'How quickly we forget.'

Eli sat down. 'Got anything good for me?'

'Depends on your definition. I managed to get DNA off the saliva that was on the pipe. I also lifted DNA off the rope, from skin cells.

It seemed to be a mixture of two distinct profiles. The first, taken from the loop, belonged to a female – your victim, I'm assuming. The second came from the end of the rope and belonged to a male.'

'Bingo.'

'Not quite,' Frankie corrected. 'The DNA belonged to a guy *other* than the one whose saliva is on that pipe.'

Eli's mind spun: assuming the pipe belonged to Gray Wolf, and if Gray Wolf had hanged Cissy Pike, shouldn't his DNA be on the rope? If it wasn't, was that enough to vindicate him? And if it *wasn't* his DNA on the rope with the victim's . . . whose was it? The investigating cop's? Spencer Pike's?

'Eli, Eli.' Frankie's voice sliced through his reverie. 'I can hear the gears going.'

'Sorry.' He shook his head to clear it. 'What about the medicine pouch?'

'The what?'

'The little leather thingy.'

'Oh, that,' Frankie said. 'I keep getting the wrong results. Something is getting screwed up in the testing, I think.'

'How do you know they're the wrong results, if you don't have any answers yet?'

'They're just weird, that's all.'

Eli frowned. 'Weird like: it's alien DNA . . . or weird like: you can't get results because it's so goddamned old?'

'Weird like: leave me alone so I can give you a report.'

'When?' Eli demanded.

'Two minutes later than it would have been if you'd let me get off the phone.'

'Thanks, Frankie.'

'Don't thank me,' she said. 'By the time I'm done, you may not want to.'

Ethan poked his head into the bathroom, where his mother was taking a bubble bath. 'Come on in,' she said, and he crept inside, studiously keeping his eyes on the tile floor. She was covered with bubbles from neck to toe, but *still*. This was his *mother* . . . and that word, along with *naked*, felt weird jammed together.

'Eth,' she said, laughing, 'I'm perfectly decent.'

He risked a glance: she was. Her face was the only body part rising above the froth of foam. 'I couldn't get this open,' Ethan said, thrusting a jar of peanut butter toward her.

'Ah.' His mother took it, twisted, handed it back. The sides of the jar were soapy now. 'What are you up to?'

'Making ants-on-a-log. For during the movie.' They'd rented something lame and Disneyfied; Ethan was hoping he could convince his mother to watch *Die Hard II* instead, which was on one of the cable stations. He glanced up at the window, streaked with rain. 'It bites that we can't go outside.'

'*Ethan.*'

'Well, it still bites, even if I'm not supposed to say that.'

When the doorbell rang, they both jumped. It wasn't just that someone shouldn't be dropping by at nine-thirty on a Saturday night. It was that nobody dropped by, *ever*. Ethan watched his mother's face go as white as the bubbles surrounding her. 'Something happened to Ross,' she whispered, and she lurched upright in the tub.

Ethan turned away before he had to see, well, *her*. She shrugged into her robe and wrapped a blue towel around her hair, then hurried down the stairs.

He could have followed her. The celery and raisins were on the counter, waiting. But instead Ethan found his mind frozen on the one piece of his mother he had glimpsed before he turned away – a foot rising from the suds.

He had no idea why, but seeing that . . . it reminded him of the night he'd gone ghost hunting with his uncle.

In his wildest imaginings, Eli could not have ever pictured himself collaborating with a paranormal investigator. In his opinion, evidence was something that could be held in your hand, not in your head. But Frankie's call tonight had changed everything. The alleged murderer's DNA had not been on the rope – yet someone else's DNA *had* been. Neither of these circumstances alone was damning or absolving . . . but taken in context, they might be. Eli needed to speak to someone who could fill in some of the historical blanks. That someone was Ross Wakeman.

He stood on the porch, the rain pounding the metal roof overhead, and rang the doorbell a second time. Wakeman had left his phone number and address behind, 'just in case,' he had told Eli, 'you change your mind about reopening that case.' Eli's keen eye had already noticed the skateboard propped up against the wall, and the pair of yellow garden clogs next to them. It surprised Eli; he had good instincts, and Ross Wakeman hadn't struck him as a family man. He knew that someone was home; the car was in the driveway and across a lighted window upstairs, Eli had seen a moving silhouette. He rapped hard on the door. 'Hello?'

There was the systematic click of locks being undone. A flash of blue crossed the sidelight window; a terry-cloth sleeve. The door swung open, and an apprehensive voice addressed him. 'Can I help you?'

But Eli could not respond. He could not do anything but stare, speechless, at the woman who'd been in his dreams.

Ethan dipped his hand into the bubbles and blew them gently. He had smelled something like this when the lights had gone out in the haunted house. He got up from where he was sitting and turned out the light, pitching the bathroom into darkness. Now, with the scent of flowers all around, and the humidity pressing in, it was just like it had been that night.

His uncle had asked him if he'd seen anything, and Ethan had said no, he was hiding. But he'd peeked out once, and there *had* been something. A movement in the dark. At first he had thought it was his uncle again, coming back, but that had not been the case. Ethan had found himself straining to see the profile in front of him, thin as fishing line. A face, or maybe not a face, he couldn't quite hold onto it then or now.

There was only one thing Ethan was certain of, one point that stuck like a knife thrown to its mark: that flower smell had been there, and then it had gone. Whatever it had been had followed Uncle Ross outside, instead of the other way around.

A streak of lightning broke the spell. 'You came back,' Ross said, not noticing that Lia's eyes were red and raw, that she was shaking her head. She had returned to him, and for this small miracle alone, he would do what it took to keep her there. He was certain, in that moment, that he could face down a hundred reporters. He could take on her husband. He could stop the thunder, if necessary.

'I came to say good-bye,' Lia answered.

Ross fielded the words like a blow. He could not explain to himself why he felt the way he did around this woman; why his skin hummed in her presence and the tips of his fingers went cold. He'd believed, on some level, that Lia had felt this too. For years, he had been looking for the answer to Aimee's death; only recently had he learned that he'd been asking the wrong question.

Before you could grab onto something else, you had to let go.

'No.' The rain matted Ross's hair and ran down his face. He did not know how to make Lia understand that a parting was a joint decision, that a person could not leave you, if you were not willing to release them. So instead, he reached for her.

Ross held her face between his hands and kissed her. He tasted doubt on her tongue and pain on the roof of her mouth. He swallowed these, and drank again. Consumed, she had no choice but to see how empty he was inside, and how, sip by sip, she filled him.

The storm whipped stronger, sparks arcing blue and thunder

drumming beneath their feet. Lia broke away from him, her eyes wide and wet. 'Wait,' Ross said, but she turned and started to run through the woods.

He followed her like a hunter, eyes marking the flashes of white from her collar. She raced across the slick, snowy clearing where Ross had done most of his research, darting between mounds of dirt that had sprung up from nowhere once again. She disappeared between a fissure of trees.

Ross had not been on this part of the property before, at least not that he could remember. His lungs were too tight, every breath a pinch, but he did not stop running. Lia had turned onto a narrow path, one overgrown with young pines and frozen scrub brush. Thorns caught at Ross's shoelaces and scraped up his calves, and then suddenly, miraculously, gave way. Beneath his feet the ground had thawed, a small patch covered with dozens of trampled white roses.

Lia glanced down at them too, but she didn't stop. And Ross, who had not taken his eyes off her, watched her legs pass directly through two stone markers, the same ones he smacked into a moment later with his boot, sending him sprawled face-first into the mud.

Winded and dazed, he struggled to his knees. It took another flash of lightning for him to be able to make out the names on the gravestones. LILY PIKE, SEPTEMBER 19, 1932. And on the larger one: CECELIA BEAUMONT PIKE, NOVEMBER 9, 1913–SEPTEMBER 19, 1932.

Ross glanced up to find Lia staring at the graves, too. Slowly, she reached out to touch the smaller stone, and her hand moved right through it. She looked at Ross, stunned.

Cissy Pike. Cecelia. Lia.

Ross had been told of ghosts who did not know they were ghosts. He'd met paranormal investigators who had been bitten, hit, slapped, and shoved by spirits. He had always assumed that the first ghost he saw would be transparent, a storybook specter, but when there was enough energy to warrant it, ghosts could seem as solid as anyone.

Ross, an insomniac, had slept like a baby after seeing Lia. He'd shivered in her presence. It had been physical attraction, in the most elemental sense: what he'd felt was a spirit, stealing his heat.

'Ross,' Lia said, and he heard the word in his mind, unspoken. 'Ross?' Over the gravestone, her gravestone, she extended her hand.

Even as he reached for her, he knew this would only bring him pain. Lia's fingers sent chills up his arm. Her features grew transparent. Ross wiped the rain from his eyes and forced himself to watch, so that this time he would know the very moment he'd been left behind.

Part Two

1932

There are two ways to be fooled.
One is to believe what isn't true;
the other is to refuse to believe what is true.

– Søren Kierkegaard

5

July 4, 1932

Running water purifies itself. The stream of germ-plasm does not
seem to.

— H. F. Perkins, *Lessons from a Eugenical Survey of Vermont*:
First Annual Report, 1927

The day after I try to kill myself, Spencer says we are going
to a celebration in Burlington. He tells me this even as he is
wrapping my wrist again, where I cut myself so deep that, for a
moment, I could tell exactly where I hurt. 'There are going to be
fortune-tellers, Cissy,' he says. 'Fire-eaters, and historical pageants.
All sorts of trinkets for sale.' He ties off the bandage, and then
gets to the point of why we're going to town for the Fourth of
July festival. 'Your father,' Spencer says, 'is meeting us there.'

Although it is so hot outside that the dandelions and black-eyed
Susans have gone weak-kneed, he helps me into a long-sleeved
white blouse, because this way the bandages won't show. 'No one
needs to know this happened,' he says quietly, and I stare at the
pink part in his hair until the shine of it makes me turn my face
away. 'You were sleepwalking, that's all. You didn't know what you
were doing.'

For Spencer, the face you show to the world is more important
than what's underneath. The end justifies the means. That is what

Charles Darwin is all about, after all, and in my opinion Spencer would pray to Mr Darwin if he didn't think it would make the biddies at the Congregational Church regard him as some kind of heathen. Spencer's long fingers curve around my jaw. 'Come on, Cissy,' he coaxes. 'Don't disappoint me.'

I would not dream of it. I smooth my face into a smile. 'All right,' I answer.

What I want to say is: *Don't call me Cissy. That's the name of a coward, a self-fulfilling prophecy, and look at where it's gotten me.* What I want to say is: *My mother named me Cecelia, which is beautiful, a river of syllables.* Once, with my head spinning from blackberry wine I'd sipped at a faculty dinner, I told my husband I wanted to be called Lia. 'Leah?' he said, mistaking me, shaking his head. 'But that's the one Jacob *didn't* want.'

He helps me stand, because my pregnancy is a condition that Spencer can accept. It's the other affliction we do not speak of. Spencer's work, dovetailing as it does with mental hygiene, keeps us from admitting that I have anything in common with those holed up in the state hospital at Waterbury.

I cannot explain to someone like Spencer what it is like to look in a mirror and not recognize the face inside it. How there are some days I wake up and it takes everything inside me to put on a mask and walk through my life like someone else. I have sat beside him, digging my nails into the skin of my palm, because if I bleed, then I must be real.

I think of what it would be like to push off on a raft in a vast ocean, fall asleep under a full sun: sweat, burn, never wake up. Believe it or not, there's a relief to that vision that feels like a cold sheet settling. If I'm going to die, I'd rather choose the where or when.

After so many years of being dismissed, it is easy to believe the world would be better off without me in it. Spencer says it's because of my condition, chemicals in my body and brain blown out of proportion, but I know better. I have never fit into this

town, this marriage, this skin. I am the child who was picked
last to play tag; I am the girl who laughed although she did not
get the joke; I am the piecemeal part of you that you pretend
does not exist, except it is *all* I am, all of the time.

And yet. There is a baby in me who never asked for any of this.
And if taking my own life means taking his as well, then I will
have twice killed someone I should have had the chance to love.

Spencer is wise; he uses this truth as a bargaining chip. He
teases me and flirts, so that by the time we have left the house
and started for town, I find myself looking forward to this celebration. I can smell the sear of fireworks on the air; I can hear
the lazy pomp of a parade. My baby rolls like the silver fish in
Lake Champlain, and without thinking about it I settle my hand
on my stomach. Spencer sees, and covers my fingers with his
own, smiling. All the way down Otter Creek Pass I think about
this fortune-teller; if she'll find my mother's face in her crystal
ball, or just the abyss I see when I try to do her job.

Q.   What is the most precious thing in the world?
A.   The human germ plasm.

Q.   How may one's germ plasm become immortal?
A.   Only by perpetuation by children.

Q.   What is a person's eugenical duty to civilization?
A.   To see that his own good qualities are passed on to future
      generations provided they exceed his bad qualities. If he
      has, on the whole, an excess of dysgenic qualities, they
      should be eliminated by letting the germ plasm die out with
      the individual.

– American Eugenics Society,
A Eugenics Catechism, 1926

The heat makes the streets ripe as fruit, pavement bruising beneath my shoes. Men in summer suits and women in smart linen dresses hold hands. There are hawkers selling lemon ices, and red-white-and-blue pinwheels. Everyone's smiles seem too wide.

'I heard there was a boxing exhibition this morning,' Spencer says. 'A soldier from the fort got trounced by an Irishman from New York City.' He steers me toward the edge of a large crowd of people, and cranes his neck to look over everyone's heads toward the Hill, where my father lives now that Spencer and I have moved into the house where I grew up. 'It's not like Harry to be late,' Spencer murmurs. 'Do you see him?'

But Spencer is nearly a head taller than I am, and he wears glasses. I try to see what he sees, but instead I notice the barefoot boy kneeling beside a puddle of manure to pick out a handful of pennies that have fallen from someone's purse. He is part of a world I do not know – people who live in the North End tenements, two hundred yards away and a world apart.

'Darling,' my father says from behind us. He kisses my cheek. 'Sorry, Spencer,' he says, shaking hands. 'I took in the boxing match. Amazing, really. If you look at the physiology of some of the immigrant stock . . .'

Science is a foreign language to me, but one with which I was raised. My father, Harry Beaumont, is a professor of biology at the University of Vermont. Spencer, a professor of anthropology, shares many of his convictions about Mendelian genetics. They are disciples of another professor, Henry Perkins, who more or less introduced Vermont to eugenics – the science of human betterment through genetic improvement. Professor Perkins once headed the Eugenics Survey of Vermont – a privately funded study of Vermont families. He now volunteers under the vast umbrella of the Vermont Commission on Country Life, just like my father and Spencer. Over the years their Committee on the Human Factor has worked on a Key Family Study, tracing degenerate Vermont families to see whether a town's social and economic success is related to the type of people who settle it. Their pedigree charts are available to social workers and probation officers to help with case work. Between that and the new sterilization law, Vermont is joining other states that are already models for the country.

It's a progressive reform movement, a thrilling one. Spencer always says it isn't about taking Vermont forward, but back – to the pastoral landscape everyone imagines when they say the word *Vermont:* a town green, a white church, a hillside stippled with fall color. My father and Spencer were among the first to realize that this picture dims when strong Yankee stock is replaced by weaker strains. Their Key Family Study sent field workers out to selected towns, to see if social and economic status had any correlation to the quality of their founding families. It was no surprise that the towns in decline were full of families whose members kept cropping up at the state mental hospitals and reform schools and jails. Recessive genes like feeblemindedness and criminal tendencies, of course, get passed on to offspring – it is all there in the pedigree charts my father used to unroll across our dining room table. By targeting these populations and intervening before they propagate, Vermont could recapture its picturesque image.

'The Ideal Vermont Family,' that's what Spencer always says his field workers are looking for. 'People like us.'

Since my marriage, I have tried to do my part. I've served on the board of the Children's Aid Society, I'm a member of the Daughters of the American Revolution, and I'm the secretary of the Ladies' Auxiliary at church. But these women, with their bobs and their shoulder pads and seamed stockings, speak the same words; they make the same suggestions; sometimes their features even blend together. And I am not one of them.

I sometimes wonder what might have happened, had I not married Spencer but rather gone off to college and joined the eugenics survey as a field worker, like Frances Conklin and Harriet Abbott. Would I have been happier? These women, they were part of a movement that would sweep Vermont into the future. They made a difference.

Spencer says that some women are meant to change the world, while others are meant to hold it together. And then there are those of us who simply don't want to be in it, because we know no matter how much we struggle, we can't comfortably fit.

My father slides an arm around my shoulders. 'How's my grandson?' he asks, as if this baby's sex is something we might know.

'Strong as an ox,' Spencer says. 'Kicks Cissy all day long.'

Everyone beams. No one mentions my mother, although her name hovers at the edges of our conversation. Had I been strong as an ox, before I was born? Had that been the problem?

Sweat runs between my breasts and down the line of my spine. Under my hat, my scalp itches. In the distance I hear the low-throated hum of barges on the lake, quivering to leave. 'Ma'am,' says a voice to my left. 'Are you all right?'

It is a young man wearing a suit, a red-tipped carnation threaded through the lapel. His hair, neatly combed to the side, is the color of molasses. His hand rests on my elbow.

'You look a little peaked.' He smiles. 'Lovelier than anything I've seen here today, but fading fast.'

Before I can answer Spencer cuts between us. 'Did you have something to say to my wife?'

The man shrugs. 'I've got something to say to the whole crowd.' As he steps up onto a small platform, he winks at me.

'Maybe next year *you* can fight the Irishman at the boxing exhibition,' my father says to Spencer.

'I will if he keeps carrying on with Cissy.' Then Spencer's voice is drowned out by the commanding baritone of the very man he is discussing.

'Ladies and gentleman,' the orator announces, 'The Legend of Champlain!'

The crowd gathers to watch the historical pageant. Musicians play Indian chords as four braves stalk about, the menacing Iroquois. They are half-dressed, in the manner of savages, with broad marks across their faces and chests. When Champlain and his Algonquin warriors arrive, a single shot from his rifle kills all of the enemies in one fell swoop. 'A dark era of savage power,' intones the orator, 'ended in that steadfast hour. As mighty Champlain crossed the water . . . and from great chaos, brought great order.'

There is a round of applause as the actors take their bows and everyone begins to disperse. 'What shall we do next?' Spencer asks. 'There's an exhibition baseball game, and a motorboat race. Or the Exposition, maybe?'

Through the weaving limbs of people I can see across to the other side of the stage, where a man is looking at me. He is as dark-skinned as the Indians hired to play in the pageant, and his eyes are so black they could only be a trap. He does not smile, or politely pretend that he is not staring. I can't seem to turn away, not even after Spencer touches my shoulder. I cannot tell what holds me more fascinated: the sense that this man might hurt me, or that he might not.

'Cissy?'

'The Exposition,' I say, and hope this is an appropriate response.

When I turn back toward the opposite side of the stage, he is gone.

Freedom and Unity.

– The Vermont State Motto

An old lot on Shelburne Street has been converted into an exhibition arena. As we sit on the grandstand and watch Bertie Briggs's Fabulous Dancing Cats, I fan myself with the program. I lift my hair off my damp neck and try to tuck it up under my hat. The circles of perspiration beneath my arms embarrass me.

Spencer must be feeling the heat, too. In his seersucker suit, though, he looks as cool and calm as ever. He and my father watch some of the Gypsies who have come to sell their wares – baskets and miniature snowshoes, herbal tonics. They camp along the banks of the river and lake for the summer, and many of them spend the winter in Canada. They are not real Rom, of course, only Indians – but are called Gypsies because they move around, have dark skin, and breed enormous families that routinely populate the prisons and institutions. 'The Ishmaelites, resurrected,' Spencer murmurs.

These Gypsies are the people Professor Perkins studied in his survey – along with a clan plagued by insanity and a depraved brood that lived in floating shanties, nicknamed the Pirates. The difference between these families, and, say, ours, is purely genetic. A transient father breeds a transient son. A promiscuous mother passes that trait along to her daughter.

'Three more operations were done at Brandon,' my father says. 'And two at the prison.'

Spencer smiles. 'That's wonderful.'

'It's certainly what we hoped for. I imagine all the patients will want to volunteer, once they understand that a simple treatment will let them live as they please.'

One of Bertie Briggs's tabby cats begins to walk a high wire. Her paws tremble on the line, at least I think they are trembling – my vision seems to be going in and out. I look into my lap, taking deep breaths, trying to keep from passing out.

The small hand that darts into my lap from the side of the grandstand might be dirty, or only dark. It leaves behind a wrinkled slip of paper, printed with a moon and stars. FREE READING – MME SOLIAT. By the time I look up, the little boy who has left this behind has disappeared into the crowd.

'I'm just going to find the ladies' room,' I say, standing up.

'I'll come,' Spencer announces.

'I'm perfectly capable of going by myself.' In the end, he lets me go alone, but only after he's helped me navigate the grand-stand stairs, and has waved me off in the right direction.

When I know he isn't watching any longer, I turn the opposite way. I sneak a cigarette from my purse – Spencer doesn't think women ought to smoke – and duck into Madame Soliat's tent. It is small and black, with yellow fabric stars sewn on the curtains. The fortune-teller wears a silver turban and three silver earrings in each ear. A wolf-dog pants beside her table, his tongue pink as a wound. 'So sit,' she says, as if she has been kept waiting.

She has no tea leaves or crystal ball. She doesn't reach for my palm. 'Don't be afraid,' she says finally, her voice as deep as a man's, when I am just about ready to get up and leave.

'I'm not.' I grind out my cigarette and lift my chin a little, to show her how brave I can be.

She shakes her head, and lowers her gaze to the baby inside me. 'About *that.*'

My mother died in childbirth. I am expecting to do the same. I will not know my baby, then . . . but there is every chance I will get to know my mother.

'You will,' the fortune-teller replies, as if I've spoken aloud. 'What you don't know is about to come clear. But that will muddy other waters.'

She is speaking in riddles, that's what Spencer would say. Of course, Spencer would never do anything as unscientific as visiting a psychic. She tells me other things that might apply to anybody: that I am to come into a sum of money; that a stranger is going to visit. Finally, I reach into my purse for a dollar bill, only to feel her fingers lock on my wrist. I try to pull away, but she's grabbing hard enough for me to feel the beat of my pulse. 'You have death on your hands,' she says, and then she lets me go.

Startled, I stumble to my feet and into the hot sun. Oh, she is right; I do, I have from the moment I was born and killed my mother in the process.

I take turns without thinking twice; I push through faces

without features. When I find myself in a crowd of young men, university students, funneling toward the entrance of a crystal palace, I try to turn against the tide. But their eagerness sweeps me forward and soon I am inside this hall of mirrors.

Spencer has told me of the movable maze that cost $20,000 to build. From behind high partitions come the shrieks of college students, taking wrong turns. The air is as thick as custard. I cannot seem to escape myself; everywhere I turn around, there I am.

Heat presses in at the back of my neck. I lean into one mirror, tracing a hand over the swell of my stomach where this baby nests. I touch my cheek, my jaw. Do I look this frightened to the rest of the world?

Trailing my hand over the panes of glass, I follow my reflection from panel to panel to panel . . . and then my face turns into something else entirely. Black eyes, blacker hair, a mouth that has forgotten how to smile. We stand inches apart, close enough to touch. Me, and the man who was watching me during the pageant. Neither of us seems to be breathing.

Oh, this heat. It is the last thing I remember thinking before it all goes black.

It is the patriotic duty of every normal couple to have children in sufficient number to keep up to par the 'good old Vermont stock.'

— Vermont Commission on Country Life,
Committee on the Human Factor,
'The People of Vermont,' in *Rural Vermont:*
A Program for the Future, 1931

'Take it easy, Cissy.'

Spencer's voice floats to me down a long tunnel. As my eyes focus, I look for landmarks: the Hall of Mirrors, the grandstand, the vendor selling salted peanuts. But instead I see the antique bowl and pitcher on my dresser, the gilded foot of our bed. A cold cloth spread over my forehead drips into my hair, onto the pillow.

He holds my hand. It makes me think of being a child, hanging onto my father to cross Church Street. I married Spencer when I was seventeen; he became the next adult to keep me safe. As I lay on my side with the bulk of my belly swelling over my thighs, it strikes me that I have never had the chance to grow up.

'You feeling better?' Spencer asks, and he smiles so sweetly something inside me breaks loose.

I love him. The smell of his hair and the bump of his nose that supports his glasses; the long lean muscles you would never expect to find beneath his pressed shirts and jackets. I adore the way he looks at me sometimes, as if love is a quantity he cannot measure scientifically, because it multiplies too quickly. I wish that we had met, however, on a busy street in New York City, or on a neighbor's porch in Iowa, or even during a trans-atlantic crossing – any circumstance at all that would make my relationship with Spencer separate from his relationship with my father.

He puts his hand over my stomach, and I close my eyes. It is impossible to not think of Spencer's Committee on the Human Factor, which advocates the careful selection of a mate. But I was picked because I am Harry Beaumont's daughter, not because I am myself.

I wonder how Spencer feels, to have made such an informed decision, and to still have wound up with something defective.

'How did I get here?' I ask, many questions at once.

'You fainted at the Exposition.'

'The heat . . .'

'Rest, Cissy.'

I feel fine. I want to shout this, even though it isn't true. There were times as a child I would climb to the roof of this very house, stand spread-eagled and yell until the whole of Comtosook heard me. It was not that I had anything important to say, but rather, that my father wanted me quiet.

I see this streak as a black curl in my blood, moving through my system and surfacing when I least expect it. Like now, with Spencer fussing over me. My smoking. This afternoon, at the fortune-teller's tent. Or last night, when I cut myself.

Sometimes I wonder if I inherited it from my mother.

'I'll send Ruby in to you.' Spencer kisses the crown of my head. 'You'll be fine.'

If Spencer says so, it must be true.

Ruby hovers at the door, waiting to be invited in. Our house girl is fourteen, close enough to my age for a friendship, and yet we are leagues apart. It is not just that she is French Canadian – I am so much *older* than she is, and not just chronologically. When she thinks no one can see, Ruby dances between the white sheets she hangs out on the line – pirouettes and the lindy hop and even a little Charleston. Me, I never forget that at any time, someone might be watching.

She comes bearing a brown-wrapped package. 'Miz Pike,' she says, 'look what came in the mail.'

She sets the package down beside me and makes an unsuccessful attempt to ignore the bandage on my wrist. Ruby, of course, knows what happened. She held a bowl of warm water for Spencer, as he cleaned the cut and bound it tightly to heal. She is part of the conspiracy of silence.

Ruby works the twine free and unwraps the box. Inside is a Sears, Roebuck order – a pair of half-boots just like the ones Spencer has removed from my feet. These are a size bigger, and maybe will not pinch so much, like all my shoes do now that I am so pregnant. Glancing over the edge of the bed, I stare at Ruby's shoes. 'You wear about a size six, don't you?'

'Yes, ma'am.'

'Why don't you take them? I don't imagine my foot's going to get smaller again.' Ruby holds my old boots in her hand as if they are a treasure. 'My sister, she used to give me hand-me-downs.'

'You have a sister?' How can I have lived with a girl for a year, and not have known this?

'Not anymore. Diphtheria.' Ruby busies herself unpacking the rest of the box. Tiny sweaters and socks and miniature undershirts in all the hues of white spill over the bedclothes, a Lilliputian bounty. These clothes seem too little to fit on a doll, much less a baby.

'Oh,' Ruby breathes, picking up a lacy cap between her thumb and forefinger. 'Have you ever seen anything so fine in your life?'

Ruby wants this baby more than I do. It's not that I am not pleased by the thought of his arrival – it is just that no one seems to understand that I will not survive this birth. Spencer taught me well; this defect is in my germ plasm. If I don't manage to kill myself first, then the day this baby is born is the day I'm going to die.

Spencer has showed me numerous obstetrical texts to convince me otherwise; he has made me speak to the best of doctors. I nod, I smile, sometimes I even listen. Meanwhile, I plot my suicide. But then I feel the baby's small feet running the curve of my ribs, as if he knows by instinct where to find my heart, and I realize I am lost.

'Oh, no, Miz Pike,' Ruby says; until then I am not aware that I've begun to cry. 'Should I get the professor?'

'No.' I use the edge of the sheet to wipe my eyes. 'No, I'm fine. Just tired. Really.'

Last night, I thought that if I cut deep enough, I might be able to see all the way down past blood and bone and marrow to the place where it aches all the time. Spencer, when he bandaged my wrist, said I must think about my baby. I have two months left before I am due to give birth, after all. He does not understand that I *was* thinking of my son. I was trying to spare him the weight I have carried all my life: the knowledge that he was the reason for my death.

I know that my actions don't follow logic; that harming myself puts my infant in danger too. But somehow, when it is just me and the dark and the night and a blade, reason never counts. I have tried to tell this to Spencer, many times. 'But I love you,' he says, as if that should be enough to keep me here.

Now, with Ruby beside me, I try to find words to explain the impossible. 'Did you ever walk through a room that's packed with people, and feel so lonely you can hardly take the next step?'

She hesitates, then nods slowly. Cocking my head, I look at her, and wonder if she might not be quite as young as I've thought. 'Miz Pike,' Ruby whispers shyly. 'Maybe we could pretend to be sisters.'

Ruby, a servant girl, and me, the wife of one of greater Burlington's most esteemed citizens. 'Maybe,' I answer.

PRINCIPLES OF HEREDITY: Prof. H. F. Perkins. Lecture course with conference and report exercises covering the principles of elementary embryology, the physical basis of inheritance, principles of breeding experiments, and eugenics, the practical application of heredity to mankind. Text used: Newman's *Readings in Evolution, Genetics, and Eugenics*.

– *University of Vermont Bulletin*, 1923–24

For years now, I have been fascinated by Harry Houdini. I've read every biography written since his death in 1926; I keep a scrap-book of newspaper articles about his amazing feats. It is not just the obvious – that, like him, I know of ties that bind and chains that keep one rooted to a certain place, or that, like him, I some-times wish to disappear. No, what is more intriguing to me is Houdini's obsession with the spirit world.

Did I mention that Houdini, too, lost his mother?

The new book I'm reading chronicles the long war between Houdini and Margery, the Boston medium. During her séances, her voice would appear from different parts of the room, a spirit

bell would ring, a megaphone was wont to fly across the table –
all while others held the medium's hands. Houdini, convinced
that she was a hoax, built her a fraud-preventer cabinet and challenged her to hold a séance from inside it. But during the séance,
a folding ruler was found at the medium's feet – something Margery
and Houdini each claimed the other had planted. In the end,
Houdini died discrediting her, and swore that if a spirit were ever
to return from the other side of the veil, it would be him.

Although séances have been held on Halloween, now, for five
years, he hasn't come back.

This is what I think about Mr Houdini: if he hadn't been so
desperate to contact his departed mother, he wouldn't have fought
so fiercely against Margery. He denounced the spirit world because
he feared it was the one space from which he could not escape.

I feel like a fool, hiding here in my bedroom closet. It's where
I've gone for privacy, dragging in a little card table that is jammed
up against my belly. Table tipping is something else I have read of;
it's a way of contacting the spirits. I should have more people sitting
here with their hands linked, but I certainly could not tell Spencer
what I am doing, and I don't know what Ruby would make of it.

The silks of my dresses brush my shoulders. I press my palms
against the table, close my eyes. 'Mama?' I whisper.

Suddenly, a hand touches my side. I jump, and then realize
that the fingers are on the inside of my skin – it's this baby, trying
to push away for all he is worth. 'Hush, now. We're trying to talk
to your grandma.'

If I can find her, if I can open a door . . . then maybe even
after I die I will be able to find my way back.

I take deep breaths to concentrate. I focus all my energy on
that table. 'Mama, if you can hear me, let me know.'

The table, beneath my hands, remains perfectly still. But then
I hear a creak. I open my eyes in time to see the doorknob of
the closet turning by itself. The brightest light appears, growing
wider and wider until it silhouettes the figure of a woman.

'Miz Pike,' Ruby asks, 'what on earth are you doing in *here?*'

My heart is pounding so hard that it takes a moment to answer. Pretending it is perfectly normal to be found sitting inside a closet, I say, 'What did you need, Ruby?'

'Your lunch with the professor . . . you're going to miss it if you don't hurry.'

My lunch . . . I have forgotten. Spencer and I have a standing summertime date, a picnic on the university grounds after his Wednesday morning graduate school lecture. We sit beneath the oaks and speak of the things that matter: Spencer's research, his most promising students, names for a son.

Ruby has already packed a basket with grapes and cold meats, sesame rolls, macaroni salad. 'Thank you,' I say, taking one last glance inside the closet before I close the door.

Spencer walked to work today – three miles to the university – and left me the car. A Packard Twin 6 with a 12-cylinder engine, it's his pride and joy. It has suicide doors, named so because they open backward and can rip you out of the car if unlatched during transit.

I've thought about it.

Spencer's graduate lecture is being held in a small classroom that smells of linseed oil and philosophy. At the front, Spencer stands with his jacket off, his shirtsleeves rolled up in deference to the heat. Lantern slides of skulls have been projected onto a screen behind him. 'Notice the difference between the dolicho-cephalic and the brachycephalic in the Negroid skull,' Spencer says. 'The prognathous jaw, the flattened nose, the apelike simi-larities . . . these all are signs of a degraded race.'

A hand shoots up. 'How primitive are they?' a student asks.

'Rudimentary,' Spencer explains. 'Think of them as children. Like children, they'll be fond of bright colors. Like children, they are capable of forming base friendships.' He glances at the clock on the wall, and his eyes skim over me, lighting briefly. 'Next week we'll be outlining the classification of all humanity into five distinct races,' he promises, as the class gathers their books and disperses. Smiling, Spencer walks down the aisle toward me. 'To what do I owe this honor?'

'It's Wednesday,' I remind him. 'Our lunch.' As illustration, I swing the basket out from behind my back, where I have kept it hidden.

A small *V* forms between Spencer's brows. 'Damn, Cissy, Harry Perkins asked to meet with me this afternoon. I don't have time for lunch.'

'I understand,' I tell Spencer.

'That's my girl.'

'Spencer?' I call after him. 'Should I wait?' But he does not hear me, or else he chooses not to. Sighing, I put down the picnic basket and walk to the front of the classroom. My boot heels click like teeth, and when I get close, my body makes a bulbous silhouette against the white screen. I hold up my hand and make a shadow puppet, a wolf. Then I send it swooping and diving along the jutting brow of a dolichocephalic specimen.

'Mrs Pike?'

Caught in the act, I whirl around to find Abigail Alcott watching me. A wide-eyed woman in her late twenties, Abigail is a social worker currently employed by the Department of Public Welfare. She is dressed for work in a smart navy skirt and a pleated white shirt. Of late, she has been meeting with Spencer to discuss the ESV records, which she uses in her investigations. Her job involves assessing which degenerate families are turning around, versus which will benefit from the new sterilization law.

'Hello, Abigail,' I say with as much poise as I can, given that she is older than I, and has a true education, instead of two years in a finishing school.

'Is the professor here?' She checks her wristwatch. 'We're supposed to be driving out to Waterbury this afternoon.'

So I am not the only person Spencer disappoints. I wonder what they are planning to do at the State Mental Hospital. I imagine her walking beside my husband, pulling threads of scientific conversation from thin air to make a verbal bouquet she might hand him – one that by its very topic is irresistible to Spencer. In this, I have always been the outsider – I do not know as much about eugenics as my father or my husband. What would it be like to sit at the dinner table with them, to say something relevant, to watch them look at me as someone to be considered, instead of something to be dismissed?

That sweet coil of insurrection swims in me. I am ten again, and climbing to the roof to shout down to the good people of Comtosook. 'Didn't he tell you?'

'Tell me what?'

'About the meeting with Professor Perkins?' There, that much is not a lie. 'Spencer was going to send you a note . . . but then he gets so preoccupied, you know . . .'

'Mrs Pike,' Abigail interrupts. 'What note?'

'The one about me going to Waterbury in his place.'

Abigail stares at me, but she is too polite to say what she is thinking: that I have never been trained in social work, that being born into a family of eugenics scholars doesn't automatically make me one. Her eyes settle on the swell of my abdomen. 'Spencer was quite sure it was safe,' I add.

That, ultimately, is what clinches it: Abigail would rather cut off her right arm than question Spencer's judgment. Her lips set in a thin line, she assesses me, and nods. 'Well, then,' she says, 'let's go.'

Vermont needs a mental survey which will locate every case of mental defect within our borders and facilities for thorough psychiatric examination of all dependent and delinquent individuals.

– Asa R. Gifford, 'Report of the President,' Vermont Children's Aid Society Second Annual Report, 1921

The Vermont State Hospital for the Insane was built in Waterbury in 1890, to ease the overcrowding at the Retreat down in
Brattleboro. Dr Stanley, the superintendent, had once come to our
home for dinner when I was thirteen, after he'd testified in support
of the 1927 Sterilization Bill that did not pass. I remember circles
of sweat around his collar, the fact that he did not eat brussels
sprouts, and the way he stood too close to me while making small
talk.

'You would think that the group represented in highest concentration at Waterbury was the Huntington's chorea family, because
of the inherited mental illness,' Abigail says as we walk up the
street from our parking spot. Now that she has taken it into her
mind to educate me on all I've missed to date leading up to this
meeting, she is chatty – friendly, almost. 'But no, it turns out
there are plenty of Pirates and Gypsies too.'

By now we have reached the front door of A Building, the new
ward where many of the female patients are kept. Abigail turns
to me, her eyes glowing. 'What is it like to wake up beside a man
who has such . . . such *vision?*' she asks, and then her face goes
as red as the brick of the building.

A memory: I am at the Eugenics Survey Office on Church
Street, come to tell Spencer that we are going to have a baby. I
open the door to his office and find him with Abigail, laughing
up at something Spencer has said. She sits on the edge of his
desk and her hand is on his forearm. 'Cissy!' he calls out, and he
is smiling, and I don't know if it is because I have arrived, or
because she has been there.

Suddenly the door of the institution opens. We are sucked
inside, because hell is a vacuum. Nurses wearing white hats
creased like Japanese paper cranes move silently, seemingly
unaware of the patient sobbing at the administration desk, or the
one who dashes naked across a corridor, her wet hair streaming
out behind her. A filthy girl not much older than Ruby sits on a
bench, wearing a shirt that secures her arms to the wooden slats

behind her. Beneath the bench is a puddle; I think it must be urine.

'Miss Alcott!' Dr Stanley approaches in his pristine white coat. I wonder how he can keep it so clean in an environment such as this. He turns to me, too close for comfort. 'I don't think I've had the pleasure . . .'

'You have,' I say, extending my hand. 'Cecelia Beaumont Pike.'

'Cissy? Cissy! You're certainly grown up.' He glances at my swollen abdomen. 'And out, I might add. Congratulations apparently are in order.'

'Thank you.'

'Mrs Pike is standing in for the professor today,' Abigail explains.

Dr Stanley hides his surprise well. 'Excellent. Well, if you'll follow me, we can speak more privately in my office.' He walks down the hall, leaving us to follow. Abigail moves in his wake immediately. I find myself rooted to the spot by the vacant stare of the woman on the bench.

'Mrs Pike!' Abigail prompts sharply, and I force myself to turn away.

Dr Stanley, seeing an opportunity to impress Spencer via me, decides to take the long route. There are spots where the halls are so congested with inmates that we have to walk single file. 'The legislature just approved the construction of a new building for the acutely disturbed female patients. You can see how overcrowded we are here.'

'What's your population?' Abigail asks.

'Nine hundred ninety-seven,' Stanley says, then notices a nurse leading a girl with angry eyes up a flight of stairs, an orderly following with a small suitcase. 'Nine hundred ninety-eight.'

The doctor gestures toward a doorway that leads into a large sunny room, one again overrun with patients. 'I believe in industrial work. Idle hands breed idle minds.' At tables, women sit weaving reeds into mangled baskets or assembling clothespins.

They look up at me and see a rich lady in fashionable maternity clothing. They don't realize that I am one of them.

'We sell the crafts,' Stanley says proudly. 'Use the proceeds for patient entertainment.'

And do they come with a stamp on the bottom? Made reluctantly, by an individual who could not cope in the real world.

The superintendent leads us further down the hall to a shut door. 'Unfortunately, not all of our patients are cooperative,' Dr Stanley says. He glances at me. 'I don't know if a woman in your condition should—'

'I'm fine.' To prove this, I open the door myself.

And then I wish I hadn't.

Two burly men stand on opposite sides of a tub of water, their hands pressing down the shoulders of a naked woman. Before she goes under, I notice that her lips are blue and her breasts have puckered like fruit dried on a vine. Over her head a steady stream of water runs from a tap. Beside her, another woman lies facedown on a table with a sheet covering her upper body. A nurse pumps a large bulb of water through a tube threaded into the patient's rectum. 'Hydrotherapy and colonic irrigation have been quite beneficial for disruptive patients,' Stanley says. 'But I brought you in here to see something else. Ladies, I'm proud to present the first patient to undergo voluntary sterilization at our institution. She's right back here.' He leads us to the rear of the room. 'The salpingectomy was done when she came into the infirmary for treatment of an irritable bowel. She comes from one of the original ten families studied in the survey, one with a long genetic history of depression and disruptive behavior. Dr Kastler and I provided the two necessary signatures.'

We stop at another table, beside which sits an attendant in a white coat like Dr Stanley's. A woman lies on top, shivering. 'She's quite healthy now,' the psychiatrist says enthusiastically. 'All this fuss . . . ,' here he waves his arm vaguely, 'has nothing to do with the procedure.' The attendant wraps a cold, soaked sheet around the patient, mummifying her as her teeth chatter. 'Wet packs tend to work on the difficult ones,' Dr Stanley says.

'What did she do?' I hear myself ask.

'Attempted suicide. For the third time.'

I see, now, that her wrists are poking through the wet pack, and are bandaged. *There but for the grace of God go I.* If my father were not Harry Beaumont, if my husband were not Spencer Pike, would I be lying on that table?

'I . . . excuse me . . .' Turning past Dr Stanley, I push out of the room and into the corridor of the hospital. I hurry past the crowded common room and the girl tied to the bench and turn the corner blindly only to collide with a patient. She is small and dark, with hair plaited in greasy braids. Her arms are scratched from shoulder to wrist. 'They'll take away your baby, too,' she says.

My arms cross protectively over my belly. As she reaches out to touch me, I turn my back and run as quickly as I can through this labyrinth to the entrance of the hospital. Throwing open the doors, I gasp in as much air as my lungs will hold and sit on the stone steps. After a few moments I pull up the sleeve of my blouse and unravel the bandage Spencer tied on my wrist. The cut still looks angry, a slash of a mouth across skin.

It is true what Spencer says, after all – some women are meant to be social workers, and I am not one of them. I am supposed to be the mother of his children, and I cannot even get that right.

This is how Abigail finds me fifteen minutes later. I can't meet her gaze; I am that embarrassed by my behavior. She sits down beside me. I see her notice my scar, but she does not comment. 'The first time I watched therapy here,' Abigail confesses, 'I went back to the office and handed in my resignation, telling my boss I didn't have the heart for a career in public welfare. Do you know what he told me? That this was exactly why I had to do it. So one day there would be fewer and fewer people who had to suffer.'

Put into those words, it makes sense. It is social welfare in a nutshell – do what you can today so that you can change the world tomorrow. And yet I wonder if anyone asked the patient before they strapped her down why she no longer wanted to live. I wonder if it had anything to do with the fact that she cannot have babies anymore.

Mostly I wonder why Abigail and Dr Stanley would advocate sterilizing that patient, but not allow her to take her own life. Either act would keep her from passing her genes along to offspring. So why not give her the choice?

'You didn't quit,' I comment.

Abigail shakes her head. 'Neither will you,' she says, not unkindly, as she pulls down my sleeve. 'Tomorrow, eight A.M. Meet me at the office on Church Street.'

Q. Why sterilize?

A. To rid the race of those likely to transmit the dysgenic tendencies to which they are subject. To decrease the need for charity of a certain form. To reduce taxes. To help alleviate misery and suffering. To do what Nature would do under natural conditions, but more humanely. Sterilization is not a punitive measure. It is strictly protective.

– American Eugenics Society, *A Eugenics Catechism*, 1926

By the time I drive home the sun is low enough in the sky to meet my gaze head on and to grace the black-eyed Susans lining Otter Creek Pass with gilded crowns. I am so filled with the need for it to be tomorrow that I might burst.

I park the car and climb the steps of the porch. As I hurry to the door, my boot knocks aside something small and light. Looking down, I find a basket no bigger than a fist. Unlike the work of the patients I saw today, these sides are intricately twisted and the weaving is neat and tight.

I slip it into the pocket of my dress and enter the house. 'Cissy?'

Spencer's voice draws me like a magnet. I find him in the doorway of his study, holding his afternoon scotch. 'Here I rush home from the university to apologize to my lovely wife for standing her up at lunchtime, and she's gone and left me.'

'Only temporarily,' I say, kissing his cheek.

'And what put you into such a fine mood?'

I notice Ruby, standing like furniture in the distance, listening when she should not be. 'The Children's Aid Society,' I lie. 'I had a meeting.'

Ruby's eyes slide away. I would have told her if there were a meeting; I always do. I give her my movements and my location at all times, just in case Spencer wants to know.

'Good news?' he asks.

'Everything,' I say, 'is looking up.'

Ruby follows me to the bedroom and begins to unbutton my dress in the back, places I can no longer reach. 'I know what you're thinking,' I say. But she remains silent as she pulls the fabric over my head and hands me a comfortable cotton sundress to put on for dinner. She ties it loosely and begins to hang up my fancy dress. The basket falls out of its pocket.

I pick it up, set it in the drawer of my nightstand. She is curious about this too, I can see, but I pretend not to notice. I do not owe her any explanations – not about the basket, not about my earlier whereabouts. And right now, I am too excited about tomorrow to worry about what might happen when Spencer realizes what I've done today.

Then I notice that Ruby is wearing my hand-me-down shoes. She steps into the closet to hang up the dress – the closet she has cleaned up since my morning séance – and walks toward the bed. Sliding her hand beneath the pillow she hands me back the biography of Mr Houdini that she has hidden on my behalf.

It is her way of telling me that my secret is safe from Spencer. Our eyes meet. 'Thank you,' I murmur.

'Do you believe it, Miz Pike?' Ruby whispers fiercely. 'Do you think someone can come back from the other side?'

I squeeze her hand and nod. After all, I am living proof.

In our study of the pedigrees of families who have been an expense to the state and towns, we have found quite a number having French and Indian ancestry with sometimes a mixture of Negro.

– H. F. Perkins, 'Project #1' ESV Archive,
'Projects – Old,' 1926

Oxbury is a tiny town on the banks of Lake Champlain that, for the purposes of protecting the innocent, has been rechristened Fleetville in Abigail Alcott's reports. 'Tracing the pedigree of this particular family,' Abigail tells me as we walk toward the Gypsy camp, 'must have been as all-encompassing as tracing the lineage of the frogs in the river.'

After the field workers had identified the families to be studied, they'd gone through the records at Waterbury, as well as the State Prison, the Vermont Industrial School, and the State School for the Feebleminded in Brandon, to see which family members had been placed where. Interviews with teachers, ministers, neighbors and even distant relatives who'd managed to elevate themselves above the delinquent behavior of their kin, all rounded out a history of the family's ill fortune, which was compiled in a final report.

Abigail has allowed me to read her notes from several visits to the area: the Delacours are a mixture of French Canadian and Indian blood, descended from two first cousins who married in the Roman Catholic Church and produced seventeen children, ten of which were feebleminded and three who had no sense of what Abigail called 'sex decency.' Subsequent generations bred alcoholics, criminals, and paupers. Members of several families lived together in one small shack. During the past six years relatives had moved from Hinesburg to Cornwall to Burlington to Weybridge to Plattsburgh, but continued to return to Fleetville during the summers, where they sold the crafts they'd made during the winter and fished for a livelihood. Their main defect, as a group, was feeblemindedness, but their close association with criminality, dependency, and nomadic habits could not be overlooked.

In Abigail's papers, the Delacours are called the Moutons – the name, she tells me, of her pet poodle. It is the policy of the social workers to keep the identities of those investigated protected from the public. 'You wouldn't believe how easy it is to get information,' Abigail says. 'Go into any town and start asking questions. Every place has a family that's an *Oh, them.*'

It seems to me that if everyone knows these people, anyway, pseudonyms are beside the point.

As we walk down toward the lake, I remember something my father taught me – the closer a person lives to the water, the less successful they are. 'Look at the River Rats,' he'd say, 'and then look at me.' His home, that is, high on the Hill in Burlington, as far away from the lake as one could get.

As Abigail approaches, it is easy to see she's been here before. Barefoot children run to her and reach into the pockets of her skirt for hard candy. A teenage boy carving a wooden paddle gives her a shy smile. 'Do they know?' I ask quietly. 'Why we're here, I mean?'

She holds her smile in place. 'They know I'm interested in their lives. People who look like me usually *aren't.* And that's exactly why they talk.'

At one shanty, we stop, and Abigail raps on the support pole in lieu of a proper knocker. 'Jeanne is expecting us,' she says, and sure enough, the flap that serves as a door lifts open. A small woman not much older than Abigail hesitantly waves us inside, inviting us to sit down at a table that has been cleared.

The small home is a single room. A bucket near the door is

filled with fresh water, and a stack of dirty plates and cups sits precariously balanced on the counter. But there is a sense that the place has been tidied for us, and that is the first note Abigail writes on her pad. 'Jeanne,' she says, offering a smile that does not reach her eyes. 'I'm so happy to meet you. This is Mrs Pike.'

Jeanne's eyes don't rise above my abdomen. 'Your first?'

'Yes.'

'I have a child, too,' Jeanne says intensely. 'A boy.'

'Yes,' Abigail replies. 'Your Aunt Louisa told me quite a lot about Norman.'

'*Oho,*' Jeanne answers, bobbing her head. 'He was her favorite. She used to take him out when she went looking for plants in the woods – juniper and black spruce and bloodroot.' Over Abigail's shoulder I see the words she is writing on her pad. *Bobbed hair – skirt fastened with safety pins. Stockings are rolled below the knee. Seems distracted.*

'Jeanne's son is in the Brandon School for the Feebleminded,' Abigail explains to me. 'Louisa said you received a letter from him, Jeanne.'

This, at least, seems to brighten her up. As she hurries off to find it for us, Abigail leans closer. 'The state was instrumental in having the boy taken away. When the social workers came, they found him sitting here, eating raw meat. *Raw* meat!'

A moment later Jeanne returns, proudly holding up the letter. 'How old is Norman now?' Abigail asks.

'He'll be ten this October.'

'Why don't you read me what he wrote?'

Jeanne falters, but only for a moment. She begins to stumble through the boy's convoluted handwriting, correcting herself as she goes along. *Illiterate,* Abigail writes. *Mother* and *son.* To Jeanne, she says, 'Well, he sounds like quite the scholar!'

Jeanne's eyes soften, thinking she has found a friend in Abigail. 'Missus Alcott, you work for the state . . . can you ask them when Norman will be brought back home?'

Suddenly I see why this woman has been so anxious to invite a stranger into her home. She wants to get as much information out of Abigail as Abigail is trying to get out of *her*. 'If you'll excuse me,' I say, 'I'm just going to get some air.'

I walk along, letting my boots sink into the soft mud. Boys play a game with a ball made of rags, the right angles of their bony arms rising against the blue of the sky as they reach for a neat catch. If I am to help Abigail, I should be asking questions. I should be learning as much about this family as I can.

An old woman sits with a pipe in her mouth at the entrance to a tent, her hands flying over a stack of reeds that begin to take the shape of a long-necked basket. I start to approach her with a smile on my face, only to have her raise her head. Although she doesn't speak or move a muscle, the look in her eyes is enough to make me change direction. Instead, I head toward a man who stands with his back to me, fishing. He casts and reels in with timing and grace, as if he is part of an elaborate dance. He wears trousers held up with suspenders, and his black hair reaches halfway down his back, making me sorry to have cut my own short in a fashionable bob.

Show interest in what they are doing; this was Abigail's first rule. 'Hello.' I walk all the way down to the water, and still he does not turn around. 'I see you're fishing.'

Brilliant, Lia, I think. *And will you next tell him he's a Gypsy?*

He turns around and unhooks a foot-long fish from a green-and-black plug. I realize this is the man I saw watching me at the Independence Day celebration. His eyes widen, and move over my face as if he has never seen someone like me before. Maybe he hasn't. Maybe Gypsies mingle with us as infrequently as we mingle with them.

Uncomfortable, I look down into the basket at his feet. It is full of writhing fish: smallmouth bass, which I recognize, and large needle-nosed speckled ones that I don't. 'Hello,' I say again, determined to put him at ease. 'I'm Cissy Pike.' I hold out my hand.

For a long moment he stares at it. Then he grabs on as if he were drowning. '*N'wibgwigid Môlsem,*' he murmurs.

Illiterate, that's what Abigail would write down. It strikes me, however, that it is not what *I* would write. 'My name is Gray Wolf,' he translates.

'You speak English!'

'Better than you speak *Alnôbak,*' he says.

He has not released my hand. Gently I pull away, clear my throat, and strike up a polite conversation. 'Do you live here?'

'I live all over.'

'Surely you have a house?'

'I have a tent.' His eyes hold mine, just like they did in the Hall of Mirrors. 'I don't need much.'

Whatever civil discourse I have planned flies from my head. 'I saw you,' I hear myself say. 'On the Fourth of July. You were following me.'

'And today?' he asks. 'Are *you* following *me?*'

'Oh, no. I didn't even know you were . . . that is, I came with Abigail Alcott.'

At that, his face falls. He starts packing up his fishing gear, his back to me. 'Then have you come to take away more of our boys to the industrial school? Or tell us we're going to hell because we pray in a different church? Or maybe to find out who got drunk in town and passed out on Church Street?'

His comments leave me speechless. I have spent my life hearing of Gypsies, but they are names on pedigree charts, not men who catch fish and whose skin is as warm as mine. 'You don't even know me.'

A shadow crosses over his face. 'You're right,' he admits. 'I don't.'

'Maybe I'm not just like Abigail.'

We stand a foot apart. 'And maybe I'm not just some Gypsy,' he answers.

Words have built a wall between us, and I can think of no easy way to bring it down other than to remove it, brick by brick. So I point to the water. 'What do you call that?'

'A lake.'

'No,' I repeat. 'I mean, what do *you* call it?'

He looks at me carefully. '*Pitawbagw.*'

'*Pitawbagw.*' I point to the sun. 'And this?'

'*Kisos.*' Bending down, I pick up a handful of dirt. '*Ki.*' Gray Wolf holds out his hand to help me to my feet. He gently touches his hand to my stomach. '*Chijis.* Baby.'

'Mrs Pike!'

From a distance up on the shore I hear Abigail calling for me. 'Sounds like your ride is leaving,' Gray Wolf says.

'Yes . . .' I shield my eyes from the sun, try to find Abigail, but can't.

'Better go. You wouldn't want to be stuck here overnight.'

'No,' I admit, and then realize what I've said. Cheeks reddening, I meet his gaze. 'How do you say "I'll return?"'

It is a challenge, and he accepts it. '*N'pedgiji.*'

'Well, then. *N'pegdiji.*'

He bursts into laughter. 'You just told me you'll fart.'

If possible, I blush even harder. 'Thank you for the language lesson, Mr Wolf.'

'*Wli nanawalmezi,* Lia.'

'What does that mean?'

He smiles slowly. 'Take good care of yourself.'

I hurry up the hill as best I can, lumbering under the weight of my baby. *Chijis.* On the drive home, I listen to Abigail tell me stories of second cousins who killed others in bar fights, of a rampant outbreak of venereal disease among a strain of Delacours. 'Did you learn anything?' she asks finally, when she has run out of things to say.

How to speak their language. And maybe, how to listen. 'Nothing you'd consider important,' I reply, and am silent for the rest of the ride home.

John Delacour, aka Gray Wolf, is of particular notoriety even for this clan. He has a history of heavy drinking, sex offense, nomadism, and criminality, and has been known to change his name several times. He was arrested in 1913 for hitting a man over the head with a brick. In 1914, he was sent to prison for a murder conviction. There is mention from several relatives about his illegitimate children. John is an absolute liar and very evasive. For this reason it is absolutely impossible to get the truth out of him.

– From the files of Abigail Alcott, Department of Public
Welfare social worker

When I come home, Ruby is waiting at the door with her heart in her eyes, and Spencer is a step behind. 'What the hell do you think you're doing?' he roars, slamming the door behind me. He grabs my upper arms so hard I know it will leave bruises.

'I can explain—'

'Explain this, Cissy. Explain why I got a call from my secretary saying that you'd been to the office to meet Abigail Alcott. Explain why my wife, who is seven months pregnant with my firstborn son, would be stupid enough to visit a state hospital for the insane where she could have been seriously hurt. And for Christ's sake, to be traipsing around some Gypsy camp—'

'It isn't some Gypsy camp, Spencer, and I'm fine.' I try to pull away from him, but he will not let me go. 'I wanted to see what it is that holds you and my father in so much thrall. Is that a sin?'

'You are in no condition to—'

'I'm pregnant, Spencer, not feebleminded.'

'Is that so?' Spencer explodes. 'Jesus Christ, Cissy, how can you expect me to trust you with your own judgment, when you try to kill yourself one night and the next day you're off at an insane asylum—'

'That's unfair,' I say, my eyes stinging already.

'Unfair? Try imagining what it's like to sit here, thinking that your wife might be injured, or God forbid, killed by some lunatic. Abigail is trained to do what she does; *you* are *not*. And you will stay in this house, goddammit, until I tell you otherwise!'

'You can't do that to me.'

'Can't I?' Spencer grabs my wrists hard enough to make me cry out. He pulls me up the stairs. The only room in the house that locks from the outside is our bedroom, and Spencer drags me into it. 'I'm doing this for your own good.'

'*Whose* good?' I challenge.

Spencer pales, as if I have slapped him. 'Sometimes, Cissy,' he whispers, 'I don't know you.'

My husband walks stiffly out of the bedroom. Inside me, the baby twines tighter. 'I'm sorry,' I whisper, and the only answer I receive is the sound of the lock being turned.

Q.   Which counts for more, heredity or the environment?

A.   They are interdependent. This question is almost the equivalent of 'Which is more important, the seed or the soil?'

– American Eugenics Society, *A Eugenics Catechism*, 1926

In the middle of the night the key turns. Even from here, I can smell the alcohol on Spencer. He slips into bed and presses his front to my back, 'God, I love you,' he says, the words settling over my skin like steam.

On our honeymoon, Spencer and I went to Niagara Falls. One night we camped out in a tent, and made love beneath the night sky. The water beat like my blood and when he moved inside me, I could swear that the stars connected in the shape of our initials.

Now Spencer pulls up the edge of my nightgown, fits himself between my thighs. We are both crying and pretending not to. When Spencer comes inside me he presses his wet face against my spine, and I imagine his features being branded there, a version of a death mask that will always be one step behind me.

He falls asleep with his arms around the breadth of my middle, hands not quite touching, as if he cannot contain me anymore.

I think we can safely say that in the sixty-two families we have studied . . . 'blood has told,' and there is every reason to believe it will keep right on 'telling' in future generations.

– H. F. Perkins, *Lessons from a Eugenical Survey of Vermont:*
First Annual Report, 1927

Blood is raining from thunderclouds. Roses burst into bloom at midnight. Water doesn't boil; words slide from the pages of books. The sky is the wrong color. And as I walk through this strange world, the ground is frozen beneath my feet.

'Cissy. *Cissy!*'

Hands on my shoulders. Breath on my neck. 'Spencer?' I say, my voice sanded and drowsy.

Gradually I become aware of the owls bearing witness in the trees, the mud on the heels of my feet and the edge of my night-gown, the summer night fermenting. I am in the woods behind our house, and I have no idea how I got here.

'You've been sleepwalking,' Spencer explains.

Sleepwalking, yes, that's what it must be. And yet this other place I have visited . . . I feel as if I can still trail my fingers along its edge. Spencer embraces me, sighs against my skin. 'Cissy, I only want you to be happy.'

A small sob catches in my throat. 'I know.'

And I am a failure, to have all this – a good home, a healthy pregnancy, a man like Spencer – and still feel as if something is missing. 'I love you,' my husband says. 'I've never loved anyone but you.'

'I love you too,' I tell him. I only wish it were that easy.

'Why don't we go back to bed,' Spencer suggests, 'and forget about all of this?'

Like we forget about everything else. Because when you don't admit out loud that something awful has happened, who is to say it ever did?

But habit holds me tight. So I nod, and follow Spencer back to the house. I keep looking over my shoulder; I cannot shake the feeling that there is something here for me to find. After we climb onto the porch, he holds the door open for me, wiping the slate clean.

It is not until I am in the bathroom, washing the dirt from my feet, that I realize I am clenching something in my left hand. I open my fist like a flower: soft and supple and honey-colored, these are the tiniest pair of moccasins I have ever seen.

6

From an exhibit at the Third International Eugenics Congress:

THIS LIGHT FLASHES EVERY 31 SECONDS.
Every 31 seconds, State taxpayers paid $100 for maintenance
only of Insane, Feebleminded, Epileptic, Blind and Deaf, in State
Institutions, Only in 1927.

In the middle of the night there is a cramp low in my belly. It
wakes me; it makes me look across the ocean of mattress to
Spencer, who sleeps as if this hotel bed fits him. I try to ignore
the teeth eating me from the inside out.

But then there is a ripping, and I am too shocked to even cry.
I watch the blood soak the front of my nightgown and the cuspid
that cuts like a knife. A scaled snout stretches through the hole
it has made in my skin; then a clawed foot, a reptile belly, a tail.
The alligator that finally hunches between my legs looks up and
smiles.

'Miz Pike . . .'

It is the voice of someone who's come to watch me be devoured
whole. The alligator's jaw ratchets shut on my thigh.

'Miz Pike . . . Lia!'

It is this, my secret name, which makes the alligator disappear. When I blink I see Ruby standing in front of me in her

nightgown, and we are in the middle of the hall at the Plaza Hotel. Her eyes are as sad as a canyon. 'You need to go back to bed.'

I have been sleepwalking again. And Ruby has been keeping watch, as she was brought along on this trip to do. She leads me to our suite, opens the door, and averts her eyes from Spencer, who sleeps undisturbed in the bed. 'No one ever gets a good night's rest away from home,' Ruby whispers, bravely making excuses. She pulls back the covers and helps me settle, as if she is the elder between us.

I swallow hard and make my eyes adjust to the darkness. I keep my feet folded up beneath me, just in case that gator is still swimming beneath the sheets.

From the program of the Third International Eugenics Congress:

  I.   Introduction and Welcome: Dr H. F. Perkins, President
       of the American Eugenics Society
 II.   'The Biological Screening of Immigrant Populations':
       Prof. Jap van Tysediik
III.   'Prevention of the Collapse of Western Civilization':
       Dr Roland Osterbrand
 IV.   'The Disappearance of the Old American: A Study in
       Human Race Improvement': Dr Spencer A. Pike

The Third International Eugenics Congress has convened at New York's Museum of Natural History, and I have been invited by default. Even with my father attending the event, and Spencer the featured speaker, I might have been allowed to stay home and fend for myself, if not for the fact that mere weeks ago I had taken a blade to my skin, and gotten myself in trouble with Abigail Alcott.

We are sitting near the lecture hall, in a room that has been converted into a private lounge for the bigwigs at the conference.

Spencer is getting ready for his presentation; my father reads the program notes. Ruby is quiet as a ghost in one corner, her lips moving silently as she knits.

We are the only ones left; the others have gone out to give their presentations, or to join the audience. So far we have met the pioneer of Michigan's sterilization program, and a Cuban physiologist who blessed me in his mother tongue and said it was the duty of gifted women like myself to rescue the world by having more children. A New York physician who smelled of garlic spent an hour with Spencer, arguing about the annual expense of caring for the offspring of two feebleminded families ($2 million) versus the one-time cost of sterilizing the parents ($150).

I peel an orange and watch through the window as visitors to the museum hurry up the stone steps. A man loses his hat in the wind, and it blows into the arms of a panhandler. A toddler sits down on a step three-quarters of the way up and begins to kick her feet with such force that her panties show, pink as a rose petal. And my father and husband argue about what, exactly, Spencer should cover in his presentation.

'I don't know, Harry,' Spencer says, pacing around a long chart unrolled like a hound's tongue across the floor. 'We've backed away from the pedigrees in the past year.'

Spencer's shoe brushes the edge of the pedigree chart. It is a long genetic octopus, a family tree with arms and legs that tangle and cross, as do those of most degenerate families. Spotted throughout are symbols, keyed on the side. A dark black circle signifies Insane. A hollow circle means Feebleminded. Black squares for those who were sent to reform school, white squares for those who were sexual offenders. This particular chart is as dotted as a leopard.

Professor Pike made the decision to stop heralding the pedigree charts as the main thrust of the Vermont eugenics movement when he, Spencer, and my father were sitting at dinner and realized that three influential swing-voting members of the legislature had unwittingly showed up on their charts, descended from some of the most degenerate families in the state. Even the lieutenant governor was linked to one notorious family by marriage. They agreed to focus instead on the best way to encourage the Old Vermont stock to reproduce, and set up another subdivision of the VCCL – the Committee for the Handicapped – to do the dirty work, advocating legislation to prevent these people from marrying and breeding. This way, any controversy that swirled over the Sterilization Bill would not be associated with the three of them, personally.

That night, we served turtle soup for dinner, which made me queasy, and I had to leave the table.

'We did what we needed to, Spencer, to get the public support necessary to pass the sterilization law. But that's done. It's time to go back to the fundamentals.' My father walks over to me and takes a slice of orange, which he pops into his mouth. He waves his fingers in front of Spencer's face. 'Smell that? You can't see it anymore . . . but you know it was there. You don't have to mention the charts if you don't want to, Spencer. Hell, you can burn them if it makes you feel better. But everyone in that room remembers the work we did to survey those families five years ago. Everyone is going to know what you're *not* saying.' Then he walks out of the room.

Spencer looks down at the chart. 'What do you think?' he asks, and I nearly fall out of my chair.

'What do *I* think?' I am so shocked to have been asked for my opinion that I can hardly find the words to give it. I think of the Gypsy whose son had been taken away by the welfare agencies. Of Gray Wolf, assuming I had come to ruin his life, simply because of the color of my skin.

Reputations, once they're made, precede you.

'I think the damage has already been done,' I reply. Through the open doorway comes Spencer's name, and a volley of applause.

Once, as a little girl, my father had taken me to a similar, smaller convocation of eugenicists in San Francisco, where I survived a small earthquake. We were told to stand in a doorway until it passed, and I tried to come to terms with the fact that something as solid as the ground beneath my feet was not quite so secure after all.

When five hundred people clap at once, it sounds like the earth is breaking to pieces all around you. Spencer rolls the pedigree chart up, tucks it under his arm, and strides into the lecture hall on this summon of thunder. 'Ladies and gentlemen,' he begins, and I don't have to listen anymore to know what he is going to say.

I stand up and walk out of the room, hurrying down the stairs into one of the exhibit halls. Children and their nannies are dwarfed by an enormous re-creation of a brontosaurus. The pin of its head is so small and distant I can barely make out the hole of its eye socket. Its brain, I believe, was no bigger than my fist. Intelligence belonged to the tyrannosaurus across the way, with its formidable jaw and fence of teeth.

And yet both of these creatures, the so-called inferior plant-eater and the ferocious carnivore, died out because of a change in the climate, or so Spencer has told me. In the end, it didn't matter who was brighter or stronger or better or could reproduce the most efficiently. Bad weather, a circumstance beyond their control, had the upper hand.

There is a distant rumbling, and I realize it is coming from overhead, as the audience applauds something Spencer has said.

I turn to Ruby, who of course has only been a few steps behind me all along. 'Let's take a walk,' I suggest.

Rosabelle – answer – tell – pray, answer –
look – tell – answer, answer – tell.

– Code devised by Harry Houdini and his wife, based on an
old vaudeville mind-reading routine, to prove his return as a
spirit after his death.

New York City, in the summer, cannot be so different from hell. The smell of sweat mixed with the brine from the pickle barrels of vendors, the tight press of a hundred people who look right through you, the newsboys selling tragedy for a nickel, the fumes of the taxis rising like wraiths – this is an underworld, and anyone in it can point you toward an escape hatch. In fact, it is the little girl living under an awning with her mother who rolls my dollar bill like a cigarette, tucks it behind her right ear, and leads Ruby and me to a brownstone three blocks away. A small, engraved sign hangs above the buzzer: HEDDA BARTH, SPIRITUALIST.

The woman who opens the door is smaller even than Ruby, with long white hair that passes her shoulders. 'Ladies,' says Hedda Barth, Medium of the Century. 'What can I do for you?'

If she is truly psychic, then she ought to know. I am about to back down the stairs when I feel Ruby push me from behind. 'We might as well go all the way,' she whispers.

Madame Hedda has been written up in the papers. She sparred with Houdini; she conjured the departed great-uncle of Mayor Walker. The chances of me being here again, and able to meet with her, are virtually nonexistent. 'We were hoping to hold a séance, with your help,' I say.

'But you have no appointment.'

'No.' I raise my chin, the way I have seen my father do, in order to make her feel this was an oversight on her part, rather than mine. And sure enough, she steps aside to let us in.

She leads us up a short staircase and holds out her hand to open the door. I wonder if I am the only one who notices that her fingers never touch it, that the knob swings open of its own accord.

A hexagonal table waits for us in the dark. 'There's the small matter of payment,' Hedda says.

'Money,' I answer, 'is no object.'

So Hedda instructs us to take seats and join hands. She scrutinizes my face and Ruby's. 'You've both suffered a loss,' she announces.

Once I read a criticism of the spiritualist movement, in which a Parisian scientist offered free horoscope readings to passersby. Ninety-four percent of those given a reading found it personally accurate. In fact, each person had received the same horoscope, belonging to one of France's most notorious mass murderers.

We believe what we want to believe; we hear what we want to hear. What Hedda Barth has told me anyone could have guessed; why else would Ruby and I have come?

But suddenly the table begins to shudder and rock, lifting up on two of its legs like a rearing stallion. Hedda's eyes roll back in her head, and her mouth gapes open. I glance at Ruby, unsure of what to do, if this is normal.

'Ma poule.' The voice is higher than Hedda's, with a ribbon of lisp. My heart begins to pound on the roof of my mouth, and the baby kicks to be free.

'Simone?' Ruby's word is just barely that, the quiet puff of shock. I recognize, now, where I have heard that cadence before – it is Ruby's own French Canadian, which creeps out when she is not careful or is tired or both.

'Cherie, you tell your friend, there's nothing to be scared of, no. We are all here waiting on her.'

'That's my sister,' Ruby says wildly. 'Simone. She's the only one who ever called me that – ma poule. My little hen.'

The one who died from diphtheria. But her message, it's lost in the translation. Waiting could signify so many things. Are they attending to my mother? Or are they expecting me?

Suddenly the baby goes limp inside me. My arms fall to my sides; my worries dissolve on my tongue. This must be how people feel the moment before their automobile crashes into a tree. This is the white light we hear talk of; this is the quiet coming.

This is something my own mother felt.

There are so many questions I have – Will I ever see my son, or is that asking too much? Will he remember me? Will it hurt? Will

I know when it's going to happen? But right now, it is enough to have confirmation, to know that my instincts have been right.

Madame Hedda is coming out of her trance. A line of drool curls down the left side of her mouth like a comma. I place a ten-dollar bill on the table, one I will tell Spencer that I lost. 'Come back,' she says, and I realize that she means from the other side.

A comprehensive eugenics survey needs to locate, first, the inadequate in the state; second, to find out, if possible, why they exist.

— Excerpt from a letter dated October 8, 1925, from
H. H. Laughlin, Director of the Eugenics Record Office,
to Harriet Abbott

Dr Craigh's office is on Park Avenue, and as I finish buttoning my blouse I stare out the window at this street trying to be something it is not. Those trees, they are not fooling anyone; it is still the heart of a city, a place where pavement has triumphed over grass. The obstetrician himself dries his hands on a towel, just as unwilling to make eye contact with me after the exam as I am with him. 'Mrs Pike,' he says gruffly, 'why don't you join us in the office when you're finished?'

When I returned to the museum, where Spencer was still riding high on the praise of his colleagues, I did not tell him where Ruby and I had been. I didn't even put up a fuss when he told me he'd made an appointment with this physician, the best in the Northeast for high-risk pregnancies. It is as simple as this: the decision has been taken out of my hands. I *know* what is going to happen, so there's no reason to fight it.

My father once invited the state medical examiner to dinner when I was a child. I remember him cutting blithely into the breast of a chicken to illustrate the nature of drowning. The horror, he said, pointing between the ribs with a knife, comes the moment you feel that your lungs will burst. But then you gasp and go under and inhale water. After that, all you feel is peace.

I have gone under for the third time. I will lie on my back on the sandy bottom, and watch the sunset through a mile of sea.

'Mrs Pike,' the nurse says, poking her head through the doorway. 'They're waiting.'

'Of course.' When I turn, I am wearing the smile I've pulled from my sleeve.

She leads me down the hall. 'You have that glow.'

Maybe the radiance in pregnancy does not come from the joy of motherhood. Maybe we all think we are going to die.

Dr Craigh's office is dark, paneled, male; a timeless cabin you might find on a clipper ship, clouded with the smoke of cigars. 'Gomez pitched a shut-out last night,' Craigh is saying. 'Between Lefty and Ruth and Gehrig, it's a lock this year.'

Spencer, who does not like baseball, surprises me. 'The Athletics are looking pretty good again, if you ask me.'

'Gehrig finished last season with 184 RBIs. You can't seriously believe – oh, Mrs Pike. Sit down right over there.' He gestures to the chair beside my husband.

Spencer takes my hand and we both turn expectantly, like children called before the principal. 'Good news,' Craigh announces. 'Your pregnancy is as healthy as any I've ever seen.'

Beside me, Spencer relaxes. 'You see, Cissy?'

'I completely understand your concerns, given your mother's experience in childbirth. But based on her medical records, which your husband took the liberty of mailing to me, the complications of her pregnancy were related to her slight frame and the size of the baby. You may be carrying small, Mrs Pike – but your hips are rather built for childbearing. Luckily, you must take after your father.'

I think of my father's tall, lean, narrow body; nothing like my own. But I smile back at him.

'Not only are you going to deliver this baby safely and without incident,' Dr Craigh continues, 'but I will expect you to bring him back here to meet me.'

I wonder how much Spencer has paid him, in advance, to lie to me.

We stand and begin the round-robin of shaking hands. Spencer helps me down the three flights of stairs. 'Craigh's considered an expert,' he says. 'Everyone, and I mean *everyone*, knows his name. You say the word *baby*, and someone mentions Craigh. So, really, I'd be quite comforted by his diagnosis.'

He stamps a quick kiss on me. His arm slides around the thick of my waist; his other hand opens the door so that we can be swallowed by the city again. The sun is too bright; I can't see a thing. I have to bring my hand up to shield my eyes; I have to let Spencer take me where I'm going.

> We know what feeblemindedness is, and we have come to suspect
> all persons who are incapable of adapting themselves to their envir-
> onment and living up to the conventions of society or acting
> sensibly of being feebleminded.
>
> – Henry Goddard, *Feeblemindedness*:
> *Its Causes and Consequences*, 1914

In the end, I want to do it somewhere familiar. I think about it during the long train ride home. I am nearly giddy with what is to come. 'I knew it,' Spencer says to my father in our private train car. 'I knew this trip would be good for her.'

By the time we arrive at home, it is nearly midnight. Peepers sing to us as we get out of the Packard, and the yellow eyes of a runaway cat watch me from the porch of the icehouse. When Spencer opens the door to our home, it sounds like a seal being broken.

'Ruby, you can unpack in the morning,' Spencer orders, as we climb the stairs to the second floor. 'Sweetheart, you too. You ought to be in bed.'

'I need a bath,' I tell him. 'A few minutes to relax alone.'

At that, Ruby turns slowly. Her mouth is round with a question I do not let her ask. 'You heard the professor,' I say, clipped. After weeks of camaraderie, these cold, sharp words are a weapon to drive her away. She hurries up the steps to the servants' quarters, ducking her head and trying to understand what has gone wrong between us.

In our room I gather a crisply folded nightgown and wrapper from my armoire. I wait outside the bathroom door until Spencer emerges. 'I drew the bath,' he says, and smiles ruefully at my belly. 'Are you sure if you get in, you'll be able to get out?'

I am committing to memory the keel of his smile, the landscape of his shoulders. All of the reasons I fell in love with Spencer swell at the base of my throat, so that I cannot say anything at all for a moment. 'Don't worry about me,' I answer finally, and I mean this for forever.

A house settles like a fat man falling asleep: first there are light twitches in the walls and floorboard, the ceiling sighs, finally there is a great rolling heave of the atmosphere, and then everything goes still. The bathroom is heavy with steam; I peel off my clothing and let the mist settle over me. My heart beats so fast I am sure that I can see it beneath the skin – but when I look, the mirror has fogged. Instead of swiping it clear, I press my hands to the glass, leaving a mark. With one finger, I scrawl a single word: H . . . E . . . L . . . P. I picture what will happen when I am found, still and white as a marble statue. I think of how everyone will say the nicest things about me; how they will look at me with nothing but regret and love.

By one in the morning, the bathwater has gone cold. My legs are drawn up on either side of my domed stomach; my wrists are balanced on my knees.

Spencer's straightedge sits on the lip of the tub.

I pick it up carefully, and press a line just below the elbow. Blood wells up and I touch it with my finger; rub it on my mouth like lipstick. It tastes sticky, salty, like a penny left on the tongue. It is no surprise to find out I've gone bitter to the core.

When that raw cut stops aching, I press the razor down again, a half-inch lower.

Two parallel lines. My life, and my son's. They will save him from the shell of me, and it will be a better life. Otherwise, from the moment he leaves my body, he will belong to someone else – Spencer, and my father. And one day, he will look at me the way they do – like someone who cannot understand the science they create; someone naïve enough to believe that a quantity as immeasurable as love might have the same combustible power as dynamite.

And if, by some miracle, this baby turns out to be a girl, I think it will be worse. I will have failed, because Spencer is expecting a boy. Not only will I have to watch him treat her the way he has treated me . . . I will have to watch her make all the same mistakes I have: fall in love with a man who loves her because of what she is, not who she is; marry for companionship, only to see it makes her more lonely; bear a child, only to realize that she will never live up to what it deserves.

Another line, and another. Blood swirls in the water of the tub, dreamy and pink. I have a railroad track on my arm. I am finally going somewhere, because there is nothing left for me here.

My last cut, on the wrist, is the deepest. The pattern for this gash is already there, a blue chalked line beneath the surface.

There will be one more knife, slicing me down the middle to save this baby. Doctors will finish the work I started here, peeling me open. They will stop and scratch their heads, stunned to discover how empty I am inside.

A beating buzzes in my ears. It takes too much now, to keep my head erect. My body, big as it is, sinks under the water.

The door bursts open, then, and Ruby leans into the tub, screaming in my face for me to hang on. She holds me when I cannot hold onto her. She is slick with my blood but somehow manages to heave me over the lip of the tub, so that I collapse wet and naked and bleeding on the bathroom floor as she shouts for Spencer. He appears in the doorway and hurries toward me. 'Cissy, God, *no.*' He wraps a towel around my wrist, and when it soaks through immediately, turns white and runs out of the room. 'You stay with her, you hear?' he cries to Ruby, who is too terrified to move. In the distance I hear him yelling into the phone for the doctor.

With the only strength I have left, I reach out for Ruby and draw her close by fisting my hand in her nightgown. 'Save the baby,' I beg, hoarse, but she is sobbing too hard to hear me. So I curl my good hand around her neck. I kiss her on the lips, so that she can taste my pain. 'Save my baby,' I whisper. 'Promise!'

Ruby nods, her eyes locked on mine. *'Promise.'*

'All right then,' I say, and I let those waves close over my head.

The rights of the individual cannot be fully safeguarded when he is being compelled to support in the midst of his community the lawless, the immoral, the degenerate, and the mentally defective.

— H. F. Perkins, *Lessons from a Eugenical Survey of Vermont:*
First Annual Report, 1927

Everything is white. The ceiling, the light, the tattoos on the backs of my eyes. The bandages, which are laced so tight up my arm from shoulder to hand that I can feel my pulse under the skin, as if I need to be reminded that I am alive in spite of it all.

The bedroom is too hot. For as long as I can remember the window has been stuck; we make do with an electric fan. But even that doesn't help, and when I kick back the bedclothes I notice them – Spencer, and Dr DuBois, standing in front of the door. 'Joseph,' Spencer says, 'I know this will stay within these walls.'

Dr DuBois is the most prominent physician in Burlington. He delivered me; he will no doubt deliver my baby. 'Spencer . . .'

'Please. I'm asking as a friend.'

'There are places, you know, in the country, where she'd be looked after. All rolling meadows and wicker rocking chairs – we're not talking Waterbury.'

'No. I can't do that to her.'

'To Cissy? Or to yourself?' Dr DuBois shakes his head. 'It's not about you this time, Spencer,' he says, and then he lets himself out.

Spencer sits down on the edge of the bed and stares at me. 'I'm sorry,' I manage.

'Yes, you are,' he answers, and in spite of the brutal heat in this bedroom, a shiver runs down my spine. Once again, Spencer has found me lacking.

Q. What is meant by negative eugenics?
A. This deals with the elimination of the dysgenic elements from society. Sterilization, immigration, legislation, laws preventing the fertile unfit from marrying, etc., come under this head.

– American Eugenics Society,
A Eugenics Catechism, 1926

It is a full week before Spencer leaves me in the house alone with Ruby, and then only because his undergraduate students have returned. 'You can call me, you know, any time,' he says.

I look up from the scone I am buttering. 'All right.'

'Maybe we could go out for ice cream tonight. If you're feeling up to it.' This is Spencer's way of telling me to be alive when he gets home. 'Well, then.' He is so handsome in his lightweight suit, with his hair slicked back and his bow tie as level as the scales of justice. I know he is staring at the butter knife in my hands, wondering whether it can do damage. Before his eyes I lick the dull blade clean, just to watch his reaction.

'I'll send Ruby in,' he says, and he flees.

Ruby, who has done her best to avoid me, drags herself into the kitchen as Spencer's car mutters down the drive. 'Miz Pike,' she says.

'Miss Weber.'

'If you were my friend,' Ruby bursts out, 'you would have told me you were going to do that.' Her eyes fix on the bandages on my wrist.

'But then, by definition, you wouldn't have let me,' I answer quietly.

I am saved from having to say anymore by a commotion outside. 'Coons,' Ruby tells me, going for the shotgun we keep behind the pantry door for things such as this.

'Then they're rabid. It's broad daylight.' I push past Ruby, gathering bullets from the sugar bowl in the cabinet. We step out the back door and look around, but the only motion comes from two dragonflies playing tag.

Ruby thumps the butt of the shotgun onto the ground. 'Whatever it was is gone now.'

I am about to agree with her when I notice that the door to the icehouse is ajar. It is a small outbuilding left from my grandmother's years in this home, before it was passed down to me through my mother's will. Blocks of ice cut from Lake Champlain in the winter get delivered every few days, and sit packed in sawdust in the shed until we chip some off for the icebox in the kitchen. Spencer is meticulous about keeping the door shut tight. 'If I want *water* with my scotch,' he says, 'I can get that from the tap.'

I pluck the shotgun from Ruby's hand. 'Stay here,' I say, so of course she follows. We climb onto the icehouse porch and slip inside, letting our eyes adjust to the lack of light. Only someone who has spent as much time trolling through darkness as I have would be able to sense that third body in the room. 'Come out,' I call, braver than I feel.

Nothing.

'I said *come out!*' By now I am imagining robbers, rapists, thieves. Because I have nothing left to lose, I raise the shotgun and fire at the closest block of ice. It explodes, and Ruby screams, and behind my left shoulder a man yells, 'Goddamn!'

Gray Wolf comes out from his hiding spot, hands up, like in the movies. His face is wreathed in a strange combination of pride and shock.

'What are *you* doing here?' Now that it is over, my hands are shaking. Ruby cowers against the doorway of the shed. 'It's all right,' I tell her. 'I know him.'

'You *know* him?' Ruby's mouth drops, a perfect *O*.

It is possible that he has come to steal from us, or to hurt me. It would have been easy enough to follow me home after that day at the Gypsy camp. But it makes more sense to have robbed our home when we were gone, in New York City. And it doesn't account for the moccasins, which I am sure he left for me to find.

More than anything, I do not want this moment to be the one where I turn out to be the sort of person he accused me of being the last time we met.

'Gray Wolf,' I say, 'this is Ruby. Ruby, Gray Wolf.' I present them to each other as if we were all British nobles at a ball. I dare either of them to comment.

'I'm going to call the professor,' Ruby murmurs under her breath.

I catch her by the elbow. 'Don't.' This small seed of trust slips from my palm into hers.

But she has been living in the house of a eugenicist. And not even Ruby's French Canadian background looks quite as dark, compared to that of a Gypsy. 'Miz Pike,' she says, her eyes sliding to his face. 'He's . . . he's . . .'

'Hungry,' I supply. 'Maybe you could get us something from the kitchen?'

She swallows whatever she is about to say, nods, and heads for the house. When we are alone, Gray Wolf lifts my arm and traces a finger down the spiral of bandage. 'You've been hurt.' I nod. 'An accident?'

Looking away, I shake my head.

He continues to examine the gauze, visibly upset. 'I brought you something to keep you safe. But I guess I didn't get here quick enough.'

He pulls a leather pouch from his pocket, which is attached to a long loop of rawhide. It smells faintly of summertime, and him. 'Black ash, ground hemlock, yellow lady's slipper.' Gray Wolf's eyes dart to my abdomen. 'For both of you.' He slips it over my neck and I feel myself leaning into him, feel the leather burning against my skin. *'Kizi Nd'aib nidali.'*

'What does that mean?'

'I have been there.'

I look into Gray Wolf's face and I believe him. This man knows what it is like to be thrown into a place that might very well kill him, if he doesn't do it himself. It is there in his eyes – black, the color that's left when all the other color in the world is swallowed whole.

'What's the word for "thank you?"' I ask.

'Wliwni.'

'Wliwni, then.' I touch the beading on the pouch, an intricate turtle. 'How did you know where to find me?'

That, finally, makes him smile. 'Everyone in Burlington knows where your husband lives.'

'You left the moccasins on the porch for me.'

'I left them for the baby.' He leans against the supporting beam of the icehouse porch. His hair spills over his shoulders.

'You shouldn't have come,' I say.

'Why not?'

'Spencer wouldn't like it.'

'I didn't come for him, Lia,' Gray Wolf replies. 'I came for you.'

I do not know what to say, which is just as well, because something catches his eye – Ruby, who has ferried a tray filled with lemonade and scones onto the porch of the house. As we walk toward the refreshments, I feel the medicine pouch sway against me. Gray Wolf and I are the only two people in the world who know it is there. I wonder how and why he has twice now called me Lia, when I have never introduced myself to him that way.

The social life of the Old Americans sets the social tone of the community. They are the charter members of society, and the rules that they make governing social intercourse are the rules that all others would follow.

– Elin Anderson, *We Americans:*
A Study of Cleavage in an American City, 1937

Forks ring against fine china, and the sound of crystal glasses singing makes me think there might be angels in the rafters. My father and Spencer and I have the best table at the Ethan Allen Club – the one uniformly agreed upon to be the choice location in the dining room for watching the sun set. Through the roses and nasturtium in the center of the table I watch my father flatter the wife of Allen Sizemore, Dean of Sciences. 'So,' Allen asks, smiling. 'When do you expect the big day?'

I do not realize, at first, that he is talking about the baby. 'Not soon enough, I bet,' his wife says. 'I remember feeling fat as a tick on a hound by the end.'

I like Mrs Sizemore, who tells it as she sees it. She reaches across the table to pat my hand. 'You hang in there, Cissy. It'll be over before you know it.'

'Over?' Allen laughs. 'Just beginning, you mean. Why, Spencer will start nodding off in the middle of lectures, after changing diapers all night long. And Harry, maybe we'll engrave *Grandpa* on your office door just for good measure.'

'This baby will be absolutely perfect,' my father promises. 'He'll have his papa's brain – which means he'll be smart enough to sleep through the night. And he'll have his mama's beauty – which means if he does wake up, he'll charm his exhausted nanny.'

'Nanny?' I turn to Spencer.

He glares at my father. 'That was going to be a surprise.'

'But I don't want a nanny.'

'Darling,' Spencer jokes, 'she's not for you.'

Everyone at the table laughs. I look down at my lap, mortified. Hiking up my sleeve a little, I make sure the bandage is showing, and then I reach for my wineglass, my eyes on Spencer the whole time.

'Mercy, Cecelia . . . did you hurt yourself?' As I have expected, Mrs Sizemore has noticed right away.

'As a matter of fact—' I begin, but Spencer interrupts.

'She burned her arm on the stove.' He stares at me with a look that brooks no argument. 'She really needs to be more careful.'

'You didn't tell me,' my father says, reaching for my wrist.

'It was nothing.' I pull away and in the process knock over my wineglass. The cabernet spills, bright as my blood, across my lap.

It seems everyone in the room summons the waiter at once. He comes out of the woodwork with a stack of snowy napkins. His face, wide and brown, reminds me of Gray Wolf's. He begins to dab at my thighs.

'For God's sake,' Spencer explodes. 'Get your hands off her!'

He takes over, mopping up the mess. 'It's only a dress, Spencer,' I say. And to the waiter, without thinking: '*Wliwni.*' Thank you.

The waiter's eyes fly to my face, as do everyone else's at the table. 'Well?' I demand of the waiter, pretending he has heard me wrong. 'Who do you think you are?' I turn to the table at large. 'Excuse me while I visit the ladies' room.' As I sweep from the sumptuous dining room I can feel the Gypsy watching. I wish I could apologize to him. I wish I could tell him I understand: the higher you raise your hopes, the farther you have to fall.

> Draft statistics showed Vermont to be almost at the top of the list of physical and mental defectives. It has been suggested that this may be due to the large number of French Canadians in the population.
>
> – H. F. Perkins, *Project #1*, ESV archive,
> 'Projects – Old,' 1926

Somehow, Gray Wolf knows when to come. I find him on my porch when Spencer is lecturing and Ruby has gone into town to the butcher. He steps out from behind a tree when I take a walk at dusk in the woods. When he does not appear himself, I discover more gifts on the porch: a small sweetgrass basket, a miniature snowshoe, a sketch of a running horse. When we are together, I wonder where he has been all my life.

I know better than to encourage this. He comes from the fraying edge of a society; he holds on by a thread. Me, I've grown up right at its woven center. He is dark and quiet and completely different from me, which is exactly why I should put distance between us. But it is also the reason I find him so fascinating.

If you walk down the street in Burlington you can see all sorts of people – Irish, Italians, Gypsies, Jews – but you learn, growing up on the Hill, to wear blinders. You notice only the people who look like you – women with the same permanent waves in their hair and children with sailor collars and men who smell of bay rum. I have not asked Gray Wolf why he keeps seeking me out, but I imagine it is the same reason I wait for him – for the risk of it, for the sheer surprise of pressing one's nose to the glass and finding someone staring back on the other side.

What would Spencer say if he knew the person I most identify with is a Gypsy, who, like me, doesn't fit into this world?

Today I don't expect to see Gray Wolf, and I am truly disappointed. I won't be at home during the day – instead, I have come to attend the Klifa Club's monthly meeting. It is the premier women's social club in Burlington; my membership was a given, based on my social standing in the community.

Spencer encouraged me to come to town today. Dressed in long sleeves, to cover my bandages, no one would be able to tell. 'Besides,' he suggested over breakfast, 'a little musical entertainment might be soothing.'

So I spend two hours listening to a harpist, and another half-hour trying not to fall asleep as a botanist drones on about the gardens of Italy. I suffer through lemonade and finger sandwiches, as women discreetly pat the mound of my abdomen and tell me what I already know – that I am carrying a boy. I fan myself with the program and slip down the stairs when the ladies are discussing next month's event.

Gray Wolf is waiting for me beneath the green awning of the bank, smoking a cigarette, as if we have agreed to meet. There is just one moment of shock that he's found me, even in town, but he only raises his dark eyebrows and offers me a cigarette too. We start walking. We don't talk, at first. We don't need to.

'The Klifa Club,' he says finally.

'Yes.'

'What's it like?'

'Magnificent, of course. We eat on plates made of 14-carat gold, and hold audiences with kings of small European countries. Why else would it be so exclusive?'

He laughs. 'Beats me.' As we come to a street corner, he takes my elbow, and I instantly freeze. Although we have met many times now, I can count on one hand the number of occasions Gray Wolf has touched me. This friendship, this easy conversation is one thing, but there are certain lines even I cannot cross.

Noticing, he lets go of me and fills the fissure between us with words. 'What's a Klifa, anyway?'

'A mistake. It was supposed to be *Klifra,* which is Icelandic for *climber.'*

'As in "social?"'

'No, these women don't have to climb. They've already staked their claim at the top.' I shrug. 'What's in a name,' I quote, before I remember that Gray Wolf would not know Shakespeare.

'Ask Juliet,' he answers dryly, fully aware of what I am thinking. 'And to answer your question, a name can mean everything. Sometimes, it's all you have.'

'You call me Lia,' I say. 'Why?'

He pauses. 'Because you don't look like a Cissy.'

'What would my name be in your language?'

He shakes his head. 'No one uses my language anymore.'

'You do.'

'That's because I don't have anything left to lose.' He glances at me, but I'm not giving up that easily. 'There isn't a literal translation. You can't always take an English word and turn it into *Alnôbak.'* Gray Wolf nods at my brooch, a small clock pinned to my white blouse. 'See, this is *Papizwokwazik.* But it doesn't mean clock. It's "the thing that ticks." A beaver might be called *Tmakwa* – a tree cutter – or *abagôlo* – flat tail – or *awadnakwazid* – the wood carrier . . . depending on how you see it.'

I love the idea that a name might change based on who you are at a given moment in time. *'Awadnakwazid,'* I repeat, rolling the syllables on my tongue. Consonants stick to the roof of my mouth. 'I wish I had a name like Gray Wolf.'

'Then give yourself one. That's what I did.' He shrugs. 'My birth name, it's John . . . Azo. But Gray Wolf describes me better. And I figured if the whole world saw me as an Indian, I ought to have a name that backs them up.'

We have turned onto College Street now, which is busy and crowded. I know the mother walking with her daughter and the businessman leaning on an ivory cane and the two young soldiers are all wondering what someone like me is doing with someone like Gray Wolf. I wonder who else will see us. It is part of the excitement.

'I used to stand on the roof of my father's house and think about jumping,' I say.

'Your father's house,' he repeats.

'Well, it's ours now, but yes. Once, I even did it. I broke my arm.'

'Why did you want to jump?'

No one has ever asked me that question. Not my father, afterward; not the doctors at the hospital who set the bones. 'Because I could.' I turn to him and make the traffic flow around us. 'Give me a name.'

He stares at my face for a long moment. '*Sokoki,*' he says. 'One who has broken away.'

Suddenly, behind me, I hear myself being called. 'Cissy?' Spencer's voice is carried on the shoulders of passersby. 'Is that you?'

Maybe I have wanted to be discovered all along; maybe I have been expecting this. But when Spencer stands in front of Gray Wolf, my insides go to water and my legs begin to shake. I would fall, if not for Spencer catching me. 'Darling?'

'I'm just a little light-headed, after the Klifa Club meeting.'

Spencer looks dismissively at Gray Wolf. 'Chief, you can move along.'

'I'm not a chief.'

With my heart in my throat I reach into my pocketbook and take out a dollar bill. 'All right,' I interrupt, as if Gray Wolf and I have been in the middle of a business deal, 'but this is all I'm willing to pay for it.'

He plays along, but disappointment shadows his eyes. 'Thank you, ma'am.' He hands me a small bundle wrapped in a hand-kerchief, the first thing he can find in his pocket for a sham transaction. Then he vanishes into the masses walking toward the university.

'I've told you not to talk to beggars,' Spencer says, taking my arm. 'Once they see you're an easy target, they'll never leave you alone.'

'It's Christian charity,' I murmur.

'What on earth did he manage to sell you, anyway?'

I peek inside the folds of the handkerchief, and go dizzy again. 'A trinket,' I say, and stuff the miniature portrait into my purse before Spencer recognizes the face, a perfect twin to the one that sits on my dressing table to help me remember my mother.

Within the ranks of the Old Americans are many individuals who transcend the group pattern, question the status quo, think creatively about community or social problems, and even consider the possibility of a different and perhaps even better Burlington. As long as they do not go too far with their questioning, the group will uphold them; and they seldom do go too far, knowing the price they would have to pay.

– Elin Anderson, *We Americans:*
A Study of Cleavage in an American City, 1937

In my dream I can even feel it, the square box of its body and the white face with a small scale of numbers and a quivering needle. There is writing on the handheld base: TriField Natural EM Meter. A man with hair as long as a woman's explains the settings: Magnetic, sum, electric, radio/microwave, battery test. He wears a faded T-shirt and denims, like a field hand.

What is a *cell phone*?

I wake up, sweating. Even the fan blowing over the surface of the bed can't make up for the fact that the windows are stuck shut. The other side of the bed is empty. Restless, I walk to the bathroom and splash water on my face. Padding downstairs, I try to find Spencer.

He is in his study. The lights are all out, with the exception of a green accountant's shade lamp on his desk. Several of his pedigree charts are unraveled on the hardwood floor like old roads, and through the open windows, bullfrogs are calling his name. When he lifts his head, I realize he has been drinking.

'Cissy. What time is it?'

'Past two.' I take a tentative step forward. 'You should come up to bed.'

He buries his face in his hands. 'What woke you?'

'The heat.'

'Heat.' Spencer picks up his glass and drains it. An ant crawls across the desk, and in one smooth move he smacks the base of the tumbler down to crush it.

'Spencer?'

He wipes off the glass with his handkerchief and looks up at me. 'Do you think,' he asks quietly, 'that they feel it? Do you think they know it's coming?'

I shake my head, confused. 'You need to go to sleep.'

Before I realize what he is doing, Spencer has twisted me onto his lap. He holds my arm fast, and touches the spot where the bandage has been taped in the crook of my elbow. 'Do you know how it would kill me to lose you?' he whispers, fierce. 'Do you have any idea what you mean to me?'

My lips barely move. 'No.'

'Oh, Cissy.' He buries his face between my breasts, his breath falling over our baby. 'You're the reason I do it.'

The small Old American group has been helped to maintain its predominant position by the strength of its traditional feeling of the racial superiority of the Anglo-Saxon.

– Elin Anderson, *We Americans:*
A Study of Cleavage in an American City, 1937

Ruby is the one who tells me he is waiting.

'Spencer's inside,' I say, panicking the minute I see Gray Wolf on our porch, with the morning sun slung over his shoulders like a matador's cape.

'Ask me,' he demands.

I glance into the house. Spencer is in the tub. And I have so many questions. 'Did you know my mother?' When he nods, it is no surprise. 'What was she like?'

His gaze softens. 'You.'

There are no words in the place where I have arrived. 'More,' I manage.

So he tells me what she looked like, standing on this very porch, in this home where she grew up before marrying my father. He paints the color of her hair, and it matches mine. He tells me how she could whistle louder than any girl he'd ever known, and that her clothes always smelled of lemons. He had worked for her father as a seasonal field laborer – back when this property was a producing farm, before that parcel of land was sold off to the current neighbors.

He tells me that once, on a dare, my mother drove a tractor onto the UVM green at midnight.

He tells me that she wanted a daughter, more than anything, so that she could grow up all over again.

I lean against the exterior wall of the house and close my eyes. I have waited my whole life for this moment. Will my child be as lucky? Will there be someone, years from now, to tell him about me?

I blink at Gray Wolf. 'I'm going to die.'

'Lia,' he says, 'we all are.'

The door opens suddenly. Spencer's hair is still wet, and there are small damp patches on his shirt where his skin pinks through the cotton. 'I thought I heard you talking to someone,' he accuses, and I wonder if Gray Wolf hears how the edge of his words are as sharp as a razor.

'This is Gray Wolf,' I announce. 'I'm hiring him.'

Spencer stares, trying to figure out why Gray Wolf's face is so familiar . . . but he will not be able to. That day on the street, Spencer had wanted nothing more than to dismiss a Gypsy. For Gray Wolf to stand out in his mind, he would have had to be important enough to leave an impression in the first place.

'The roof needs work. Both here, and the icehouse. You told me to hire a handyman to take care of it. Gray Wolf, this is my husband, Professor Pike.'

Spencer looks one last time between Gray Wolf and myself. 'There's a ladder in the garage,' he says finally. 'Go on, then. You can start with the drainpipes.'

'Yes, sir.' Gray Wolf's expression is blank. He strikes off toward the shed to start working a job he never asked for.

Spencer watches him leave. 'Where did you find him?'

'The Hardings,' I lie.

'Cal Harding?' This will impress Spencer; our neighbor is a stickler for detail. 'Did they check his references?'

'Spencer, he's patching a roof, not signing on as the nanny.'

From a distance comes the clatter of things being moved in too small a space. 'I don't like him,' Spencer says.

'Well,' I answer. 'I do.'

Eugenics is the scientific projection of our sense of self-preservation and our parental instincts.

– O. F. Cook, 'Quenching Life on the Farm:
How the Neglect of Eugenics Subverts Agriculture and Destroys
Civilization,' from a review by E. R. Eastman in the *Journal of
Heredity*, 1928

As a child, I used to go to my father's office at the university and pretend his big leather desk chair was a throne, and I was the Queen of Everything. My subjects – pencils, paperweights – lined up at attention on the desk to hear me speak and watch me twirl in circles. My court jester, a typewriter carriage with a bell at each return, sat at my elbow. I was only three-and-a-half feet tall, and I pretended I could fill this space with as much command as my father.

He is sitting at the desk, laboring over a legal pad, when I let myself inside. Seeing me, he puts down his work. 'Cissy! This is a nice surprise. What brings you to town?'

For the past few days, my belly has been stretched to breaking, my skin on the verge of splitting. 'Your grandson wanted to pay a visit.'

He sees me looking at his chair, and he smiles slowly. 'Did you want to take a spin, for old time's sake?'

Ruefully, I shake my head. 'I wouldn't fit.'

'Of course you would. I've seen Allen Sizemore stuff his considerable, er, assets into that seat.' When I don't laugh along with him, he stands and reaches for my hand. 'Tell me what's the matter.'

Oh, God, where would I even start? With the way I look at a blade as a silver opportunity? With the nightmares I have of my own father and Spencer, pulling this baby out from between my legs? Or should I appeal to him as a scientist: *Hypothesis – fear is a room six feet by six feet, without any windows or doors.*

What comes out of my mouth instead is a single word. 'Mama,' I whisper.

'She would have been so proud of you. She would have loved to see this baby.' He pauses. 'It's perfectly natural to worry. But Cissy, you're a different woman from your mother, God rest her soul. You're stronger.'

'How do you know?'

'Because part of you came from *me*.' Suddenly he tugs me into his leather chair. He spins it slowly, a carousel.

'Daddy!'

'What? Who's here to see?'

So I lean my head back and try to find the eye at the center of the cyclone. My feet fly out in front of me, my hands rest heavy on the armrests. 'That's my girl,' my father says, and he brings me to a stop. 'I might come out to your place this afternoon. I hear you're having some work done by a Gypsy.'

'Yes.' I wonder what else Spencer has told him.

'Never hired one, myself.' My father leans against the desk. 'There was an Indian in grade school with me. Linwood . . . good God, I can't believe I remember his name. This kid was as Indian as the Indian on a buffalo head nickel. Braids and all. Of course, every boy back then played cowboys and Indians. The highlight of the summer was heading up to South Hero, where there would be Indians at camp to teach us to make trails in the woods and such . . . but that was all for *play,* you know. Linwood, though . . . he lived it. He could actually trap and hunt and shoot a bow. Hell, he could *make* a bow.' There is a strange tone of admiration in my father's voice. 'He wore moccasins to school,' he says faintly. 'He did all sorts of things the rest of us couldn't do.'

I wonder if something as simple as this could have been the raw splinter that stuck in my father's mind, the one that brought him to eugenics in the first place. A chance meeting that means nothing at the time might bloom into an event of enormous importance. You don't think twice about an Indian boy's coveted leather shoes, but you may never forget them. You ignore the man staring at you across the stage of a July 4th historical pageant, until it seems he was fated to be there.

I study his face. 'What about Mama? Did she know any Indians?'

The light leaves my father's eyes. 'No,' he answers. 'They scared her to death.'

June 13, 1933

Miss Martha E. Leighton
Agricultural Extension Building
City

Dear Miss Leighton:
I think I shall choose 'Registered Human Stock' as the topic for discussion with the 4-H older boys the last of the month.

Sincerely yours,
Henry F. Perkins

– Correspondence from H. F. Perkins, ESV
and VCCL papers, Public Records Office, Middlesex, VT

The town diner looks the same, a squat clapboard eyesore sitting like a blister on the lip of the town. What makes no sense, though, are the odd things surrounding it. There are more cars than I have ever seen in all of Burlington, in the sleekest of shapes. A boy with wheels on his feet rattles past me. When I turn the corner, the long-haired man stands up, and he hands me his heart.

Waking abruptly, I stir in Spencer's arms. 'What is it?' he murmurs.

'A dream.'

'What were you dreaming?'

I have to think about this for a moment. 'The future, I think.'

Spencer's hand splays over our son. 'That's a start,' he says.

Styla Nestor, a cousin by marriage to Gray Wolf Delacour, relates his heavy periodic drinking and sex immorality to his Gypsy-like travel, due most likely to the fact that overseers and townspeople wanted to get rid of him. The only semi-permanent address she could recall for her cousin, in fact, was the State Prison.

– From the files of Abigail Alcott, social worker

The afternoon sun is a cat, tickling me beneath the chin. Bolting upright in bed, I check the clock, and then check it again. I am shocked to have slept so late; I wonder why Ruby has not come in to wake me.

I wash and dress and run a comb through my hair, in a hurry to get outside. The steady beat of the hammer overhead tells me Gray Wolf is already working on the roof, and there is so much I want to ask him.

'Coffee?' Ruby asks, as I come into the kitchen.

'Not now.'

'Miz Pike—' she says, when I am already halfway out the back door.

I shade my eyes with a hand, heading in the direction of the noise. 'Gray Wolf?' I call, and nearly lose my footing when my husband's face peers over the edge of the roof instead. 'Spencer, what are you doing here?'

'Finishing what I should have done myself. I don't have to teach until this afternoon.' He tucks the hammer in the back loop of his belt and begins a careful climb down to the porch, leaving the ladder propped against the house near the sealed bedroom window. 'I fired him,' he says, when we are facing each other.

'What . . . what did he do?'

'What *didn't* he do, Cissy?' Spencer hands me a paper from his pocket. It is a carbon copy of a court conviction from nearly two decades years ago, in which John 'Gray Wolf' Delacour was sentenced to twenty-five years in jail for murder. Stapled to it is a second page – the paroled release of Gray Wolf from the Vermont State Prison, dated July 4th of this year.

'He was here alone with you and Ruby, for God's sake!'

'He isn't like that,' I blurt out.

'Cissy. Did he tell you he'd served time in prison?'

My gaze slides away. 'I didn't ask.'

Spencer's hand cups my cheek. 'That's why you have me.'

John 'Gray Wolf' Delacour is alleged to be the grandchild of Missal
Delacour, the old Gypsy. John does not show the colored blood
quite as dark as his ancestor, but has the loose, shambling walk
of the Gypsy. He is considered by his own relations to be arrogant,
ignorant, and immoral, although he has managed to learn to read
and write. If you are interested in Evolution you won't have to
trace back very far from John Delacour to find the Missing Link.

          – From the journals of Abigail Alcott, social worker

As anyone who's ever contracted it knows, lies are an infectious
disease. They slip under the almond slivers of your fingernails
and into your bloodstream. Maybe this is why it comes so easily
to me – the fabrication of a doctor's appointment to check the
progress of the baby, the hurried drive into town, the turn I take
to bring me to the camp on the edge of the lake.

This time as I walk through the labyrinth of tents, I notice the
color. A woman steps outside to shake wrinkles from a rainbow-
ribboned coat, brillliant silks spilling like paint across the dust. It
is Madame Soliat, I realize – the fortune-teller from the Exposition
on the Fourth of July. A few tents away an old woman hunches
over a stool, lashing a thin ash splint to a wide-lipped basket. A
calico cat plays at her feet; a splash of canary sits on her shoulder.
Men who work the carnival circuit pack their wares in brightly
painted boxes, loading up for the next journey to a country fair.
My whole life, it seems, is pale by comparison.

When I walk up to the basket weaver she pretends she can
see right through me. 'Excuse me,' I say. Her cat yowls, and runs
away. 'I'm looking for Gray Wolf. John Delacour?'

Maybe it is my advanced pregnancy; maybe it is the wildness
in my eyes – but this old woman gets to her feet and plucks the
canary from her shoulder to sit on the back of her chair. Leaving
the unfinished basket on the ground, she begins to limp toward
the woods.

We walk for several minutes, past the point where the Gypsy tents thin out. The old woman points me toward a copse of pine trees that grow up the base of a steep hill, and she leaves me to my own devices. My legs begin to burn with exertion; I am not certain I will make it. I am even beginning to have doubts that this woman understood who I was looking for, when suddenly the forest opens into a small clearing. The ground is uneven, as if the earth is boiling just under the crabgrass. In the middle of these mounds sits Gray Wolf.

He gets up when he sees me coming and a smile washes over his face. 'I didn't know when I would get to see you,' he says, relieved.

Uneasy, I fold my arms across my stomach. 'You lied to me. Spencer found out that you were in jail. And my father says that my mother never knew you. That she was terrified of people like you.'

'People like me. Did it ever occur to you that maybe *I'm* not the one here who was lying?'

'What reason would they have to lie?'

'Why does anyone?' he says. 'Down by the river, you go ask any of those people who they are, and they're gonna tell you they're dark French. Or that they're cousins, six times removed, from someone Irish or Italian. I know one family that passes themselves off as Negro or Mohawk, because even that's not quite as bad as being Abenaki. You should understand, Lia, that there can't be any *Indians* around. Because that would mean someone lived here before all those old Vermonters who think they came first.'

'That has nothing to do with going to prison for murder,' I argue. 'You don't get convicted of a crime if you didn't do it.'

'No?' He takes a step toward me. 'Did Spencer tell you about the man I killed? He was a supervisor at the granite quarry, and he was beating a man for not hauling stone fast enough. A man who was seventy-nine years old, and who happened to be my grandfather, and who died in front of my eyes.'

I recall Abigail's reports: *John Delacour is an absolute liar . . . it is impossible to get the truth out of him.* 'A jury would understand that.'

'Not when there were people who wanted to get rid of me,' Gray Wolf says. 'People jurors listen to.'

Immediately, I think of my father, dining with Governor Wilson shortly before the passage of the Sterilization Bill in the legislature. Of Dr DuBois, who could not convince Spencer to send me to an institution . . . and who would dare not breathe a word to the community about Professor Pike's suicidal wife. 'You didn't serve your whole sentence,' I realize.

'No. Believe it or not, I finally had something they wanted, something I could bargain with.' He looks down and stamps at a patch of grass with his heel. 'The warden, he was real excited about the new sterilization law. Inmates who volunteered for a vasectomy got to shave five whole years off their time. For me, that was *freedom.*'

It is one thing to have Spencer talk of sterilization in the abstract; it is another thing entirely to discuss a vasectomy with a man who has had one. 'But at what cost,' I murmur, my cheeks flaming.

'I wasn't thinking of what they would do to me, or of the family I'd never have. I was thinking that if I got out, I might get to meet the child I already knew about, the one born after I went to jail.' Gray Wolf lifts my chin. 'Lia,' he says, 'you were worth it.'

7

September 1, 1932

We have seen more than once that the public welfare may call upon the best citizens for their lives. It would be strange if it could not call upon those who already sap the strength of the state for these lesser sacrifices, often not felt to be such by those concerned, in order to prevent our being swamped with incompetence . . . Three generations of imbeciles are enough.

– Justice Oliver Wendell Holmes, delivering the opinion of the Supreme Court of Appeals of the State of Virginia, in the 1927 case of Buck v. Bell, which upheld the sterilization of a 'probably potential parent of socially inadequate offspring.'

Once upon a time, when my mother was my age, she fell in love. Not with one of the long-faced boys who held their straw boaters like wheels in their hands, boys who walked down from the university clutching bouquets, boys who called my imposing grandfather Sir. Not with Harry Beaumont, a young professor who stood first in line for the prize that was my mother; a scientist nearly ten years older than she was who spoke of love and natural selection in the same sentence. My mother was courted by Harry and these other young men on the porch, and meanwhile she looked over their shoulders at a Gypsy laborer who worked in their fields.

His skin was the color of the polished piano she played for her mother's friends at teatime; his hair was longer than hers. His eyes were as sharp as a hawk's, and sometimes when she was in the privacy of her bedroom with the curtains closed she knew that he could still see her. When she brought water out to the Indian workers – the only contact she was allowed – she could feel him swimming through her veins.

She had spent seventeen years being an exemplary daughter. She had attended finishing school; she crossed her legs at the ankles; she washed her face each night with buttermilk to make it glow. She was being groomed to be an exemplary wife, something she had known all along, but now the concept seemed like a fancy coat tucked away in a hope chest: trying it on after all these years, it did not fit quite as well as she had expected.

One day in the field, he was the last one to turn in his tin cup. Sweat ran down his bare chest, and there was a streak of dirt across his brow. He smelled of the blueberries he'd been picking. His teeth seemed too white when he spoke. 'Who are you?' he asked.

She could have said, *Lily Robinson*. Or, *Quentin Robinson's daughter*. Or, *Harry Beaumont's intended*. But that wasn't what he had been asking. For the first time in her life she wondered why she defined herself as part of someone else.

He began to leave her small gifts on the porch: a pair of tiny moccasins; a sweetgrass basket; a sketch of a running horse. She learned that his name was John.

On their first date, she lied and told her parents that she was spending the night at a girlfriend's. He met her halfway down the road into town. He took her hand, as if they had been doing that forever, and told her that his home was the world, that the sky was its roof. They walked to the edge of the river and pulled the stars close as a blanket. When he lay her down to kiss her, his hair fell over their faces, a curtain for privacy.

He was a year younger than she was, and nothing like the

Gypsies she'd been hearing of her whole life. John wasn't dirty or stupid or dishonest. He understood how it felt to be boxed in by a label someone else had slapped on you. Lily started to live her days only as a means of getting to the nights. She talked back to her father and ignored her mother. She began to dream in rich reds and blues. And on the evening that John fit himself to her and taught her how to bloom, Lily cried because someone loved *her*, not the person she was supposed to be.

Her first mistake, when she became pregnant, was to see it as an opportunity instead of a crisis. She hovered like a hummingbird outside her father's study while John, wearing a collared shirt and tie he had borrowed for a dime, asked permission to marry her.

What happened after that Lily could not remember, or maybe she could not let herself remember. There was John, unconscious and beaten bloody, being dragged out of her father's study. There was her father's fist shaking above her as he ordered her to play the whore again by marrying some unsuspecting fool. The stiff kiss that sealed her engagement to Harry Beaumont; the awful moment at the church where she almost told her new husband the truth; the joy on his face later when she told him, instead, that she was expecting.

She tried to find John, but it was difficult to locate someone who had no permanent address. She heard rumors that he worked at a bar in Vergennes, that he had become a horse thief, that he was a quarry laborer. By the time she realized this last tale was true, John Delacour was no longer employed there. He was in jail pending trial for the murder of a supervisor.

She wrote him one letter, a small square of paper that he folded and wore in a pouch around his neck. It did not mention her marriage, or her health, or the child. It said simply, *Come back*. John did not write in return; he knew better. After the first month, Lily stopped waking up with the taste of him on her lips. After three months, she could no longer remember the wood-smoke in his voice. After six months, she began to have nightmares that her baby would arrive with hair dark as a crow's wing, with cinnamon skin.

Lily Robinson Beaumont died in apparently premature childbirth, having slipped into unconsciousness after forty hours of labor. She held John's name between her teeth to take with her. She did not know that John would, one day, come back – even after he learned from bribing a prison guard that his love had gone to the spirit world. She did not know that the daughter she left behind, Cecelia, had golden hair, and skin as white as a miracle.

A great deal is known about human heredity – enough to make eugenical sterilization a safe policy, provided the standards for sterilization apply only to the most patently degenerate individuals who are definitely demonstrated to be cacogenic. In the future, as more is learned about heredity, the standards can be shifted to include those individuals who now constitute situations described as 'border-line.'

– Excerpt from a letter dated September 24, 1925,
from H. H. Laughlin, director of the
Eugenics Record Office, to Harriet Abbott

In my dreams I give birth to the Devil, to Jesus, to a Titan that tears me apart. I bleed from my pores and wake to find the sheets wet with sweat. For several nights, Spencer tries, unsuccessfully, to raise the stuck window in the bedroom. I cannot bear to look at him.

Tonight when I startle out of sleep Spencer doesn't wake with me. I inch back the covers and get out of bed, careful to walk around the few floorboards that gossip. The carpet runner muffles the sounds of my steps down the stairs. Spencer has left the door to his study open.

I turn on the green accountant's lamp. A thousand times I have come into this room, but never with the intent of finding something. Where would Spencer keep it?

On his desk are neat piles of papers – letters he has received from colleagues in the field of eugenics, books in several languages, photographic slides scattered like cards across an illuminated table. His blotter is covered with illegible notes. I read some of the words: *twins, custodial, epidemic.* As I maneuver around the desk, I bump into the corner and send a paperweight crashing to the floor. Immediately, I freeze and look up at the ceiling, waiting with my heart in my throat. When there is no answering sound, I take a deep breath and inch toward the long table pushed against the wall.

One genealogy map is partially unrolled on its surface, a family with a surname I don't recognize. I scan the thick lines that link one insane relative to another, profligates to prostitutes, reform school students to convicts. I follow one trail of family members, seemingly unaffected by any degeneracy for an entire generation. And yet the children of these children have all landed in the industrial school, at Waterbury, in the state prison – they are as depraved as their grandparents were. How many times have I heard Spencer say it? Inherited traits might skip a generation . . . but blood eventually tells.

My hands steal over my belly, which freezes up hard beneath my hands. False labor, it is called. I force myself to sift through the scrolls of other pedigree charts tucked into an umbrella stand beside the table. They are labeled Delaire, Moulton, Waverly, Olivette – there is no Delacour to be found. Could my father – my *father?* – have logged the survey of Gray Wolf's family under a different surname?

Weber/George.

This tag leaps out at me. With great care I pull the chart from the stand and unroll it over the table. It is not hard to find Ruby's name among those at the bottom; Spencer has marked it with red ink. There are mathematical calculations and notes in his narrow hand, speculating on Ruby's chance at turning out as badly as the rest of her family.

Her beloved sister, the one who died, has a mark as dark as a brand next to her name. *Sx*, for Immoral.

It is the same symbol, I realize, that would have been given to my mother.

'Cissy.'

Spencer's voice is so quiet it simply tips into my mind, and yet I jump a foot. He stands in silhouette in his dressing gown, watching me. Taking a step inside, his gaze falls to the table.

For one excruciating moment when he looks at me, I think he knows exactly what I have been searching for. But for whatever reason, Spencer's face smooths into a mask. 'Sweetheart, you've been sleepwalking again.'

'Yes.' I clear my throat.

He offers me his arm and escorts me out of the office, locking the door behind us. 'Blame it on the baby,' Spencer says, his eyes never leaving my face.

We are speaking two conversations at once, and we both know it. 'No,' I answer. 'Not him.'

I call your attention to the fact that the number of our insane and feebleminded is constantly increasing with a corresponding increase in the burden cast on the community and the State. We are doing our duty about the care of these unfortunates, but practically nothing to prevent a further increase in their number. Medical science points out some definite course which has been followed successfully in some states. . . . You will do well to give this matter serious consideration.

— From Governor Stanley Wilson's inaugural message to the Vermont General Assembly, *Journal of the Senate of the State of Vermont*, 1931

The next morning I am sitting at the dressing table in front of my mirror when Spencer leans down to kiss my neck. 'How are you feeling?' he asks, as if last night never happened.

I set down my brush. 'Fine.'

Spencer's hand steals down my robe, onto the swell of our son. 'And how's he feeling?'

'Heavy.'

We are a beautiful couple. Somehow the long lines of Spencer's jaw and the pale blue behind his glasses are the perfect complement to my heart-shaped face and honey-brown eyes. Our child, a combination of the best of us, should be stunning. Except that he might not look the way Spencer is expecting him to look.

'Spencer,' I whisper, a beginning. 'We have to talk.'

But he has slid his hands down my arms by now, and his gentle fingertips are playing over the healing ridge of skin at my wrist. With his head bent, in silence, it is simple to read his mind: if he didn't love me, this would be so much easier.

Then again, he doesn't love *me*. He doesn't even really know who I am. If Spencer is too ashamed to admit to a wife who cannot manage to keep herself alive, how will he feel about a wife who is half-Indian?

Would he add my name to the bottom of the Delacour genealogy chart? Or would he burn it? Spencer has done an admirable job of hiding the truth about me from his friends and colleagues. Maybe he could continue to do so. All babies, I could tell him, look dark and round-faced when they are newborn.

'You know,' Spencer says, 'I don't think we *should* talk. Talking . . . *thinking* . . . that's what gets your mind in knots, Cissy.' His fingers smooth my brow in tiny circles. 'What you need is a distraction. A task to keep you busy.' He takes a small piece of paper from his pocket, inscribed with the names of ten couples, and sets it beside my bottle of French tea-rose perfume. 'A dinner party. A pre-birthday, maybe, for our baby. You and Ruby can come up with a menu, decorations, a theme.' He kisses my cheek. 'What do you think?'

I smooth the list of names with one hand and tuck it into the corner of my mirror. *We will have rib roasts and sweet potatoes in maple syrup and candied carrots. We will drink red wine and laugh at jokes that aren't funny and toast a baby who will break my world in half.* 'I'm not supposed to think,' I say.

We are so careful in breeding our cattle to get good breeds yet we give this human procreation no thought.

– Mrs Bickford, of Bradford, quoted in the *Burlington Free Press* on March 21, 1931, during the debate in the Vermont State House regarding the Sterilization Bill

I begin to create complications. Each morning I say there is something else bothering me about this pregnancy – a pinched nerve, a lack of fetal movement, a heartburn so severe it makes me weak. My nervousness about giving birth feeds this fire, and so Spencer does not question me when I tell him I am headed to Dr DuBois's office every other day. *Better him*, I am sure he is thinking, *than me.*

Instead of going into town, however, I go down to camp on the lake. After several days of seeing me in Gray Wolf's company, the people who live there have stopped staring. Some know me by name. 'This,' Gray Wolf says when he introduces me, 'is my daughter.'

The familiar Abenaki phrase for 'my father' is *N'Dadan*. Spoken, it sounds like a heartbeat.

Today, it is raining. We sit in Gray Wolf's tent at a scarred table. While he reads the sports page of the newspaper, I sift through a small cigar box. A cameo, a violet hair ribbon, a lock of hair – these are the things my mother left him. Each time I come I study them, as if they might hold a clue I haven't yet discovered. Sometimes I think of Houdini; of what more one could possibly need to return from the other side.

He tells me I can have all of these, if I would like them. He says he doesn't need *things* to recall her, because unlike me, he met her. I do not know how to tell him that what I really want is something of his – something to remember him by, just in case.

He makes a small sound of dismay. 'Sox just blew their chance at the Series,' he sighs. 'It's the Curse of the Bambino. The worst trade in history since we swapped Manhattan for a few shells and beads.' I stand up and pretend to wander around the small tent. I touch his shaving brush, his razor, his comb. With his back to me, I take a pipe from his nightstand and slip it into my pocket.

'I thought you preferred cigarettes,' he says, without turning around.

I whirl. 'How did you know?'

He glances over his shoulder. 'I can smell how nervous you are. I would have given the pipe to you if you'd asked.' Grinning, he says, 'My daughter's a thief. Must be all that Gypsy blood in her veins.'

My daughter. Once again, the title makes me feel as if I have swallowed a star. 'You haven't asked me,' I point out, 'if I'm going to tell Spencer or my . . . Harry Beaumont.'

Gray Wolf studies his newspaper. 'That isn't my choice to make. I didn't tell you so I could claim you. Nobody belongs to anyone else.'

I think of him in prison, making the decision to be sterilized so that he would be free to search for me. Whether he wants to admit it or not, people do belong to each other. Once you make a sacrifice for someone, you own part of his or her soul. 'But you must want me to.'

When he looks up at me, I take a step back; there is that much passion in his eyes. 'I wanted *you*. On any terms. I was willing to trade anything just to see you. Would I like to hear you say you're my daughter, to have you shout it to anyone who'll listen? God, yes, there's a part of me that says that's why I did what I did. But there's a bigger part of me that only wants to make sure you're safe.' He folds the sports page, pleats it neatly, as if he will be judged on the result. 'And if you go out and tell people about me, they won't hear how proud you are. All they're gonna hear is that you're Indian.'

'I don't care.'

'That's because you've never been one. You haven't spent years wearing someone else's clothes, taking someone else's name, living in someone else's houses, and working someone else's jobs to fit in. And if you don't sell out, then you run away . . . proving you're the Gypsy they said you were all along.' He shakes his head sadly. 'I want you to have a better life than the one I had. Even if that means keeping your distance from me.'

The baby does a slow roll inside me, unsettled. 'Then why would you bother to look for me? Why didn't you just stay away?'

He stares at me for a long moment. 'How could I?'

'Then how,' I say, 'can you ask *me* to?'

He looks out the flap of the tent, into the rain. 'You'll understand, when that baby is born. There's an old phrase, *Awani Kia*. It means, "Who are you." Not your name, but your people. You hear it a lot when you move from place to place. Every winter, when I go up to Odonak and someone asks me, I get to tell him about my great-grandfather, who was a spiritual leader. Or my Auntie Sopi, who was the best healer in her day. Every winter when I answer I remember that it doesn't matter what people call me, as long as I know who I really am.' He hesitates. 'This winter, I'll tell them about you.'

It is the first time he's talked about his departure from the camp. He is a wanderer, an itinerant – I have always known this. But for the first time I realize that when he leaves for Canada, he will be leaving *me*.

'What if I come?' I blurt out.

'To Odonak? I don't think you'd be happy there.'

'But I'm not happy *here*.'

'Lia,' he says quietly. 'I won't tell you not to go; I'm too selfish for that. But the minute you get to Canada, you'll be thinking about what you left behind here.'

'You don't know that.'

'Don't I?' He glances at the table, at my mother's cameo. 'A person can't live in two worlds at once.'

'But you just found me!'

Gray Wolf smiles. 'Who said you were lost?'

I duck my head. Without being conscious of it, I rub my fingers over the scars at my wrist. 'I'm not as brave as you,' I say.

'No,' he answers. 'You're braver.'

No one has a right to become a parent who has so sinned that their children must suffer.

— Mr Harding, of W. Fairlee, quoted in the *Burlington Free Press*
on March 21, 1931, during the debate in the Vermont State
House regarding the Sterilization Bill

In the billiards room, the balls strike each other with precision. 'Spencer,' my father laughs, 'you're not going to let an old man beat you!'

'Harry, shut up and take your turn, will you?'

I smile and press my hand to the small of my back. At the sideboard in the adjoining hall, I am counting the silver. Spencer has me do it once a month. We never come up short, but he says you can never be too careful.

I am on the seventh teaspoon when I hear the word *Gypsy*.

'Actually,' Spencer responds, 'I had to finish the job myself.'

'Can't say it's any surprise.' There is a neat click as my father hits another ball with his cue. 'Stealing, lying . . . I wouldn't be surprised to find unreliability an inherited trait.'

'Well, this one also happened to have served time for murder.'

'Good God—'

'Exactly.' Spencer scratches, curses. 'I'm all for believing in the rehabilitation of criminals, but I'd rather not test the theory at the expense of my own wife.'

There is a sharp crack, a muffled click, and then the sound of my father racking up the balls for another game. 'The problem with the Sterilization Law is that it doesn't get rid of the degenerates that have already been born,' he says. 'That's what needs to be addressed next.'

All the blood drains from my head. He does not say this with malice; for his statement to be hateful he would actually have to know some of the people he wants to eliminate. He and Spencer, they are only trying to change the world, to make it a better place for their children.

By getting rid of someone else's.

I stare at them through the open doorway; it is like seeing a saucer of milk go sour before your eyes. Spencer grins amiably. 'Genocide's not legal.'

'Only if you get caught,' my father laughs, and he picks up his cue again. 'Stripes or solids?'

Before I know it I have pushed myself into the doorway. I am white as a sheet; Spencer's cue rattles to the ground and he is at my side in an instant. 'Cissy?' he says frantically. 'What's wrong? Is it the baby?'

I manage to shake my head. 'The baby . . . is fine.'

My father frowns. 'Darling, you look like you've seen a ghost.'

Maybe I have, because I have just watched something that clearly has been here all along, even if I was too blind to bear witness before. Spencer pries the teaspoons from my hand. 'You aren't up to this. That's why we have Ruby, isn't it? Come. Let's get you off your feet.'

'I don't want to be off my feet,' I say, my voice escalating. 'I don't want . . . I don't . . .' As I push Spencer away, the teaspoons clatter to the floor. I burst into tears.

My father grasps my shoulders firmly. 'Cissy, you're over-wrought. Sit down, *now*.'

'Listen to your father,' Spencer agrees.

The problem is, I *have* been. And I no longer know who I am.

'Call Dr DuBois,' Spencer says quietly to my father, who nods and lifts the telephone receiver.

Spencer kneels beside me and puts his arm around my shoulders. What does one do with an insane wife? 'Cissy?' he says, his bewilderment twisting my name like ribbon candy.

Silver winks at me, a conspiracy at my feet. 'Oh, Spencer,' I sob. 'Look at what you've done.'

Every woman in the Vermont House, with the exception of Mrs Farr of Monkton, who was absent, favored the [passage of the 1931 sterilization] bill.

– *Burlington Free Press*, March 25, 1931

Dr DuBois sets his stethoscope in his ears. As I lay back on my pillows, he shields me with his body for privacy and begins to unbutton my blouse. I remember too late that I am still wearing the medicine pouch Gray Wolf gave me.

My eyes meet the doctor's. Before he can touch the pouch I grab the edges of my blouse and pull them together. I shake my head once, sharply, staring hard at Dr DuBois, whose brow has furrowed in a frown. Without breaking my gaze, I slide the buttons back into their holes, and wait for him to make the next move.

He is Spencer's puppet, but I am his patient, and to my surprise, that actually counts for something. Dr DuBois tugs his stethoscope from his ears and hangs it around his neck. His eyes pose a question I have no intention of answering. 'Well, your baby is fine,' he says briskly. 'I think all you need is a good rest.' He shakes two sleeping pills from a medicine bottle and watches carefully as I put them into my mouth and take a drink from the cup of water he's holding out. 'That's a good girl. You should feel better in no time. But you know, Cissy, that you can call on me whenever you have anything you need to . . . ask.'

With that, he rises and approaches Spencer, hovering in the doorway. As they begin to speak quietly, I roll onto my side and spit out the pills I've tucked high in my cheek. I slip them into my pillowcase.

I cannot take a nap, because then I won't be able to meet Gray Wolf as I am supposed to this afternoon. Of course, now that Dr DuBois has come to visit, I will have to concoct some new excuse. Maybe I will say I'm going to the stationer for vellum, to write invitations to our dinner party. What they do not understand is that I don't need pills, and I don't need rest. What I need is someone who does not want me to sleep through my own life.

The bed sinks as Spencer sits down beside me. I roll toward him, my eyelids half-lowered. 'I'm already getting tired.'

'You aren't the only one,' Spencer answers, and his voice is full of edges.

In that moment I forget how to breathe.

'Why is it that Dr DuBois – the physician you've gone to see six times in the past two weeks, for various aches and pains – has no recollection of these visits?' His face is stained crimson, which makes the blond roots of his hair stand out like platinum. 'What on earth could my *wife* be doing that would make her lie to me?' He has my shoulders in his hands, and shakes me. 'Not just once, but over and over?'

My head snaps back on the stalk of my neck. 'Spencer, it's not what you think . . .'

'*Do not tell me what I think!*' he roars, and then suddenly collapses into himself. 'Cissy, God, what have you done to me?'

Seeing him fall apart, I push myself into a sitting position and cradle his head in my lap. 'Spencer. I was going out for walks. By myself. I just wanted to be by myself.'

'Yourself?' Spencer murmurs against my skin. 'You were by yourself?'

I stare square into his eyes. 'Yes.'

Stealing, lying . . . I wouldn't be surprised to find unreliability an inherited trait.

'*Look* at me,' I say wryly, gesturing at the swell of my belly.

'I do,' Spencer answers. 'I am.' He cups my face in his hands and kisses me lightly. When he pulls away, he is holding an apology between his teeth. 'I'm sorry, Cissy.' I squeeze his hand as he gets to his feet. It is not until he takes the key to the bedroom door from his dresser that I realize he has not been asking forgiveness for what he has done, but for what he is about to do. 'Dr DuBois agrees with me – you can't be left alone. Especially not now, when your emotions are running so high with the pregnancy. He says that you're at risk to . . . to hurt yourself again.'

'And God forbid I do it where someone else could see. What would people say if they knew Spencer Pike was married to a woman who belonged with the rest of the feebleminded in Waterbury!'

Spencer's hand strikes my cheek with a sound like thunder, and shocks me into submission. He stares at his palm, as surprised by his actions as I am. I touch the pads of my fingers to my face, feeling the print of him rising like a second skin. 'I'm doing this,' Spencer says stiffly, 'because I love you.'

The minute the door closes behind him and the lock turns into place, I get out of bed. I try the windows, which are stuck as always. I bang on the door. 'Ruby!' I yell. 'Ruby, you get me out of here this instant!'

I hear her scratching on the other side of the door. 'I can't, Miz Pike. The professor, he says so.'

I beat my fist one last time against the panels. Thrashing around has only made the close room even hotter; my hair sticks to the back of my neck and my shirt is damp. A princess in an ivory tower, that's what I am. But if the prince knew, at heart, that I am a toad, would he fight so hard to keep me?

Crawling around on my hands and knees I plug in the electric fan and hold my face close. Immediately I am cooler. I wonder if this is what the air in Canada is like. I wonder if Gray Wolf will worry, when I do not come.

As the fan spins I speak into it, a child's trick, so that my voice sounds like someone else's. 'Nia Lia,' I say. I am Lia. 'N'kadi waji nikônawakwanawak.' I want to go home.

Henceforth it shall be the policy of the state to prevent procreation of idiots, imbeciles, feebleminded or insane persons, when the public welfare, and the welfare of idiots, imbeciles, feebleminded or insane persons likely to procreate, can be improved by voluntary sterilization as herein provided.

– 'An Act for Human Betterment by Voluntary Sterilization,' *Laws of Vermont*, 31st Biennial Session (1931), No. 174, p. 194

'I'm thinking about caramelized onions,' Ruby says.

She sits on a chair beside my bed, my only visitor. Outside, on one of the trees in the backyard, a bird is making a nest. A red thread unwinds from its beak, like a magician doing sleight-of-hand with a handkerchief. 'Fine.'

There is nothing sharp in my bedroom. Nothing I could swallow or use to string myself up. I know, because Spencer has had Ruby canvass the space. What he doesn't understand is that I will not try to kill myself, not yet. Just in case, just in case . . . oh, I cannot finish the sentence, and jinx it.

Ruby flips through another cookbook. 'Or else, a pepper crust.'

'Yes,' I say. 'Wonderful.'

Ruby frowns. 'Miz Pike, I can't put them *both* on the roast.'

Spencer is not a tyrant. When he comes home from work, he takes me out for a walk on the edge of our property. He buys me books. He brings me dinner himself, and holds bits of chicken and potato up to my lips as if we are on a picnic. He brushes my hair for me, long lean strokes that make me forget where we are and who I am. But in the morning, when he leaves, he turns the key in the bedroom door. And the only person I see, until he comes home again, is Ruby.

I drag my attention toward her. 'You said you need two roasts, for that many guests. Do one of each.' *Or serve it raw. I don't care.*

'We don't have room in the icebox for two roasts, plus a dessert. Some of it, I'll have to store in the icehouse.' Ruby makes a note to her checklist. 'What do you think about a seven-layer cake? Or baked Alaska?'

Her words blend together at the edges. I turn away. The robin has woven the thread through the rest of his nest. It looks like a line of blood.

Why go to all that trouble, when soon he will be flying south for the winter?

'Miz Pike.' Ruby sighs. 'Miz Pike?'

The robin is no more than ten feet away from where I am. I have no idea how to get from here to there.

Ruby touches my hand. 'Cissy?'

'Go away,' I tell her, and pull the covers over my head.

> When a Doctor wants a boat
> On the broad highway to float
> He will find a place where sapheads congregate
> He will chase them to a shed
> And at fifty bucks a head
> He will freeze his conscience out and mutilate.

> – E. F. Johnstone's 'Authority to Mutilate,'
> from newspaper clippings on sterilization,
> Henry F. Perkins Faculty File, UVM archives

By the third day of my imprisonment, I have stopped bothering to dress myself. I lay on the bed with my hair a rat's nest, my nightgown hiked high. Ruby has gone to the butcher's, Spencer is at the university. The radio warbles band music that beats like my baby's heart.

When I hear the lock turn, at first I wonder how Ruby has made it back from town so quickly. But even the way Gray Wolf moves through a room is different from anyone else. I sit up, unable to speak as he kneels beside the bed and embraces me. 'You told him?'

'No.' He smells of the outdoors. I drink him in.

'He locked you in for something *else?*' Gray Wolf says, shocked.

Before I can explain, he starts speaking, his words tumbling like avalanche stones to land at our feet. 'When you didn't show up, I thought maybe you had listened to me after all about staying away.'

'I wouldn't—'

'But it came to me pretty quick that you would still say good-bye. And when you didn't come, not that day, or the next . . . I went into town. No one there had seen you, either. And then, with the camp . . .'

'What about it?'

He looks at me. 'There is no camp, anymore. After I was in town overnight, I came back to a ghost town. Empty tents, laundry hanging, toys scattered on the ground – like everyone had left in a hurry, right in the middle of everything.'

'Why would they go without taking their things?'

'Because someone made them,' Gray Wolf says flatly.

I think about the old woman who smoked in front of her tent while weaving sweetgrass baskets. About the toddler who drew in the dirt with a stick, and cried when a puppy ruined her artwork. About the girls who giggled behind their hands at the smooth-chested boys. Had they been rounded up? Put into institutions and sterilized? Killed?

'When you went missing . . . and then so did everyone else . . .'

He squeezes my hand. 'Well, a person's got to have a lot of anger in him to do that much harm.'

I realize what he is implying. 'You're wrong,' I tell Gray Wolf. 'Spencer would never hurt anyone like that.'

'Not even if he found out the truth?'

We stare at each other, a stalemate, until a voice in the doorway breaks our concentration. 'And what truth would that be?' Spencer asks softly.

He stands with the gun from the pantry, pointed straight at Gray Wolf. 'You son of a bitch,' he says. 'I saw you break into the house. I thought you were here to steal something, and I was going to catch you red-handed.' He looks at our joined hands. 'But you didn't have to steal a goddamn thing, did you? It was handed to you on a silver platter.'

'Spencer, stop!'

Before I can get to my feet Gray Wolf has lunged for Spencer, knocking the gun out of his hand. Spencer wrestles him onto the ground, pinning him. He has the advantage of youth and rage; his fist pounds into Gray Wolf's face until blood runs from his nose and mouth and his eyes roll up in his head.

I pull at Spencer's arm and he flings me away, so that I fall onto my side. A sharp pain runs beneath my belly and around my back; I wince. 'Please! Let him go!'

Spencer hauls Gray Wolf to his feet by the collar of his shirt. 'The only reason I won't kill you is because that would bring me down to your level,' he pants, dragging my real father down the stairs. I follow them, slipping on the blood, trying to ignore the pain shooting up my spine. When Spencer opens the door to toss Gray Wolf out Ruby is on the other side of it. She takes one look at the battered face and screams, dropping her sack of groceries on the porch.

'Lia.' Gray Wolf twists in Spencer's hold. 'Come with me.'

The baby seizes inside me, reminding me of the answer I have to give. 'I can't.'

Spencer shoves him so that he flies off the porch, landing face-first on the ground. 'If you are still in Comtosook tomorrow,' he vows, 'I will make sure you spend the rest of your life at the State Prison. Say good-bye to your lover, Cissy.'

'He's not my lover!' I cry, but my voice splits apart on the words. Spencer turns just in time to see me double over, to watch my water break like a lake on the floor.

> The immediate need is to lessen the distress of body or mind in those about us. Common humanity calls for that. . . . [n]o hamlet is so small as to be exempt and every state and town has problems of its own concerning its unfortunate, its underprivileged, its handi-capped. . . . How can a community, after caring to the best of its abilities for those who suffer from devastating ills, proceed to govern itself in such a way as to better its chances for the future?
>
> – H. F. Perkins, 'Eugenic Aspects,' Vermont Commission on Country Life, *Rural Vermont: A Program for the Future*, 1931

So this is how my mother died: cracked wide as a hinged jaw, pressing a century between her legs, unable to breathe for fear of what might come next. Fire races from my back to my belly, and my insides wring tighter with every contraction. Ruby, just as scared as I am, whimpers at the foot of the bed, hoping to catch a miracle in her outstretched hand.

It is too early – for this baby to come, and for me to leave.

I have been in labor for eleven hours. All this time, Ruby has been by my side. And Spencer has been in his study, drinking. I do not know if he called Dr DuBois. I am afraid to hear the answer, either way.

'Ruby,' I call out, and she comes to my side. 'You listen to me. You promised me that you'd take care of this baby.'

'You'll be able to—'

'I won't.' I know it, too – my sight waffles gray at the edges;

my arms are so weak I cannot move them. 'Tell him about me. Tell him I loved – oh, God!' I break off as another contraction tightens its hold on my belly. Everything inside me spirals low, and I hike myself up to let it happen. 'Ruby,' I whisper. 'Now.'

My vision goes crimson and the ocean beats in my ears. My body is a tide, and I am swept away in pain, in rapture. I open my eyes and expect to see my mother, waiting for me now that I am on the other side, but instead I find myself looking into the face of my baby.

My baby *daughter*.

I have spent so long certain that giving birth will be the death of me; I have been sure that this child I carried was a boy. Yet neither of these things has come to pass. In one breathless second, my entire world has been turned inside out.

She cries, the sweetest sound I have ever heard. As Ruby delivers the placenta and cuts the cord, diapers and swaddles the baby, Spencer bursts into the room. His eyes are an unholy red; he reeks of whiskey. 'You're all right,' he says hoarsely. 'Cissy, God, you're all right.' Then he notices the tightly wrapped infant in Ruby's arms.

'Mr Pike,' she says. 'Come see your little girl.'

'Girl?' He shakes his head; this cannot be.

I hold out my arms and Ruby gives her over. I think of my mother, who did not feel the bliss of this. Now that I have felt this baby, heard her, it seems impossible to think I would have willingly ended my life without watching her live her own. There will be the moment she smiles for me, the moment she strikes out on unsteady legs, the first haircut, the first school day, the first kiss. How could I miss any of that?

I tuck her into the crook of my arm. After eighteen years of struggling to find my place in this world, I realize that I've always belonged right here, holding fast to my daughter.

'Her name is Lily,' I announce.

Spencer comes closer and glances down at our baby. At her face – dark as a nut, round as the moon, with the flat features of her grandfather's people.

When Spencer looks at me, I realize that he has been hoping this baby would be a fresh start, instead of fuel for the fire. 'Lily,' he repeats, and swallows.

'Spencer, it's not what you think. Gray Wolf – that man – he's my *father*. You know how heredity works . . . you understand why she looks the way she does. But she's yours, Spencer, you have to believe me.'

Spencer shakes his head. 'Dr DuBois said you might be irrational after giving birth . . . We should call him, to come look after you.' He lifts the baby out of my arms and turns to Ruby, his eyes flat, his voice even. 'Why don't you take the car and find him, Ruby?'

'Take the . . . ?' She has never driven the Packard, but she knows better than to talk back to Spencer right now. 'Yes, sir,' Ruby murmurs, and she sidles past him.

Spencer starts to follow her, still carrying the baby.

'No,' I call out. 'Spencer, I want to hold her.'

He stares at me for so long that I imagine he is seeing our history like a movie, looped to lead up to this point. His eyes shine with tears. But then he pulls up a chair beside the bed and sits in it, holding Lily so that I can see her face. He smiles a little, and for just a moment I let myself believe that Spencer might come to understand it is not blood that connects a family, but the love between its members. 'You rest, Cissy,' he tells me. 'I'll take care of her.'

We pay full price for the virtues our culture develops at any particular period. . . . The very ethnic and religious prejudices which still live in the community may be forged into the tools by which a demagogue can further divide the population and stultify human development.

– Elin Anderson, *We Americans:*
A Study of Cleavage in an American City, 1937

In my mind's eye, I am running. The rain sluices over my face and muddies my feet and yet I know I have to get away from whoever is chasing me. When I look over my shoulder I see him – the same man who has been in my other dreams, with the long brown hair and quiet eyes. He calls out my name, and I turn again, and a moment later he trips and sprawls across the ground. I stop to make sure he has not hurt himself and then I see it – the tombstone with my name on it, the tombstone that I have run right through.

Jerking awake, I feel something heavy on my thigh. Spencer is draped across my lap. At first I think he is asleep and then I realize he is sobbing. His eyes are so bloodshot it frightens me, and his skin gives off the steam of alcohol.

'Cissy,' he says, rising. 'You're awake.'

My body feels as if it has been beaten for days. My legs are too tender to shift on the mattress. Someone – Spencer? – has pressed cold compresses between my thighs to stanch the bleeding. 'Lily,' I ask. 'Where is she?'

Spencer takes my hand and raises it to his lips. 'Cissy.'

'Where is my baby?' I push myself up in the bed.

'Cissy, the baby – she was too young. Her lungs . . .'

I go perfectly still.

'The baby died, Cissy.'

'Lily!' I scream. I try to get off the bed, but Spencer holds me down.

'You couldn't have done anything. No one could have.'

'Dr DuBois—'

'He's doing a surgery in Vergennes. Ruby left word for him to come as soon as he gets home. But by the time she came back the baby was . . .'

'Don't say it,' I threaten. 'Don't you *dare* say it.'

He is crying too. 'She died in my arms. She died while I was holding her.'

All I want is my baby. 'I have to see her.'

'You can't.'

'I have to see her!'

'Cissy, she's been buried. I did it.'

I throw myself out from beneath the covers and hit Spencer in the chest, the arms, the head. 'You wouldn't. You *wouldn't!'*

He grabs my wrists hard, pulls me back, shakes me. 'We couldn't have baptized her. We couldn't have buried her in conse-crated ground.' A sob rounds from his throat. 'I thought, if you saw her, you would try to follow her. I can't lose you, too. Jesus, Cissy, what did you want me to do?'

It takes a moment for his words to sink it. We couldn't have baptized her, we couldn't have buried her in the church graveyard, because to Spencer she was illegitimate. Spencer gathers me into his arms while I am still stiff with shock. 'Sweetheart,' he whispers, 'no one has to know.'

My eyes burn, my throat aches. 'How about the next time I have a baby, Spencer, and it looks the same way? How many Gypsies will you accuse me of sleeping with before you realize I'm telling you the truth? Before you send me off to an institu-tion to be sterilized?' I shake my head. 'My mother fell in love with an Indian. Blame her for that, not me. All I ever did wrong was fall in love with you.'

How does it feel, I want to ask, *to find yourself at the bottom of one of your own genealogy charts?* But instead I pick up the swad-dling blanket at the foot of the bed. 'Take me to the grave.'

'You're too upset. You need to—'

'I *need* to see my daughter's grave. Now.'

Spencer stands up. He picks up from a tray beside the bed the scissors Ruby used to cut the umbilical cord, a knife she had sterilized just in case. He tucks these into his breast pocket, for safekeeping. 'Tomorrow,' he promises, and then he kisses my forehead. 'Cissy. Let's start over.'

I stare at him so long that everything inside me goes to

stone. 'All right, Spencer,' I answer, in a voice that sounds much like the woman I used to be. My hands are shaking in my lap, but I can play his game. I am already thinking of my next move.

In the voelkisch State the voelkisch view of life has finally to succeed in bringing about that nobler era when men see their care no longer in the better breeding of dogs, horses and cats, but rather in the uplifting of mankind itself, an era in which the one knowingly and silently renounces, and the other gladly gives and sacrifices.

– Adolph Hitler, *Mein Kampf*, from Volume II, written in prison in 1924 prior to the 1933 'Law for Protection Against Genetically Defective Offspring' passed as part of the Nazi Racial Hygiene Program

Lily isn't dead. Now that I have thought about it, this is the only way it can be – why else would Spencer refuse to show me the body, the coffin, the grave? A hundred scenarios have run through my mind: he has hidden her until he has a chance to leave her on the steps of a church; he gave her to Ruby to bring to the orphanage; he is waiting for Dr DuBois to come and spirit her away. Another reason I did not die in childbirth: it is my responsibility to find my baby.

I wait until I am certain Spencer has closeted himself in his study again and then I get dressed. It is slow going – my head is heavy with fever and my legs shaky. I slip Gray Wolf's pipe into the pocket of my dress and double-knot my boots – above all, I have to be ready to run away. I turn the knob of the door with the care of a military spy and creep into the hall.

My first stop is the bathroom. Quietly I rummage through the clothing hamper; I check inside the tub. I even force myself to look in the tank of the toilet. When I cannot find her I go to

Ruby's room on the third floor, and empty the insides of the closet and drawers, mess the bed, toss the shelves. By the time I finish I need to sit down.

Think, I command. *Think like Spencer.*

On the ground level of the house I sneak from small cubby to cornerhole, peeking in places too small to fit anything but a sleeping newborn. I take care to tiptoe around Spencer's study, where the clink of glasses places him at the sideboard. By the time I reach the kitchen I am on the verge of tears. She must be hungry by now; she must be cold. *Cry, and I will find you.*

I will carry her tight against my chest; I will keep her warm. On the way to Canada, I will tell her of the sights we pass – the cows marooned in fields, the violet fireweed exploding along the road, the mountains that curve like the line of a woman's body. We will stand beside Gray Wolf at the settlement at Odonak when he is asked, 'Who are you?' so that he can point to the two of us.

I walk into the dark kitchen, thinking of the wine cabinet, the flour bins, the root cellar. There are twenty places alone to hide in this room. I have just taken a step inside the cool, black pantry when someone bumps into me from behind.

I stifle a scream and pull the cord above me to flood the room with light. Then everything comes clear. 'Ruby, what are you doing in here?'

She is shaking like an aspen leaf. 'Getting some . . . sometimes I can't sleep at night and I make myself a little cup of that fancy chocolate of yours. I'm sorry, Miz Pike. I know it's stealing.'

I narrow my eyes. 'Where is she?' My hands begin to run over the shelves, under stacks of clothes, pushing aside bins.

'Who?'

'The baby. You're helping him hide the baby.'

'Oh, Miz Pike,' she says, her eyes wide and wet. 'There is no more baby.'

'Ruby, you don't understand. She's fine, the baby is fine. I just have to find her. I have to find her, and I have to take her away from here.'

'But the professor, he said—'

I grab Ruby by the shoulders. 'Did you see a body? Did you?'

'I saw – I saw—' Ruby's teeth are chattering. She cannot cough out the answer I want.

'Dammit, Ruby, speak up!' I shake her a little harder, and she wrenches away from me, her arm striking a shelf lined with canned beets and beans. One jar tumbles to the checkerboard floor and shatters. As the pungent stink of vinegar spreads, I push aside bins of oatmeal and biscuit mix, soap flakes and powdered milk.

Strong hands pull me away from the shelf, into the main room of the kitchen. 'Let me go, Spencer,' I say, trying wildly to free myself.

He turns to Ruby. 'Call Dr DuBois's service again. Tell him we need him here *now*.'

'Let go of me! Ruby, he's lying. Let go of – Lily!' I scream. *'Lily!'*

It takes all Spencer's might to wrestle me out of the kitchen. Frozen, Ruby watches him drag me, screaming, up the stairs by my wrists. 'This is not any of your business, Ruby,' Spencer calls over my cries. 'You can see that Mrs Pike isn't herself now, and I'm going to make sure she calms down.' He grunts as one of my kicks lands squarely in his shin. 'Call the doctor. And then do what I asked you to do earlier.'

'Don't listen to him, Ruby!'

She seems to shrink before my eyes. 'Go,' Spencer bellows. 'Now!' Suddenly I go limp in his arms. He catches me before I hit the floor and carries me the rest of the way. I do not open my eyes, not even when he modestly checks the pad between my legs to make sure I have not hemorrhaged, not when he sighs like a man who has given up hope. Then Spencer tucks me into bed and removes my boots and locks the door firmly behind himself.

I do not consider this a failure.

After all, now I know that Lily is hidden outside.

Why not drop the whole works? . . . We have carried on for several
years and what have we accomplished? It was good fun as long
as we could afford it, but now it is a different matter. If Hitler
succeeds in his wholesale sterilization, it will be a demonstration
that will carry eugenics farther than a hundred Eugenics Societies
could. If he makes a fiasco of it, it will set the movement back
where a hundred eugenic societies can never resurrect it.

— Excerpt from a letter dated February 1, 1934, from Henry H.
      Goddard to H. F. Perkins, in response to financial assistance
      requests, ESV papers, Public Records Office, Middlesex, VT

The hardest part is breaking the glass. To do it soundlessly is
nearly impossible; I have to wrap the chair in the blanket from
the bed and hope that the fabric will muffle some of the sound.
I pick the window closest to the ladder that Gray Wolf, and then
Spencer, used to fix the roof. After that, it is almost too easy. To
shimmy down to the ground level, to sneak beneath the light in
Spencer's study window, to see by the midnight moon.

We have so many acres, and she could be anywhere.

I check beneath the shrubs that line the front porch, under
the porch itself, around the pile of firewood to the east. In back
of the house, I move through the forest, walking in circles, in
patterns, until finally I sit down on the ground and let myself
cry.

It's devastating, Spencer will tell Dr DuBois when he gets here.
*I found her digging in the dirt. No, it's not the first time she sleep-
walked . . . but this is the first time she could not snap out of it.* I
wonder if, at private mental institutions, they tie patients to
benches or drown them, like they did at Waterbury.

But is it crazy to search when you know there is something
to find?

I look back at the house. There is no light in Ruby's bedroom,
no silhouette in Spencer's study. I close my eyes and think of

whales and dolphins, bouncing sound off the bottom of the ocean.

When I blink again, the wall of the icehouse rises out of the black of the night. One sliver seems darker than the others – someone has left the door ajar again. I stand up, reeled by an invisible line into the chilled belly of the shed.

The soles of my boots slip on the sawdust. Luminous blocks of ice sit shoulder to shoulder, a glowing row of giant's teeth. There are Ruby's roasts, for the dinner party we will not have. And on a cutting block sits an old apple crate, with the top set off to the side.

Inside is the smallest, stillest doll I have ever seen.

'No. *No*. Oh, no.' I grip the rough edge of the crate, tiny coffin, and look down at the face of my baby.

Her eyelashes are as long as my pinky nail. Her cheeks are a pale, milky blue. Her fist, impossibly small, is curled tight as a snail. With one finger I touch her dimpled jaw, her embryo ear. 'Lily,' I whisper. 'Lily Delacour Pike.'

In this frozen nursery, I lift my daughter from her cradle. I wrap her blanket tighter, to keep her warm. I rock her against my breast, so that she can hear my heart break.

Spencer cannot take her away from me. To do that, I would have to agree to let go.

Awani Kia, I think. In this other world, they will ask her who she is. 'You tell them about your grandma, and your grandpa, who built a bridge out of love,' I say against her skin. 'You tell them about your father, who thought he was doing the right thing. And you tell them about me.' I kiss her, letting my lips rest for a moment. 'You tell them I'm coming.'

Then I put my daughter back in her crib and press my fist against my mouth to hold in all the sorrow. I will spend forever wondering if Spencer told me the truth, or only half. If Lily stopped breathing in his arms, or if he made sure of it. Maybe one day he will explain: *I only did it because I loved you.*

'Me too,' I say aloud.

Soon Spencer will wake and come looking for me. And I will make him pay for this. There are ways to show the authorities what really happened. I will do what it takes, even if it kills me.

There isn't much time. So I reach into the crate again, where my baby's face fits in the palm of my hand. Her nose and her chin push up against it, a memory to carry. 'Sleep well,' I tell her, and I move to the doorway of the icehouse.

I think of Madame Soliat at the Fourth of July, with her wolf dog and her tent. I think of her shaking out her many-colored coat on the banks of the lake where she lived for a summer. *Don't be afraid,* she told me. Among other things.

I do not need a fortune-teller anymore. I know what comes next.

Part Three

2001

The dead continue to converse with the living.

– Thomas Hardy

8

On nights that Az Thompson didn't work at the quarry, he spent hours cleaving through the barnacled facts that cluttered his head. Live a century, and you know a lot of things: how to navigate by starlight, what to say to a grieving widow, where bear hide in the winter. Under all this flotsam you could scrape down to the barest truths – that, for example, it was not blood you passed down to your children, but courage. That you might find love in the most unlikely places – under stones in the shallows of the river, at the bottom of a bowl of shelled peas. That even when you least expected it, you could go on.

Doctors called it insomnia, but Az knew better. He didn't go to sleep because then he didn't have to wake up and wonder why he hadn't died overnight. He'd read of Egyptian kings and Ponce de León and Tithonus, who had tried so hard to live forever. But what good was eternity, when you outlived everyone you loved? When you watched your body fall apart piece by piece, like a rusting automobile, even though your mind could snap like lightning? These fools with their elixirs and their golden tombs . . . he would shake his head and think, *Be careful what you wish for.*

Az was tired at the cellular level, but he didn't lie down on his cot. Instead he watched the raindrops charge the roof of his tent like an old-time picture show. In another four hours, the sun would rise, and he would still be here.

Suddenly, he heard a cry. It seemed to come simultaneously from both the distant forest and inside Az himself, an ache more than a sound. He wondered if it were possible to throw one's emotion so that it spoke back to you, a ventriloquism of pain.

There – the sound, again.

It wasn't thunder. It was too deep for a child, too guttural for a woman. No, this was the requiem of a man who had lost so much he could no longer find himself. Someone like . . . well, himself.

Az sighed. He didn't believe in a lot of mystical bullshit – that was the province of New Age wanna-be Indians, in his opinion – but he also knew that your past could return in a number of disguises, from the shrill whistle of an owl to the eyes of a stranger that followed you down the street. And he knew better than anyone that turning your back on your own history only made it that much easier to be blindsided.

Then again, it could just be some guy who'd tripped in the dark and hurt himself.

Either way, Az thought wearily, he was going to have to go see.

Ross sat on the floor of the tent with Az Thompson's Hudson Bay blanket wrapped around his shoulders. His pants and shirt were thick with mud. His wet hair dripped into his eyes as he sipped the instant coffee the old man had made with a battery-powered immersion heater. He could not seem to stop shaking, although this had nothing to do with the dampness that soaked through to his core. No, that was due to a woman who smelled of roses. A woman who – *say it,* he demanded silently – he had fallen in love with. A woman who was not alive.

'You all right?' Az asked.

You look like you've seen a ghost.

Ross couldn't answer. He bent his head to the mug and took a swallow of coffee that burned his throat. It brought tears to his eyes.

He had watched as her skin went translucent, as the trees grew

more solid than Lia herself. He had seen the shock on her face
when she looked down at the gravestone and saw her own name.
She hadn't been aware, any more than Ross had. Ross, who had
studied the paranormal, who understood that a demon carried a
rotten stench and that a poltergeist drew its energy from a teenage
girl, had not known the simple fact that a ghost could kiss you
back.

Ghosts were not the norm. They were the ones who, for one
reason or another, still had one foot in this world and could not
seem to shake it free. Ross had heard Curtis Warburton speak of
ghosts who return to avenge their own demise, and ghosts who
came back because they'd forgotten to pay the electric bill. Ross
remembered Curtis telling stories about ghosts who'd returned
for a love they'd left behind.

Could a ghost return for a love she had not yet met?

The cot creaked as Az sank down onto it. He folded his hands
on his lap and stared at Ross, his black eyes burning. 'You want
to talk about it?' Az asked quietly.

Ross shook his head. He couldn't. The words, the memory:
that was all he had left of her.

Eli waited on the couch while Shelby Wakeman was upstairs
dressing. He sat on the left-hand side, but then worried he might
look too comfortable slung over the arm when she got back, and
moved into the middle, twirling his uniform hat in his hands
until she stepped into the room and took all the air away just
like that.

'I'm sorry; I don't usually answer the door without a chance
to titivate.'

'I beg your pardon?' Eli swallowed. 'Titi-what?'

'Spruce up.' Shelby smiled uncomfortably and sat down across
from Eli, tucking her hair behind her ears. 'You're sure Ross
isn't . . . in trouble?'

'Not with me,' Eli assured her. Like everyone else who received a police visit in the dead of night, she'd assumed the worst. If Eli had been thinking clearly, he might even have waited until morning. But he'd been so intent on the puzzle he'd unraveled with Frankie's DNA report that he needed someone who might be able to help him put the pieces together. Gray Wolf's DNA was not on that rope, but it did not necessarily exonerate him from a murder charge. Spencer Pike's DNA *might* be on the rope, but that didn't necessarily incriminate him. The question was, who had actually killed Cissy Pike? And was she the only victim that night?

Eli tried to remind himself of this, and that the reason he had come to this house had nothing to do with the fact that, against all reason, Shelby Wakeman had slipped into his subconscious for the past three weeks. She smelled of apples, just like his bedroom did in the mornings after he dreamed of her. She looked even more lovely in person. He found himself reaching out a hand toward hers before he remembered to stop himself.

Eli cleared his throat. 'I, um, I believe your brother might have some useful information about a case.'

She shook her head. 'I doubt it. Ross doesn't get out very much, and lately when he has, he's been working.'

'Ghost hunting,' Eli stated.

'Yes.' Shelby lifted her face. 'You must think he's crazy.'

Eli started to nod, to tell her that yes, he could not in his wildest imagination picture spending your life looking for something that seemed only to exist previously in your mind. But then he stared at her sea green eyes and the place where her chin came to too sharp a point, and he felt every inch of skin on his body tighten. 'I don't know what I think,' he managed.

Heat rushed Shelby's face, and she stood abruptly, muttering something that sounded like *xerothermic* as she struggled to raise a window that was stuck. 'Here,' Eli said, and he went to help her. They stood side by side at the sash, their shoulders touching.

Eli yanked the window up with too much force, and a cool draft fell like a guillotine between them.

'Thank you.'

Eli stared at her. 'My pleasure.'

Whatever else Eli was going to say – and at that moment he truly could not have formed words, much less the letters of his own name – was lost in a hail of footsteps bounding down the stairs. 'I'm sorry. I didn't know anyone was asleep upstairs.'

'Ethan wasn't asleep,' Shelby said, as the boy came into the room. He was a small kid, skinny, wearing far too many damn clothes for this time of year. A hat shaded his eyes, but even with his face half-covered Eli could see how the boy's skin was as milky as china. One hand was bandaged, and the other was blistered in spots, as if it had been plunged into boiling water. He had his mother's skittish smile.

'Ethan, you can go out,' Shelby ordered.

'But it's raining—'

'Not anymore. *Go.*' She waited until the door closed and the throaty roll of skateboard wheels scraped the driveway. Then she turned to Eli and crossed her arms, a completely different woman from the one he'd seen moments ago. 'That's my son.'

Eli watched her fingers bite into the skin of her own arms. Her posture was so rigid he thought she might snap in half.

'You're thinking there's something wrong with him,' she accused.

He wanted to run his hand down her spine. He wanted to hold her between his palms until she went soft again. 'Actually,' Eli said, 'I was thinking he looked like you.'

The sound was as round as a nut, as tiny as a pebble, but it rang in Spencer Pike's skull. No matter how many pillows he piled over his head, he could hear the cry of that baby. Spencer writhed, scratching at his ears until blood ran into the collar of his pajamas.

'Mr Pike! Oh, sweet Jesus. I need some help in here!' the nurse screamed into the intercom.

It took two orderlies to pull Spencer's arms down to his sides and secure them to the bed with straps, like they did with Joe Gigapoulopous, the delusional man two doors down from Spencer who tried to eat his own fingers every now and then. 'The baby,' Spencer gasped, as the nurse dabbed at the deep furrows around his ears. 'Get rid of the goddamned baby.'

'There is no baby here. You must have been having a nightmare.'

By now, tears were streaming down his face. That sound, it was splitting his head in two. Why couldn't they hear it? 'The baby,' he sobbed.

The nurse injected him with a tranquilizer. 'This will help.'

But it wouldn't. It would put him to sleep, where that baby would be waiting for him. He lay very still, staring at the ceiling, as the drug slid through his system. He felt his hands relax, and then his legs, and finally his jaw fell slack. 'When will I die?' Spencer thought, but it turned out he had spoken aloud.

The nurse stared at him, her brown eyes steady. Cissy had had brown eyes. 'Soon,' she said gently.

Spencer sighed. Her answer was more powerful than this sedative; it eased him like no medication ever could. Truth could do that to a man.

Men, Meredith figured, were an accessory, like a belt or purse or shoes. You didn't necessarily need one to complete your look. Granted, if you walked around barefoot you got a few odd stares every now and then, but the important parts of you were covered. And after a string of meeting men she really didn't want, and wanting men she couldn't seem to meet, the scientist in Meredith had simply said to cut her losses.

She was driving home, now, at nearly 11 P.M. The commute from the office – forty-five minutes, without traffic – was the only time of her day when she let the gates free in her mind and allowed herself to reflect on anything but the task at hand. Tonight, by studying cells from four viable blastospheres belonging to a family carrying sickle-cell anemia, Meredith had avoided accompanying a colleague to a dinner honoring cutting-edge scientific companies. Martin was definitely her type – tall and cerebral, with the long fingers of a researcher. In her first year of working at Generra, Meredith's crush on Martin was so severe that sometimes after speaking to him at the copy machine she'd have to hide in the bathroom until her cheeks stopped flaming. Her prayers were answered a year ago, or so she thought, when her boss sent her to a funding dinner with Martin, who drank enough champagne to float a horse and introduced both her and her breasts to the master of ceremonies.

It was raining up and down the whole East Coast, or at least that was Meredith's guess from the ache in her leg. Her left one – the one she'd been having set in an ER when she was told the news about Lucy's existence – was as good a barometer as any meteorologist's tool. As she got off at her exit, she drew her thoughts away from her nonexistent love life and focused instead on Lucy, who had been taken off the Risperdal but hadn't shown any signs of improvement. If anything, her daughter had gotten more fanciful – speaking at the breakfast table to people who were not there, buckling the seat belt beside her around nothing at all. Meredith was an aficionado of scientific fact, but told herself that her daughter was genetically predisposed to fiction. She, who had made a living out of defining 'normal,' had broadened the category so that it would include Lucy.

She pulled into the driveway. The only light on in the house was in the parlor; everyone had already gone to sleep. Meredith got out of the car stiffly and put her weight on her good leg. For a moment she stopped breathing, struck by the sheer beauty of a night littered with stars. She spent so much time looking at the most minute elements of humanity that she sometimes forgot how simple the world could be.

Meredith let herself in with her key and found Lucy on the

stairs, fully dressed and staring straight ahead, a suitcase at her feet. 'Luce?' she said, but her daughter didn't respond.

'She can't hear you.'

Ruby was descending the steps. Her long white hair was a cloud behind her; her hands clutched the banister for support. 'She's sleepwalking.'

Sleepwalking? Lucy's eyes were open. 'Are you sure?' Meredith asked her grandmother. 'Did you ever sleepwalk?'

Ruby bent toward Lucy and helped her to her feet. 'I used to know someone who did.'

Lucy followed Ruby upstairs, docile as a lamb. Meredith went after them, and tripped over the forgotten suitcase. It fell open at her feet, spilling its contents. Inside were dozens of dolls – dolls that ate or cried or swam, dolls Lucy had not played with for a few years, dolls that stared up at Meredith with their glassy eyes like so many broken babies.

There is a feeling that runs like a current through the heart when you pull up to the house that holds people you love and see a police cruiser sitting outside. Ross barely slammed his car into park before racing up the driveway and throwing open the door, shouting Shelby's name.

She stood up immediately. 'Ross!' He looked at her and at Ethan, who'd come up from behind Ross, on his skateboard, and then he looked at the cop standing in the living room.

Belatedly, he became aware of Shelby taking in his ruined clothes and wet hair. She must have called the police because she was worried about him – something his sister would definitely do. 'It looks worse than it is,' Ross said, thinking that if she could see how scarred he was on the *inside* she'd be horrified. 'But I'm fine. You can call off the search party.'

At that, Eli Rochert stepped forward. 'Actually,' he said, 'I came here asking you to join it.'

*   *   *

Ross wanted to be in his bedroom at Shelby's place, with the lights off and a bottle of Jameson's at his side, as he carved Lia's name into his arm with the tongue of a knife. Maybe he would bleed, maybe it would hurt – although Ross would bet on neither of these. He knew what no one else seemed to be able to figure out – he was already dead; his body just hadn't caught up to the rest of him.

Sitting in the interrogation room at the Comtosook Police Department with Eli Rochert and his behemoth dog, he supposed, offered torture of a different sort. Scattered across the conference table were evidentiary pictures of Lia's body after the hanging, boots she had worn, even the dress that she'd been wearing when she appeared to him. Seeing each of these was a cut deeper than any Ross could have made himself.

'You, uh, said when we last met that you had started to investigate the history of Cecelia Pike's death,' Eli said.

'Lia,' Ross murmured. 'She likes to be called Lia.'

The cop resisted rolling his eyes, but just barely. *Well, fuck him,* Ross thought. *I don't want to be here either.*

'You . . . saw her, then?' Eli asked.

'You're not going to believe me if I say I did, so why are you even asking?'

'Look. I'm not crazy about consulting a psychic—'

'I'm not a psychic,' Ross interrupted. 'Sensitive, maybe.'

'Jeez, no matter what you're doing in this state, it always comes back to Civil Unions.'

'Not *that* kind of sensitive.' Ross couldn't stand it anymore; he turned over one gruesome autopsy photo of Lia so that it was no longer visible. 'The kind of person who's receptive to spirits. *This* one, in particular.'

Eli hesitated before speaking. 'Mr Wakeman, a week ago, you begged me to reopen a seventy-year-old case. Against my better judgment, I did. And I'm interested enough to keep digging, even though it's something I have to do on my own time, instead of the department's.' He flattened his hands on the table. 'You indicated there might be foul play involving Spencer Pike. What made you say that?'

'The Abenaki claim to the land. Pike's absolute fit when I brought it up. And the fact that there was a ghost at all – from everything I've been taught, ghosts only come back for a reason. I assumed that if there was a ghost on the property, it was a Native American – maybe even the one accused of murder. But the one I found turned out to be Lia.' He turned away. 'I'm sorry you wasted your time.'

'It may not have been a waste,' Eli said. 'According to what you just told me, if Lia Pike came back as a ghost, then something about her death probably didn't sit right.'

Her face flashed in front of Ross's eyes, and he got to his feet, intent on leaving before he fell apart in front of this cop. 'Being murdered when you're eighteen usually *doesn't* sit right. Now, if you'll excuse me, Officer Rochert . . .'

'Can I show you something, before you go?' Eli handed Ross a piece of paper, one he recognized as a crime-scene report dated from the 1930s. 'Pike says Gray Wolf hanged her. According to the officers on the scene, there was sign of a struggle. There are photos of the porch where the body was found hanging, photos of footprints, photos of a broken window in the master bedroom. I've got DNA matching the victim's blood, plus DNA from two different males who were also placed at the scene.'

Ross swallowed around the brick in his throat. 'Sounds like you're well on your way to proving Pike right.'

Eli continued as if Ross had not spoken at all. 'But there's also evidence that doesn't add up. Things that make me wonder if you aren't right about Spencer Pike getting rid of Gray Wolf. And possibly his own wife.'

'Listen.' The room was swimming in front of Ross. 'I can't talk about this right now.'

'I don't want you to talk. I want you to help.'

Ross looked up. 'I'm not a detective.'

'No,' Eli agreed quietly. 'But you apparently know how to find things the rest of us can't see.'

SEARCH INVENTORY: Pike Homicide, Sept. 19, 1932

SEIZED FROM THE ICEHOUSE PORCH:
Noose, cut
Leather pouch
Pipe
Photographs: sawdust on porch w/footprints, body cut down

SEIZED FROM VICTIM:
Boots
Dress
Underwear/sanitary napkin
Photographs: autopsy

SEIZED FROM MASTER BEDROOM:
Photographs: broken glass window
Photographs: interior of house – ransacked
List of names – dinner party following week
Sheets, pillows, coverlet, nightgown – stained
Swaddling blankets
Metal basin

By the time Ross got home, it was daybreak. He walked inside, thanking a God he no longer believed in that Shelby did not seem to be around. Making a beeline upstairs, he shut the door of his room behind him, crawled into bed fully clothed, and finally let himself go to pieces.

Most of the time when Ross thought about his life, he imagined living it alone. The very concept of a family did not appear to be in the cards for him. He was not commitment-shy, or unattractive, or too free-spirited to settle; but whenever he tried to give his heart away, he found himself holding it out to a person who was no longer there.

There were women. The waitress in Duluth who took him home with the extra beef stew one night; the soccer mom who had never been told by her businessman husband that she was worthy of more than that life; the scarred breast-cancer survivor who had to be reminded how beautiful she still was. But these were women who needed him for a night or two, who dropped him the moment they saw how much Ross needed *them*. After all, who could love someone like him – a man who sometimes could not get out of bed even though he had not slept for weeks, a man who had tried to kill himself so many times that he believed he was invincible, a man who could not even love himself?

Ross pulled a pillow over his head. He wanted a woman who would feel about him the way he felt about her – as if she'd been missing something until they met, willing to give up everything to follow him from one world to another, certain that every disastrous second she'd spent alone had only been leading up to this moment.

He wanted a woman who did not exist.

There was a knock on his door, which Ross ignored. Maybe Shelby would think he was asleep. He ducked further beneath the covers.

'Hey.' She sat down on the edge of the bed, her hand resting gently on the blanket covering his shoulder. 'I know you're not asleep.'

He tugged down the blanket. 'How?'

'Because you *never* sleep.'

'There's always a first time,' Ross said.

He watched Shelby pleat the edge of the sheet into a fan, then let it fall apart. 'What did the police want?'

'Nothing.'

'He came all the way here, and took you all the way to the station, for nothing?'

'Leave me alone, Shelby. If you want to be a mother, go practice on your son.'

'My son isn't the one who's crying.'

Ross touched his fingers to his cheeks – Christ, he hadn't even noticed. 'I can't do this now.'

'Ross, *talk* to me . . .'

He fell onto his back, his arm covering his eyes. 'Shel, look. I haven't found out that I have six weeks to live, unfortunately. I didn't commit a felony. I just had a really shitty night that made me remember why it's no use falling in love. So go back to your room or the library or wherever and let me lick my wounds, all right?'

'You got dumped by that woman you've been seeing?'

'I haven't been seeing anyone.' But he had. Just not in that way.

'Who is she?'

Ross came up on an elbow. 'She,' he said, 'is the ghost of a woman who was killed seventy years ago.' He had the satisfaction of watching Shelby's jaw drop, and he sank back onto the pillows. 'Exactly.'

'You saw a ghost?'

'I saw a ghost. I touched a ghost. I kissed a ghost.'

'You *kissed* a ghost?'

'I fell so hard for a ghost that everything inside me is still black and blue.'

'Ross, come on—'

'Don't, Shelby. Just don't. I'm absolutely, a hundred percent, totally aware of what did and did not happen to me out there.'

His voice was riding high, his eyes wild. 'Ross,' she said gently, 'there's no such thing as ghosts.'

He turned on her. 'How do you know? Maybe if you can't see something, it doesn't mean it's not out there. It only means your eyes aren't tuned quite right, or it's too well camouflaged, or you just haven't been lucky enough to find it yet.'

He was speaking of himself, but to Shelby, he might as well have been speaking of Ethan, and what the future might hold for the scientists searching for a cure to XP. She suddenly understood that whether or not Ross's ghost was real, right now, it was what he needed to believe. What he needed *her* to believe.

She had been there, herself.

Ross pressed the heels of his hands against his eyes. 'God, maybe I *am* crazy. Maybe I should have myself locked up.'

'You're no crazier than anyone else. We all do it.'

'See ghosts?'

'Fall for someone who doesn't exist.' Shelby stroked his hair. 'Infatuation's just another word for not seeing clearly. When you start to love a person – that's when they become real.'

Ross turned toward his sister on a sob. 'She left,' he choked out. 'She left me.'

Shelby bent low, kissed him on the crown of his head. 'Then find her,' she said.

Date: September 21, 1932
Time: 1:15 PM
Interview of: Mrs Wilmetta Sizemore
Interview by: Officer Duley Wiggs
Location: Comtosook Police Department

Q. When did you last see Cissy Pike?
A. At the Ethan Allen Club, a week ago, when we were having dinner with our spouses and her father, Harry Beaumont. I've known Cissy for years; she was the perfect wife, so enamored of Professor Pike and so clearly anticipating the birth of her baby.
Q. Was there anything unusual about her that night?
A. I don't think so . . . no, wait. There was a moment where poor

Cissy spilled a glass of wine. One of the help, a Gypsy boy, came over to assist but took liberties, touching Cissy's person while trying to clean up the mess. Professor Pike, well, he quite rightly ripped the waiter up one side and down the other. [Pause] I don't know the Gypsy boy's name. But you all might want to find out.

'God*damn*,' Eli said, when he heard the crash. He ran downstairs from the bathroom, half his face still lathered with shaving cream, to find Watson hiding under the coffee table. One quick look at the living room told him there either had been a recent B&E, or a 150-pound dog chasing something. The TV had been knocked off its stand, the pillows tossed from the couch, and one ladderback chair was now tipped over beside a broken window. Eli crouched down near the dog. 'Give it up.' He held out his hand, and Watson sheepishly opened his mouth so that the mouse dropped into it.

Eli tossed it out of the shattered window. 'Well, this is great, Watson. We can open a McDonald's drive-through in our very own home.' The dog's ears flattened. 'I suppose you're going to tell me it wasn't your fault. Oh, that's right, you're smarter than that. You're not going to say anything at all.'

The dog whined and snuffed his nose further into the carpet. Eli put the couch to rights, and then gently set the television back on its pedestal. This, at least, wasn't smashed. Sighing, he walked to the window and moved the chair that had broken it. A rainbow of shattered glass lined the sill, but since the window had been broken from the inside, most of the shards had landed somewhere in the azalea bushes.

Suddenly, he turned and charged up the stairs, this time with the dog at his heels. In his bedroom, Eli overturned a pile of folders on his nightstand until he found the manila envelope containing the crime-scene photos. The photographs taken after the Pike homicide were seventy years old, but they had been made with 4x5 negatives – still the best source around for excellent detail. Eli squinted at the shot taken inside Cissy Pike's bedroom. The focal point of the picture was the bed, but the window was just behind. Something sparkled on the sill. What about the floor?

Eli scratched his jaw, surprised to remember he was still covered with shaving cream. 'When I finish, Watson,' he said, 'we're going for a drive.'

Rod van Vleet put his face very close to Ross's. 'Let me get this straight,' he enunciated. 'You actually found a ghost?'

Ross nodded. 'Isn't that what you asked me to do?'

'No!' Rod threw up his hands and walked away. 'I asked you to come check out the property. I never actually expected you to *find* anything.' He sat down across from Ross in the narrow on-site trailer. 'So what am I supposed to do now? Douse the place with Holy Water? Wait until my foreman's head starts doing 360s?'

'It's not a demonic possession. Just a ghost.'

'Oh, well, fabulous,' Rod said. 'I'm glad you've cleared that up. And what do I do when it starts coming after my workers?'

'That probably won't happen. Curtis Warburton always said that ghosts tend to do their own thing.'

'Then she should be willing to move somewhere else.'

Ross shook his head. 'According to Curtis, human spirits only leave if they want to. If they're comfortable where they are, or emotionally tied to the place, or just stubborn, they don't budge.'

'*Curtis* said. According to *Curtis*. What do *you* think?'

For a long moment, Ross was silent. 'I don't really know anymore,' he said finally.

'Well, let me tell you what *I* think, then. If a judge happens to believe in this crap and thinks there's a spirit floating around here, I lose my permit to build. That means one of us is going to have to disappear . . . and for a nominal fee, I'm sure I can count on both of you to do that.'

The color drained from Ross's face. 'I can't make her leave.'

'Then I'll find someone who can.'

They stared at each other, and then, without another word, Ross slammed out of the trailer. Rod stood in the doorway and watched him go. The workers he passed didn't even bat an eye. Then again, they were being paid to do a job – and minor setbacks like frozen ground in August, or shovel handles that split at the touch of a hand, or nails that simply would not burrow straight, were all just a path to fat overtime checks. So he had a ghost in his strip mall. So what? Maybe he could even capitalize on it. Launch a breakfast café called 'Restaurant In Peace,' and sell boogels and scream cheese. When the press interviewed him, he'd deadpan and say the place was a great undertaking.

Or maybe . . . he wouldn't build a strip mall at all. New England was full of creepy old B&Bs stuffed to their dusty rafters with stories of hauntings. If he already had a ghost, why not build a hotel around it?

After, of course, he had found someone to officially evict the thing.

Just in case.

Rod whipped his cell phone out of his pocket and dialed 411. 'Angel Quarry,' a voice answered.

He checked the number, then hung up and redialed. When the operator picked up on the other end, Rod exhaled. In truth, he'd been expecting the quarry again. 'Yes,' he said. 'I'm trying to find a Mr Curtis Warburton.'

The Forensic Lab in Montpelier prioritized cases depending on severity. Which meant that although evidence from a homicide that needed processing might be returned in just a day's time, a simple burglary might not yield results for several weeks. Eli knew this well, which was why he was even now holding a conversation with Tuck Boorhies, a technician he'd worked with in the past. 'A murder?' Tuck said. 'In Comtosook?'

'That's right,' Eli said. He did not mention that the event had occurred seventy years ago.

Tuck took the print from Eli. 'Jeez. What's with the black-and-white?'

'Crime-scene photographer is a purist. How long is this going to take?'

'How long are you going to stand there breathing down my neck?' Tuck answered, but he scanned the print into the computer programmed with Adobe Photoshop. 'Now, what part do you want blown up?'

Eli showed him on the screen, and the computer zoomed into the bedroom window and the wooden floor in front of it. The technician punched buttons, highlighting the contrast between light and dark. 'What do you see?' Eli asked.

'A floor.'

'What do you see on the floor?'

'Nothing,' Tuck said.

Eli grinned. 'That's right.'

Ten minutes later, he had a print of this enlargement, as well as some others, including a zoom taken from a photograph shot outside the house below Cecelia Pike's window. There on the grass, near the feet of the ladder still propped against the house, were small winking chips that looked like broken glass. 'There's no glass inside,' Eli said to Watson, a half-hour later on the drive home, as the bloodhound panted beside him in the cab of the truck. 'But there *is* glass outside. That means no one took her out; she broke out. But if she was being abducted, why would she have broken out?'

Eli slowed as a car passed him. 'She wasn't abducted, that's why. She was running away. Why else would you go out the window, instead of using the bedroom door? Because you don't want someone to see you leaving. Or because you try going downstairs, and can't, since the bedroom door and window have been locked by someone trying to keep you there.'

He turned to the dog. 'Next question: why was the downstairs of the house wrecked? Pike says on the police report that Gray Wolf entered the bedroom through the broken window. If that's true, then he wouldn't walk downstairs with the victim to make his escape – he'd go out the way he came. Which means that house must have been tossed by someone else.' He thought about staging this crime, and what it might accomplish. Then Eli put on his blinker, turning off at the exit. 'All roads,' he said, 'lead to Spencer Pike.'

CORONER'S REPORT
CAUSE OF DEATH: HANGING
MANNER OF DEATH: SUICIDE
Significant associated findings:
Recent childbirth, at or near term.

EXTERNAL EXAMINATION
External exam: The body is that of a well-developed well-nourished white female who appears the stated age. Hair is blond. Irides are brown. Pupils are equal and measure 6mm each. The body measures sixty-two inches in length and weighs 124 pounds. No scars are identified. There is moderate rigor. Moderate livor is noted in the hands, forearms, feet and legs. There is slight livor noted on the back of the trunk.

The eyes are prominent. A 2cm red groove is noted in the neck, more prominent anteriorly. It extends from just above the level of the thyroid cartilage to the level of the ears. Petechiae are noted in the skin above the groove. Bloody mucus exudes from the mouth and nares. The tongue is protruberant and the protruding tip is dusky and dry. Linear scratch marks are noted in the skin of the neck.

Examination of the thorax reveals the breasts are engorged. No ecchymoses are identified.

Examination of the abdomen reveals a protruberant abdomen with striae noted. The uterus is palpated four inches above the pubis.

Examination of the extremities reveals multiple ecchymoses on both shins and wrists.

INTERNAL EXAMINATION

The body is opened through a standard Y-incision. The thoracic and abdominal viscera are in their appropriate positions. There is no measurable pleural or peritoneal fluid. Examination of the neck reveals no evidence of fracture of the thyroid cartilage or hyoid bone. There are ecchymoses only underneath the externally noted groove.

The right lung weighs 300 grams and the left lung weighs 280 grams. There is minimal congestion in the posterior aspects of the lower lobes bilaterally. The heart weighs 350 grams. No abnormalities are identified.

The liver weighs 1200 grams and on sectioning it contains 600cc of liquid blood. The liver otherwise shows mild nutmeg appearance. The pancreas, gallbladder, and biliary tree are unremarkable. The spleen weighs 100 grams. It is unremarkable externally and on sectioning. Examination of the stomach reveals a small amount of partially digested food. No pills are identified. No abnormalities are noted in the intestines.

The kidneys, ureters, and bladder are normal in location and contour.

The uterus weighs 450 grams. The endometrial lining is thick and hemorrhagic. The wall measures 2cm in thickness. Examination of the ovaries reveals a 2cm corpus luteum in the right ovary. The left ovary is unremarkable.

The abdominal aorta and vena cava are unremarkable. There is minimal postmortem hemorrhage. Examination of the brain and spinal cord shows no significant gross abnormalities.

MICROSCOPIC EXAMINATION

Sections of the ecchymotic area over the right flank show small numbers of segmented neutrophils around the extravasated red cells. Sections of the lungs show mild congestion and edema.

> There is no evidence of pneumonia. Sections of the liver hematoma
> confirm the gross impression of blood without significant organ-
> ization. Sections of the other viscera are unremarkable.

'Translate for me, Wesley,' Eli said. He sat on the porch of the old
man's house, holding a sweating glass of lemonade. Watson had
turned himself into an area rug beneath the hanging cedar swing.

Wesley Sneap had been the town doctor back when there were
town doctors – and by default, the county coroner until 1985.
The coming of HMOs, plus a shaking scalpel hand, had pushed
Wesley into retirement. However, he still kept a microscope and
makeshift lab in his basement. And sitting on a sideboard in his
parlor was his old black medicine bag, just in case someone
should call for assistance.

'Well,' he sighed, 'she was hanged, all right. You could see it
in her face, and in the way she scratched at her neck.'

Eli leaned forward, hands clasped. 'What else?'

The doctor skimmed the report again. 'Lot of the notes just
confirm a recent delivery of a baby . . . the thickness of the uterus,
the colostrum, the size of the heart. Oh, and she had a fight with
someone a few hours before the hanging. There are bruises on
her shins and her wrists, but only the wrists show inflammation
in reaction to the injury. The bruises on her shins don't, because
she died before there was time for a cellular response. Probably
was kicking like the devil to get free.'

'What was the time of death?'

'Let's see.' Wesley frowned. 'Nothing in her stomach, but then
again she was busy giving birth. We can guess the hanging interval
though . . . it was long enough for there to be livor – blood
pooling, that is – in the legs and lower arms . . . at least four or
five hours. But she wasn't hanging much longer than that, because
it would have been fixed. Instead, there was some redistribution
of blood to the back of the trunk after she was cut down.'

'The husband told the cops he cut down the body around

ten-thirty in the morning . . . but that the killer came into the house in the middle of the night.'

Wesley shook his head. 'Doesn't fit. Based on the autopsy report, if she was cut down at ten-thirty in the morning, then she was hanged at around six A.M.'

'What if she was hanged in the middle of the night?' Eli asked.

'Then she was cut down by six or seven A.M. Otherwise, the livor would have been fixed and wouldn't have redistributed to the back of the trunk.'

He picked up one of the slides that had been tucked into the autopsy report, holding it up to the light. 'Huh.'

'What'd you find?'

'Well, the old ME mentioned a bruise on the right flank, and then he talks about a liver hematoma. He seems to have chalked those up to some physical trauma. See here, when he talks about that nutmeg liver? He thought they were expanded blood vessels, from right-sided heart failure.'

'So what?'

'Imagine it like a backed-up drainpipe: when the heart isn't working well, everything jams up in the liver. But she died instantaneously . . . and there wouldn't have been time for this kind of reaction.' He squinted at the slide. 'Come downstairs with me. I want to take a closer look.'

Eli followed Wesley down to the basement. Where most men had a workshop or an exercise room, Wesley had a stainless-steel examination table and a counter full of instruments and microscopes. 'I remember this case,' he said, pulling stain from a shelf. 'When I came to Comtosook in 1943, folks still talked about it. In fact, I can recall how teenage boys used to hide in the woods at the Pike place on Halloween night, so that they could live to tell about it in the halls of the school the next day.'

'Yeah? What did they say?'

'Not much, come to think of it. They'd go out there as a dare, and come back quiet as church mice. I once treated a fellow, a football star, who couldn't speak for the whole month of November. Had him go to Boston, to have his larynx checked out by a hoity-toity specialist and everything.'

'What was wrong with him?'

'Not a thing, physically. Started talking again one day as if there'd never been a problem.'

'You think something happened to him at the Pike property?'

Wesley shrugged. 'I think things can happen to a body that never make it to the medical books. Like how grief can kill you, or how falling in love can give you the bed spins. I never thought that boy had any damage to his vocal cords, no matter how many fancy tests those city doctors sent him for. And I was right all along – that's what had come of swallowing sadness.' He slipped the slide beneath the microscope and sucked in his breath. 'Aha.'

'What is it?'

'Fibrin deposition within the periportal sinusoids, and microscopic areas of hemorrhage. And coagulative necrosis in the periportal hepatocytes.'

'Jesus, Wesley. English.'

Wesley took off his glasses, then rubbed his eyes. 'Preeclampsia is a serious complication of pregnancy. It gets even more serious when it causes the HELLP syndrome – that's short for hemolysis, elevated liver enzyme levels, and a low platelet count. They've only been diagnosing it for about twenty years – and it's treatable, now that they know what it is. But back then, it was a different story . . . and could escalate quickly. It looks to me like this liver hematoma developed as a result of the HELLP syndrome . . . not the knocking around your old medical examiner seemed to think.'

'Does that affect my investigation?'

The doctor shook his head. 'Not really. It just means that if Cissy Pike hadn't been hanged, she probably would have died of natural causes within a couple of days.'

*　*　*

Spencer Pike's skin had gone a dull shade of yellow, like rotting parchment. Tubes piped oxygen into his nose. He watched Eli start his tape recorder with the disappointment of a man who knew he had limited time left on this earth and was not willing to share it with a stranger. 'Last I heard, it wasn't a criminal act to sell a piece of land that belongs to you.'

'It isn't,' Eli agreed. He glanced at the other residents of the home sitting in this cafeteria, eating an unidentifiable lunch best suited to a mouth without teeth. 'I wonder, though, what made you decide to sell at all.'

Pike chuckled. 'I just want to be able to continue to live in the sumptuous style to which I've become accustomed. You can tell those Gypsies that it's mine, Detective. If I want to set up a carnival there, I have the right to do it. If I want to donate it to white supremacists, I can. And if I feel like letting some fool developer give me cash for it, instead of waiting for the state of Vermont to take it as part of my estate when I'm gone, then that's my prerogative too.'

Eli realized two things at that moment: Spencer Pike thought he'd come to smooth out relations with the protesting Abenaki, and Spencer Pike did not realize Eli was part-Native American. He seized on this. 'It sounds like you've had some run-ins before with the Abenaki.'

'Damn right I have! One of them killed my wife.'

'Yes, that's what it says in the police report. That must have been very difficult.'

'She was the love of my life. No one should have to bury his wife and his baby the same day.'

'I understand their graves are on the land?'

'Yes.'

Eli tipped his head. 'Not at the church cemetery? Years ago you were quite active in the Congregational assembly . . .'

'My daughter was stillborn,' Pike said. 'And my wife was dead. I . . . wasn't ready to let them both go. I wanted them in a place where they could find me, and I could find them.' He turned away, but not before Eli noticed that he was crying.

Nowhere in the original police report was there any mention of the infant's body. Eli had read this and counted it up to sloppy police work – any self-respecting medical examiner would have conducted an autopsy. On the other hand, if an influential rich man called in to report his wife's homicide, the last thing an officer was going to want to do was cause him any more suffering. If Pike said the baby had been stillborn, they would take his word for it.

People see what they want to see, Eli knew, and police officers were no different. 'You found her,' he repeated.

'I was the one who cut her down. I knew enough to realize that you folks would want to see the way . . . it had been done. But I couldn't stand to see her like that. It looked like . . .' His voice trailed off. 'It looked like she was in pain.'

'What about her father?'

'Harry? He lived on the Hill. He was in Boston at a conference and came home immediately. Never was the same after Cissy was killed . . . drank himself to death two years later.'

He was in Boston. Which ruled him out as a suspect. 'Did you see a step stool anywhere?' Eli asked. 'Something that your wife might have climbed up on by herself?'

'My wife was *murdered*,' Pike corrected, his voice dry as flint. 'If she committed suicide, then she must have flown up to the rafter – it was ten feet off the ground, and there was nothing for her to stand on to reach it.'

Eli met the old man's gaze dead on. 'I'm just trying to understand what happened, Mr Pike. With all of the controversy surrounding the sale of your land, we've had some new leads regarding Gray Wolf. As far as I'm concerned, this case wasn't solved to my satisfaction.'

'Mine either.'

Eli waited, aware that silence could exert the strongest pressure, but Pike confessed nothing. A nurse approached, smiling. 'Time for physical therapy.'

Eli put his hand on the wheelchair. 'Do you have any idea where Gray Wolf might have gone after that night?'

Pike shook his head. 'But if you're looking for him now, Detective, you might as well start in hell.'

Eli stood as the old man was wheeled out. He waited until the nurse turned the corner with the wheelchair, until the other residents seemed to have nodded their heads into the mush on their plates. Then he removed a pair of latex gloves from his pocket, opened up a Ziploc bag he'd taken from home, and plucked the old man's water glass off his tray.

In Comtosook, things started returning to normal. Clocks that had stopped running at the stroke of midnight weeks earlier began ticking again; the swings at the playground no longer moaned when a child sat down; butterflies that had gone gray bled with fresh color. Cautious mothers crept out of the house and let their toddlers play on the sidewalks. The glowing beetles that had infested the birch trees near the town offices vanished. Images that had slipped right off the paper in photo development shops now stuck fast, proof of change.

But the local undertaker, who had grown accustomed to finding one perfect peony inside the mouths of his clients, still checked behind their lips and teeth out of habit. Abe Huppinworth swept the porch of the Gas & Grocery every morning although it was bare as a bone. Middle-aged businessmen who, of late, had overslept on the tails of dreams now woke to their alarm clocks and pulled the covers over their heads, as if finding fantasy might be that simple. And in general, the residents of the town wondered why they all felt hollow just beneath the throat, the result of missing something they had never been able to name in the first place.

* * *

Shelby barely made it out of the attorney's office before running to the bushes and vomiting. Afterward, she wiped her mouth on a Kleenex and sank to the curb, berating herself. Having a will drawn up was perfectly normal, something any adult would do at a given point in her life, especially when she had a son.

Except Shelby knew, for a fact, that the estate and its entirety that she had just signed away to Ethan would never be his.

Shelby had gone into labor in the middle of a thunderstorm. Thomas drove to the hospital in their old convertible, the one with the top that got stuck when open and was stuck even then, so that on the highway, ripped with contractions, she found herself being soaked. When they took her newborn and placed him on her chest, boneless and sticky as a tree frog, Shelby could not tear her eyes away. 'Look,' she had said to Thomas, over and over. 'Have you ever seen anything like him?'

Ethan had been the most beautiful boy. Strong and dark-haired, with the fists of a fighter and eyes as pale as turquoise, he turned heads from the moment Shelby brought him home. 'That,' people would say, stopping her on the street, 'is a perfect baby.' Ethan's defects, it turned out, were the ones you could not see.

The first time he'd been badly burned by the sun, he was six weeks old. Thomas and Shelby had been living in New Hampshire at the time, near the shore, and drove out to the Plum Island Bird Sanctuary in October, when no one was on the beach. On this long, desolate stretch of sand, with seagulls stealing their crackers, they lay a sleeping Ethan down and kissed, their hands moving beneath each other's sweaters and their hair going stiff with the salt in the air. 'I feel like a high school kid,' Shelby said when Thomas unbuttoned her jeans and slipped his hand between her legs. And Thomas had laughed. 'High school kids don't own infant car seats,' he'd answered.

Lost in each other, they hadn't noticed the alarming mulberry of their baby's skin, deepening under the eye of the sun. They did not realize that what they thought was a rash might actually be blisters. And late that night, when not even cool compresses could soothe a screaming Ethan, Shelby understood that this moment was only the beginning.

The doctors had never been able to tell her whether it was her DNA or Thomas's that carried this fatal flaw, but to Shelby, it wouldn't have mattered anyway. She assumed that Ethan's condition was her fault, and because she had not prevented it, she would spend the rest of her life trying to make up for her shortcomings.

Nobody could tell her how long Ethan had left. She asked the dermatologist at every visit, and each time he said that it depended on how much damage had been done to Ethan's skin before his diagnosis – every minute he'd been outside and uncovered as a baby might have stripped days off his life. Shelby imagined cancers like jellyfish that slipped through the sea and sometimes rose to the surface – you knew they were there, and were dangerous, even if you could not see them at first sight.

How on earth did you lower your baby's body into the ground and then keep on living?

Shelby buried her face in her hands. Her pocketbook strap fell to the side. In spite of this crisp new will tucked into her pocketbook, it was not Ethan who would sort through her china, her photographs, her old love letters. It was Shelby, who would fold small shirts into smaller squares to pack up to Goodwill, who would open the windows of his bedroom and let free the smell of him until anyone at all, and not this incredibly special boy, might have lived there.

She heard the growling approach of a vehicle, but didn't look up. In the first place, she was a mess. In the second, she had precious few places where she was allowed nervous breakdowns, and if she used a public street to do so it was no one else's business. The windows of the car were open; she could hear the twang of a guitar on the radio.

'Ms Wakeman?' The tires rolled to a stop beside her. Shelby

didn't lift her head at first, until she heard panting. She glanced up out of curiosity, to find the most enormous dog she'd ever seen lolling its head out the window of a black truck. A hand pushed the skull to the side, revealing the cop who had come to her house last night.

Eli. That was his name.

She swiped at her cheeks, trying to minimize the damage. 'Uh, hello.'

She could feel him staring at her. Was this what it felt like for Ethan in sunlight – all this incredible heat rushing to the surface of her skin? To her surprise, though, the policeman didn't mention the obvious – that a crazy woman was sitting on the curb, bawling. He said, 'Watson is on his way to get a cup of coffee.'

'Watson?'

Eli touched the crown of the dog's head. 'Watson.'

Shelby felt her mouth curve into a smile as she stood. 'The dog drinks coffee?'

Covering the dog's floppy ears, ostensibly to keep him from hearing, Eli confided, 'He's trying to stunt his growth.'

At that, a laugh burst out of her. It hung before Shelby, obscene as a belch, and she held her hand to her chest, stunned to realize that she could produce such a sound.

'Watson would be honored if you'd join us.'

Shelby tentatively put her hands on the open frame of the window. 'Watson should learn to speak for himself.'

Reaching around the dog, Eli pulled the passenger door handle, so that it swung open in front of Shelby; a red carpet, a beginning. 'What can I tell you,' Eli grinned. 'He's shy.'

Ross took a long drag of his cigarette and tossed the butt into the bushes edging the porch. It turned out that being present at the moment you lost someone you loved didn't make it any easier. It turned out that being numb on the outside didn't keep you from bleeding internally.

Ross no longer knew what to believe. Could he love Lia, and still love Aimee? Could Aimee have come back, as Lia had, but chosen not to? And if that was the case . . . was the connection he'd thought to be so strong between them not anything special at all?

If he let his mind trip down this road, it negated everything he'd done for the past ten years. Ross had chased after his fiancée – first by courting his own death, later by investigating the paranormal. Yet maybe a relationship he'd chalked up to fate had only been a matter of coincidence. Maybe he'd met Aimee, had loved Aimee, had lost her – simply so that at some point later in his life he would be ghost hunting, and would meet Lia.

But Rod van Vleet was going to get rid of Lia's ghost. Maybe not the first time he got some hack to try – maybe not even the second – but eventually, there was a good chance that Lia, wherever she was now, would leave. After all, what did she have to stay for, now that she knew who . . . and what . . . she was?

If finding a ghost had taken Ross several years, he imagined that locating a specific one who didn't want to be found would take him several lifetimes.

Why not end this one, then, and start the next?

He stared at the cigarette burn he'd made on his flesh weeks ago. Just a few inches farther down his arm was the scar that reminded him how close he'd come, once, to dying. It wouldn't be hard to do it again. There were pills as bright as marbles in Shelby's bathrooms. There was a Swiss Army knife in Ethan's nightstand drawer. He had canvassed the house weeks ago, a traveler making sure he knew the quickest path of exit in case of emergency.

Except, Ross knew, he wouldn't pass easily to the other side. He'd become a ghost, held to this world by the pain he'd have caused his sister, by what he *didn't* do for Lia.

Maybe he would help Eli Rochert after all. Maybe then, if Lia was somewhere where she could see him, she would have reason to stay . . . no matter what van Vleet did to make her go.

Frustrated, he jammed his hands into his shorts, and felt his fingers brush something. From each pocket he withdrew a bright copper penny, dated 1932, so shiny it might have been minted that morning. He had a vision of himself in a coffin, these pennies on his eyes, payment for crossing the River Styx. Would Lia be waiting? Would Aimee?

'What are those?'

Lost in his thoughts, Ross was startled by the sound of his nephew's voice. 'What are you doing up?'

Ethan was wrapped in clothing from head to toe, even though the porch was protected from sunlight. 'I don't know. You don't sleep, either, do you?' Ethan approached, looking at the pennies. 'Those and a dollar'll get you a cup of coffee.'

'When did kids turn so cynical?'

'When the world started going to crap,' Ethan answered. 'We're Generation Z.'

Ross raised his brows. 'What comes after that?'

'I guess they just start over again.' He sat down on the porch swing and set it rocking, as Ross lit another cigarette. 'Can I have one?'

'What do you think?' Ross shook his head. The very things that branded him such a failure in the eyes of society made him seem positively cool to boys Ethan's age.

'Mom says you shouldn't smoke around me.'

'Then don't tell her.'

'I won't.' He grinned. 'Besides, dying of lung cancer instead would be a surprise.'

Ross leaned against the porch railing. He was exhausted; he couldn't sleep if he tried; and now he had to make polite conversation with a nine-year-old when he really wanted to go into hibernation or stick his head in a gas oven or both.

'I heard you and that cop talking about a ghost last night.'

'You weren't supposed to be listening.'

Ethan shrugged. 'I guess there really *is* a place you go to . . . afterward,' he said. 'What do you think it's like there?'

A small ache winced across Ross's breastbone at the realization that Ethan wasn't asking out of curiosity, but preparation. He remembered the first time he'd held Ethan as an infant, how he had looked into his blue-black eyes and thought, *I already know you*. 'I don't know, bud. I'm not expecting harps and angels.'

'Maybe it's different for everyone,' Ethan suggested. 'Like, I'd have a half-pipe and get to be out in the sun all the time. Enough awesome stuff so that I totally forget about what it used to be like down here. What would you want?'

What sort of world order would let a kid like Ethan die – a kid with his whole life in front of him – yet keep Ross alive and miserable, although there was nothing left for him and never would be? This world, which he would throw away in a heartbeat, was something rare and precious to people who could not afford to take it for granted.

Purgatory, he thought, was just a synonym for *tomorrow*.

Ross sat down on the porch swing and slipped an arm around Ethan's narrow shoulders. 'What I'd want,' he said, 'is to come visit.'

Like Lia had.

'I can't believe it.' Shelby stood on the porch at the Gas & Grocery and watched Eli's bloodhound lap tepid coffee from a borrowed bowl.

'Well, this is easy. It's when he starts getting the urge for sweet-meats and escargots that it gets to be a drag.'

Watson seemed to have an excess of skin. It fell over his forehead in a roll that nearly obliterated his eyes. He glanced up at Shelby and poked his snout into her stomach. 'Watson!' Eli scolded.

'It's all right.' Shelby rubbed behind the dog's ears. 'He just thinks I'm esculent.'

'Would that be a good thing?'

'It means edible.'

'Smart dog,' Eli murmured, lifting his own cup of coffee to his mouth and swallowing his words.

They were distracted by a station wagon, crunching on the gravel and rolling to a stop. A handsome man with a white streak in his hair and a woman dressed as flamboyantly as a tzigane stepped out of the car. 'For the love of God,' the woman said. 'Haven't these towns ever heard of Ralph's?'

'Relax, Maylene. All I need is a Sterno and matches. They must stock them for the folks who don't have electricity yet.'

Shelby took a combative step forward. She couldn't stand city folk who came to Comtosook expecting archetypal Vermonters to wear overalls and go barefoot, or possess only seven teeth, or raise Holsteins in their living rooms. 'Excuse me,' she began, but Eli grabbed her hand and every single word flew out of her head.

'She wanted to say that you'll find the Sternos on the third aisle on the right,' he finished smoothly. The couple nodded at them, surprised, no doubt, to find someone in town with an IQ in the double digits, and entered the general store. 'That's Curtis Warburton,' Eli said, the moment they were out of sight. 'He hosts a paranormal cable show about hauntings.'

'I know. My brother worked for him.' Shelby hesitated. 'But that doesn't make him any less of a moron.'

'A famous moron, though. And one who probably came to Comtosook for a reason. Watson!' The dog raised his massive head. 'Go keep tabs on them.'

To Shelby's amazement, Watson padded into the store. 'Do I pay taxes for his salary?'

'He comes cheap. A good steak every now and then.'

'He can't possibly tell you what the Warburtons do in there . . .'

'Of course not,' Eli said. 'But how else was I going to get a minute alone with you?'

Shelby felt the blush start at her throat and spread upward. She took another sip from her coffee cup, and realized it was empty. 'I should walk back home. Ethan's there with Ross, and you, uh, probably have a lot to do with the Pike case . . .'

'Your brother told you?' Shelby nodded. 'Then you also know it's not a priority for the department.'

His eyes did not leave her face. Even when Shelby tried to turn away, he pulled her back, a moon beholden to gravity. 'What does that mean?'

Eli smiled slowly. 'That I've got all the time in the world.'

WITNESS STATEMENT
Date: September 19, 1932
Time: 11:36 PM
INTERVIEW OF: John 'Gray Wolf' Delacour
INTERVIEW BY: Officer Duley Wiggs and
                  Detective F. Olivette of the
                  Comtosook Police Department
LOCATION: Comtosook PD
SUBJECT:

1.   Q.   Can you state your name for the record, and your
            date of birth?
       A.   Gray Wolf.

2.   Q.   Is that your given name?
       A.   John Delacour. My birthday's December 5, 1898.

3.   Q.   Where do you currently reside?
       A.   I'm between places.

4.   Q.   Can you tell us where you were last night?
       A.   At the Rat Hole. A bar in Winooski.

5.   Q.   What time did you arrive?
       A.   About eight, I guess.

6.   Q.   And what time did you leave?
       A.   I don't know . . . maybe midnight? One?

7. Q. Which was it? Midnight or one?
    A. One.

8. Q. Is there anyone who could vouch for you?
    A. The bartender. His name's Lemuel.

9. Q. Do you know a Mrs Spencer Pike?
    A. [Pause] I do.

10. Q. Why?
    A. I've been doing some work at her house.

11. Q. When was the last time you saw her?
    A. Yesterday afternoon.

12. Q. What time yesterday afternoon?
    A. About three.

13. Q. Are you aware that Mrs Pike was found dead this
       morning?
    A. She . . . she . . . oh, no. Oh, Jesus.

14. Q. How come you killed her?
    A. I . . . God, no, I didn't do it.

15. Q. We know you came back yesterday, after three
       o'clock.
    A. I didn't. I swear it.

16. Q. John, John. You should know better than to lie to
       us.
    A. I – Jesus Christ, don't hurt me! – I didn't!

17. Q. You are one lying piece of shit Gypsy.
    A. I'm not lying . . .

18. Q. No? That's funny, because we know you killed her.
       You missing some personal property lately?
    A. No.

19.   Q.   Really. This photo look familiar?
       A.   My . . . that's my pipe.

20.   Q.   It was at the scene of the crime. Just like you were.
             With your filthy hands all over a lady—
       A.   I wasn't—

21.   Q.   Stop the tape, Duley. [STOPS]
       A.   [TAPE RESUMES] God, please . . . I'll tell you the
             truth. I'll tell you the truth. She was . . . I would
             never hurt her, never.

22.   Q.   Just like you didn't hurt the last person you
             murdered, John?

Taken aback, Ross stopped in front of the closed door on the
second floor of the police department. The secretary had directed
him upstairs to find Eli Rochert, but surely the detective wasn't
getting high on inhalants – although, for all intents and purposes,
it smelled that way right now. The scent made Ross dizzy; he
knocked once and then pushed open the door to find Eli bent
over a box with Plexiglas windows, removing a glass with one
gloved hand. 'You don't want to come in here. I'm fuming.'

Ross ignored him, taking a step inside. 'What pissed you off?'

Eli set the glass on a work counter. 'No, I'm *fuming*. Super-
Glue. The stuff's noxious, but it develops the best latent ridge
impressions.'

'No kidding?' Ross stepped over the ubiquitous hound that
seemed to be the detective's favorite accessory, and peered at the
glass. 'Who figured *that* out?'

'Some film company over in Japan, I think. The vapor released
from heating glue makes Cyanoacrylate Ester adhere to the spots
where there was moisture left on the surface. For a while there,
before it started costing too much, forensic detectives were putting
up tents and fuming dead bodies to see if they could get fingerprints

of perps.' Eli nodded at his makeshift glue chamber. 'Me, I have to settle for the small stuff.'

He took out a small jar of black powder and something that looked like the makeup brush Shelby used. As Eli swirled powder over the glass, the fumed fingerprints rose into stark relief. 'Of course,' he said casually, 'I couldn't really discuss this procedure with someone who wasn't involved in the case.' He glanced up, waiting.

Ross sat down on a lab stool in response.

'Spencer Pike's drinking glass,' Eli said, setting it down again to take a photograph of the print. 'Filched after an interview at the rest home. I'm getting the print off it before having it tested for DNA.'

'Why do you need to test it, if you know it was his?'

'The scientist I have working on the DNA evidence from the murder can compare this to the stuff she's got from back then. And that just might incriminate the good professor in a way that wasn't possible seventy years ago.'

'Whatever happened to hunches?' Ross murmured.

'We still get them,' Eli said. 'But now we back them up.' He pushed an index card in Ross's direction. 'This is a print I lifted from a stone pipe before I sent it off to Frankie for DNA analysis. It's Abenaki; my grandfather had one just like it. It was found under the porch where Cecelia Pike was hanged. Now, common sense says it belonged to Gray Wolf. But these are Gray Wolf's prints, courtesy of the State Prison . . . and they don't match.'

Ross squinted at the second card, with its ten tiny boxes set like teeth, and a fingerprint in each one. He tried to liken one of these to the print that Eli had taken from the pipe, but the latter one was far less distinct, and seemed to be missing its bottom half. 'How can you tell?'

'Look at the shape of the fingerprint,' Eli suggested. 'Whether it's an arch, a loop, or a whirl, the position – which finger it's on, the size – the ridge count of loops, for example. What you'll notice about Gray Wolf's prints is that they're pretty unique – the guy's got arches on eight of his fingers, which only five percent of the population has. The print I lifted off the pipe isn't great, but you can still tell it's a loop. And check out the ridge detail.'

'Ridge detail?'

'Right there.' Eli leaned over Ross's shoulder and pointed to a spot on the fingerprint where the lines forked. 'A bifurcation, for example. Or a ridge that just ends suddenly. Or a dot. Finding eight similar characteristics in two different fingerprints happens about as often as tossing a rock up in the air and not having it come back down.' He took away the prison fingerprint card and set down the new print he'd taken from Spencer Pike's glass. 'The point is – even if that pipe did belong to Gray Wolf, his prints weren't the ones on it. And I'm awfully curious to see whose *were.*'

Wheels began to turn for Ross. 'If Spencer Pike handled the pipe, he might have planted it.'

'There you go.' Eli leaned forward, elbowing Ross out of the way as he scrutinized the two prints with a magnifying glass. 'It starts to add up, if you look at it . . . according to the police report, Pike fired Gray Wolf and threw him off his property that afternoon. He was pissed off at the guy – maybe pissed off enough to pin a murder on him. I had the lab in Montpelier working on some of the old crime-scene photos. You can see how the window was broken in the bedroom – it was smashed from the inside.'

Ross had gone still. 'I thought her husband was beating her,' he said softly. 'But she told me that he just loved her too much.'

'You can love something to death,' Eli answered. 'I see it all the time.'

'So you think she was running away from him?'

'I don't know,' Eli admitted. 'But I do think she fought with him that day. The autopsy report showed bruising on the wrists that happened hours before the death.'

'Do you think . . .' Ross swallowed. 'Do you think he killed
her some other way and then made it look like a hanging?'

'No. The autopsy proves it, and the photographs . . . well,
anyway, the answer is no. Plus, those photos I enlarged – on
the sawdust, beneath where the body was found hanging –
there are two sets of footprints. One boot sole is smaller, and
seems to correspond to the footwear taken off the victim's body.
The other sole is larger, presumably a man's. Now, Pike admits
to cutting down his wife's body. But he also says that someone
else hanged her. So then where are Gray Wolf's footprints?'
Swearing, Eli put down the magnifying glass and pushed away
the fingerprint cards. 'Shoot. Pike wasn't the one holding the
pipe.'

Ross pulled the card closer, staring at the whirlpool of
parallel lines. He was familiar with crime-scene linkage, which
said that any person who came into contact with an object or
another person left a piece of himself behind. Detectives, like
Eli, would use this to document that a suspect was in a
certain place at a certain time, to find the cause that led to
this particular effect. But the same theory could be used to prove
the existence of a ghost. Or to make a man rethink suicide.
Or to explain why love felt like a phantom limb, long after it
was over.

Forensic detectives already knew what most people spent a
lifetime learning: you couldn't pass through this world without
affecting someone else.

Ross's chest suddenly felt so tight he thought he might pass
out. 'You okay?' Eli asked, staring at him curiously. Even the dog
cocked its head. Ross grabbed the first thing he could on the
table – another set of prints that had been tucked underneath
some crime-scene photos. He bent down, pretending to be
absorbed by the lines and dips that made up the fingerprints.

'This is what I'm thinking,' Eli mused. 'Pike's an influential guy.
He told the investigating officers a story, and they believed it

because it was far easier to blame an Indian than to stand up to a guy who was so well-respected in the town. The question, of course, is why Pike killed his wife, if that's the way it went down.' He snapped on latex gloves and began to pack the glass for transport to his DNA scientist. 'Money, maybe. He *did* inherit the land.'

Frowning, Ross glanced from one of the index cards to the print that had come off the pipe. 'Uh, I'm not sure about this . . . but don't these two match?'

Eli took the cards out of his hands and began to bob his head back and forth. 'Hmmph.' Settling down on a stool, he picked up his magnifying glass and began to scrutinize them. After about five minutes, he rubbed his jaw. 'I'll be damned. I'm going to have to have the experts at the lab take a second glance, but yeah, I'd say this is a match.'

'So whose prints are they?'

Eli looked at him. 'Cecelia Pike's. They were rolled postmortem. Standard procedure.'

'If Gray Wolf wasn't even there, what was she doing with his pipe?'

'Holding onto it, apparently,' Eli said. 'Among other things.'

'Like?'

'Maybe Gray Wolf himself. Say the wife was having an affair . . . getting rid of her and framing her lover would kill two birds with one stone.'

'Shut up,' Ross said, his voice rising. 'Just shut up, all right? There was no lover. There was no one. You have no idea what you're talking about.'

'Easy . . .' Eli held up his palms, placating. 'I'm not the bad guy here.'

Ross forced himself to relax, realizing how crazy he must have sounded. 'It's just . . . she was *not* having an affair. You didn't know her.'

Eli stared at him. 'Neither did you.'

WITNESS STATEMENT
Date: September 22, 1932
Time: 8:15 AM
INTERVIEW OF: Lemuel Tollande
INTERVIEW BY: Officer Duley Wiggs and
Detective F. Olivette of the Comtosook Police Department
LOCATION: Comtosook PD
SUBJECT:

1. Q. State your name and address for the record, please.
   A. Lemuel Tollande, 45A Chestnut Street, Burlington.

2. Q. Where do you work, Mr Tollande?
   A. The Rat Hole in Winooski. I tend bar.

3. Q. Do you know John Delacour, aka Gray Wolf?
   A. Sure. He's a friend, a regular.

4. Q. Did you see this man on the night of September 18th?
   A. Yeah. He came in about eight, eight-thirty, and left near one.

5. Q. At any point did he leave the bar during that time?
   A. I think he went out to get some smokes . . .

6. Q How long was he gone?
   A. I can't say. The bar was awful busy that night.

7. Q. Well, are we talking five minutes? An hour?
   A. I . . . I really can't tell you. All's I know is he was gone and then he was back.

8. Q. Did he tell you he'd been fired from his job?
   A. No . . . but Gray Wolf's a pretty private fella. He keeps his business to himself. [Pause] He ain't no murderer, though. Wasn't the first time around, and not this time neither.

9.   Q. Mr Tollande, have you seen Gray Wolf lately?
     A. Not since that night in the bar.

10. Q. Do you know where we might find him?
     A. He moves around a lot.

11. Q. Your people always do. And you lie, too, don't you?

What Eli first thought, stepping into the musty, stuffed room that made up the Comtosook Public Library, was that someone with all the bright bloom of Shelby Wakeman didn't belong in such a closeted place. He imagined her sitting, instead, among a kaleidoscope of tulips in the Netherlands, or swimming with a rainbow of Caribbean fish, and then drew himself up short at being caught in such a flight of fancy.

Watson, unused to being on a leash, yanked so hard all of a sudden that Eli went flying, nearly jackknifing himself on the front desk. The resulting noise caused Shelby to look up from the computer terminal where she sat. 'Well, hello,' she said, getting up and coming around the counter. She looked at Watson, who was wagging his ridiculous tail so hard it made his face shake. '*You* aren't allowed in here,' she scolded, but she was patting him all the same. 'Then again, who am I to tell a cop what to do.'

When she smiled at him, Eli's heart raced like a Roman candle. 'Hey,' he managed.

Brilliant, Rochert. She works in a library, she knows the whole dictionary, and that's the only word you can scrape out?

'Were you looking for something in particular?' Shelby asked, and Eli opened his mouth only to realize that she was speaking to Watson. '*Hound of the Baskervilles,* maybe, with your namesake? Or Robert Stone's *Dog Soldiers?*'

'Actually, he just came to keep me company,' Eli said. 'I was looking for town records from the thirties.'

He was not particularly looking for town records from the thirties. In fact, he'd come expressly to see if Shelby was working today. But the murder case was on his mind, and that excuse was the first to pop into his head. It occurred to Eli that, between his investigation of a seventy-year-old murder case and his itch to see this woman, he was clocking precious little time for police work.

She was staring at him curiously, wondering, no doubt, why a policeman wouldn't know that all municipal records were stored next door to the department in the town clerk's office. 'I know exactly where they are . . . but it's not here.'

'Any chance you can show me?'

Before Shelby could even pose the question, the other librarian on duty – one who'd been so still and wrinkled Eli hadn't realized she was animate – waved her along. They walked down the steps with Watson between them, Shelby squinting in the sun.

'Beautiful out, isn't it?'

She nodded. 'I forget how bright it gets, sometimes.'

'You mean working in the library all day?'

'That, and staying up all night with Ethan. It's the only time he can go out to play.' They began to walk down Main Street, Watson sniffing at cracks in the sidewalk and patches of gum stuck to the ground.

'When do you sleep? You must be exhausted.'

She smiled tightly. 'You do what you have to do.'

A kid on a scooter passed them on the left, pushing Shelby toward Eli. He felt the charge that came from being so close. He could trip, blame it on Watson, and brush up against her. He could even push Watson into her, and then catch her when she fell.

What would she feel like in his arms?

Then they were at the municipal offices, and Eli felt a slow roll of frustration. Had the buildings in this town always been so close together? He followed Shelby up the stone steps and into the first room on the right. 'Lottie,' she said to the colossal town clerk, 'have you lost weight?'

If she'd lost an ounce, Eli would eat Watson's grain for a week. But the woman beamed. 'I think that diet's working,' she tittered, waving them into the bowels of the building without question.

The basement was dark and moldy, with spiderwebs festooning the ceiling. Watson immediately tugged free of his leash to chase a rodent behind a stack of boxes. Unerringly, Shelby crawled over a small bunker of crates into a narrow aisle of filing cabinets that had not seen the better half of this century. She opened a drawer and pulled out a yellowed stack of cards. 'These are from 1932.'

Stupefied, Eli could only stare at her. 'Are you psychic too?'

'Ross isn't psychic,' Shelby corrected. 'And no, I'm not either. I found them the hard way the last time I was here – by going through every other drawer before I hit this one.'

He moved into the narrow aisle to stand beside her, only to realize there wasn't really space for two. They were pressed up against each other from chest to hip; Eli could feel her breath against his shoulder. In this basement, with the air thick as blood around them, Eli thought time might have stopped. After all, lately, stranger things had happened.

'Why are you doing this?' Shelby asked quietly. 'It isn't going to solve anything.'

It took him a moment to realize she was talking about the murder case. Eli shrugged. 'People do all sorts of crazy things every day.' A shaft of sunlight fell onto her cheek from the one window in this cellar, as if it had sought and found the only object of beauty worth illuminating. Eli leaned forward, toward that halo. Would it be warm, there?

Shelby reared back so suddenly that a short wall of boxes tumbled to the ground, spilling their contents. She thrust the stack of cards into Eli's hand. From across the room, Watson sneezed. 'The one, um, that you want should be in front,' she murmured.

Eli took her lead, forcing himself to concentrate on the brittle pile of death certificates he now held. He glanced down at Cecelia Pike's, signed by the same ME who had done the autopsy. He had responded to a call placed to the Comtosook Police department at 10:58, concerning an alleged homicide. The time of death had been certified at 11:32 A.M. Stuck to this card with what could only be blood was one for the newborn, also certified at 11:32. His mind scrambled back to his talk with Wesley Sneap, who'd said Cecelia Pike had been hanged near midnight, and cut down to a horizontal position about 6 or 7 A.M. But the police hadn't been called in until eleven . . . which gave Pike plenty of time to stage the scene.

He glanced up at the sound of footsteps. 'Hello? Hello down there?'

There was a clatter, and the whump of Watson finding someone new to greet. 'Whoa, Pilgrim. Down! News flash – you're not a Pomeranian,' said Frankie Martine. She wore jogging pants with a white stripe, and a formfitting T-shirt that read hotbod. Her blond hair was pulled back in a ponytail, and in spite of her lack of makeup, she could have given any model a run for her money. That was Frankie's cross to bear – she was Marie Curie trapped in Marilyn Monroe's body. 'Eli Rochert. What's a girl gotta do to find you in this town!'

A smile split his face. 'Jeez, Frankie, I never expected door-to-door service. What are you doing here?'

'No way was I gonna get into this on the phone.' She peered over his shoulder, and he belatedly remembered Shelby.

'Frankie Martine, this is Shelby Wakeman. Shelby's—'

'Leaving,' Shelby murmured. 'I, uh, have to go.' And without even looking at him, she backed out of the pile of cartons and fled up the stairs.

*   *   *

'Your girlfriend's gonna be ma-a-ad,' Frankie sang as Eli escorted her into his makeshift lab. She took a seat and propped her feet up on Watson.

'She's not my girlfriend. Yet.'

'Yeah, well, you just blew that one back about three months.'

Eli scowled. 'Is it my fault you're beautiful?'

'Gee, was that a compliment?' Frankie leaned forward, plucking a particular page from the sheaf. 'C'mon. Admit. You love me.'

He did. Because all the sharpest detective work that Eli did amounted to nothing at all if Frankie couldn't take the traces of evidence a perp had left behind, and make heads and tails of it. She was leafing through his evidence – the clothing and articles that hadn't been sent to her. 'Nice print.'

'I took it off the pipe before giving it to you,' Eli said.

'Yeah? Whose is it?'

'The victim's, strangely enough.'

'Hmm,' Frankie said, but did not elaborate. 'How come I didn't get this?' She was holding up the victim's nightgown, with a small brown splotch on one side.

'How much blood did you need? You had the rest of her clothing.'

'It's the wrong color.' Frankie pursed her lips. 'I mean, I don't get to see seventy-year-old blood very often, but still.' She rolled it into a ball and tucked it into her black bag. 'Just in case I get bored when I go to visit my friends at the lab in Montpelier.' Then she tossed him a file. 'Look at this.'

Description	Amelo-genin	CSF1PO	TPOX	TH01	vWA	D16S539	D7S820	D13S317	D5S818
Gray Wolf	X , Y	11, 12	8, 11	7, 7	16, 16	11, 12	11, 11	9, 11	11, 11
Cecelia	X, X	10, 11	11, 12	7, 7	16, 17	11, 12	11, 12	9, 9	11, 11
Spencer Pike	X, Y	9, 12	8, 8	7, 9.3	17, 18	9, 10	10, 10	8, 13	10, 12
Pipe	X , Y	11, 12	8, 11	7, 7	16, 16	11, 12	11, 11	9, 11	11, 11
Rope end	X, Y	—	8, 8	7, 9.3	17, 18	—	10, 10	8, 13	10, 12
Rope loop	X, X	—	11, 12	7, 7	16, 17	11, 12	11, 12	9, 9	11, 11
Medicine pouch A	—	—	—	—	—	—	—	—	—
Medicine pouch B	X (Y)	11 (10)(12)	11 (8)(12)	7, 7	16 (17)	—	11 (12)	9 (11)	11, 11
Medicine pouch C**	X (Y)	11, 11	11 (8)	7, 7	16 (17)	—	11, 11	9 (11)	11, 11

Table 1—Amelogenin Typing Results

KEY: Types in parentheses ( ) are lesser in intensity than types not in parentheses.

— No conclusive results

** Drop-out may have occurred due to limited amount of DNA

She took one look at Eli's face and rolled her eyes. 'Crash course?'

'Please.'

'OK. Basic DNA – everything you've got came from either your mom or your dad. She gives you one allele, and he gives you another. The result – a baby with big feet or dimples or curly hair. All those physical traits are on your DNA strand, but they don't do a lot of good in criminal investigations. So we test the DNA for different traits – like vWA or TH01. At those spots, every person's gonna have a type: one number from Mom and one from Dad. The DNA we extract from evidence – even really old, difficult evidence like the stuff you sent me – narrows the pool for who might have left that DNA behind.' She smoothed out the corners of the chart she'd handed Eli. 'Each of these columns here with the weird number on top is one of those traits. At each trait, there are two numbers – the alleles – which came from the mom and dad of whoever left that DNA behind. *Capisce*?'

'So far.'

'OK. Before we can analyze evidence, we need control samples – that is, DNA profiles we can compare to the ones we're about to find on the rope or medicine pouch. The first control sample came from the victim's blood, which was all over the evidence thanks to her recent labor and delivery. The results I got I labeled as Cecelia. As for your missing perp – well, you got lucky. Making the assumption that the saliva on the pipe was his, I concentrated the DNA yield and was able to get all eight loci . . . which I titled Gray Wolf. Finally came the glass you just sent – that saliva was the basis for the eight numbers that make up the profile of someone different than Gray Wolf's profile . . . they're listed as Spencer Pike.'

'Hang on. So that means that we definitely have the DNA of these three people?'

'Two out of three are a lock. The third is a little less of a sure thing. I can't tell you that this particular DNA belonged to Gray Wolf, because I never had a control sample.'

'So all you really know is that you've got DNA on the pipe that's male, and different from Spencer Pike's.'

'Actually, I've got a little more than that.' Frankie trailed her finger down the page. 'One of the byproducts of DNA testing is that we've got charts, now, of subpopulations, which show how alleles tend to crop up with frequency in various ethnic and racial groups.'

'You lost me,' Eli said.

'We can generate statistics collected by typing people of a certain background – white, black, Native American. Say you've got a white Rolls-Royce. Rolls are only two percent of the entire car population.'

'And you know this . . . why?'

Frankie shook her head. 'Shut up, Eli. Two percent. White cars are fifteen percent of the total car population. To approximate how many white Rolls-Royces there are, we say fifteen percent of two percent of the car population . . . which means that .3 percent, or three out of every thousand cars, is a white Rolls. That's the same thing we do when we look at the way types tend to crop up with frequency in various subpopulations. For example, the rope end – the profile I got there is found in one in 1.7 million Caucasians, but only one in 450 million Native Americans. That means if I filled a football stadium with 450 million Indians and another stadium with 450 million whites, I'd expect 264 Caucasians in that stadium to have a matching profile . . . but only one Native American to have it.'

'So whoever handled the rope end was more likely white than Native American?'

'Right. But now, look at the numbers from the pipe. The chances of finding a D5S818 combo of 11,11 is fourteen percent in the Caucasian population, seven percent in the African American population, and twelve percent in the Hispanic population. But the chance of finding an 11,11 combination there in the Native American population is thirty-five percent – that's more than twice as common as the Caucasian population. If you look at the whole profile on the pipe, the chance of it coming from a Caucasian is one in 320 million; from an African American it's one in 520 million; from a Hispanic it's one in 41 million. From a Native American, though, it's only one in 330,000.'

'So whoever smoked the pipe was an Indian.'

'That would be my unofficial assumption.'

Eli nodded. 'What else?'

'There was no surprise when I tested the rope loop, with the epidermal cells that came from the victim's neck – if you compare the row to Cecelia's control sample, they're identical. I only got seven of the eight systems when I tested the noose, but I'd still call it a success. Then I tested the end of the rope, as a different sample. I wasn't expecting much, and even after scraping for

E-cells I had no luck. So I used a PCR procedure to replicate billions of copies of discrete areas of the DNA, and managed to get six loci, which was pretty much a miracle. And of those six systems, every single one is a match to the DNA taken from Spencer Pike's drinking glass.'

It didn't necessarily mean that Pike had hanged his wife, but it at least meant that he'd handled that rope. Eli looked at the empty row on the chart. 'What happened with the medicine pouch?'

Frankie narrowed her eyes. 'What happened is that your favorite DNA scientist nearly came here and committed a felony against the detective that begged for her help. You have no idea what a bitch this was, Eli. I would have scrapped it, if you didn't have such a dearth of evidence to begin with.'

'I'll take you out to dinner.'

'No, you'll buy me a yacht,' Frankie said. 'The first time I tested it I came up dry. I wound up taking a second cutting off the string that came in contact with the neck. I got two profiles – both similar, both consistent with a mixture.'

'Meaning?'

'That there was more than one or two types in most of the systems. Look at that line on the chart . . . see the spots where there are three numbers, instead of two?'

'Yeah.' Eli frowned. 'What's up with that?'

'You know how you get one allele from Mom and one from Dad? If you wind up with three or four, either you're a freak, or there's a mixture of DNA from at least two people. And given their genetic makeup, neither Cecelia Pike nor Gray Wolf can be excluded as cocontributors to this mixture.'

Eli whistled softly. 'But not Spencer Pike?'

'Nope. See the D7S820 location? He's a 10,10. But the medicine bag is an 11, (12) or an 11,11. That's not in Pike's genetic profile . . . so it couldn't be him.'

Eli exhaled heavily. This would throw a wrench into his theory about the crime, because now DNA evidence placed Gray Wolf at the scene, too. But maybe Pike's staging didn't extend to the medicine pouch. Maybe, for whatever reason, Gray Wolf had worn it for some time and given it to Cecelia as a love trinket, which she ripped off her neck during the hanging . . .

'There's something else, Eli.' Frankie hesitated. 'It bothered me enough that I actually went back to that damn pouch and tested at six more loci. See?'

Description	FGA	D8S1179	Penta E	D18S51	D21S11	D3S1358
Gray Wolf	19, 25	13, 13	—	13, 16	30, 30	15, 15
Cecelia	19, 19	13, 14	—	13, 16	30, 30	15, 15
Spencer Pike	20, 22	12, 14	—	14, 17	29, 30	17, 18
Medicine pouch B	—	13 (14)	—	13, 16	30, 30	15, 15
Medicine pouch C**	—	—	—	—	30, 30	15, 15

Table 2—Typing Results

KEY: Types in parentheses ( ) are lesser in intensity than types not in parentheses.

— No conclusive results

** Drop-out may have occurred due to limited amount of DNA

Frankie traced the rows with a scarlet fingernail. 'At not a single location did I come up with four types. In these tests, I didn't even come up with *three* types.'

'So what?'

'So, if you and I were to grab hold of something and leave our skin cells all over it, chances are that at one of fifteen spots, we'd have four separate types. I mean, you get two from your parents, and I get two from my parents, and the likelihood of us having the same types more than once or twice in a profile is pretty slim.'

'You said that the DNA was hard to extract. Maybe there was some snafu.'

'No. That's why I went for the extra tests.' Frankie tucked her hair behind her ears. 'When I see profiles of mixtures where there are only three types, or even two, they're usually between direct descendants. Since the parent always gives one allele to the offspring, the parent and offspring will always have at least one allele in common. If Cecelia Pike was Gray Wolf's daughter, this is exactly what I'd expect a mixture of their DNA to look like.'

Eli shook his head. 'No way. Cecelia Pike was white.'

Frankie pulled another piece of paper out of her folder. 'Statistically speaking,' she said, 'I don't think so.'

9

As far as Ross was concerned, Eli Rochert could go to hell. You did not have to meet a person, flesh and blood, to *know* them. Couldn't you read a diary, and feel a kinship? Sift through yellowed love letters, and bring a romance back to life? Connect two distant keyboards in an Internet chat room? Ross *had* known Lia, and the cop was wrong – if she were having an affair, he would have known.

Because it would have been with him.

At this very moment, Rod van Vleet might have some hack reciting scripture around the property, trying to reduce the amount of space Lia's spirit had to roam. By now, he might even have started reasoning with her, explaining that this was no longer a world where she belonged.

With a growl, Ross pushed off his bed and began to pace the small bedroom, a caged animal. He had known Lia, but he hadn't known what it was like to feel her body close around his, to have her dig her nails into his shoulders as the night began to move around them, a living thing. He had known Lia, but not enough.

These were the moments when Ross believed in God. Not a kind God or a just God, but one with a wicked sense of humor. One who punished someone who'd made an irreparable mistake by dangling the treat he wanted above all else, and then snatching it away so that Ross would fall flat on his face.

The walls were folding in on him, and there was a knot in his throat that kept any air from getting through. He had aimlessly picked up one of Ethan's CDs from the computer hutch, and had been holding it so tightly that the plastic container had cracked. Steam rose off his skin. His skull was too tight for his brain.

'Okay,' he said to no one. 'Okay.'

Already, it was happening – he was looking at the mirror on the dresser not as a reflection, but as a potential weapon. He could feel the seams on his wrists itching. He could picture a world he was not in.

Bursting out of the bedroom, Ross raced down the stairs past Shelby. 'Where—' she began.

'*Out.*'

He barreled past Ethan, still waking with the moon. His car peeled out of the driveway and through the winding dirt roads of Comtosook. It was five minutes before he realized where he was driving, and by the time he parked at the blockade on Otter Creek Pass, night had fully fallen.

The protesting Abenaki had gone back to camp for the night; the few reporters who had not been called back to their city papers were holed up in the Best Western in Winooski. Rod van Vleet was nowhere to be seen, thank God, nor were there any paranormal investigators with bells and whistles. The massive excavators and cranes slept, their necks extended.

Ross crawled over the construction tape and fencing to stand in the center, where the house still partially stood, having knit itself back together after Rod van Vleet had knocked it down. The developer had given up on setting his strip mall just there; a hundred yards to the left, now, excavators were trying to dig deep enough into the frozen ground to pour concrete. Ross took a deep breath: this is where Lia once sat down to dinner, or had a morning cup of coffee. Here, she fell asleep on stagnant Sunday afternoons. She placed Spencer Pike's hand on her belly, told him she was carrying their child.

'Lia!' Her name unwound from his throat, conjuring.

He stayed that way for a moment. The old Pike property had

an uncommon stillness to it, an absolute lack of activity. No chipmunks skittered up trees, no birds traded secrets, no bullfrogs spied through the grass. If a paranormal investigator wanted Lia's ghost to leave, he'd have to find her first.

Ross walked back to the car in silence, thinking hard. She wasn't here; he would have felt it. And whoever van Vleet hired would be expecting a ghost – but not necessarily Lia. After all, Ross was the only one who had actually seen her.

What if he gave them a ghost, a different one, to get rid of?

He made a straight beeline for his car. He was three-quarters of a mile away from the house clearing when a single rose petal fell from a starless sky, drifting to settle in the footprint Ross had left behind.

Meredith couldn't have asked for a nicer day – seventy-five degrees, the sky a brilliant blue, and the mall not nearly as crowded as she'd expected for August. Add to this the fact that her daughter was free and clear of the antipsychotic medicine – which had made no difference in her behavior – and there was plenty of reason to celebrate.

They were walking slowly, because Ruby was with them, and even if she was too proud to complain about her hips, Meredith had noticed the slight wince on her face with every footstep. They'd been to meet the new giant pandas at the National Zoo, to the Natural History Museum to sigh over the Hope Diamond, in the Air and Space Museum to touch the moon. Now, they headed toward the parking garage, each holding a soft-serve ice cream cone.

'It is my opinion,' Meredith said, 'that the streets of heaven are paved with chocolate.'

'Which just goes to show you it can't be hot and humid there,' Ruby pointed out. 'Yet another gold star in the travel guide.'

A family was walking toward them – tourists, from the looks of their cameras and FBI T-shirts. They split up as they passed, funneling around Meredith and Lucy and Ruby like a river, catching together again once they'd gone by. 'Mom?' Lucy said. 'I've got a question.' Lucy had been asking questions all day – from the bathroom habits of the dinosaurs featured in one of the museums to where the president stayed when all the tourists were invading his house. 'How come you didn't marry anyone?'

Meredith stopped walking. She had explained the facts of life to Lucy at her own lab, showing her live sperm and a real egg and then the resulting embryo that turned into a human fetus. Taken in scientific terms, love had nothing to do with procreation. A father was nothing more than a donor, and that description suited Meredith just fine.

Ruby gave Meredith a pointed look over Lucy's head.

'Well. I didn't need to get married. I already had *you.*'

Lucy rolled her eyes. 'Mom, a husband's good for more than just making a baby. Maybe if you had one you'd be at home more.'

'You know why I work so hard . . .'

Lucy turned away. 'It's because of me, right? No guy wanted to marry someone who already had a kid.'

'Lucy, no. Hey.' Meredith caught Lucy by the arm and tugged her toward the supporting wall. 'Sweetheart,' she began, and suddenly Lucy shrieked.

'Don't sit on him!' She backed away as passersby turned to stare. 'Mommy, what's wrong with that boy?'

She pointed, but there was no boy. 'Lucy, what's the matter?'

Her eyes were wide and wild. 'The boy sitting there, in the jail suit, like they wear on cartoons. And the woman who's bald, and the babies . . . they're skeletons, but they're still moving. Can't you see them?'

A man tapped Meredith on the shoulder. 'Do you need help?'

'We're fine,' she said brusquely, never turning away from Lucy. 'Take a deep breath, and tell me what you see.'

The man, intent on being a Good Samaritan, spoke again. 'I'll get a guard,' he said, and ran off. Meredith looked up long enough to watch him enter the building in front of them: the Holocaust Memorial Museum.

'They're the ones,' Lucy whimpered, 'who stayed behind.'

The warrant to exhume remains from the Pike property was burning a hole in Eli's pocket, but he kept it there like a coal close to the heart, to remind him what he was doing and why. Frankie's DNA analysis had twisted his investigation. Presumably, if Gray Wolf was Cecelia Pike's natural father, then they were not having an affair. The medicine pouch and even the pipe might have been gifts. But Eli was still leaning toward Pike as the murderer. Gray Wolf had only just been released from prison, and immediately sought out the daughter he had never met. If Cecelia had been told of her true paternity, she might have kept it a secret from her husband – leading Spencer Pike to jump to the wrong conclusions when he found his wife keeping company with an Indian. Or maybe Pike had found out about his wife's ancestry – and afraid of what it might do to his career, had simply gotten rid of the evidence.

Either way, the Abenaki's complaint about a burial ground had been valid.

He found Az Thompson on the banks of the Winooski at dawn, pulling up muskies. The old man's thin shoulders moved beneath the fabric of his shirt as he reeled and cast. 'My grandfather caught a sturgeon in Lake Champlain,' Eli said, coming up behind him.

'They run in there,' Az said.

'You ever get one?'

He shrugged.

'My mother used to tell me how he had to tie it to his canoe and let it pull him around until it got tired out and he could get to the shallows and club it.'

'Patience is a hell of a lure,' Az agreed.

Eli watched him toss another fish into his pail. 'I need your help. Turns out, Cecelia Pike was half-Abenaki.'

Poking over a small container of bait, Az hesitated for only a moment. 'Abenaki,' he repeated softly. 'Do you think the dawn's just as beautiful to the people who aren't named for it?'

Eli understood that the old man wasn't expecting an answer. 'I know there should be some kind of – well, isn't there a cere-mony? A place you can . . . move her and her daughter?'

Az looked up. 'What's going to happen to the property?'

'I don't know,' Eli admitted.

The answer seemed to satisfy the old man. 'I'll take care of them,' he said.

'Not those,' Ross said to the clerk at the Gas & Grocery, a green-haired teen in overalls with so many piercings along her eyebrows and nostrils that he wondered if she took on water when she showered. 'The Merits.'

He paid for the cigarettes, watching the girl make change. Ross tore open the package to light a smoke and inadvertently knocked his book of matches onto the floor. It landed near the shoe of the man waiting in line behind him, who bent down to pick it up. 'Thanks,' Ross said, and then the man straightened. 'Curtis?'

His former employer's lips thinned. 'Ross.'

'What are you doing here?'

'The same thing you are, I imagine. Looking for a ghost.'

Ross's knees went weak. Rod van Vleet had indeed found himself someone to get rid of a spirit . . . and Ross had been the one to give him the lead. 'Curtis, listen—'

'No, you listen, you son of a bitch. You signed a non-compete clause when you started working for us, and don't think I won't ride you all the way to court if you decide to show me up. You are an amateur, Ross. You have no idea how to run a show like this.'

The inside of Ross's mouth was as dry as dust. 'This isn't a show.'

'It will be.' Curtis jabbed a finger into Ross's chest. 'I'm going to find that ghost, and I'm going to get rid of it, and the whole damn thing's going to win me my time slot.' He shoved past Ross, thrust a dollar bill at the clerk, and took a stale bagel from a basket on the counter before slamming outside.

'He's got issues, huh?' the clerk said, and she clicked her tongue ring against the ledge of her bottom teeth.

'Yeah.' Ross lit his cigarette, inhaled, and stepped onto the porch of the Gas & Grocery. It was so bright out he found himself squinting. From here, past the 1950s-style gas pumps and the antique Moxie sign, you could see the edge of the town green, with its requisite white church. You could just make out the hill that was the quarry and the valley that became Lake Champlain. This was the world Lia had known.

He would need mirrors, and fishing line. Speakers, and batteries, and Shelby's laptop. If Curtis wanted to oust a ghost, he'd give him one.

It just wouldn't be Lia.

Duley Wiggs had been twenty years old and a policeman for eight days when Cecelia Pike was murdered. Now, he was in the early stages of Alzheimer's and living in the Northeast Kingdom with his daughter Geraldine. 'Some days are better than others,' she told Eli, standing at the sliding-glass door that opened out to the patio where Duley sat in a wheelchair. 'And then some days he can't figure out what you do with a spoon.'

She looked, to Eli, like a teabag that had been used several times over, to the point where it had lost all flavor. 'I appreciate your letting me talk to him.'

'You can talk as much as you want,' Geraldine said, shrugging. 'But he confuses everything. I'd take whatever he tells you with a grain of salt the size of Lot's pillar.'

Eli nodded and then followed her outside. 'Daddy?' she said loudly, as if the old man was deaf too. 'Daddy, there's a man here to see you. Detective Eli Rochert, from Comtosook. Remember when you used to live in Comtosook?'

'You know, I used to live in Comtosook,' Duley said. He smiled, his face cracking like porcelain. He shook Eli's hand.

'Hey, Duley.' Eli had worn his dress uniform, in the hopes of jogging the memories even more. 'I have a few questions to ask you.'

'Miranda, why don't you leave us two men alone?' Duley said.

'I'm Geraldine, Daddy.' She sighed, and then retreated back to the house.

Eli sat down. 'I was wondering if you might remember any murder cases from your time on the job in Comtosook.'

'Murder? Oh, yeah, sure. We had a lot of murders. Well, no, it wasn't murders exactly. It was burglaries. Yes, I do recall those. A rash of them in the forties that turned out to be two teenagers, who fancied themselves to be Bonnie and Clyde.'

'But the murder cases . . .'

'There was one,' Duley said. 'I don't suppose anyone could ever forget something like what happened to Cissy Pike. I knew her personally. We went to school together. She was younger than me by a couple of years. Pretty thing, and smart, too. Got it from her father. He was an astronaut.'

'He was a professor, Duley.'

'That's what I said!' The old man frowned, annoyed. 'Listen, will you?'

'Yes. Right. Sorry. So . . . you were talking about her murder . . .'

'She was married to some bigwig at the university. Pike. Had a reputation around town for being a little holier-than-thou, if you get my meaning. But he treated Cissy like she was a queen. When we got there — to the house, after he called us — well, I'd never seen a grown man weeping like a baby.' He shook his head. 'And then to have him turn the gun on himself, right before our eyes . . .'

'Duley,' Eli said gently, 'Spencer Pike didn't commit suicide.'

'Suicide? Oh, that's right, now. That was a hostage thing up at the post office in the late fifties.' He rubbed his forehead. 'Sometimes . . . sometimes it all just slides together up there.'

'I understand.' Eli twirled his hat on his hand. Maybe this hadn't been such a great idea.

'The medical examiner, he wanted to do an autopsy on the baby.'

At that, Eli's head snapped up. 'He did?'

'Yeah. And Olivette – he was the detective-lieutenant at the time – wouldn't let him dig up the grave. Said that you didn't cause a man like Spencer Pike any more grief if you didn't have to.'

'So the baby was already buried when you got there?'

'Uh-huh. Off in the woods a ways. Fresh dirt and even some flowers. Pike told us that the baby came stillborn, and it sent his wife over the edge. Said he buried the baby just to give her some peace of mind.'

'Pike told *me* he buried his wife and his baby on the same day.'

'Nope, I know that for a fact. I was at Cissy Pike's funeral. Weren't many of us – me and Olivette, and her father, and Pike, just enough to lower the coffin. It was a pretty big scandal at the time – he wasn't up for the church ladies bringing casseroles, even though he could have used the help, with his girl gone. Buried Cissy right next to the grave where his baby already was.'

'Did he tell you what took so long? To call the cops?' Eli asked.

'Oh, he didn't have to tell us. We could still smell the booze on him. Pretty much pickled himself the night before.' Duley looked toward the house. 'I got three girls, you know, and I can't even imagine what I'd have felt like if they'd been born dead. I figure Pike was trying to take the edge off. But he did such a good job of it he passed out . . . didn't hear anyone coming in to take his wife, or trashing his house. And by the time he woke up half the morning was gone. He called us just before lunchtime, which was a good thing, because I had less in my stomach to toss up when I saw Cissy.'

Cecelia's body had been cut down hours before lunchtime, according to Wesley.

Eli rolled this thought around his head like a marble. 'Tell me about Gray Wolf.'

'Shifty son of a bitch. He was a Gypsy, you know – what you'd call a Native American today. Lying, thieving, it all came easy to him. Everyone knew of him, and his family, and he'd only just got out of jail for killing someone else. Pike said he'd been harassing Cissy the past few weeks. Between the personal belongings of his we found at the crime scene, and the condition of the house – plus a big fat hole of time in his alibi – it made sense. And then, of course, when he vanished, it was like having our suspicions confirmed.'

Eli scratched his head. 'Yeah, I'm wondering how he *did* vanish.'

A blush spread upward from the old man's neck. 'That, well . . . that would have been my fault. I was one week on the job, you know, and I thought I could bring him in and put the screws to him, and make myself a hero in the meantime. So I went out in the middle of the night like Columbus—'

'Columbo?'

'Yeah, him. I found Gray Wolf drinking at a bar and dragged him in for questioning. But Olivette, he chewed my ass out – said we didn't have enough to hold the perp yet, and bringing him in for questioning was just gonna make him suspicious. We knocked him around a little, the way we used to do things, but he wouldn't confess. Olivette set me to tailing him, watching his every move . . .' Duley looked out over the vista of the backyard. 'And I lost him. He was there one minute, and the next one, you'd have thought he never existed at all.' He licked his lips and leaned forward to whisper. 'I have my theory about what happened to him, mind you.'

'Do you?' Eli came closer.

'I think . . .' Duley cupped his spotted hand around Eli's ear. 'I think there was a second shooter on the grassy knoll helping

Oswald out.' He leaned back and folded his arms across his chest. 'You get what I'm saying?'

Eli sighed. 'Perfectly.'

When Ethan woke up, it was still light out. He slipped the blackout shade back and closed his eyes the way his uncle had taught him, trying to ferret out the activity in his house by sixth sense.

His mother was working at the library, which suited him just fine, because she'd been a real pain in the neck to live with, lately. Everything Ethan did seemed to rub her the wrong way – from the way he left his dirty clothes inside out in the hamper, to the amount of time he spent surfing the Net. He would have gotten a complex about it, probably, if not for the fact that she'd been a total witch to Uncle Ross too – and for that matter, any tele-marketer who had the misfortune of getting the Wakeman household on their calling list – and one neighbor kid who committed the cardinal sin of hitting a baseball into the garage window. *What is wrong with you?* Uncle Ross had even asked yesterday night, when they were all eating breakfast. And his mother had been so busy ignoring him that she burned her hand on the stove, burst into tears, and cried, 'Do you see what you made me do?'

She was screwed up, all right.

Ethan swung his legs over the edge of the bed. He put on yesterday's clothes, still on his floor (inside out, which actually *was* a pain, now that he had to do something about it). He opened the door quietly and crept down the hall to his uncle's room. The door was locked, the way it had been since Uncle Ross had swiped his mom's computer and holed up in there, probably breaking into the Pentagon or something. He was *supposed* to be baby-sitting, but then again, Ethan was supposed to be asleep.

Downstairs, Ethan pulled on his jacket and hat and put sunscreen on his hands and face, because old habits died hard. Then he let himself out the side door, the one that didn't squeak.

The sun was a kiss on the back of his neck, and who knew that an afternoon could be so bright? Ethan picked up his skateboard and carried it under his arm. He walked down the driveway and turned right, then set his skateboard on the pavement and began to roll. A boy on a BMX bike rode past him, wearing a backward, upside-down visor. 'Hey,' the kid said, as if Ethan was just like everyone else.

'Hey,' he replied, stoked simply to be having a conversation.

'That's a bitchin' board.'

'Thanks.'

'What's with the winter clothes?'

Ethan shrugged. 'What's with the stupid hat?'

The boy spun his wheels. 'I'm heading to the skate park. You want to come?'

Ethan tried to keep his face as blank as he could, but it was hard, being this real. You didn't truly exist in the world, he now understood, until you could get out and make it take notice of you. 'Whatever,' he said indifferently, smiling beneath every inch of his skin. 'I've got nothing better to do.'

What if she'd kissed him?

After three days now, that question had become unavoidable, caught like a thorn in Shelby's mind. She relived in excruciating detail the moment where she and Eli had been too close in too tiny a space; what his skin had smelled like, how she had seen the smallest of scars beneath his right ear. She had lain in bed imagining how he'd gotten it: chicken pox, a fistfight over a girl, a fall on the sharp edge of a hockey skate.

Frankie Martine. Shelby supposed when you looked like *that,* it didn't matter if you had a boy's name.

She had told herself that, really, she wasn't jealous. In the first place, she hardly knew Eli Rochert. In the second place, in Shelby's limited experience, romantic love was selfish – linked to want and yearning. Maternal love was the other end of the scale – all about sacrifice. She had given herself entirely to Ethan; certainly there was nothing left to offer to anyone else. And yet, she wondered if love – as rare a commodity as gold – might not share the same properties, capable of being hammered so thin it might expand exponentially.

Had Eli and Frankie Martine spent the past seventy-two hours together?

Shelby sat at the reference desk, her hands poised over her computer keyboard, as if she expected a patron to come up any moment with a challenging inquiry. *How do our lungs screen out carbon dioxide? How did the dinosaurs die? How many World Series have the Yankees won?* She knew all the answers. She was just afraid to ask questions.

But it was dinnertime, and the last visitor to the library had left two hours ago. Shelby had to stay until seven, although no one would come in. With a frustrated sigh, she set her head down on the desk. She could sit here forever, and neither Eli nor Watson would enter.

So when the bell above the library door twinkled, Shelby snapped upright, hoping in spite of herself. 'Oh, it's you,' she said, watching the town clerk stagger in beneath the weight of a yellowed box nearly as large as herself – and that was saying something.

'Well, that's a fine how-do-you-do!' Lottie huffed, wiping her dirty hands on her skirt.

'It just . . . I was expecting someone else.'

'That gorgeous cop?' Lottie grinned. 'I don't know as I've ever seen anything so delicious *and* calorie-free.'

Laughing, Shelby came around the desk and helped her haul the box onto the checkout counter. 'Trust me, he's still bad for your blood pressure. What's this stuff?'

'We had the boiler replaced yesterday – and found about thirty boxes of records no one even knew existed . . . which tells you how old that boiler was. Anyway, I know you were looking for

things from the 1930s. I thought maybe you and your detective
might want to sort through them.' She raised a brow. 'You could
make a night of it.'

Shelby opened the top of the box, coughing as the dust flew.
Inside were dozens of rolls of paper. 'Blueprints?' She reached
inside and began to unroll one, using two Hardy Boys mysteries
to anchor the ends.

PEDIGREE CHART of the WILKINS FAMILY
Eugenics Survey of Vermont, 1927

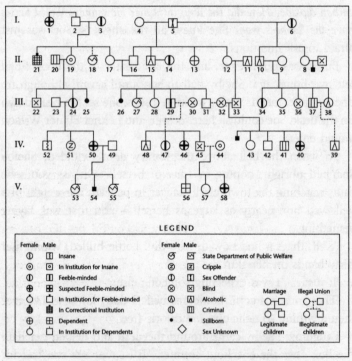

The key seemed to link alcoholics and cripples and sexual
offenders and illegitimate children and criminals. Shelby peered
closer at some of the symbols. *In Institution for Feebleminded.*

Feebleminded. Suspected Feebleminded. Oddly, the records were curled into a clock-dial format, so that it seemed that all of these social ills were spreading with subsequent generations, and rooted to the two unfortunates in the center who'd married and procreated. A second chart, a bar graph, reorganized the family by 'Social' and 'Unsocial' individuals, according to the legend. *Social: Those who seem to be desirable citizens – law-abiding, self-supporting, and doing some social work. Unsocial: insane and suicides. Undetermined: Those who, while not definitely showing either of the defects, do not seem to show any socially desirable tendencies, and those about whom too little is known to make any judgment possible.* 'Lottie,' she said, 'where did you find this?'

She unrolled a second chart on top of the first. PEDIGREE OF A GYPSY FAMILY, the DELACOURS. A handwritten message floated down to the floor. 'Tell Harry – sex-deficiency seems to be holandric. Perhaps use charts in hearings for Sterilization Bill?' The stationery was printed at the top: Spencer A. Pike, Professor of Anthropology, UVM.

The box was filled with more genealogies and correspondence and index cards written in a careful hand, which seemed to be case studies of the people who had figured into these pedigree wheels: Mariette, a sixteen-year-old girl at reform school, had a history of petty larceny, an inability to control her temper, an abnormal interest in sex, and a slovenly disposition. Oswald had dark skin and shifty eyes, had retained his tribe's roving tendency, and, as a result of an 'illegal union,' had produced seven subnormal children in as many years. Shelby pulled out the Fourth Annual Report of the Vermont Committee on Country Life. It fell open to a dog-eared page, an article cowritten by H. Beaumont and S. A. Pike. 'Degenerate traits do not breed out,' Shelby read aloud. 'But they may be held at bay and diluted with a favorable choice of mate.'

'Eugenics,' Lottie read, holding up another annual report. 'What on earth is that?'

'It's the science of improving hereditary qualities by control-
ling breeding.'

'Oh, you mean like they do for cattle.'

'Yes,' Shelby said, 'but these people did it to humans.'

Eli had gone off duty at nine, but years ago he'd made it a habit
of doing a final check before he went home – sort of like tucking
his town in for the night. Normally, when he felt like things were
settled, he'd drive back to his place . . . but tonight, with Cecelia
Pike's murder weighing on his mind, he just didn't feel like his
work was finished.

He drove aimlessly down the access road to the quarry, Watson
at his side. Solving this case wasn't going to get him a citation.
It wasn't going to bring Cissy Pike back to life. And no prosecutor
was going to try a nonagenarian with advanced liver disease. So
why did any of this matter?

Watson turned and butted Eli on the arm. 'It's too cold out.
I'm not rolling down your window.'

The answer was: Cissy Pike had gotten him thinking. About
what it meant to belong – to a family, to a lover, to a heritage –
and what it cost to hide the truth. He knew, as a detective, that
even people you thought you knew could surprise you with their
actions. But it turned out that you could surprise yourself, too.

Eli wanted to go to the ceremony that Az Thompson would
perform to gather the remains of Cissy Pike and her child. Not
because he was a cop involved in the case . . . but because, like
her, he was half-Abenaki. And because, like her, he knew what
it felt like to keep that hidden.

Watson sidled closer on the seat, burrowing his nose in the
neck of Eli's shirt. 'All right,' he conceded, and opened the window.
Watson liked driving that way, the wind flapping his loose lips
up and down like small wings. Suddenly, he raised his nose and
began to howl.

'Jesus, Watson, people are sleeping.'

The dog only keened a higher note, then stood up on the seat and began to wag his tail in Eli's face. Faced with the possibility of driving off the road, Eli pulled over. Watson leaped through the open window as they rolled to a stop, and loped to the fence that surrounded the eastern wall of the quarry. He started to bark, then stood on his hind legs and caught his claws in the chain links as someone on the other side stepped forward. The kid was wearing gloves. It was cold out, but not *that* cold. Squinting, Eli tried to make out a face beneath the brim of the baseball cap, but all he could see was skin that glowed as white as the moon. 'Ethan?' he called out.

The boy's head came up. 'Oh,' he said, deflating before Eli's eyes. 'It's you.'

'What are you doing here? Who let you into the quarry?'

'I let myself in.'

'Your mom know you're here?'

'Sure,' Ethan said.

Eli knew that the quarry was blasting tomorrow at dawn – they always let the police department know, for the sake of safety – and that having Ethan in the vicinity of explosives was not a good idea. 'Climb over,' he ordered.

'No.'

'Ethan, it's just as easy for me to haul ass over the fence and get you myself.'

Ethan took a step back, and for a moment Eli thought he would bolt. But then he tossed his skateboard into Eli's hands, and hurtled toward the chain-link. Scrambling effortlessly as a spider, he dropped to the ground beside Eli and held out his wrists. 'Go ahead. Cuff me for trespassing.'

Eli stifled a smile. 'Maybe I'll break protocol. I'm assuming this is your first offense.' He started walking to the car. 'Want to tell me how you wound up here?'

'I went outside and just kind of kept going.'

Eli looked down at the gloves on Ethan's hands again.

'Didn't she tell you?' the boy said bitterly. 'I'm a freak.'

'She didn't tell me anything.' Eli pretended that he couldn't care less whether Ethan chose to continue the conversation. He dropped Ethan's skateboard, walked to the back of the truck, and whistled for Watson. 'Well. See ya.'

The boy's mouth dropped open. 'You're leaving me here?'

'Why shouldn't I? Your mom knows where you are.'

'You mean you believed me?'

Eli raised a brow. 'Is there a reason I shouldn't?'

In response, Ethan threw his skateboard into the pickup and got into the passenger seat. Eli started to drive. 'When I was born, my fingers were webbed together.' He felt Ethan's gaze shoot to his hands on the steering wheel. 'The doctors had to cut them apart.'

'That's gross,' Ethan said, and then he blushed. 'Sorry.'

'Hey, you know, whatever. It's just the way I was made. Didn't keep me from doing what I wanted to do.'

'I have XP. It's like being allergic to the sun. If I go out during the day, even for a minute, I get burned really badly. And it *does* keep me from doing what I want to do.'

'Which is?'

'Swim in a bathing suit and dry off in the sun. Take a walk outside during the day. Go to school.' He glanced at Eli. 'I'm dying.'

'So's the rest of the world.'

'Yeah, but I'm going to get skin cancer. From all the exposure to the sun before anyone knew what I had. Most kids with XP die before they're twenty-five.'

Eli felt his stomach tighten. 'Maybe you'll be the one who won't.'

Ethan stared out the window for a few miles, silent. Then he said, 'I woke up early, and no one was around. So I went outside. Hung out at the school, skateboarding. But then the other kids had to go home, to bed. And I wasn't even tired, because I'd been

sleeping all day. I just kept walking, and I wound up here. I'm
a freak,' he repeated. 'Even when I try, I don't fit in.'

Eli turned to him. 'What makes you think it's different for
anyone else?'

Ross had fallen asleep over the keyboard, where he was currently
inventing a ghost. He woke up, ran his tongue behind his teeth,
and tasted despair. Even after brushing and rinsing with Listerine
he still couldn't shake it – bitter as licorice, with small crystals
that melted on the tongue and left it the sunset color of hope-
lessness. Grimacing, he padded downstairs to the kitchen to pour
a glass of juice and realized he'd forgotten about Ethan. It was
nearly midnight – and his nephew would have been up for hours.

'Eth?' he yelled, but the house was silent.

When he glanced out the window, Shelby's car wasn't in the
driveway. That was strange, too – she should have come home
from work by nine, at the latest. The message light on the
answering machine blinked like an evil eye; he hit the button.
'Ross, it's Shel. I'm caught up in something you won't believe.
Just tell Ethan I'll be there soon, and make sure you're
home . . . I've got a lot to tell you.'

So she hadn't taken Ethan somewhere. Ross opened the door,
but he wasn't skating in the driveway or holed up in the backyard. Inside, he took the stairs two at a time and opened the door
to Ethan's room. His bed was made; his pajamas twisted in a
Gordian knot on the floor. Where *was* he?

Panic slid down Ross's throat. Any nine-year-old kid could get
into trouble, but for Ethan, the world posed a whole different set
of dangers. 'Ethan, this isn't funny,' he shouted. 'Get your ass over
here.'

But he knew, even as he was calling out, that Ethan wasn't there
to hear. He grabbed his car keys from his bedroom and hurried
downstairs again. Maybe if he could find Ethan before Shelby got
home, no one would have to know that he'd ever been lost.

He had only just gotten into his car when a truck pulled in behind him. Eli Rochert's dog leaped out as if he belonged at Shelby's house, and then Ethan got out of the cab. Ross's eyes did a quick inventory – all in one piece, smiling. Then he considered throttling the kid himself. He looked from Ethan to Eli, who crossed his arms but didn't say a word. 'You want to tell me where you were?'

Before Ethan could answer, Shelby pulled into the driveway. An enormous box was in the hatchback of her car. 'What's going on here?' she asked.

'Nothing,' all three men said simultaneously.

'Then what's a policeman doing at my house at midnight?'

Eli stepped forward. 'I, um, came here because I knew you'd be up. With Ethan. But when I got here, you weren't. Here, I mean.'

Shelby stiffened. 'Did you need more help with research?'

'No, I wanted to ask you out.'

The words seemed to surprise even Eli. Ethan nudged Ross in the side, and he shrugged to show that he didn't know what was going on either. But in that moment, when Eli did not rat out Ethan, Ross's respect for him doubled.

And that wasn't even taking account of what it did for Shelby. She pinked, then looked away, and finally met Eli's eyes. 'I'd like that,' she said.

From the way they were locked onto each other, as if a homing device had pinned them both, Ethan and Ross might as well have been on Jupiter. 'You would?' Eli said.

Ethan snorted. 'I'm gonna hurl,' he announced, and slipped into the house.

His departure broke the spell. Shelby cleared her throat, then opened the hatchback of her car. 'Carry this in for me, will you?'

'What is it?' Ross hefted the box, stumbling under its weight.

Shelby dusted off her hands on her shorts. 'History.'

*   *   *

'It was called *An Act for Human Betterment by Voluntary Steriliza-tion*,' Shelby explained, 'and it was passed on March 31, 1931. Vermont was the twenty-fourth state out of thirty-three to pass sterilization legislation. From what I could dig up, it seems like Henry Perkins was the mastermind behind the genealogical surveys done on families believed to be a burden to taxpayers . . . and Spencer Pike and Harry Beaumont were his right-hand men.'

They had spread out a few of the pedigree charts on the floor of the kitchen, and were sitting cross-legged around them. 'They thought that delinquency and degeneracy were something you could inherit from your parents, like eye color or height. And the best way to make Vermont a showplace for the nation was to make sure its gene pool was as strong as possible. Which, following that logic, meant preventing the folks who were diluting it from having any more kids.'

'Why would anyone have believed them?' Ross asked.

'Because the eugenicists of the thirties were doctors, lawyers, teachers, judges. They were people like Oliver Wendell Holmes, President Coolidge, Margaret Sanger. People who truly felt that what they were doing, in the long run, was best for everyone.' She pulled out papers from the Vermont Industrial School, the Waterbury Hospital for the Insane, the State Prison. 'They started out targeting three families whose individual members kept crop-ping up at state institutions. The Chorea family was chosen because of a recurring neurological disorder. The Pirate family lived on houseboats and in waterfront shanties and was known for loose living and abject poverty. The Gypsy family was nomadic and often in trouble with the law . . . and there were so *many* of them. They weren't even necessarily related – the eugenicists called them "families" just to create that closeness where it didn't always exist. Anyway, in the late 1920s, six thousand people were recorded by the survey's field workers, and organized into sixty-two notorious lineages. The idea was to sterilize these people, so that they wouldn't create more like themselves.'

'Who would be naïve enough to talk to them? Eventually, even these families had to figure out what was going on,' Ross said.

'I imagine that when you live in a tent and have ten children and no money, and a fancy white woman arrives one day and asks to talk to you, you are too surprised to do anything but let her in. And when she asks to see pictures of your children, you show them out of pride. And when she asks about your relatives, you tell family stories. You never know that the whole time, these women are writing down comments about how slovenly your home is and how stupid you are because you can't speak English well.'

Eli had told Ross and Shelby everything he'd learned from Frankie – genealogy, again, of a different sort. Shelby's discovery had been the missing link, the reason why Gray Wolf and Cecelia Pike's kinship might have led to her death. Pike's reaction to that news, given his eugenical convictions, would have been extreme. But would it have made him commit murder?

He hunkered down over one wheel-shaped chart. It was hard to read, but simple to understand – dotted from generation to generation were all the flaws that had made this kinship network a target. Some of the relations at the tail ends of the chart were men and women Eli still knew, most of whom had suffered more than their share of hard times. Was this just a matter of bad luck . . . or had shame kept them in their place? 'How many people were sterilized?' Eli asked.

Shelby shook her head. 'That was the one piece of information I couldn't really find. As of 1951, there were 210 reported sterilizations in Vermont – mostly in institutions for the feebleminded, or the insane asylum, or the jail. Of course, the people who were in those institutions were there in the first place because they weren't living the way society thought they should: their marriages weren't valid, for example, under Vermont law . . . so social services would take their children to the industrial school, the wife to a mental institution for having loose morals, and the husband to jail for being a sexual offender.'

'But the operation was voluntary,' Ross said.

'In theory. But there were different levels of "voluntary." Sometimes the only consent needed was that of two doctors. The patient apparently didn't always know what was best for himself.'

Eli could feel a headache building behind his left eye. In all the years he'd been in this town, he'd never heard of the eugenics project. The site of the survey office, 138 Church Street, was now a shop that sold incense and candles.

He thought of old Tula Patou, who lived down by the river, and had no children in sixty years of marriage. Of uncles and aunts of his own who had remained childless, though not for lack of trying. Had they been sterilized?

Did they even *know*?

There would be people in Comtosook still haunted by the memory of what had happened in the 1930s. People who'd straddled both sides of the debate. Victims who were too afraid to speak of it, for fear that it might happen again. And proponents who kept silent out of guilt.

If the dispute over the Pike property had seemed volatile, then this discovery was incendiary.

Suddenly Eli remembered standing with his mother in line to register for school. He couldn't have been more than five, and the sun was strong on the neat part she'd made in his hair. She held his hand like all the other mothers, but when they were coming close to the secretary at the table, she kissed him on the cheek and told him she would wait for him outside. 'With your looks, you can pass,' she told him cryptically, when he caught up with her afterward.

It was not that the Abenaki didn't remember the days when they were mistakenly christened Gypsies; it was that they remembered too well.

Eli bent over another pedigree chart. 'What if Pike didn't know? What if his beloved wife gave birth . . . to a baby a little too dark-skinned?'

'And she was in Gray Wolf's company, because she'd found out he was her natural father—' Ross interrupted.

'And Pike assumed, incorrectly, that the baby was Gray Wolf's.'

To a man who had spent his career proving that the Abenaki were genetically inferior, this would not sit well. It explained why Pike might have buried the stillborn before any authorities could see its face. And it explained why he might have killed his wife.

'What happened to the project? Why did it stop?' Ross asked.

Shelby began to gather some of the documents again. 'They ran out of funding. And then along came Hitler. The Nazi Law for Protection Against Genetically Defective Offspring was based on American models for sterilizing the unfit.'

'So when was the Vermont law repealed?'

'That's the thing,' Shelby said. 'It wasn't, entirely. It was challenged by the ACLU in the seventies . . . and the original language has been changed . . . but there *is* still a sterilization law in effect.'

Suddenly a name on this particular chart leaped out at Eli. Pial Sommers, married to Isobel DuChamps, who was feebleminded. Their children: Winona, Ella, and Sopi, who had died at age seven. Ella Sommers had married a man she met while working as a waitress in Burlington. His name was Robert Rochert, and he had been Eli's father.

Pial Sommers had been one of seven children, the only one who was not, according to this chart, insane or criminal or perverse. One short dotted line separated him from his mother's side of the family, and ten first cousins, the youngest of whom was named John 'Gray Wolf' Delacour.

Ethan rolled over on his bed as his uncle opened the door to his bedroom. 'You still up?' Ross asked.

He had been staring out the window, watching the sun come up. As always, a thick pane of glass was protecting him. He knew he'd totally lucked out; if Eli Rochert had decided to be honest and if his mother hadn't come home with that box of old papers, he'd have been reamed up one side and down another for sneaking away.

'I know what you're going to say,' Ethan sighed. 'And it's not like I wanted you to get in trouble too.' He picked at a stitch on the quilt that covered his bed, a lame blue thing with babyish trucks on its hem. Didn't anyone except him realize that he was growing up? 'It's just that she doesn't get it. Not like *you* would.'

Ross sat down on the bed, and put the laptop he'd been carrying on the floor. 'Why me?'

With shining eyes, Ethan turned to his uncle. 'Because you've skydived, and played chicken with a train, and fought back when someone pulled a knife on you. All those stories you tell me about things you've done. Sometimes I wake up and think I want to run until there's nowhere left to go, and that if I *don't* do it I might as well just croak right here and now.'

Ross shook his head. 'When I do those things, it's not for the thrill. It's because sometimes I get so down that I need to feel something, anything. And since a pinprick isn't cutting it, I've got to try a meat cleaver.'

'I know,' Ethan breathed. 'And that *rocks.*'

'The thing is, Eth, I'd give anything to be sitting on a bed in a house that was safe, knowing that on the other side of the wall was someone who would rather die than think of me being hurt.' He pulled at the same stitch on the quilt that Ethan had toyed with, and unraveled one appliquéd truck. 'Don't try so hard to be me,' Ross said, 'when all I'm trying to be is someone else.'

Suddenly Ethan felt like a sock was stuck in his throat, and those stupid tears were coming. 'I just want to be normal,' he said.

'Yeah, well . . . if it weren't for you and me, normal people would have nothing to measure themselves against.'

Ethan hiccuped on a laugh. 'I guess we'd better stick together.'

'That's good,' Ross answered, opening the laptop so that Ethan could see the screen. 'Because I'm counting on your help.'

* * *

By the time Eli got home from Shelby's house, and this new package of nightmares, it was after three in the morning. The blasting at the quarry started at five, but he managed to get back to sleep with a pillow over his head. So when his doorbell rang at 6:30 A.M., he seriously considered taking his piece and shooting in that general direction, just to make the caller go away. Then he weighed the time he'd be stripped of his shield, and the ridiculous amount of paperwork he'd have to file for the simple discharge of a bullet, and dragged himself out of bed in his boxer shorts.

Frankie exploded into the apartment the minute he unlocked the door. 'Wait'll you hear this,' she said, making her way into the kitchen, where she held up the empty coffeepot and tsked. 'I tested that nightgown at the state lab for you.'

'Frankie—'

'You know that stuff you thought was the victim's blood?'

'Yeah.'

'Well, it wasn't. Don't you keep your coffee in the freezer, Eli, like the rest of the modern world?' She turned around, holding the coffeepot aloft. 'You're wearing your underpants, for God's sake.'

'Underwear. Grown men don't wear underpants.'

'Grown men usually get dressed before they answer the door.'

'Frankie,' Eli sighed, 'I've had about three hours of sleep. Don't screw with me.'

She unearthed the coffee, which was – of all places – in a box with his black shoe polish on top of the fridge, and began to measure it out. 'It's meconium.'

'No, I think it's Colombian.'

'The stain, you jerk. On the nightgown.'

Eli yawned and scratched his chest. He was too tired, at this point, to even care about covering himself for Frankie, who was far more interested in whatever her tests had yielded than his body anyway. 'So what's meconium? Something radioactive? You're not gonna tell me aliens hanged her, are you?'

'It's feces. Baby poop.'

'Yeah, well, we already know she gave birth that night. So what.'

The coffeemaker sputtered, and Frankie found two mismatched mugs. 'You told me the woman gave birth to a dead baby. Dead babies don't pass stools.'

Her last sentence cut through Eli's senses, and he swam out of his fog. 'Hang on—'

'Hello,' Frankie said. 'That baby was alive.'

Today was Bingo Day, and although Eli had absolutely no intention of playing, some well-meaning staffer at the nursing home had plunked a card in front of him. 'B-11,' said the activities co-ordinator, a large woman in a jumpsuit that made her look like a prize-winning pumpkin. 'B-11!'

He saw Spencer Pike before the old man saw him, and approached the intern who was wheeling him into the room before he reached the table. 'I can take care of this,' Eli said, taking the handles of the chair and repositioning Pike in a corner, away from the grainy speakers of the Bingo caller.

Eli was unprepared for the way hate spread through him viscerally. This was the man who had tried to erase his family. This man once thought he had the right to decide what kind of life was worth living. This man had played God.

Eli had cringed when he'd read the 1932 police reports, where brutality was the order of the day and Miranda wasn't even a gleam in some detective's eye. But cruelty came easily, it turned out, when you had so much anger swimming in you that you risked floating away on the tide.

'Go away,' Spencer Pike said distinctly.

Eli leaned closer, pinning Pike's shoulders to the back of his chair. 'You lied to me, Spencer.'

'I don't even know who you are.'

'That's bullshit, and you know it. Your brain's just fine. I bet you remember everything you did in your life. I bet you even remember their names.'

'*Whose* names?'

'O-75,' the activities coordinator chirped. 'Do we have a Bingo?'

'You thought you were so smart, telling the cops you'd only just cut down your wife's body. But you'd cut it down hours before you called them.'

A vein throbbed in the old man's temple. 'This is ridiculous.'

'Is it? I mean, I wasn't there. I wasn't even *alive*. So how could I possibly know?' Eli paused. 'You ever heard about forensics, Spencer? You know how many things a dead body can tell us these days? Like when she was killed. How it was done. Who was stupid enough to leave clues behind.'

Spencer pushed at him ineffectively. 'Get away from me.'

'Who'd you kill first, Spencer? The baby, or your wife?'

'Nurse!'

'It must have made you crazy to know that you'd married one. That your child was one.'

Pike's face had gone white. 'One what?'

'*Gypsy,*' Eli said.

Almost immediately, Pike struggled halfway out of his chair. His skin darkened, and his watery eyes fixed on Eli. 'You . . . you . . .' he wheezed.

'I-20. Anyone?'

Pike clutched his chest and scrambled to grab at the armrests, but missed and fell forward, landing on the floor. The activities coordinator cried out and came running from the front of the room. Two burly interns headed toward them. Eli leaned down beside Pike. 'How does it feel, not being able to fight back?' he whispered.

In the melee that followed, Pike battled the staff trying to help him, shouting obscenities and scratching a nurse deep enough to draw blood. Pandemonium broke out in the activities room, with some patients egging Pike on, others weeping, and two coming to blows over who had called Bingo first. Eli slipped out of the room unnoticed. He walked down the main hall of the rest home and out the front door, whistling.

Maylene Warburton moved a crystal an eighth of an inch to the right and lifted her face to the sky with expectation. A moment later, she swore and turned to her husband. 'Curtis, I can't conjure anything with him standing here. The negativity is keeping all the spirits away.'

From his spot on a folding camping chair, Rod van Vleet exploded. 'It's been four hours, and Wakeman didn't seem to have this much difficulty. Did you ever think maybe it's *you*?'

'You see what I mean?' Maylene cried.

'Cut!' Curtis called, and he clapped the cameraman on his shoulder as he walked into the clearing of the Pike property. 'Johannes, take five.' He smiled at his wife, placating, and pulled her toward Rod. 'If we aren't all on the same page here, it's no wonder the spirits won't come.'

'*Spirit*,' Rod clarified. 'Getting rid of one is enough.'

He was beginning to believe his original premise – namely, that all paranormal investigators were nutcases and that ghosts were about as real as the Tooth Fairy. The Warburtons had seemed a natural choice, since Ross Wakeman had touted Curtis as a mentor and since *Bogeyman Nights* was one of the better-known supernatural shows on cable. Plus, Curtis had asked to bring a camera, and to interview Rod on film. Who could resist that kind of PR?

But after a lot of hoo-ha and posturing and some grand cere-mony that involved Warburton's so-called psychic wife sticking rocks all over the place, no ghost had appeared. There had been no chains dragged, no bumps in the night, not even a faint moan. The EMF meter that had been set in stationary position beside a rock – after everyone had removed their watches and phones and everything else that might affect the magnetic field there – remained inactive. Next, Curtis Warburton would tell him that sometimes it took several sittings for a spirit to warm up to an investigator.

'You know,' Curtis said, 'sometimes, we need to spend a few consecutive nights in order for the ghost to feel comfortable enough to show itself.'

Rod rolled his eyes. 'Yeah. Well. The fact of the matter is, maybe it decided to up and leave without any help from—'

Whatever he had been about to say was interrupted by a flash of light that originated from nowhere and seemed to bounce around, skimming the toes of Rod's loafers before growing brighter.

'Johannes,' Curtis yelled. 'Get your ass back here!'

The light was so bright now that Rod could see his shadow, as if it were daylight. Speechless, he squatted down toward the ground.

His shadow didn't.

'Oh my God,' Rod whimpered. 'Oh, holy shit.'

The black mass moved across the field of light and raised its arms. Overhead, pale pink globules of light began to rise into the night. A breeze rolled over the clearing, plunging it into darkness again, and scenting the air with a lady's perfume.

'By any chance,' Maylene asked, 'is your ghost a woman?'

Rod's insides had begun to quake. 'It's her. It's the wife that was killed.'

'This isn't your place anymore,' Curtis said loudly. 'This isn't your time.'

The only warning he had was a rustle of leaves overhead, as a heavy limb from the tree beside him came crashing down, narrowly missing his head, and crushing the cameraman's knapsack. 'God*damn*,' breathed Johannes.

'You need to go to the light,' Curtis urged.

Rod felt something stir in his hands, and suddenly the jacket he was holding flew out of his arms and flung itself into the middle of the clearing, as if it had been possessed. 'Hey!' he cried, standing abruptly. 'It took my coat!'

'I think she's trying to convey how she feels about you taking over her land,' Curtis explained.

Rod turned in a frantic circle. 'It's *my* land!'

'Curtis, the temperature's dropping.' Maylene waved a digital thermometer in the air. 'And look at this.' On the ground, their EMF meter was blinking wildly. A thick white fog spilled from the sky, concentrating itself into the clearing.

'Keep filming, Johannes,' Curtis whispered, and then more loudly, 'You can't live here anymore. You can cross to the other side. Show us a sign of departure!'

The mist dissipated, and Rod glanced down to find the ground covered with rose petals. He knelt and picked one up, rubbing it between his thumb and forefinger, and looking up at the clear sky.

At the sound of a click, all three of them jumped. 'Sorry,' Johannes said. 'That's the end of the tape.'

'Well. I think we both got what we need,' Curtis said, smiling at Rod.

He stood up, looking around. 'You mean that's it? She's gone now?'

'It's what you wanted, isn't it?'

Rod nodded. 'But what keeps her from coming back?'

'Once she finds her way to the other side, there's no reason for it. Unless, of course, your check bounces.' Curtis grinned at his own joke, then began to gather the equipment his production crew had brought. Maylene repacked her crystals in a small silk pouch.

Rod handed Curtis Warburton an envelope with his prearranged fee, and followed him out toward the front of the property, where their cars were parked. 'So . . . that's it? I can build on it now?'

'You could have built on it before,' Curtis said. 'But now you won't have a roommate.'

'Curtis.' Maylene reached out the passenger-side window of their van. 'Can we please get out of Mayberry and find a Starbucks?'

'Coming.' He shook Rod's hand. 'Do me a favor, will you? When you see Ross Wakeman again, tell him what happened tonight.' He got into the van, waving as he drove down Otter Creek Pass.

The van passed another vehicle on its way, and Rod squinted into the headlights until they switched off. A sheriff's car, its motor still humming, sat a few feet away from him. 'Mr van Vleet?' the deputy said.

'Yes?' Rod's heart began to pound. Was it illegal to evict a ghost? 'This is for you.'

He slit open the sealed envelope from the county court, read the contents, and swore under his breath.

Now that he'd gotten rid of his ghost, Rod was being evicted too.

As Ethan rappelled down the trunk of the tree, Ross caught him by the waist. 'Easy,' he said. 'You don't want to break anything.'

He had waited to reveal himself for a full hour after he'd heard Rod van Vleet drive away, just in case. Ross reached up and stretched out the kinks in his body as Ethan swung his feet onto solid ground. 'Got it all,' he promised, patting the backpack he wore. Several of the half-filled helium balloons – their globules – were tangled around his waist, floating at half-mast. 'I didn't leave anything up there.'

The scent, the globules, the roses, the fog – these were all things Ross had seen when Lia had first come, organic signs of a spirit. Except this time, they'd been hand-made. 'You got the projector? The wires? And all of the mirrors?'

'I even took the fishing line.' Ethan grinned widely. 'Did you see that dude's face when his jacket went flying?'

'I *told* you not to try that. What if he'd moved, and gotten a hook in his palm?' Ross glanced around at the equipment he and Ethan had set up before the Warburtons' arrival tonight. There was a sweet irony to perpetrating a hoax upon the man who had built a career of doing just that – but Ross had known all along that the odds of pulling this off were in his favor. In the first place, Warburton wanted to look like a success, so he wouldn't have been hunting for anything fishy. Add to that the darkness, and the fact that the haunted area was outside rather than in the confines of a room – and it had been simple enough for Ross to jerry-rig mirrors and lights and balloons.

'I couldn't breathe from the dry ice,' Ethan said, still animated. He watched Ross bend down to sweep up rose petals shaken loose from Shelby's pillowcases. 'If you get those dirty, my mom will kill you.'

'She's already going to murder me for using up a bottle of her perfume,' Ross pointed out. He headed toward a small patch of white petals that he had missed.

'The coolest thing was the thermometer. How'd you get the temperature to drop?' Ethan asked.

Ross hefted the Styrofoam-packed dry ice onto his shoulder and started walking through the woods, to the spot where he'd hidden his car. 'That wasn't me,' he admitted. 'I think we just got lucky.'

He had wondered, too, while he was sitting in the upper-most branches of a tree and watching the ground show below, at the stroke of good fortune that had caused the air to cool at just that moment. It was certainly something that could be explained meteorologically, from a sudden wind to a swift weather front moving through. But the EMF meter reading was another story. Ross had held that very EMF meter in his hand; it was sensitive enough to pick up the presence of a person on the other side of a wall, or the approach of a thunderstorm.

He had made certain that he and Ethan would be too far away to trigger the EMF with their equipment . . . yet it had still signaled. There had been no approaching physical body to set it off, no inclement weather. Chalk it up to a glitch in the system, a battery failure, a mistake.

Or, Ross thought, a wish blossoming, *maybe not.*

Eli stood beside the chief of police, decked out in dress regalia because the chief knew a photo-op when he saw one, and squinted as the camera flashes went off in his face. He wasn't watching the main event, however – Chief Follingsbee giving Az Thompson the court order from a district judge that officially halted development on the Pike property, pending the removal of Abenaki remains from the site. Instead, Eli scanned the faces of the crowd – people he had known all his life who suddenly looked entirely different.

Winks, for example, had a drinking problem and a wife who'd left him for one of the students she'd taught English to at the high school. But today he was smiling to beat the band, this triumph made sweeter by the fact that he'd had so many runs of hard luck. Old Charlie Rope had come out for this, and had his granddaughter balanced on his shoulders. 'You watch,' Eli heard the old man say, bouncing her lightly. 'This is something we need to remember.'

Even stoic Az Thompson, the unofficial Abenaki spokesman, seemed moved by the occasion. This was a victory, and there had been few. Every time the Abenaki had mustered the effort to purchase lands, or win fishing rights, they were defeated on the grounds that they had not been federally recognized as a tribe and therefore had no rights to speak of. According to the Bureau of Indian Affairs, to be a tribe an indigenous group needed to show a continuous cultural history for hundreds of years.

For the Abenaki, there was a gaping hole that began in the 1930s.

Eli had always assumed that this was due to the Abenaki's seeming lack of organization, or drive, or both. But now he wondered if they'd been put in a catch-22 of their own making.

As Shelby had said the night before – to keep from being targeted by the eugenicists in the thirties, the Abenaki had intermarried and taken on white names and jobs. They'd moved out of state and blended in with other existing tribes. They'd hid their own traditions behind closed doors, to keep from losing it forever. And now, they were being punished for it.

Eli watched some of the Abenaki drift back to the big drum they'd carried in for the occasion. Their voices, deep and urgent, plaited together in the most unlikely melody. Indian songs did not follow a set course; they were more like rivers, which went where they needed to. Eli could remember summers on the banks of the lake with his mother's family; how this music would seep through the crack in the tent at nighttime, how it would carry him to sleep.

This song, it was their history. Like the rest of Abenaki memoir, it was oral – written words, like that paper that Az was holding now, meant nothing until they created a legend, told by Charlie Rope's granddaughter to her own children. Eli wondered how many of these men and women remembered what had happened in Comtosook under the direction of Spencer Pike. The very fact that there had been such a conspicuous silence about it was meaningful – it had not been passed down, for some reason. This story, Eli realized, was all the more important for what had not been said.

'This,' said a voice at his shoulder, 'is an outrage.' Rod van Vleet looked ready to spit as he stood on the fringe of the media that was immortalizing this moment. 'This is my land, and frankly I don't care if it's owned by retarded bald eagles in wheelchairs – I paid for it, fair and square.'

'I'm sure you'll get your money back,' Eli said, although he wasn't sure of this at all. 'The last thing they'd want to be accused of is being a bunch of Indian givers.'

Van Vleet narrowed his eyes, not at all appreciative of Eli's joke. He pushed his way through the knot of reporters and took his contract from Spencer Pike out of his pocket. 'The hell with you,' he said.

He tore up the paper and tossed the pieces into the air. They fluttered down, light as feathers. When they landed, Eli noticed one small root poking through the dirt. It looked to be a crocus. At some point, apparently, that frozen ground had begun its thaw. Who else knew what lay hidden?

Eli put his hands in his pockets and walked toward the group of Abenaki who were singing. Words rose from his throat, refrains he had forgotten he ever knew. And even people miles away in Swanton and Morrisville, who had been listening to the song of the wind without even realizing it, suddenly stopped mowing their lawns and wiping down their kitchen counters, somehow aware that the melody had changed.

The transformations were gradual, but because they had been expecting them this time, people in Comtosook took notice. When Scotch tape failed to stick, they smiled knowingly. When the melons in the Gas & Grocery grew so ripe that the smell of summer rolled onto the sidewalk like fog, everyone understood. They found four-leaf clovers in their wallets, pressed between the largest bills; they heard bobcats sobbing in the hills; they found their pillows too soft at night – all things that could have been chalked up to any number of causes, but that instead were attributed to their ghost.

And so it was that when Ross came outside onto Shelby's porch and saw what he did, he thought twice. It could have been squirrels; it could have been a neighbor kid's prank. Or it could have been something else entirely that had meticulously arranged seventeen tiny stones in the shape of a heart.

This was not his mother. Ethan watched the imposter getting ready for her date from his nest on the bed, humming as she snapped on her holiday earrings, using that goop girls wiped on their eyelashes if they were in the habit of wearing makeup, putting perfume on in places that made no sense – the backs of her knees, the pucker of her belly button.

'Are you two going to hook up?' Ethan asked.

'Hook up?'

'Yeah, you know. Do it.'

His mother, in the process of slipping into a high-heeled shoe, stumbled. 'What kind of a question is that?'

He thought for a minute. 'A smart one.'

'Well,' she said. 'I haven't decided yet.'

Ethan began to pick at the knotting on the quilt. 'If I were you, I'd do it. But only if he lets you shoot off his gun once or twice.'

His mother got that look, the one where she did a really bad job of trying not to smile. 'I'll tell him you suggested that.'

Ethan considered what he knew of making out – it seemed to him about as gross as some girl spitting into a glass, and then giving it to him to drink. 'Then again, it might not be worth it.'

She tugged at his cap, so that it twisted around backward. 'Get back to me on that when you're older.'

'I'm never going to kiss any girls.' Ethan watched her stand up, check herself out in the mirror. He had to admit, she looked . . . pretty. And something about that made him feel like the room was spinning.

'Trust me . . . it's irrefragable. One day you're going to want to do that more than anything else in the world.'

'And who,' Ethan said, 'is going to want to do that with *me?*'

His mother paused, then came to sit beside him on the bed. She touched his face as if it were the most beautiful thing she had ever seen, instead of the chalk-white mask of a monster. 'Many, many smart women,' she answered, looking into his eyes. 'We may have to beat them off with a stick.'

'As if,' Ethan answered, ducking away, when what he really meant was: *I hope I'm here to see it.*

She hugged him, and for some reason, he let her, although

he'd given up that kind of lovey-dovey stuff a year ago. Her eyes were bright with a world that did not include Ethan. And because it was going to be that way sooner or later, he found the strength to let her go.

In the dark of his room at Shelby's, Ross was kissed awake. He felt the soft pressure of a mouth against his, the sigh that breathed into his own lungs, and he raised his arms from the cocoon of covers to pull this moment tight against him before it could bleed into the next. He reached out, and found himself grabbing at nothing.

He knocked over the alarm clock and flicked on the lamp, suddenly alert. Sitting up, he confirmed what he already knew: he was alone in his bedroom, the door locked just the way he'd left it the night before. And his bed was now spotted with hundreds of rose petals.

'Where *are* you?' He jumped to his feet in only his boxers, yanking the covers off with one good tug. He lifted the mattress and threw it onto the floor. He shoved at the footboard, sliding the bed away from the wall. Frustrated and breathing hard, he sank to the carpet and buried his face in his hands. *Just once,* Ross thought, *I would like to be the kind of guy who gets lucky. Just once I'd like someone to live for.*

The knocking on the door grew louder. 'Ross? You in there? I thought I heard something fall down.'

He dragged himself to his feet and unlocked the door, opened it just a crack. In the hall his sister stood dressed to the nines, trying to see over his shoulder. 'I tripped,' he lied.

'Oh. You're okay?'

'Great. Fantastic.' Ross nodded at her dress. 'You look nice.'

She blushed. 'Thanks. The date. You said you'd watch Ethan.'

'Yeah, I remember,' Ross said, although he hadn't. 'Give me a minute.'

He closed the door and reached for the jeans that he'd left on the floor before going to sleep. How could he not have fallen for Lia, a woman who – like Ross himself – would have given anything to change the circumstances of her existence . . . but could not figure out how?

He could still taste her.

He was about to leave when he turned back, walked to the puddle of linens on the floor, and shook them out onto the bed again. The sheets floated down, still fragrant with the scent of roses. But the petals themselves had vanished, disappearing without a visible trace.

Sometimes, being a public servant paid off. Such as tonight, when Eli had wanted to do something special for Shelby – like providing her with a memorable date at approximately two in the morning, when most restaurants were closed. He unlocked the door to the Italian bistro and held it open so that she could step inside. She sniffed at the traces of oregano and garlic wafting from the kitchen. 'You moonlight as a chef?'

'No . . . I just know the right people.' He led Shelby to the table he'd set up earlier this evening. A bottle of red wine sat beside a single candle. A rose was draped over her plate.

Eddie Montero had come to Eli a month ago, asking for his help in nailing an employee who was stealing from the cash register. A few surveillance cameras had done the trick – although Eli imagined that Eddie hadn't had the heart to reprimand his mother, a part-time substitute waitress who also had kleptomaniac tendencies. Still, he'd been happy enough to loan Eli his establishment off-hours, and even went so far as to prepare a meal that was waiting in the warming oven for them. A heart-healthy meal, unfortunately, without any goddamned red meat.

'You know,' Shelby said, as he pulled out her chair, 'I could have come out at a normal hour.'

'But then I wouldn't have been the only guy staring at you.' In heels and a tight black dress, Shelby Wakeman looked nothing like the brown mouse she pretended to be at the library, or the harried mother she actually was. She'd tumbled her hair into a knot at the top of her head, which only made her eyes more luminous and her mouth seem softer. If Eli had felt some primal pull between them before, he was absolutely captivated by her now.

He served the salad and antipasto, and poured the wine. 'Eddie picked the vintage,' Eli admitted. 'I can't tell a Riesling from a Riunite.'

'I'm pretty sure the Riunite is the one with the twist-off cap.'

'Ah, right. I knew there was a clue.' Eli tipped his glass against Shelby's, listening to the crystal sing. 'To first dates,' he toasted.

Shelby shook her head and put down her glass. 'I can't drink to that.'

A sinking feeling started in Eli's stomach. 'You can't?'

'No. I've been thinking about it, and I don't really want to have a first date. By definition, they're awful, aren't they?'

It took Eli a few moments to find an appropriate response. 'What do you think we ought to do, then?'

Shelby smiled. 'I want to have a second date.'

'By definition,' he repeated, 'doesn't that imply that we've had a first one?'

'Well, it certainly suggests that we know all the bare facts about each other already.'

'Which we don't . . .'

'We know enough to have gotten us here.'

A smile stretched across Eli's face as understanding dawned. 'What did he do . . . throw up in your lap? Talk about how your eyes reminded him of his ex?'

'Who?'

'Whoever it was that ruined first dates for you.'

Shelby pleated her napkin. 'Actually, this is my first date. I'm going strictly on hearsay.'

'I find that hard to believe.'

'Oh, I could tell you stories that would—'

'No,' Eli interrupted. 'I mean, I find it hard to believe that this is your first date.'

'Well, I meant since having Ethan.'

Eli feigned nonchalance. 'What happened to Ethan's dad?'

'Last I heard, he was living in Seattle. We don't really connect much.' Shelby moved her food around her plate. 'He divorced me after Ethan was born. He couldn't handle having a kid with XP.'

'XP,' he repeated.

'That's the condition Ethan's got – the one that means he can't be out in the sunlight. It's a genetic abnormality – and very rare.'

Eli had talked with Ethan about it . . . but briefly. The only thing he remembered the kid saying was that he wasn't going to live long. 'Is he . . . is he going to be okay?'

'No,' Shelby said softly. 'He's not.'

Her chin came up, but she did not say anything else. Eli set down his fork. 'There's nothing doctors can do?'

'The only thing they can do is tell you ahead of time. So you know what to expect, although I don't think you're ever ready for something like this. But most genetic counselors don't even think to look for XP. I wouldn't have even gone to one, if Thomas hadn't had cystic fibrosis in his family.'

'Didn't the doctor flag it?'

'She. And no, she didn't. It turned out that my appointment was canceled. When I got down there, I was pretty annoyed, like most of the other patients who had been left high and dry. One of them had heard the receptionist talking on the phone – apparently the reason for the snafu was that the doctor had taken the day off to get an abortion herself.' Shelby's hand crept to her abdomen unconsciously. 'I thought about that, a lot. It was certainly her choice to do what she needed to do, and I have no idea what her reasons were. But I also realized that I wouldn't give up on that baby inside me – not even if it had cystic fibrosis, or XP, or anything else. Nothing that geneticist was going to tell me would change my mind . . . so it didn't make any sense to reschedule my appointment.'

Eli and his wife had not had children before she ran off with another man. He wondered, now, what he would have done if she'd not only taken herself away, but also his baby. He imagined that no matter how it came about, losing a child was something that you kept coming back to, like the hole in your gum when you lost a tooth or a scar you'd worry with your fingertips – a disfigurement that you felt over and over. 'Ethan seems like a great kid,' Eli said.

'A handful of years with him still beats a lifetime with anyone else.' She smiled. 'He had some advice for me about this date. So did Ross.'

'Oh, yeah?'

'Ross told me never to trust a man who makes people confess for a living.'

'And Ethan?'

'I may just hang onto his pearl of wisdom for a while longer,' Shelby laughed.

Eli leaned back in his seat. 'Your brother, he's interesting.'

'That's a nice way of saying it,' Shelby replied, buttering her bread. 'More often, I hear terms like *drifter* and *fuck-up.*'

'You don't think of him like that.'

'No. I think he's lost. And that's a circumstance that only lasts as long as it takes to be found by someone else.' A curl fell out of her topknot; she tucked it behind her ear. 'Happiness comes easier to some people than others. Ross wants to be happy; he wants it more than anyone I've ever met. But asking him to actually find his way there . . . well, that's like asking him to spread his arms and fly. He just can't, is all.'

'What about you?' he asked. 'You take care of Ethan and you stand up for Ross. But who's watching out for you?'

Eli reached for Shelby's hand, which was wrapped too tightly around the stem of her wineglass. He watched her mouth relax, and then, in the moment it took for her to remember herself, she pulled away. 'Here I am confabulating about myself—'

'Why do you do that?' he asked.

'Do what?'

'Use words no one else understands.'

'It means—'

'I don't care,' Eli said. 'I just want to know why you never say what you really mean.'

He thought she would sidestep the question, but she met his gaze. 'With words, you know what you're getting. When I know the right thing to say, there aren't any surprises.'

He leaned in a little. 'Go ahead. Ask me the *wrong* thing.'

She hesitated, then lowered her voice, as if there were other people around. 'Why *me,* Eli?'

He stood up and drew her close, as if this might be the way to answer her question.

'Why?' Shelby repeated.

'Because dancing's what you do on the second date,' Eli said, deliberately misunderstanding her. He tucked her tighter, feeling her head beneath his chin, her jaw against his collarbone.

'There isn't any music.'

'You think?' Eli said softly, and he rocked Shelby in his arms until she too heard the silver sound of nothing at all.

Ross stood at the highest ledge of the granite quarry, watching his nephew scramble over huge chips and pillars left by yesterday's blasting that hadn't yet been mined. It surprised him, after being so reckless with his own life, to feel so incredibly nervous watching someone he loved taking a risk. But in return for helping Ross at the Pike property, Ethan asked to spend one night living on the edge – literally. And because he deserved it, Ross had been determined to make it happen.

He had gotten the permission of the security guard – Az Thompson. With Shelby gone on her date, Ross knew he had a good few hours to take Ethan on this field trip. Az stood beside Ross, watching Ethan shimmy up a long sloping piece of rose-colored granite. 'You won't get in trouble for this, will you?' Ross asked.

'Only if the kid hurts himself.'

'He better not.'

'Will *you* get in trouble for this?' Az asked.

'Probably,' Ross admitted. 'I'm supposed to be taking care of him.' He kicked at a pebble, which fell over the lip of the quarry to strike hundreds of feet below. 'Speaking of which, I never thanked you for the other night.'

'No need.'

Ross shook his head. 'I . . . well, a lot happened just before you got to me. I found my ghost.'

'I heard.'

'You don't seem surprised.'

'I wasn't the one who needed convincing,' Az said.

'Eli Rochert said you're going to do some kind of ceremony?'

'Friday, at dawn. You coming?'

Ross could not speak for a moment. Eli had explained that the ritual would be a private one, limited to the officials needed to dig up the remains and the Abenaki spiritual leaders. He was not an official, and he was not Abenaki; therefore, he had no illusions about being invited. He had even told himself that seeing the remains of this woman who'd come alive only for him would be like losing her all over again.

Yet there was a part of him that wanted so badly to be present. Because if Lia's body was being put to rest, chances were that her spirit would come to bear witness. And if she saw Ross, maybe this time she would not leave.

'I'll be there,' Ross said quietly.

Az crossed his arms over his chest. 'What they should be doing, instead of digging up this grave, is burying Spencer Pike alive.'

Ross looked hard at Az. Az, who had protested the development of the Pike property before there was any concrete proof. Az, who was old enough to have heard about Spencer Pike's crusade for sterilization. Eli had told him that the old man had moved to Comtosook in the seventies, and that he'd come from the Midwest. But Shelby had said that in the 1930s some of the Abenaki had migrated to escape what was happening in Vermont – joining up with the Ojibway in Michigan and Minnesota and Wisconsin. They had taken their stories. And Az would have listened.

'How much,' Ross asked, 'did you know?'

Az shrugged. 'Enough.'

'You didn't tell anyone. You could have walked right up to Eli and told him about Spencer Pike and eugenics.'

'Why bring up something that hurts so much, if it's not going to change anything?'

'But it does. It keeps it from happening again.'

Az raised a brow. 'Do you really believe that?'

Ross started to nod, but then realized he would be lying. The truth was, history repeated itself on a daily basis; mistakes were made over and over. People were haunted by what they had done, and by what they hadn't had time to do. 'Gray Wolf,' he said suddenly. 'You know what happened to him, don't you?'

The old man stared up at the yellow eye of the moon. 'Where I used to live, every few years, there would be rumors about people seeing him. In line at the bank, or sitting in the back of a bus, or dealing in a casino.'

'Like Elvis.' Ross smiled. He should have known better. Reality sometimes morphed into legend, but the equation never went the other way. 'Well, I suppose it doesn't matter, really. The guy's probably dead by now.'

'I'm 102,' Az said softly, 'but who's counting.'

10

'I killed her.' Az pressed the small wad of gauze to the spot on his arm where blood had just been drawn and looked calmly at the detective sitting across from him in the examination room.

Eli didn't even blink. 'The evidence doesn't suggest that.'

'Far as I know, there's still a warrant out for me.'

Ross put down the tongue depressor that he'd dressed with a cotton ball hairdo, a makeshift puppet. After confessing his identity, Az had agreed to meet with Eli. Ross half expected him to skip town again – but he'd been waiting on the steps of the police station when Ross had arrived. He'd allowed Eli to fingerprint him, and even Ross could see those telltale arches, the same ones that had been on Gray Wolf's fingerprint card from the State Prison. And when Eli had gone one step further and asked Az for a blood sample for DNA typing, the old man was the one who suggested they do it right away.

But why confess after seventy years?

'I killed her,' Az repeated. 'I found a girl who grew up like royalty, and explained she wasn't a princess after all. It doesn't matter if I wound that rope around her neck, if I was even there that night. She wouldn't have died if I hadn't told her she was my daughter.'

'You must have realized that finding out the truth wouldn't be easy for her,' Eli said.

'I wasn't thinking of the choices she'd have to make. I just wanted to get to know her, because she was what I'd be leaving behind in this world. Only it didn't work out that way.'

'Did you tell Pike, too?'

'No.'

'Do you think Lia told him?'

'I think she was afraid to,' Az said. 'He'd locked her up the week before. She had been suicidal — and he said he wanted to keep an eye on her, keep her from hurting herself. In Spencer Pike's mind, announcing you were a Gypsy was just as self-destructive.'

'Why didn't you take her out of there?' Ross accused. 'You could have saved her.' And yet, he knew that even if Az Thompson had spirited Lia off to Canada to have her child, she still would not be his. She would be an old woman. The only reason he had ever met her at all was because she *had* died when she did.

'Her husband beat me up and threw me out. By the time I came back for her, the place was a murder scene . . . and Spencer Pike was telling the cops I'd done it. The reason I've lived so long is that it's my punishment. I met her, but then had to spend the rest of my life without her.'

Ross stared, surprised to hear Az voice the very same pain that *he* felt.

Eli shook his head. 'I remember when you moved here, Az. I was a kid. You came back to Comtosook, knowing that you could still be arrested for something you didn't do?'

'I came back because I promised someone I loved that I would.' Az pulled the Band-Aid from the crook of his elbow, where only the tiniest dot indicated the question of his identity. 'You ask me, that's all it takes.'

It turned out that sneaking into a rest home wasn't very difficult if you happened to be the same age as most of its patrons. He moved through the halls like the ghost he nearly was, squinting at the names on the doors until he found the one he wanted.

Inside, Spencer Pike lay twisted in his sheets, his face as white as the belly of a whale, his IV hooked up to a patient-controlled analgesia pump. His thumb pressed hard on a nurse's call button, and his breath came in small shallow pants. 'I need more morphine!'

The answer was tinny, distant. 'I'm sorry, Mr Pike. You can't have any more tonight.'

With a roar of pain, he threw the PCA button down. He lay on his side, his features twisted with agony. Even after the other man slipped out of the shadows, it took a few moments for Pike to focus on his face. And then, there was no sign of recognition. 'Who *are* you?' he gasped.

There was no right way to answer. In his life, he had been so many different people: John Delacour, Gray Wolf, Az Thompson. He had been called an Indian, a Gypsy, a murderer, a miracle. Yet the only identity he had ever wanted was the one that had been denied him – Lily's husband, Lia's father.

Maybe Spencer Pike was delirious from the narcotics or the haze of his illness; maybe he saw courage in Az's eyes and mistook it for understanding. But something made him reach across the six inches of physical space and miles of distance between them to grasp Az's hand. 'Please,' he begged. 'Help me.'

It rocked Az to the core to realize that he and Spencer Pike had something in common after all: they would die alone, and their grief would die with them. He looked at the broken man in front of him who had ruined so many lives. 'Help me die,' Pike breathed.

It would be so easy. A pillow, held down for thirty seconds. A hand covering the parched and bitter mouth. No one need ever know, and Az would have his biblical justice: a life for a life.

But it was what Pike wanted.

Az felt the bands around his heart break free. 'No,' he said, and he walked out of the room without a second glance.

* * *

The Comtosook Police department had hired six part-timers to keep the media away from the site of the disinterment. Gathered around the open graves were Wesley Sneap, Eli, Az and several hand-picked Abenaki, and Ross. The stench of time rose from the earth, thick as cinnamon.

That should be me, Ross thought, at the moment Az murmured the same words aloud. The old man's hand trembled as it reached toward the coffins. 'Where will you take her?' Ross asked.

'To the top of a mountain, a sacred place. The Abenaki are always buried facing east.' Az looked up. 'That way she can see what's coming.'

Ross tried to swallow around the knot that had lodged in his throat. 'Will you . . . will you show me where she is?'

'I can't. You're not Abenaki.'

Ross had known that would be the answer, but it did not keep tears from springing to his eyes. He nodded, pretended to kick at a stick beside his shoe. Suddenly he felt something being pressed into his hand. An envelope.

Inside was a faded clipping from the *Burlington Free Press,* the obituary of Cecelia Beaumont Pike. A picture of her sat off to the side. In it, she was smiling faintly, as if the photographer had told a joke she did not find funny but was too polite not to laugh just a little. 'You keep it,' Az said.

'I couldn't—'

'She'd want that.' Az tilted his head. 'She told me she'd dreamed of you, you know.'

'She . . . *what?*'

'Of a man who looked like you look. Who had gadgets and things she didn't recognize. You would come to her, when she was sleeping.' Az shrugged. 'It's not so strange, really. You can be haunted for years by someone you've never met.'

'You ready?' Eli asked gently, and the old man nodded.

Wesley Sneap helped Eli position a crowbar and crack open

the lid of the larger coffin. Ross fell backward, and two of the Abenaki blanched. Eli peered into the pine box at the yellowed puzzle of long bones and joints in a bed of dirt and dust. Only one entire limb remained intact – the right arm, a continuous line from shoulder to elbow to wrist to hand, which lay on top of the sternum that once covered a heart.

He stood with his hands clasped, feeling his childhood unspool as Az started to speak a language that ran through his veins. *Kchai phanem ta wdosa* . . . the mother and daughter. *Kchi Niwaskw* . . . Great Spirit. *Nosaka nia* . . . follow me. Eli did not know if Cecelia Pike, or her baby, were in a place where they could hear this ceremony, but he hoped so.

'*Olegwasi,*' Az said. 'Dream well.' Then he turned to face the others. 'The Ojibway – the people I went to when I left here – they hold a ceremony when a baby is born.' He took a twist of tobacco from a canvas bag he'd carried into the gravesite and lit it on fire. 'It's so the Spirit World can recognize a child, and make a place for her when it's her time to go. Today I want to give my granddaughter her name.'

Az looked around the circle of people, daring them to say that it might be too late after seventy years. 'Lily,' he called, facing to the east.

Eli felt the response drawn from his throat. 'Lily,' he repeated.

Az turned to the north. 'Lily.'

'*Lily.*'

To the west, to the south, he offered up her name for safekeeping. By the time Az turned to Eli again, it was snowing. Eli touched the top of his head and brushed off a few flower petals. 'Now,' Az said.

Just then the sky darkened, until it was the color of a bruise beneath the skin. Ross Wakeman turned in a circle, as if he were expecting something to materialize, and damned if Eli didn't think that just might happen.

But just then Wesley jimmied open the smaller coffin, an apple crate, with a crowbar. Ill-preserved and eroded with time, the wooden box broke into pieces. The contents spilled, and Eli ran forward too late, thinking there might be something he could do.

A hush fell over the small group. The bones that fell out, twisted and brown, were a scramble of points and edges. But even Eli, who had no training in this kind of thing, realized that the skull was missing. 'Uh . . . Wesley?'

The medical examiner creaked down to his knees, poking through the remains with a gloved hand. 'The ribs and vertebrae are here,' he said, 'but they're too large to be from an infant. I don't even think this is *human*.'

'Then what the hell is it?'

Wesley looked up at Eli. 'Looks to me like a rib roast,' he said.

Years from now, Eli would know this was the moment he had truly forsworn red meat. He knelt beside the coffin and felt Az come up behind him. They all watched the sky split at a seam, letting forth a steady rain of rose petals that covered the ground, the grave, the bones inside the coffin. A rogue wind whipped between Eli's legs, caught the petals in a funnel draft. They drifted down to the ground, spelling out initials: *RW.*

In her dreams, Ruby was reaching. Anticipation was a lion crouched on her chest, clawing at her collarbone. She woke with a start and tried to sit up, but that lion had her pinned to the mattress, and now that she tried, she couldn't catch her breath, either.

Was Lucy crying?

No, this was a baby. The thin wail snaked under the door of Ruby's bedroom, through the crack where the hall light shone through. Ruby struggled upright, but not before the lion on her chest took a vicious swipe.

She clutched the burn over her left breast and fell heavily to the floor. In the moment of clarity that sometimes comes with great pain, Ruby suddenly knew who that baby was. And she realized that in her dream, she had been reaching out for Cecelia Pike.

Ross drove in circles, and when he could not fool himself anymore he pulled onto the side of the road and got out of his car, laying on the hood and the windshield and smiling up at the sky. 'RW,' he said aloud. 'RW.'

He had seen it, clear as day, and whether anyone else had noticed hardly mattered – the flowers had taken the shape of his own initials. Ross let the sun wash over his face. The sky was printed blue on the backs of his eyelids and the clouds were a kaleidoscope – flat-bottomed giraffes and teapots and porcupines. It was possible to find all sorts of things, if you were in the mood to see them. Ross shifted to the right, so that half of the car's hood was left empty. Room for someone to sit, should she choose to.

'What do you mean, the body was missing?' Shelby, sitting beside Ross on the porch, was incredulous. 'There was a death certificate.'

From the end of the driveway, where Ethan had just executed a series of G-turns, he took a bow. 'Ma! Did you see?'

Shelby clapped. 'Eximious!' Then she turned to Ross. 'Didn't the medical examiner have to sign off on a body?'

'Who knows? Eli's working from transcripts and testimonies and public records, but you can only construct so much of what actually happened. It's like doing a puzzle when you've only got half the pieces.'

'He seems to know what he's doing,' Shelby mused.

'Eli?' Ross took one look at his sister's face. 'Are we still talking about the murder, here, or do you have something else you want to share?'

She pulled her feet back as Ethan whizzed by, skating within inches of her toes. 'He's thorough, that's all.'

'I'll bet.'

Shelby gave him a withering look. 'It doesn't add up ratiocina-tively. If the body of the baby was missing, then presumably, it was either buried somewhere else . . . or it was never buried. Pike wouldn't have buried it in a different grave, because if the medical examiner had insisted on digging up the baby to see it, he wouldn't have been able to explain a rib roast. But then again, he doesn't seem like the type to leave it on the doorstep of a church, either.'

'Why would you leave a dead body at a church?'

Shelby looked at him. 'Who said the baby was dead?'

'Spencer Pike,' Ross replied, and then blinked. '*Shit.*'

'Exactly.'

'So if he lied . . . and the baby was alive . . . then maybe someone tried to save it. It would explain why they'd stick the rib roast in the coffin instead . . . they were trying to fool Pike into thinking that the baby had died.'

'Which Pike would probably have been more than willing to believe,' Shelby added. 'What if the reason your ghost was haunting the property had nothing to do with the way she died? What if she came back to find her child?'

Ethan skated by, his eyes bright with constellations. He executed three 360s, missed the fourth, and fell down. Lying on the driveway, he laughed the deep-belly way only children can, bubbling up from the core. 'I guess you'd come back for that,' Ross said.

'No,' Shelby answered. 'I never would have left.'

It was too fine a setting for Spencer Pike. In his wheelchair, with a blanket on his lap and the white slats of the gazebo behind him, Eli wished for something more suitable – fire and brim-stone, tar pits, a cell from the Middle Ages. This, after all, was a man who had gotten away with murder.

Eli leaned back against the railing of the nursing home's gazebo, trying to keep his cool. Getting Pike to confess had become a personal mission. 'How would you like it if you went in for a sponge bath,' he said evenly, 'and came out with a vasectomy?'

'Can't say it would cramp my style these days.'

'Unfortunately,' Eli said, 'I doubt some of your sterilization victims would say the same.'

'Hitler gave eugenics a bad name, and you liberals swarmed all over us. But we were just like you. We were making the world a better place, too.'

'By keeping the poor and the different from multiplying. *Very* humane.'

'You have no idea. Their children were growing up without four walls to call a home. They had no moral direction. The ones we could save, we did. The others, well, it was for their own good.'

'Did you ever think to give them a second chance?'

'Of course. But they kept making the same mistakes again.'

'And you?' Eli said. 'You've never made a mistake?'

Pike narrowed his eyes. 'You want to tell me what that has to do with my property being developed?'

'Funny you should mention that, since your property isn't going to be developed.' He handed Pike a copy of the injunction that had been given to Rod van Vleet.

'This is . . . this is ridiculous,' Pike sputtered. 'My land's no Indian burial ground.'

'Actually, it is.' Eli came a step closer. 'Tell me, Spencer, did she fight you? Did she beg you to stop while you were putting that rope around her neck?'

'She was my *wife.*'

'And she was half-Abenaki,' Eli countered. 'Which wasn't going to reflect well on a card-carrying member of the American Eugenics Society, was it?'

He watched Pike's face, the shock that unraveled across it. 'You said that the last time you were here.'

'Because it's true,' Eli said.

The old man shook his head, as if that might keep the fact from sinking in. 'Cissy wasn't . . . her hair, it was blond, and her skin was like milk . . .'

'And her father was not Harry Beaumont, but an Abenaki man named Gray Wolf.'

'Her *father* . . . ?'

'She had the bad luck to not be what you needed her to be, and you took care of that problem the way you took care of everything else that didn't agree with you – by simply getting rid of it.' By now, Eli was leaning down over the old man. 'Tell me the truth, Spencer. Tell me what you did.'

Pike closed his eyes, silent for so long Eli wondered if he'd suffered a stroke. 'I thought she loved him,' he whispered. 'I thought the child was his.'

'What did you do with the baby?'

The old man's throat knotted, and his mouth worked soundlessly before the words burst free. 'I killed it. I smothered it. Hid the body in the icehouse and told Cissy it had just died. I thought maybe, this way, we could start over. But I didn't touch Cissy. I swear it, I loved her. I *loved* her.'

Eli thought of the apple crate in the ground, the one that had not held an infant. 'What did you do with the baby's body?'

'Buried it,' Spencer said. 'The next morning, I found Cissy . . . and I buried the crate before I called the police. I had to, or they would have found out what I did.' He grabbed for Eli's sleeve. 'I did it because I loved her. All I wanted was—'

'A second chance?' Eli interrupted, unsympathetic. 'The question is, did you make the same mistake again?'

The hardest part for Meredith was trying to keep from breaking down as she listened to the cardiologist who'd treated her grandmother after the heart attack. They stood in front of the hospital bed, where Ruby lay lit like a Christmas tree and strung with all manners of tubes and intravenous equipment. 'She's not out of the woods yet by any means,' the doctor said. 'Reduced cerebral blood flow secondary to a myocardial infarction leads to ischemia . . . and delirium. I think it's best to keep her here for a few days, just for monitoring.'

Meredith mumbled something – praise? thanks? – and sat down on the chair she'd pulled up to the bed. Outside this cardiac care room, a saint of a nurse had Lucy drawing Magic Marker faces on ballooned latex glove-puppets. Meredith rested her forehead on the synthetic blanket and held Ruby's hand, which glowed at the forefinger with a pulse-oxygen monitor. 'Don't leave me,' she begged.

She felt the paper-thin skin of Ruby's fingers twitch in her own. Meredith sat up, hopeful, to find her grandmother's eyes wide open. 'I'll be fine in time for that dinner party,' Ruby said, her voice sliding into a French Canadian dialect.

Dinner party? Meredith frowned, and then remembered what the doctor had said about delirium.

'You take care of that baby.'

Lucy. 'She wants you to get better too.'

Ruby's eyes drifted shut. 'I will,' she murmured. 'I promise, Miz Pike.'

Shelby's face bloomed the moment she realized it was Eli ringing the doorbell. 'I'm glad you came by,' she said, stepping aside to let him in.

'I am too.'

'I had a wonderful time the other night.' Shelby thought of the way they had ended their date in Eli's truck; how he had leaned over and asked if he could kiss her before Watson beat him to it; how incredible it felt to be held by someone, instead of doing the holding.

'Good. Since I came by to propose, and all.'

'To . . . *what?*'

Eli grinned. 'I figured after your aversion to first dates, you might not be crazy about second ones either. So I thought maybe we'd just skip ahead.'

'Maybe we should jump to our silver anniversary,' Shelby said. 'Play it safe.'

'All right by me,' Eli replied, and amazingly, Shelby thought he was only half-joking. She imagined sitting next to him, doing absolutely nothing, because they had spent years together doing it all and now could fill the spaces simply with each other's company. She thought of what a bed would feel like when it was not empty on the other side.

'Can I get you something?' Shelby asked. 'A cold drink?'

'Ross.'

Her face fell. 'Oh. You came to talk to him.'

The uncomfortable moment was interrupted by the boisterous arrival of Watson, who pounced through the open door and between them. 'I told you to stay in the truck,' Eli said, trying in vain to grab the dog's collar.

'It's okay.' Shelby watched the bloodhound begin to case her parlor and move into the living room. Watson stopped, turned toward Shelby, and gave an enthusiastic swipe of his tail – which managed to send a candy dish, a television remote, and several books off of the coffee table. Eli and Shelby both ran forward to pick up the mess. 'I'm sorry—'

'Don't be—'

'—He's a pain in the ass, sometimes—'

'—No worse than a nine-year-old boy, believe me.'

As Shelby examined the crystal candy bowl for hairline fractures, Eli collected the books, which had splayed open on the carpet. One was a coffee table pictorial of Vermont. The other was a scrapbook. Curious, Eli flipped through the pages. 'What's this?'

Shelby read over his shoulder, her cheeks pink with embarrassment as Eli skimmed the stories she went back to time and time again. On the page he'd opened, there was an article about a six-year-old boy bitten by a shark off the coast of Florida. His leg had been severed and successfully reattached, but the blood loss had put him into a coma. After weeks of assuming the boy was brain-dead, he'd awakened just as good as new.

The most recent article involved a Canadian toddler who'd wandered out of his house and had fallen asleep in a six-foot drift of snow. 'I remember this one,' Eli said. 'He was pronounced dead, and brought to the hospital—'

'And the doctors gradually warmed him up and he came back to life.' Shelby took the scrapbook from him. 'It's stupid, I know, but I keep track. I clip stories where death turns out to not be . . . well, so final. Maybe one day someone will clip a story about Ethan for the same reason.'

Suddenly Ross came pounding down the stairs, his hair still wet from a shower. 'I thought I heard your voice,' he said to Eli, as Watson did his best to leap into his arms. 'How'd it go with Pike?'

But Eli was still riveted by the story of the Canadian toddler. 'The doctor's from McGill,' he said. 'That's right over the border in Montreal. The family must be nearby. Shelby, come with me?'

She did not consider Ethan, or her job, or her brother. She didn't consider the logistics of staying overnight with a man she'd gone out with only once. And she didn't wonder why, spontaneously, Eli seemed as interested in near-death experiences as she was. All Shelby knew was that when you are given the chance to meet a miracle, you do not think twice.

From the *Burlington Free Press:*

Burlington, VT – Dr Thomas Smalley, president of the University of Vermont, announced plans to rename the Beaumont Biology Library and the Pike Museum of Anthropological History. 'The University of Vermont wants to make clear that the ideas espoused by these professors during Vermont's eugenics studies were theirs alone, and did not represent the views of the university community as a whole,' said Smalley, in a written statement. Potential new names for these buildings are under review by the Alumni Committee.

When Eli was a boy, he had been certain that state boundaries and the equator were lines drawn on the ground, just like on a map. 'The first time my mother took me to Canada, I asked her to pull over so I could see it,' he told Shelby.

'You must have been disappointed.'

'Nope.' He grinned, thinking back. 'She took a piece of chalk out of the glove compartment, and started drawing. Said that all the car tires on the highway must have rubbed it right off.'

'And you believed her?'

He glanced at her from the corner of his eye. 'I think people believe what they need to, don't you?'

'I suppose you can't be a cop unless you're cynical.'

'Not true. We continue to be amazed every day.'

He pulled the truck into a highway motel, one just over the city line of Montreal, according to the map. *Avec HBO,* promised a billboard.

They had made it to Canada in record time. However, it was nearly 8 P.M. – which meant that Eli would not be seeing Dr Holessandro until the following day. 'Sorry it's not the Ritz,' Eli apologized. 'But the Ritz doesn't take dogs.'

'I hope you were referring to Watson. And don't worry on my account. I'd be just as happy camping out in the flatbed.'

The thought of Shelby pressed against him from toe to shoulder in the rear of his truck was enough to make Eli suddenly as hard as a rock. He got out of the rig, turned away, and adjusted his jeans. Shelby followed him into the office of the motel, where a boy with a green mohawk was playing Scrabble against himself. 'Do you speak French?' she asked Eli.

'Nothing to worry about.' As Eli walked up to the desk, the boy made no effort to even look at him. 'Hello.' He rolled his eyes. 'Bonjour.'

'Bonjour,' the boy said, smirking at Eli and Shelby – and their lack of luggage. 'Vous desirez une chambre?'

Shelby opened her mouth and stepped forward. 'I'll take care of this,' Eli said. 'Oui, deux chambres, s'il vous plaît.'

The boy looked at Shelby, and then back at Eli. 'Deux? Vous êtes sûr?'

'Oui,' Eli said.

The boy raised a brow. 'Et Madame? Elle est sûre aussi?'

'Bon, d'accord. Avez-vous des chambres ou non?'

'Oui, oui . . . ne vous fachez pas. D'abord, j'ai besoin d'une carte de crédit . . .' Eli slapped his MasterCard on the counter. 'Voilà les clefs pour les chambres 40 and 42.'

'Merci.'

'Ou, préférez-vous plus de distance entre les chambres? Deux étages différents peut-être . . . ?'

'Non, ça va comme ça.' Eli grabbed Shelby by the arm and pulled her toward the front door. 'Bonne nuit, alors . . .' the clerk called after them, laughing.

Outside, Eli made a beeline for his truck. If his dick had been hard before they'd gone into the motel, by now he could be the body double for a jackhammer. 'Eli—'

'I want to get the dog. You know what they say about leaving animals in cars . . .'

'Eli!' Shelby planted her hands on her hips in the middle of the parking lot. 'Goddammit, listen to me!'

He turned slowly, exhaling heavily. 'What.'

'The reason I asked you if you speak French in there . . . was because I do, and I could have checked us in. *Would you prefer more distance between the rooms?*' she translated, mocking the clerk. '*Two different floors, maybe?*'

Mortified, Eli swore. 'Shelby, it's not like you think . . .'

'You have no idea what I'm thinking,' she countered, then added quietly, 'I was thinking that he was right. You could have gotten one room.'

Eli took a few steps forward, until he was standing just inches away from Shelby. 'No, I couldn't have,' he said.

He watched the light go out of her eyes, and realized she had misunderstood him. In that moment, he wished for her facility for words. He wished for a lot of things. 'You know how sometimes when you're reading a really great book or watching a really great video you stop, just to make it last longer? There is nothing I want more than to, uh, oscillate with you. But that's gonna lead to more than that . . . pretty damn quick. What I feel right now – what we feel – it's eviscerant enough. We can't get that back, once it's gone.' He kissed her on the forehead. 'I don't want to go slow, but I'm gonna make myself do it.'

'*Evanescent?*' Shelby smiled slowly. '*Osculate?*'

Eli winked. 'You're not the only one who can read a dictionary.' And over her shoulder what had been just a crack in the pavement, a line of trees, and a picket fence suddenly reconfigured into a city boundary line, clear as day.

The hospital was a little too clean and a little too quiet, swimming with so much false cheer that it made the tiled floor shine. As Lucy climbed on the bed, she concentrated on not making any sound – not only because her mom and great-grandma were sleeping but because the crinkly covers and plastic sheets were already covered with people who Lucy could see, even if no one else seemed to be able to.

She didn't like touching them, didn't like the way their arms and legs moved right through her and made her so cold inside that her bones ached. She didn't like the way they stared at her, as if they were jealous that she was someone who could walk into a room and be noticed without even trying. So Lucy curled herself into as small a ball as possible, and watched her great-grandmother rest.

Her mother had told her that Granny Ruby's heart was broken, and it made Lucy think of a vase she'd knocked over once and tried to glue back together. Every time she saw it, now, she knew it wasn't as good as it had been.

Lucy felt the hair on the back of her neck stand up as a girl beside her with long black braids and a funny striped apron poked at her with one long finger. She looked to be about sixteen, and sickly, her cheeks nearly blue. *'Ma poule,'* the girl whispered.

Suddenly Granny Ruby blinked awake. 'You're here,' she said, reaching for Lucy.

'My mother brought me.'

At that, Ruby looked around wildly. 'Mama? She's here too?' But before Lucy could answer, her great-grandmother touched her cheek. 'Simone,' she said, not Lucy at all. 'You came back.'

'I'm not Simone,' Lucy whispered, but by then her great-grandmother was no longer listening. The see-through girl with the black braids reached out, and with one shove, pushed Lucy off the bed.

On January 3rd, 2002, Alexandre Proux had awakened before his mother, Genevieve. He opened the back door, whose doorknob he had only been able to reach for a week, now, and wandered onto the porch in his Spider-Man pajamas. It was snowing, and he wanted to play.

By the time his mother woke up and realized he was gone, Alexandre had been buried beneath the snow. For six hours, the police followed kidnapping leads and looked everywhere but in Alex's own backyard.

Now, Alex was three and torturing the beagle puppy his mother had bought him last Christmas. The dog had been trussed up in a kerchief, and Alex was trying to tie reins onto its collar. 'I keep thinking that the dog is going to bite him,' said Genevieve, smiling.

'But he seems to have the same trouble saying no to Alex as the rest of us.'

'You are so lucky.' Alex handed his mother the cap gun and then galloped off astride his long-suffering makeshift steed.

'There is nothing like it,' Genevieve added, now that Alex was out of earshot. 'Seeing your baby, not moving like that. Alex was still, and Alex is never still. I kept thinking, *He will wake up now. He will open his eyes and look at me and be fine.*'

Shelby understood. If you lost a child, grief wasn't just part of the equation. It *was* the equation. Suddenly the beagle raced into the room, the cowboy hat clamped firmly between his jaws, Alex trailing behind. 'You have a son, *oui?*'

'Ethan. He's nine.'

'Then you understand.'

Alex veered left, flying into his mother's arms. She kissed him on the soft spot behind his ear. 'Yes,' Shelby said, watching them. 'I do.'

Dr Gaspar Holessandro had a bad toupee and a weakness for sardines. 'I'm sorry,' he said, licking his fingers after plucking another one from a Tupperware container on his desk. 'I don't usually eat in front of guests.' Too busy to schedule a meeting, Holessandro had agreed to meet Eli during a lunch break. His office was a closet attached to the pristine research lab at McGill where, three days a week, the doctor studied SIDS by implanting probes in the brains of infant pigs. The other four days, he worked at the hospital where Alexandre Proux had been brought in stiff and blue and presumably dead.

Eli had, again, bent the truth. He explained to Holessandro that he was a detective in Vermont, that there was an open investigation into a baby's death, one that shared characteristics with young Alex's situation. He'd wanted to know if there was some regenerative process caused by extreme cold – one that might explain why a baby who had been smothered might suddenly

come back to life after being stuck in an icehouse. He didn't tell
the doctor that all this had happened in 1932.

Holessandro bit the tail off a sardine. 'Smothering,' he explained,
'would cause asphyxiation . . . and make a person hypoxic. Now,
if you're an adult, that means you'd breathe more – hyperventi-
late. Infants, though – their bodies are physiologically quite
different from ours, and for them hypoxia inhibits breathing. So
if a baby was smothered, it might stop breathing for several
minutes . . . and then would autoresuscitate.'

'You mean it wouldn't stay dead?'

'When you stop the part of a baby's brain that's responsible for
normal breathing, another part of the brain takes over . . . which
makes the infant gasp a few times. The purpose is to get some
oxygen in there to jump-start the heart and lungs again.' He
smiled. 'It's actually very hard to kill an infant.'

'But whoever was doing the suffocating – surely he'd have
noticed an infant gasping for air.'

'That depends on how quickly he left. It happened in an
icehouse, you said?'

Eli shrugged. 'Yeah.'

Holessandro shook his head. 'And I thought Canadians were
provincial. Well, the icehouse adds another twist to it. Say the
baby was asphyxiated . . . and then gasped . . . *and* was stuck
in a cold environment. In that case, what happened to Alexandre
would start to happen to the infant. The skin would cool, which
in turn would cool the blood flow, which cools the brain, which
causes the hypothalamus to lower the metabolic rate to basal
levels. Perhaps even more so – the younger the child, the more
potent the reflex that makes bodily systems shut down that
way.'

'So the baby would look dead, but wouldn't *be* dead?'

'Exactly. It's like energy-saver on a computer . . . the screen
shuts off but you haven't lost your data. Likewise, as the blood
flow was directed only to essential organs, the baby's skin would

get blue and cold. It wouldn't be breathing visibly; its pulse would be indistinguishable. Like Alex.'

'How long could an infant live like that?'

'It can't,' Holessandro said flatly. 'Scientifically, according to textbooks, it doesn't happen. But the rules of biology aren't like the rules of physics, and as we've seen with Alex – sometimes it does.' He popped the last of the sardines in his mouth. 'So did your baby live?'

'My baby?'

'The infant. The one from this case.'

'Oh, right,' Eli said. 'We don't know, actually.'

'Well, if it did, someone or something must have come along to warm it up. That's the only way to come out of that hibernation, so to speak. *Especially* an infant – neonates can't shiver, so they can't warm themselves up.'

Who had been there that night to warm the baby? Spencer Pike, for one . . . who'd confessed to killing the infant. Why admit to murder – a more serious crime – if instead he'd squirreled the baby away somewhere, alive? It was possible that Cecelia Pike had managed to hide her child in the hours before her death. Maybe Az Thompson had even taken it, and knew more than he was letting on.

But if that infant *had* come back to life . . . where the hell was she now?

'Hope this helps you find some answers,' Holessandro said.

'Definitely,' Eli replied. But he could not shake the feeling that he had not yet asked the right question.

'We're good to go,' Ross said, as he handed Ethan a vase filled with popcorn, then flopped into the beach chair beside him. They were sitting on the driveway at midnight, watching a video that his uncle had rigged to project on the white doors of the garage. It was some shoot-'em-up flick, R-rated and so full of dead guys and bullets that Ethan figured his mother would have a cow if she found out, which of course made it all the better.

'What's with the vase?' Ethan asked.

'We ran out of clean bowls.' Ross grinned as the opening credits started to roll. 'Is this, or is this not every bit as good as a drive-in?'

Ethan nodded. 'The only thing that's missing is a girl in the backseat.'

His uncle choked on a piece of popcorn. 'Jesus, Ethan. Aren't you a little young to be thinking about that?'

'Well, that depends. On account of most guys get into that stuff when they're fourteen or fifteen, and I'll be dead by then.'

Ross turned, so that the movie played over his cheek and brow, distorting his face. 'Ethan, you don't know that for sure.'

'That guys have sex when they're fourteen?' Ethan said, deliberately misunderstanding. 'How old were you when you had sex for the first time?'

'I wasn't nine and a half.'

'What's it like?'

On the screen, two cops were shooting at a bad guy in a convertible. The convertible rolled on an embankment and burst into flames. Ethan knew that the stuntman who'd done that scene had gotten out of the fire and walked away in his flame-retardant suit, perfectly okay. People died all the time in movies and then got right back up and did it again, like it was some kind of joke.

He could see that his uncle was trying to edit whatever he had decided to say, but he also knew that Ross would tell him the truth. Unlike his mother, who only wanted to keep him a kid as long as possible, Uncle Ross understood exactly how much you needed to cram into the measure of a life before you checked out. 'It's pretty amazing,' Ross answered. 'It feels like coming home.'

Somehow, that description just didn't do it for Ethan. He thought he might hear words like *round* and *wet* and *burst,* dialogue from the Playboy Channel that came through the speakers on the

TV even though the picture was scrambled. He wondered if his mother, in Canada, was doing things that were round and wet and bursting with that guy Eli, who made her glow every time he came over. That detective was all she thought of these days. He remembered how he had been talking to her while she was making pancakes a few nights ago, about this wicked cool pogo stick he'd seen advertised on TV that not only counted how many times you jumped but egged you on and called you by your name. 'It sounds great,' his mother had said.

'Maybe I could get it for my birthday,' Ethan suggested, and she had turned to him, all confused.

'Get what?'

'The pogo stick?'

'What pogo stick?' she'd asked, and then she'd shaken her head and flipped the pancakes again, when they were already done cooking anyway.

Uncle Ross still seemed to be coming up with his explanation. 'I think when you sleep with someone, you take a part of her with you. Not just the physical stuff – cells and all that. But part of what makes her *her*.'

Everyone had someone, Ethan thought. Everyone but him. 'Maybe I could just kiss a girl, so that every now and then she'd think of me. You know, *Oh, that was the kid I kissed who had that disease and died.*'

'Ethan, you're not—'

'Uncle Ross,' he said wearily. 'Don't you lie to me too.'

Most of the time, the truth that he was going to die sat in his stomach like something that would not digest – a stone, a ball of wire. He understood that he'd drawn the short end of the stick genetically, that an early death was not an option, but a fact. He did not want to find Jesus, or make out a will, or do any of the things people did when they knew they were going to pass away. He just wanted to *live*.

In the movie, someone got his arm cut off with a chain saw.

Ethan reached for his uncle's hand. He pushed up the sleeve of his sweater, to the spot where a scar swam beneath the surface of his wrist. 'Why?' he whispered.

'The difference between us is that you're a hero, Ethan, and I'm a coward.' Ross pulled his arm away and rolled down the sleeve. 'I will personally make sure you kiss a girl before you die, if I have to hire one,' he said, and he wasn't joking, and that made Ethan feel like crying.

There was a hail of bullets on the soundtrack. Ethan sifted his fingers through the popcorn, which rustled like autumn. 'Do you feel like you want to die right now?' he asked.

Ross shook his head. 'No.'

'Me neither,' Ethan said, and he turned his face up to the screen.

Eli had always been the kind of cop who couldn't sleep well while a case was still at loose ends. Add to this a healthy dose of sexual frustration, and it was no wonder that he found himself walking around the edge of the parking lot of the motel shortly after a rainstorm at midnight. Watson lay just beyond an empty spot, his head on his paws, his eyes following Eli as he paced on the muddy ground.

Shelby was asleep. At least, he figured she was asleep. She'd kissed him good night so thoroughly he could still feel the imprint of her breasts and hips against him, hours later. Then she'd closed the motel room door in his face. It was a punishment of sorts, he was sure, a look at what he was missing by virtue of taking it slow.

He wondered what she slept in. Silky nightgowns? Flannel pajamas?

Nothing?

Why *was* he taking it slow, anyway? She'd all but told him flat out that she was interested, and ready. If he went inside and knocked on her door, she might answer it wearing only a sheet.

Eli had no doubt that if anything could get his mind off this murder case, it was making love to Shelby Wakeman.

But the last woman he'd felt so much for in so little time had been his wife. He'd married her within months of their first meeting, certain that her love for him ran as deep as a trench in the Atlantic, too. And she had left him for another guy.

Eli wasn't going to let that happen to him again. And the easiest way to keep from getting burned was to keep a safe distance from anything that looked like a potential fire.

'Milk.'

Eli turned to find Shelby standing a few feet away in a tank top and a pair of drawstring pants printed with cherries. She came closer, barefoot, on the wet earth. The sight of her narrow feet alone made Eli start to sweat. 'What?'

'Milk. Warm. It'd do the trick.' She smiled at him. 'You can't sleep, right?'

She didn't know the half of it.

'It's what I do when my biorhythms are all screwed up – you know, from being awake during the night with Ethan, and then having to go to bed in bright daylight.'

Eli heard nothing in that sentence except the words 'go to bed.' He nodded at her and wondered if his whole hand would be able to span the flat plane between her hips. Her tank top rode up in the front, exposing the thinnest line of skin, and Eli felt himself stop breathing.

Hypoxia, he thought.

Eli stared down at the ground, fighting for composure. One of Shelby's footprints, delicate and full-bottomed, had landed by chance right across one of his – bigger, broader. It was the most erotic thing he'd ever seen.

Jesus, he was a basket case.

The hell with it, Eli thought, moving across the muddy stretch toward her. He could have her in bed in less than three minutes, and he'd deal with the consequences later. He stepped over Watson, over the double footprint that had gotten him hot and bothered in the first place – and he stopped short.

Double footprints, like the ones that had been photographed at the crime scene after Cecelia Pike's murder. The first time Eli had noticed that, he'd used it to blow holes in the theory that Gray Wolf had been there to hang Cecelia. It stood to reason, too, that if Cissy had been abducted from her bedroom after child-birth, she would not have been wearing boots to leave a tread behind. She, like Shelby, would have come right from bed.

Pike's shoes had been predominant . . . after all, he'd cut the body down. But there had been one print where the woman's sole had been stamped down on top of the man's, like the foot-prints that he and Shelby had just made – the woman's smaller foot superimposed across the man's larger one, the step made after the man had made his.

Dead women don't walk away.

'I know where to find the baby,' Eli said.

Ross believed in past lives. Moreover, he believed that the person you fell in love with in each life was the same person you fell in love with in the life before, and the one before that. Sometimes, you might miss her – she'd be reborn in the post–World War I generation, and you wouldn't come back until the fifties. Some-times, your paths would cross and you wouldn't recognize each other. Get it right – that is: fall madly, truly, deeply – and perhaps there'd be an eternity carved out solely for the two of you.

What if Lia Pike had been the one for Ross? If she'd been killed before she could find him, and then had come back as Aimee . . . only to die accidentally after falling in love with him? What if she was haunting him now because there was no other way to connect?

What if the reason he thought about killing himself so much was not depression, or chemical imbalance, or borderline person-ality disorder, or the dozen other labels shrinks had slapped on him . . . but only a means of ending this life so that he could start another one with the woman he was supposed to be with?

He stared down at the obituary in his hand, the one that Az Thompson had given him days ago. By now, Lia's body was where it belonged. The rest of her, though, was waiting for him. She'd even said so, with his initials.

'Ross!'

Shelby's voice rose like smoke from downstairs. He folded the picture of Lia again and tucked it into his pocket, then came into the living room to find Eli Rochert and his sister beaming, that behemoth dog between them.

'Where's Ethan?' Shelby asked.

Ross looked at the clock. He didn't wear a watch – why bother, when he couldn't seem to speed up his time on earth anyway – and hadn't really noticed that nearly all the night had passed. 'I guess he's still skating out back.'

'I'll check.' Shelby started through the kitchen, then turned to Eli. 'Go ahead. Tell him.'

'Tell me what?' Ross said.

Eli sank onto the couch and spilled a mess of papers on the cushion beside him. 'Pike smothers the infant, or at least he thinks he does. He leaves it in the icehouse while he breaks the news to his wife. It autoresuscitates—'

'It what?'

'Just trust me on this. It starts breathing again, but then it sort of goes into standby mode since its body is so cold. It looks dead, but it's not.'

Ross sank down. 'Okay,' he said, listening more closely.

'Cecelia Pike wants to see her newborn's body. She breaks out of the bedroom he's locked her in, and finds the baby in the icehouse, where it's cold and blue and looking pretty damn dead. She picks it up and cries over it . . . which is how Pike finds her. He goes off the deep end – here she is mourning for what he thinks is her lover's child – and hangs her. *But the baby's not dead.*'

He tosses a photograph at Ross, a grainy study of footprints. 'Someone walked on that sawdust after Pike did, someone who was wearing boots that were awfully similar to the ones taken off Cecelia Pike's feet – a girl named Ruby.'

'Ruby?'

'Yeah. She was the housekeeper, some kid who lived with them. When I met with Duley Wiggs, that old cop, he mentioned it – although I didn't realize it at the time. Said that Pike wasn't up for a big funeral celebration at his house, with his *girl* gone. I thought he was talking about Cissy . . . but now I realize he meant the hired help.'

'Why hasn't anyone mentioned her?'

'Because she was a servant, and servants are supposed to be invisible. And because she disappeared that night. Pike wouldn't tell me about her, because she probably knows that he killed his wife.'

'So if Ruby took the baby and disappeared that night—'

'The baby might still be alive. In her seventies, and about to inherit a nice tract of land,' Eli finished. 'Plus, Ruby might be able to fill in the blanks. I did a little digging on the Internet. A woman named Ruby Weber was born in the Northeast Kingdom, moved to Comtosook with her family in 1925, and disappeared from Vermont records in 1932. Now she lives at 45 Thistlehill Lane in Gaithersburg, Maryland.'

Ross could not seem to force the woman's name out of his throat. Ruby Weber. *RW*. Lia had not been trying to tell everyone gathered at her grave that she loved him. She had only been pointing Eli and the others in the right direction.

When Meredith had been about Lucy's age, her dog had been run over by a truck. Her mother had taken Blue to the vet to be put down, and instead of crying, Meredith had thrown herself into the art of prestidigitation. She made quarters vanish, red rubber balls slip out of sight, small paper bouquets of flowers disappear – before retrieving them magically from her ears, the cookie jar, the silverware drawer. She put on these shows for Ruby, who saw right through her. 'Honey,' she had said to Meredith, 'there are some things you just can't bring back, no matter what.'

Years later, Meredith knew she was lucky to have reached the age of thirty-five and still have her grandmother around. After all, she had experienced firsthand her mother's premature demise, and she knew how loss could eat away at you like a termite, tiny and insidious until your heart was nothing but dust.

She thought of death like the seam of a hem: each time you lost someone close, it unraveled a little. You could still go along with your life, but you'd forever be tripping over something you previously took for granted. If Ruby passed away, there would be no one but Meredith and Lucy. There had never been aunts and uncles and cousins; no family reunion or gala Christmas dinner. They had had each other, which had been enough.

'You are not allowed to die,' Meredith said, matter-of-fact. She squeezed her grandmother's hand. 'You are not allowed to die until I say so.'

She nearly jumped out of her seat as Ruby squeezed right back. Looking down, she saw her grandmother's open eyes – and even better, the yellow heat of recognition in them. 'Meredith,' Ruby answered, her voice faint and thready, 'who said anything about dying?'

After Eli left and Ethan went to bed, Ross holed himself up in his room. Shelby knocked on the door to bring him some food, which he turned away. She tried an hour later, hoping to just sit and talk, but he came to the door in his underwear, and said he really didn't feel up to company.

She hated herself for doing it, but when there was no sound of movement from inside the room, Shelby jimmied the lock, checked Ross to make sure he was only asleep, and slipped his razor into her pocket.

She slept fitfully that night, dreaming in black-and-white about walking on a ground so hot it burned the soles of her feet. When she woke up, it was nine in the morning, she had a skull-splitting headache, and someone was playing a radio too loud.

Determined, she stomped down the hall toward Ethan's room first, certain that he was to blame. But he was fast asleep, curled under the blankets and completely oblivious to the racket that was coming from down the hall. Shelby moved along to Ross's room, and knocked on the door. 'Ross,' she yelled, 'turn that thing down!'

But the music did not stop. She pushed on the door, and found it unlocked. The radio blared on, a preset alarm.

The bed was made, the dresser clear, and Ross's small duffel missing.

On the pillow was a piece of paper.

Shel, she read, *I'm sorry for leaving this way. But then, if I ever did do something right, I wouldn't be the brother you know.*

A scream rolled inside her. Ross had just left her a suicide note.

Ross sat in his car, looking at the neat line of Japanese maples and listening to the language of birds and thinking that it was fitting for everything to come to an end at a spot like this. He took a deep breath, aware that what he was about to do would change the lives of many people other than himself. But then, how *couldn't* he do it?

He'd driven around Comtosook for a few hours, until he'd come to a decision and had gotten everything he needed to make it happen. He could say he was doing this for Lia, but it wouldn't be the truth. Ross was doing it for himself, to prove that there was something – at last – at which he could succeed.

He reached along the passenger seat, picked up the piece of paper that had Ruby Weber's address scrawled across it, and then got out of the car.

The mailbox said weber/oliver, and Ross found himself wondering if this woman might have a male companion, or for that matter, a female one. He walked up the brick path to the front door and rang the bell.

'They're not home.'

Ross turned to see a neighbor watering the adjacent lawn with a sprinkler. 'Do you know where they went?' he asked. 'I'm sort of dropping in unannounced . . .'

'Are you family?'

Ross thought of Lia. 'Yes.'

The neighbor came closer. 'I don't know how to tell you this,' she said sympathetically, 'but Ruby's in the hospital.'

Ross wandered the hospital's administrative floors until he reached an office that had a secretary absent on a coffee break and a doctor's extra lab coat hanging on a coat hook just inside the door. Costumed, he moved with purpose to the cardiac care unit and asked for Ruby Weber's chart, which he scrutinized for a few minutes, memorizing her age, her condition, and the room into which she'd been put. When he got there, however, a woman was sitting with Ruby on the edge of the bed.

Not wishing for an audience, Ross busied himself in the hallway until the woman left the room, holding a little girl by the hand. As they headed away from him, Ross slipped inside. 'Mrs Weber,' he said, 'I'd like to talk to you.'

She had battleship-gray hair and eyes as blue as the center of a flame. Her skin, so finely wrinkled, reminded Ross of rice paper. 'Well, that would be a novelty. Being that all your friends seem to want to poke and prod me and take my blood.'

Ross tugged his arms from the sleeves of his coat, folded it, and set it on a chair. 'That's because I'm not a doctor.'

He watched her face as she struggled with the decision to push the nurse's call button and have him evicted . . . or to simply hear him out. After a very long moment, Ruby hiked herself up on her pillows. 'Are you a patient? You look like you're in pain.'

'I am.'

'What hurts?'

Ross thought about how to answer this. 'Everything.' He took a step forward. 'I want to talk to you about 1932.'

'I knew it was coming,' she murmured. 'That heart attack was the warning.'

'You were there. You know what happened to Lia.'

She turned her head in profile, and Ross was struck by how noble she looked. This woman, whose ancestors had been prominently featured in one of Spencer Pike's degenerate family genealogies, could have been the prototype for a queen, the face on the bow of a ship, the figurehead on a golden coin. 'There are some things that shouldn't be talked about,' Ruby said.

Well, he couldn't be blamed for trying. With a sigh, Ross picked up the borrowed lab coat and started to walk away.

'Then there are some things that shouldn't have been kept secret in the first place.' She looked at Ross. 'Who wants to know?'

He thought about explaining the development, and the Abenaki protest, and Eli's investigation. But in the end, he simply said, 'Me.'

'I worked for Spencer Pike. I was fourteen. Cissy Pike was only eighteen, you know – her husband, he was eight years older than she was. That night they'd fought, and she started in having her baby, even though it was three weeks early. Tiniest little girl you ever saw. When the baby died, Miz Pike went a little crazy. Her husband locked her in her room, and I was so scared I just picked up what I could and left.' She pleated the blanket between her hands. 'I heard afterward that she had been killed that night.'

'Did you see her body?' Ross pressed. 'Did you see the baby's?'

Ruby opened and closed her mouth, as if trying to reshape her words. Color rose to her face, and one of the monitors began to beep more fervently.

The door swung open. 'Granny? What's that noise? Are you all right?'

Ross turned, an explanation on his lips. And found himself staring into the face of Lia Beaumont Pike.

11

'Who the hell are you?' Lia said to Ross, or not-Lia, or whoever she was. She didn't wait for an answer, though, before she stuck her head back out of the door and screamed for a nurse. Suddenly the room was crowded with hospital personnel, jockeying for position in front of Ruby's bed and assuring themselves that she was not going into cardiac arrest again. Lia turned her attention to the medical team, soaking up their technical jargon like a sponge. She stood rigidly until the monitor began to sway to its simple rhythm again, the crisis passed. Only then did she let her shoulders relax, her hands loosen from fists.

Ross slid out of the room, unnoticed. It wasn't Lia. He knew this, because she didn't recognize him. There were subtler differences too – this woman's hair was longer, and curlier, more honey-colored than wheat. She had a little girl with her; there were fine lines of age bracketing her mouth. But those remarkable brown eyes were the same, and the sorrow in them.

She was too young to be Lia Pike's daughter. But she was too much of a dead ringer for Lia to be anything but a direct relation.

The whitewashed nurses and doctors began to file out, a string of pearls. Ross peeked back inside the room. 'He's an old friend,' Ross heard, before the door swung shut and cleaved the conversation in two.

This much he knew: Ruby Weber was a liar. She was not an old friend of his.

And she had not left the Pikes without taking that baby.

Shelby learned that you cannot put out an APB on someone until they have been lost for twenty-four hours; that there are five major routes out of Burlington by car; that if you leave from the airport, you can get to Chicago, Pittsburgh, Philadelphia, New York City, Boston, Cleveland, or Albany.

And that 2,100 people are reported missing, daily.

Her brother being one of them.

She had not let go of his note, not since finding it five hours ago. The ink now tattooed the palm of her hand like hieroglyphs, a diary of loss. Eli had come at her call, and had promised to personally search every inch of Comtosook, and lean hard on the cops in Burlington. But Shelby knew that if Ross did not want to be found, he would simply make himself invisible.

Once when they were in high school, a football jock had killed himself by jumping off the edge of a gorge. The news had been all over the papers; guidance counselors had set up shop in the hallways of school; memorials of flowers and teddy bears decorated the site. Ross had wanted to go see where it happened. 'Jesus,' he'd said, over the raging water and the broken rocks. 'If you're going to do it that way, you're pretty sure.'

'How would *you* do it?' she had asked, with a morbid curiosity that, now, she could not believe they'd ever discussed. She also could not remember, although she'd tried so hard her head throbbed, how Ross had answered. Would he use pills, or a gun, or a knife? Would he lock himself in an anonymous motel room, jump from a train bridge, do it in his car?

When Ross had been in the hospital after the last suicide attempt, she had gone to visit him. Since he was doped up on medication, Shelby was certain he did not remember their conversation. 'Try living on dry land,' Ross had said, 'when you are a fish.'

The phone rang, and Shelby flew from Ross's bedroom down the hall to her own. 'Shelby?'

'Eli?' Her heart sank.

'Has he called you yet?'

'No.'

'All right, well . . . leave the line free for when Ross calls.'

She loved him, because he'd said *when* Ross calls, not *if*. 'Okay,' she promised, and she hung up to find Ethan standing in the doorway of her bedroom, looking miserable.

'I think it's my fault,' he confessed.

Shelby patted the bed so that he'd sit beside her. 'It's not, Ethan, believe me. I used to think that I was the one to blame, too, because I wasn't doing something Ross needed me to do.'

'No, that's not what I mean.' His face twisted. 'We were talking about it the other night – dying.'

Shelby turned slowly. 'What did he say to you?'

'That he was a coward.' Ethan worried the seam of the quilt. 'I asked him about his scars. Once I made him remember, maybe he couldn't stop thinking about it.'

She felt her shoulders relax. 'Ethan, you didn't give Uncle Ross any ideas. They were in his head long before he got here.'

'Why would he do it?' Ethan exploded. 'Why would he even *want* to die?'

Shelby thought for a minute. 'I don't think he wants to die. I think it's that he doesn't want to live.'

They sat in silence for a few seconds. 'He also said he would bring me a girl.'

'He *what?*'

Ethan blushed. 'To kiss. So, you know, I could see what it was like.'

'Ah. And where was your uncle planning on finding this girl?'

'I don't know. Isn't there someplace you can pay them to do that stuff?' He shrugged. 'I guess there's a chance that he's off doing that, instead.'

Shelby thought of Ross walking the theater district in New York City, soliciting whores in heels and snakeskin skirts to come and kiss a nine-year-old boy. It was a frightening image, but not nearly as terrifying as the mental picture of Ross dying alone. 'Let's hope,' she said.

For two nights, Ross slept in the backseat of his car, parked in the Wal-Mart lot behind the pools and barbecues. During the days, he haunted the hospital, slipping in to see Ruby whenever her granddaughter – he'd learned that her name was Meredith – was not there. Ross did not press Ruby for information about the Pikes, and Ruby did not volunteer it; in fact, their conversations tiptoed around this by filling in instead all the details they did not yet know: where they lived, what they did, how they'd come to be at this point. Ross discovered that he liked Ruby – she was sharp and outspoken and had memorized the batting average of every player on the Orioles. He knew that they were both getting something out of these daily visits – Ruby was deciding whether or not to trust him with the history she carried like a stone beneath her breastbone, and Ross was meeting the woman who had raised Lia's baby.

She would not talk about Lia, or that baby, but she told him about Meredith, a single mother who worked too hard. About Lucy, scared of her own shadow. She laughed when Ross imitated the cardiologist who walked like he had a full diaper. And whenever Ross arrived, Ruby's face lit up.

Not unlike Lia's.

Meredith left the hospital at three to pick Lucy up at summer camp, and returned at around four-thirty, so Ross timed his visits accordingly. Today, he pushed through the swinging door to find Ruby sitting in a chair by the window.

'Well, look at you,' Ross said.

'I was hoping to run a marathon today, but the nurse suggested this instead.'

'It suits you.' He dropped a small wrapped gift into her lap. 'Open it.'

'You didn't have to bring me anything,' Ruby demurred. But Ross had brought her a present the last two times he'd seen her – a collection of wild purple loosestrife he'd picked from the side of the highway, a stack of magazines he'd found in someone's recycling bin. Gifts that she could enjoy . . . but tell Meredith had come from a friendly candy striper.

Her hands worked the ribbon on the package until she pulled free a deck of cards. 'I used to be quite the poker champion in my day,' Ruby said. 'I played it with the other girls who worked at the mill, on our cigarette breaks.'

'I only just learned. My nephew taught me.'

She began to shuffle, her knotted hands more nimble than he would have thought. 'I'll be gentle, then. What about the pot?'

'I didn't realize you indulged,' Ross joked. 'Maybe I can find some for next time.'

'Spoken like a man who's afraid to put his money where his mouth is.'

'The truth is, Ruby,' he admitted, 'I have about forty dollars to my name.'

Ruby didn't react to this; she just kept ruffling the cards and frowning. 'It isn't five-card stud without a prize. I suppose we could play strip poker, but something tells me I'd have the better end of the deal there.'

'There's something else we could play for. Something free.'

'If you're thinking of sexual favors, I ought to tell you I'm not that kind of woman.'

Ross caught her eye. 'How about the truth?'

The air stilled around them. Ruby tapped the deck around and around in a square, aligning the edges. 'But then nobody wins,' she replied.

'Ruby,' he said. 'Please.'

She looked at him for a long time. Then she shuffled the cards. 'Ante up.'

'I'll give you the answer to one question,' Ross began.

Ruby nodded in agreement, and dealt them each two cards, one facedown. Ross had a ten of jacks, Ruby a queen of hearts. She raised a brow, waiting for him to make an opening bet. 'Two answers,' Ross said.

'I'll call.' She dealt two more cards faceup. Ross got a two of clubs, Ruby the queen of diamonds.

'You're winning,' Ross said.

'I told you so.'

He looked at his hand. 'Three questions of your choice.'

Ruby matched again, and continued to deal, until they each had two more cards – Ross a six and ace of clubs, Ruby a pair of kings.

With the best hand showing, Ruby made the final bet. 'I'll tell you everything,' she said soberly, and Ross nodded. They flipped over the cards they'd had in the hole. Ross looked at her three of hearts. 'Does that beat a two of clubs?'

'Not by itself,' Ruby said. 'But your flush beats my two pair.'

'Even though you have people with crowns? And mine don't even go in order?'

'Even though. Beginner's luck, I guess.' She reached for his cards, and Ross noticed that her hand was shaking. 'So,' she said, looking up at him.

'So,' he answered softly.

One of the pumps on her IV began to beep, the Ringer's solution having run low. A nurse would come in to fix it. And by the time she was finished, Meredith and Lucy would have returned. 'I'm being discharged tomorrow morning,' Ruby said.

'Then I'll just have to come to your house to collect.'

'I'll be expecting you.' He stood up and started for the door as the nurse entered the room. 'Ross,' Ruby called. 'Thank you for the cards.'

'My pleasure.'

'Ross!' He turned, his hand on the panel of the door. 'I threw that game,' Ruby said.

Ross smiled. 'I know.'

Shelby was dreaming of blood, thick as molasses, flooding a city street, when the telephone woke her. 'Aw, damn,' Ross said when she picked up the receiver. 'It's noon and you're asleep. I've been keeping other hours, so I forgot.'

She sat up instantly, the sheets pooling around her waist. 'Ross? Are you all right? I thought you were dead!'

'I'm not dead. I'm just in Maryland.' Ross seemed genuinely stunned. 'What made you think that?'

'Oh, gee, I don't know – a whole catena of misinformation, apparently. The suicide note you left me? The fact that you've tried to kill yourself before?'

'That wasn't a suicide note. It was sort of a quick good-bye.' When Shelby was silent, Ross added, chagrined, 'Well, I see your point. Listen, by any chance is Eli there?'

'Eli is out looking for your *body*,' Shelby said pointedly.

'Ah. Maybe you could relay a message. Tell him I found Ruby Weber.'

It took Shelby a moment to wade through the past three days and place the name. 'The house girl? What did she tell you?'

'Nothing,' Ross admitted. 'Yet.'

'When are you coming back?'

'I don't know.'

Silence stretched between them, the thinnest filament. 'But you *are* coming back?'

Before he could answer, an operator got onto the line, announcing that Ross had run out of money. 'Tell Eli,' he said, just before the line went dead.

Shelby was left holding the phone. In her bedroom, the sun pushed at the backs of the rolled-down shades, threatening to burst through. Shelby threw back the covers and pulled open the curtains, letting the light spill over her bare feet.

Her brother had not said he was coming back. But then, he hadn't said he *wasn't,* either.

On the doorstep of Ruby's house, Ross rang the bell and stuck his hands in his pockets, only to find them filled with rose petals. 'I know,' he said aloud. 'I'm anxious, too.'

The woman who answered the door was a six-foot Amazon in scrubs with cornrowed hair that reached her behind. 'We don't want any,' she said, and started to slam the door.

'I'm not selling anything. I'm here to see Ruby. Tell her it's Ross.'

'Ms Weber is asleep now.'

A voice, from the belly of the house: 'No, I'm not!'

The home health aide narrowed her eyes and then stepped aside to let Ross into the house. She muttered something under her breath in a language Ross didn't understand, and was certain he didn't want to. Ross followed her into a living room, where Ruby sat on a couch with a crocheted afghan covering her legs. 'Welcome home,' he said.

'Welcome *to* my home.' Ruby turned to the health aide. 'Tajmalla, could you give us a minute?'

With a bearing that made him think of African priestesses wearing kente headwraps, she glided from the room. 'The agency sent her,' Ruby said, watching her go. 'She's been teaching me Swahili. Gorgeous language. It feels like a river running over your brain.'

Ross sat down across from Ruby. 'Go ahead. Impress me.'

She concentrated. '*Miya* . . . no wait, that's *Liya* . . .'

Lia?

'*Liya na tabia yako usilaumu wenzako,*' Ruby said in a rush.

'That means hello?'

'No. It means, "Do not blame others for problems you have created yourself."'

Ross shook his head. 'I think I would have started with "Hi, my name is Ross."'

'Actually,' Ruby said, 'I asked her to translate that particular sentence.' She reached for the remote control, and turned off the soap opera on the television. 'I thought it might help, you know, to have it in my head.' *Before I tell you the rest.* 'You need to explain something first. Why would you want to bring this up, now?'

Ross thought of Lia, haunting the property; of Shelby unrolling those genealogy charts; of the rose petals that filled his pockets. 'Because I need to know what happened to someone I love,' he said.

Ruby pulled the afghan higher. 'He told me to bury the baby.'

'Spencer Pike?'

She nodded. 'You need to understand, the professor – well, I've never met anyone like him, since then. He had a way of talking to you and before you knew it you were nodding right along with him without knowing how you'd even come to agree. I always figured that was what made Cissy Pike marry him.' Ruby looked at Ross. 'She made herself a friend, an Indian, and they kept sneaking off to see each other. The professor, he knew something was going on between them. He found the Indian up in her bedroom one day, threw him out, and knocked around Miz Pike . . . which made her go into labor.'

'Was the baby born alive?'

Ruby seemed surprised by the question. 'Oh, yes. I'd never attended a birthing before, I was only fourteen. And after all that work, to hear that baby cry . . .' Her voice trailed off. 'Professor Pike took the baby, so his wife could get her rest. I was cleaning up inside when he came back and said that the baby had died. He'd left her in the icehouse, and he wanted me to bury her in an old apple crate before his wife woke up.'

'Did he tell you how the baby died?'

Ruby shook her head. 'He didn't tell, and I didn't ask. I think I knew the answer, already. I went out to the icehouse, and found her there, just like a doll wrapped in her blankets. There was something about putting her in the ground, when she still looked like an angel, that I just couldn't do. So I put her in the apple crate, but left the lid off. I figured that he could bury that baby himself if he felt a need to.

'By the time I got inside, he was drinking in his study. I went up to bed. And in the middle of the night I heard a baby crying. I got up and went outside, following that noise.' She shivered. 'Sometimes, I still hear it, just before I fall asleep at night. I went out to the icehouse, toward that sound. But when I stepped up onto the porch, I bumped into Cissy Pike's legs.' Ruby's voice dropped to a whisper. 'She was tied to a rafter, her eyes wide open and bright red . . . I screamed. I thought that the professor had killed her – and that I was going to be next. I decided to run away, right then and there – and then I heard it again. That cry. The baby I'd seen dead with my own two eyes was just inside the icehouse, in the apple crate, kicking and screaming.'

'You took her.'

Ruby glanced up at Ross. 'I had made a promise to care for that baby, if anything happened. So I took a roast we'd been saving for a dinner party, and put it in the crate instead, and nailed the lid shut, like Professor Pike wanted me to do in the first place. Then I grabbed the baby and ran.'

'Where is she now?' Ross asked.

Ruby glanced away. 'The baby was young and sickly. She died on the way to Baltimore.'

Ross thought of Lia, of Lily, of Meredith. And suddenly he understood why Ruby was lying. 'You haven't told her,' he said quietly.

Ruby's eyes met his, in that small cramped space where no words can fit. After years of keeping this secret, big as Atlas's burden, Ross had come to offer a shoulder. But just because she'd told him did not mean she was going to be willing to tell anyone else.

Suddenly there was a thunder of footsteps, and the little girl Ross had seen days earlier in her mother's company rounded the corner. 'Granny Ruby, we're back!'

A moment later, Meredith stood in the doorway, trailed by Tajmalla. 'How are you feeling?' she asked Ruby, before her eyes homed in on Ross. '*You.*'

Ross stood up. He would have introduced himself, but again he was struck by this woman's uncanny resemblance to Lia Pike. He wondered what she would do if he reached out his hand and touched her cheek to make certain she was real.

'I don't know who you are, and what business you have with my grandmother,' Meredith said, 'but I don't think—'

'His name is Ross, dear,' Ruby interrupted. 'He's come to take you out to dinner.'

'*What?*' Ross and Meredith spoke at the same time.

'I'm sure I mentioned it. Last week.'

'Last week you were in the hospital, talking to people who weren't in the room.'

Ruby smiled tightly at her. 'Ross is an old friend . . . of a friend. And I've told him so much about you.'

Ross felt Meredith size him up, and find him sorely lacking. Then she looked at the woman she believed to be her grandmother – a woman who'd almost died – and her eyes softened. Was this Ruby's way of getting rid of Ross? Of pushing him to tell Meredith the truth? Or was this Ruby's way of making him understand why she *hadn't*?

Either way, Ross knew, he would go out with this woman in a heartbeat. If only so that he could sit across the table and stare at a face that he could not forget.

'Will you, um, excuse me?' Meredith said politely, and she turned to Ruby, lowering her voice – but not enough that Ross could not hear. 'Ruby, he's not my type . . .'

'Merry, you have to actually date to *have* a type.' Ruby smiled. 'I have Lucy and Tajmalla to keep me company.'

'Coffee,' Ross heard himself say. 'Just a cup.'

Meredith turned to Ruby again. 'When you're all better again, remind me to kill you,' she murmured, and then she turned to Ross. 'Just a cup.'

She moved stiffly to his side. Ruby stared at Ross, but she had on her poker face. And as he walked with Meredith out of the living room, two strangers who each thought they knew the other better than they truly did, Ross realized that her perfume smelled faintly of roses.

The only reason she was doing this, Meredith told herself, was because she didn't want Ruby getting all worked up again. She watched with distaste as Ross swiped empty coffee cups, cassette cases, and cigarette packs off the passenger seat of his ancient rattletrap and tossed them into the backseat. 'Sorry,' he said, and he held the door open for her.

It smelled of smoke. Meredith watched him walk to the driver's side. His hair was long – all one length, nearly to his shoulders; he wore a short-sleeved bowling shirt open over a man's tank-style T-shirt; his jeans had a hole on the left thigh. He looked like the kind of guy you'd find strumming a guitar for tips in a subway hollow, or writing bad poetry in the rear of a rundown café. The kind of guy who scribbled notes to himself on gum wrappers and stuck them in the pocket of his jacket, only to forget what they were about in the first place. The kind of guy who drove taxis while people like her were busy getting their doctorates. The kind of guy she would never have given a second glance.

The car started right up, a small miracle. 'So,' he said, smiling. 'Where to?'

'Somewhere close.' Meredith gave him directions to the first Starbucks that came to mind, and when he turned away she told herself that she had imagined the flash of disappointment in his eyes.

Those eyes. She'd give him that. They made her think of the sort of pool you'd stumble across in a rain forest, so jewel green and rich that once you fell in, you'd be immediately over your head and unable – unwilling – to drag yourself out.

He held up a pack of cigarettes. 'Do you mind?'

She did, greatly, but this was his car. She unrolled the window as he lit a cancer stick and drew deeply. It hollowed out his cheekbones even more, casting the planes of his face in stark relief. 'Just so you know,' Meredith announced, 'I am not in the habit of being fixed up by my grandmother.'

'Of course not.'

'What's that supposed to mean?'

Ross blew a stream of smoke out his window. 'That someone like you can get her own dates.'

In spite of herself, Meredith felt heat rise up from her neck. 'Like me,' she repeated, immediately putting up her guard. 'How do you know anything about me?'

'I don't,' Ross admitted.

'Then why don't you just stop making assumptions.' And yet, Meredith thought, hadn't she been doing the very same thing about him?

He drove with his right hand, the cigarette in his left. The end glowed like a game-show buzzer, an evil eye. 'It's only that you remind me of someone I used to know. She was just as beautiful as you are.'

In her lifetime, Meredith could count on one hand the number of times she had been complimented on her looks. *Accomplished, intelligent, groundbreaking* – those were all adjectives that had often been tethered to her name. But she'd set her physical attributes on a back burner, choosing instead to play up her mental acuity, and the world had followed her lead. *Beautiful,* she thought again.

She wondered what had happened to this woman he used to know, if she had died or gotten into a fight with him or walked out of his life. Meredith looked at Ross again across the front seat of the car and this time, instead of seeing a loser, she saw someone who had a story to tell.

To her great surprise, she wanted to hear it.

'So?' Ross asked, and she thought maybe he could read minds, too.

'So what?'

'So . . . are we going in?' He glanced out the window, and she realized that they had pulled into the parking lot of Starbucks. He had a dimple in his left cheek when he smiled.

'Yes. Right.' Ross came around to her side of the car and opened the door for her. They walked into the café to find several people in line in front of them. 'Do you know what you'd like?' he asked.

For the first time in years, Meredith didn't have a ready answer.

Bruno Davidovich had been a pro linebacker, a bouncer, and, in one career aberration, a television chef, before getting into lie detection work. The trick, he'd told Eli, was to never take your eyes off your subject. He kept time with Swiss precision, and always arrived at the exact scheduled hour to perform his tests, which was one reason Eli liked to employ him. The other was that Bruno's sheer size often scared people into telling the truth.

'Try to relax,' Bruno said to Spencer Pike, as the old man sat trussed up to the polygraph. Pike had agreed to the test when Eli asked, saying he wanted this over and done with, already. Now two pneumograph tubes were attached to his chest and abdomen, two metal plates hooked onto his ring and index finger, a blood pressure cuff around his thin upper arm. 'Is today Wednesday?' Bruno asked.

Pike rolled his eyes. 'Yes.'

'Is your name Spencer Pike?'

'Yes.'

'Are you a healthy man?'

A pause. 'No.'

'Have you ever told a lie?' Bruno asked.

'Yes.'

'Have you ever told a lie about something serious?'

'Yes.'

'Have you ever lied to get out of trouble?'

'Yes.'

Eli listened to Bruno continue through the questions, working his way up to the relevant ones. It was not as if this polygraph test would be used in court, nor was it considered accurate enough to acquit or condemn Pike. But Eli needed to know for his own peace of mind why Spencer Pike seemed to think that he was responsible for the death of a child that hadn't been killed, yet innocent of the murder of his wife.

'Was the baby born dead?' Bruno was asking.

'No.'

'Did you hold the baby after it was born?'

'Yes.'

'Did you kill the baby after it was born?'

Pike's breath left his body in a thin stream. 'Yes,' he said.

'Did you have a fight with your wife before the baby was born?'

'Yes.'

'Did you fight with your wife after the baby was born?'

'No.'

'Did you harm your wife?'

Pike bowed his head. 'Yes.'

Bruno stared at Pike. 'Did you hang your wife?'

'No,' he answered.

'Thanks,' Bruno said. He pulled the printout from the polygraph and walked into the hallway, Eli following.

While Eli waited, Bruno scored the charts. 'So?'

'Look here. When I asked him if he hurt his wife, and he replied affirmatively . . . that was the control question. Then I asked him if he killed his wife, and his physiological response wasn't as strong as it was to the previous question.'

'He didn't do it,' Eli said softly.

'Seems that way.' Bruno hesitated. 'You want me to scare him up a little bit, see if we get something different?'

Eli glanced through the door. Pike's watery eyes were fixed on something outside the window. His hands flexed on the arms of his wheelchair. 'No,' Eli said. 'He's done.'

It was not until the clerk from behind the Starbucks counter took off his apron and began to swish a mop around the table where Ross and Meredith had settled that she realized they had been sitting there for five hours. 'Designer babies are the norm in nature,' she argued. 'Look at gorillas, okay? Grayback males are the ones all the ladies go for, because they've lived long enough to go gray. So when it comes time to picking your mate, you choose someone who's going to give your offspring the best chance for longevity.' Meredith felt her brain snapping with the challenge of defending her work, and she knew it wasn't only because this was her fourth caramel macchiato. 'All we're doing in the lab is making nature run a little more smoothly.'

'But how big a leap is it from discarding embryos because they carry cystic fibrosis,' Ross countered, 'to getting rid of anything that doesn't have blue eyes?'

Meredith thought for a moment. 'Well, technically, blue eyes are a one-gene defect, so that would be possible. But most traits that parents would consider undesirable involve hundreds of genes acting in tandem. That was where Hitler was categorically wrong. You can't pinpoint stupidity or frailty or ugliness at one place on the DNA strand.'

'Not yet,' Ross qualified. 'But once you figure that out, it's only a matter of time before stem cell therapy is used to get rid of those . . . *undesirable* traits. And suddenly you've got a whole world full of Stepford people.'

'First off, there's a difference between curing someone who is already sick, versus engineering someone who can't get sick. Second, 99.9 percent of the scientists doing this kind of research are in it for the right reasons – not because they're megalo-maniacs set on creating a master race. Third, you can't criticize me until you talk to a woman whose three babies have died of leukemia, a woman who's come to beg for a baby that won't die this time around.' Meredith shook her head. 'I have this sign on my office door that says *The Last Resort*. I put it there because that's what the parents who meet with me think they've come to. And to have those same parents show up with a healthy baby months later – well, no parent should have to suffer through having a sick child.'

'And who gets to define *sick*?' Ross swirled a stirrer in his coffee mug. 'My nephew has XP. You ever heard of that?'

'Sure.'

'He's just the sort of child PGD would have recommended discarding. But Ethan's the smartest, sharpest, bravest kid I've ever met. And even if he can only be smart and sharp and brave for ten years or thirteen years or thirty, who's to say that time isn't better than none at all?'

'Not me,' Meredith agreed. 'That would be up to the parents.'

'But there are plenty of parents out there who would have gotten rid of Ethan—'

'—Who was not Ethan at the time,' Meredith argued. 'Barely a clot of cells.'

'Whatever. The point is, parents draw the line at all different places. What if PGD diagnoses a disease that won't come out until a person's thirties or forties? Or if it screens a predisposition to heart disease or cancer . . . which still might never develop in the course of a lifetime? What if you find a way to tell that a child will grow up to be suicidal?' Ross's gaze slipped away from hers. 'Do people have the right to get rid of those embryos too?'

Meredith raised her brows. 'And what if deaf parents used PGD to be able to have a child with the same inherited condition? That would be *endorsing* a disability.'

'You can't tell me that's what most of your clients do.'

'No,' she admitted. 'But it *does* happen. And it's exactly why my job is not evil incarnate. Is it so wrong for a parent to know what her child will be like in advance?'

'How about when a kid finds out that the circumstances of her birth aren't what she thought they were?' Ross asked, looking at her carefully.

'It's up to the parents to tell her, or not. If things go well, either way, she's happy . . . because she's got parents who love her for the way she turned out.'

'Love has nothing to do with science,' Ross said. 'Love's not a *because*, it's a *no matter what*.'

'But why take the chance?' Meredith argued. 'Can you honestly say that there's one thing about yourself you don't wish could have been changed for the better before you were born?'

For a moment Ross did not respond. Then he asked, 'Have you found the gene for happiness yet?'

She fell silent, looking at him, wondering about the genesis of an answer like that. The only sound was the quiet swish of the mop, rasping its tongue along the tile floor behind them. Meredith realized, in that moment, what was so different about Ross Wakeman – in the five hours they'd spent in each other's company, this was the first glimpse into himself that he'd offered. They had talked about Lucy, about Ruby's health, about Meredith's career . . . and not at all about him. Meredith could not recall a single date that hadn't centered on the man she was with. Ross – well, Ross was doing what *she* usually did.

She did not know anything about this man who caused her mind to spin, except that he had a nephew with XP, knew her grandmother, and made the seam of her pulse lose a stitch every time he smiled. 'I'm sorry,' Meredith said. 'I've completely monopolized this conversation.'

'No. I wanted to know about you.'

'I want to know about you too,' Meredith admitted.

'Nothing very interesting, I'm afraid.' Ross took out a pack of cigarettes, lighting up.

She waved away a cloud of smoke. 'Those things will kill you.'

'I wish.'

'Why?'

'Because I can't die,' Ross admitted.

In spite of herself, Meredith grinned. 'Unless I take out my kryptonite necklace, you mean?'

'No, really. I've been hit by bullets, thrown from a car crash, fried by lightning, and every time I come away without a scratch.'

'You're kidding.'

'I've got the doctor bills to prove it.'

Meredith was stunned for a moment. 'That's a pretty remarkable gift.'

'Not when you want to save someone other than yourself,' Ross said.

'Your nephew.'

'Among other people.'

She leaned forward, drawn by the flicker of pain at the back of his eyes. 'The person you said I look like?'

He didn't answer – he didn't seem capable of answering at that point. Meredith wondered what it would feel like to have a man so enamored of her that even after her death, he might still carry a torch. He might look for her face in the faces of others. The Starbucks worker approached their table. 'You can't smoke in here.'

Ross turned to him. 'I guess self-immolation is out of the question, then.'

The kid blinked. 'Dude, whatever perverted stuff you do on your own time is your own business.'

Meredith covered her laugh with a cough. 'Maybe we ought to go.' She hesitated. 'I've really enjoyed being with you. I think the last time I told that to a guy and meant it, I was making mud pies in the nursery school sandbox.'

'And you didn't even get your hands dirty tonight.'

'Imagine.' Meredith looked up at him shyly. 'Are you in town for a while? Maybe we could, you know, get together. For a whole meal this time. Or just the appetizer, if you want to work up to that.'

'I can't.'

Immediately her eyes flew to his left hand. Bare. 'You're gay,' she said.

'It's not that.'

The old reflex kicked in – she had been at this juncture of an evening before, where she was found unattractive or lacking in some other way. Meredith felt herself separating by degrees. 'Yes. Right.' She briskly held out her hand. 'Well, it was very nice to meet you.'

He took her hand with reverence, turning it over between his own for a long moment, as if she were made of the finest crystal instead of ordinary flesh and blood. 'Meredith,' Ross said quietly, 'I like you. I like you a lot. But there's someone else.'

The woman, the one Meredith looked like. She ducked her head. 'I'm sorry,' she muttered. 'I didn't realize you two were still—'

She felt something being pressed into her hand. A newspaper clipping, yellowed and faded, but it was still possible to see the face of the woman in the center. A face that was a mirror of Meredith's. *Lia Beaumont Pike,* said the caption. *1914–1932.*

'This was your biological grandmother,' Ross said. 'And I'm in love with her.'

It was a war, Ross realized, and Meredith was losing. She stood with her arms crossed tight, her back straight, her eyes the color of anger. Ross and Ruby, on the couch, took turns fielding her outrage and tossing it back, in the hopes that she would start to believe what they were trying to say.

'When I told your mother that she was not my child, not even named Luxe, but *really* Lily Pike,' Ruby said, 'she had a heart attack and died. Can you blame me for not wanting to bring it up again?'

'Yes!' Meredith exploded. 'You don't hide something like that from a person!'

'You do if it saves their life,' Ross pointed out.

She turned to him, lashing out like a wounded bear. 'Explain something to me. How could you possibly have known a woman who died before you were born?'

'I met her at work.'

'Work. What do you do for a living, raise the dead?'

Ross exchanged a glance with Ruby. 'I don't raise them. I just sort of find them.'

'Great. You hunt for ghosts, when you're not getting hit by lightning and managing to stay alive. Ruby, I don't know how this guy walked in and convinced you the way he did, but he's crazy. Wacko. I think—'

'I think you'd better listen to him, Meredith,' Ruby interrupted. 'He's telling you the truth.'

'The *truth*. So now you believe in ghosts, too? Fine, then. Conjure this grandmother of mine. If she floats in here and tells me the same thing, I'll believe you.'

'It doesn't work that way,' Ross explained.

'How convenient.'

The corners of Ruby's mouth turned down. 'Don't shoot the messenger.'

'Then what would you like me to do? Thank him for coming here to tell me my entire life has been a lie?'

'It hasn't been a lie,' Ross said. 'It just . . . hasn't been what you thought it was.' He walked toward Meredith. 'You are the direct descendant of Lia Pike. And that means you own a really nice piece of real estate in Comtosook, Vermont.'

He wished he could tell her that from this property, you could see mountains so green it made your eyes hurt, and that the air smelled cleaner than anything you could ever imagine. He wished he could show her the spot where he'd fallen in love with Lia.

'I don't need real estate in Vermont,' Meredith said.

'Well, there are a boatload of Abenaki Indians who do, who've been fighting to keep the land from being developed.'

'That's not my problem.'

'No, but if you own the land, you get to decide what's done with it.'

'Ah, see, now we're getting somewhere. You're an Indian-rights activist.'

'I'm—'

'And naturally, if you can convince me I'm part Abenaki, I'm supposed to side with my relatives. Am I the only person here who can see what's right in front of her eyes? Look at me.' Meredith yanked her hair out of its neat bun. 'I'm blond. I'm pale. Do I look like I have even a drop of Native American blood in me?'

'No, but neither did Lia. Listen, you're a scientist,' Ross argued. 'Your great-grandfather, Az Thompson, is still alive. Let us run a DNA test to prove it to you.'

'And then what?'

Ross looked at Ruby, and then back. 'Then it's up to you.'

Meredith narrowed her eyes. 'What do you get out of this, exactly? Some kickback from the Abenaki? A book deal?'

'Nothing.' Ross glanced at the table, at Lia's obituary. 'I just want to help her.'

Suddenly he was aware of small hands pushing at his knee, moving him out of the way. Lucy – Meredith's little girl, who was supposed to be asleep – had been eavesdropping. 'Lucy!' Ruby said. 'What are you doing up?'

'Go back to your room,' Meredith ordered.

But Lucy pointed to Lia's moon eyes, to the white bow of her cheek. 'She lost her baby.'

He felt everything inside him freeze.

'Lucy.' Meredith squatted down. 'I don't know how much you overheard, but—'

'Let her talk,' Ross murmured.

'She tells me every time.' Lucy hesitated. 'She told me you were coming.'

Ross's voice was tight, stretched, like the flight of a bird. 'Who?'

'That lady,' Lucy said, pointing to Lia's photograph. 'She's the one I see in the middle of the night.'

Eli hadn't realized what a pit he lived in until he saw it through Shelby's eyes. 'It's not much,' he'd warned, throwing open the door, and looking with dismay at the scarred wooden floors and the dormitory-quality couch, hiding its shabbiness under a floral sheet that had seen better days itself. A stack of dishes waited in the sink, as it had for the past week; a pile of mismatched shoes walked over themselves at the side of the door. 'I, uh, didn't know you were coming,' Eli apologized.

'Wow!' Ethan pushed past them. 'Can I have a place like this one day?' Without waiting for an answer, he followed Watson upstairs, and suddenly there was a squeal of delight.

Eli glanced at the ceiling. 'He must have found the shooting range.'

'You have a *shooting range?*'

'Kidding,' Eli said. 'But I do have a PS2.'

'Aha. Is Watson addicted to Gran Turismo?'

'Of course not. He doesn't have a thumb to work the joystick.' Eli led her into the kitchen, setting down the bag of groceries with which, Shelby had promised, she would make him a culinary feast.

So what if it was three in the morning?

Shelby immediately began to bustle around his knot of a kitchen, setting vegetables in the sink to be washed and organizing the rest of the groceries for refrigeration or oven cooking. Now that her brother had called to say he wasn't lying in a ditch somewhere, she was a different person. She'd explained how she'd once interrupted Ross in the middle of a suicide attempt – a facet of his personality that had come as a surprise to Eli. Sure, the guy was a little gloomy, but he hadn't seen him on the verge of taking his own life. Or maybe he hadn't wanted to see him that way.

So Ross was off in Maryland looking for Ruby Weber, and Eli was having dinner cooked for him by a beautiful woman. All in all, he thought he was getting the better end of the deal. 'You know, we could get a frozen pizza.'

'But then I wouldn't be able to impress you.'

'You already have.' Eli suddenly remembered how, before his ex-wife had taken everything with her, she'd had a designer into the house, who'd encouraged her to build a room around a certain piece – a rug, a table, a chandelier. He'd thought at the time it was the stupidest advice he'd ever heard, but now Eli understood. He would have happily built a room around Shelby. A house. A life.

He watched her line up peppers on his sideboard – just the smallest splashes of color, and already his kitchen looked a hundred percent better. She turned, a Styrofoam tray of chicken in her hand. 'Let's put this in the fridge,' she said, in the instant before Eli leaped up and flattened himself against the door.

'All right,' Shelby said slowly. 'You'd rather get salmonella?'

'No.' Eli reached behind his back and plucked a photo from beneath its magnet. Then he stepped away and opened the refrigerator door.

By then, though, Shelby could have cared less about the chicken. 'What's that?' she asked, pointing at the picture in his palm.

'Nothing.'

'Nothing, nothing? Or nothing, like an old girlfriend?' In a move that any police academy instructor would have found impressive, she stuffed the chicken into his hand, extricated the photograph, and screamed.

Eli took it from her and tried very hard not to say *I told you so*.

'I hope that's not an old girlfriend,' Shelby said weakly.

He glanced down at the shot of Cecelia Pike hanging from a beam on the icehouse porch. Her face was aubergine, her tongue protruding, her eyes bloodshot and bugged. 'Sorry,' Eli murmured. 'Like I said, I wasn't expecting you.'

'Because then you would have taken the cadaver photos off the fridge? Good lord, Eli, what is that doing up there in the first place?'

'To make me remember. I do it every time I'm thick in the middle of a case.'

Ethan flew into the kitchen. 'You know what Eli's got?'

'A twisted work ethic?' Shelby said.

'No, a PlayStation.' He turned to Eli. 'I would totally kill for one of those.'

'Knock yourself out,' Eli said, and Ethan left as swiftly as he'd arrived.

Shelby had taken to slicing mushrooms. Eli sat down, watching the way the muscles shifted beneath her thin T-shirt as she cut and diced. 'Is that really what happens to you when you hang yourself?'

'Yeah.'

'Then I guess I should feel grateful with Ross, there was only all that blood.' She looked up for a second. 'No, actually, I'm not grateful about any of it.'

'First rule of being a homicide detective: Death isn't pretty. *Ever.*'

He watched her hand still over the cutting board, and realized that he'd put his foot in his mouth. 'Shelby—'

'How come when we really, really want something, we say we'd *kill* for it, or we'd *die* to have it?'

'I suppose because it's the ultimate tradeoff.'

Shelby began to mix the ingredients for a salad dressing. 'It is. Tropologically. As in: *I'd die to keep my son alive.*'

Not sure what to say, Eli looked down at the picture on the countertop. Cecelia Pike had been killed, and somehow or other, her child had been spared. But if it was a murder, he didn't know who was to blame. The evidence told him it wasn't Gray Wolf, and his gut told him it wasn't Spencer Pike. Ruby Weber, if she'd been there that night, wouldn't have had the strength to hoist Cissy's noose up over the beam of the icehouse porch. And yet you could see right there on the bottom of the photo, the long crooked mark in the wet sawdust that came from the dragging of something – a heel or a boot? – during a struggle.

He certainly hoped Ross would come home with his pockets full of missing puzzle pieces.

'Taste this,' Shelby said, and before he could even shake his mind back to the present she pressed her mouth against his.

Along with the sweetness, there was something bitter. Tart. Oily.

Did disappointment have a flavor?

She drew back. 'Wait, don't tell me. You prefer French.'

'I don't like any dressing at all,' Eli said.

'Huh. I never would have figured you for a salad purist.'

Eli smiled. He drew her close, so that the confetti of peppers in her soft palms spilled between them and the photograph fluttered to the kitchen floor, forgotten. 'Were we talking about salad?' he asked.

It was *Temezôwas,* the time of the Cutter Moon, and that was enough to make Az nervous. A season that was all about things coming to an end . . . coupled with the milk-blind eye of the full moon – well, it just wasn't a good time to be laying charges to blast granite at Angel Quarry, is all. No matter that the actual detonation would happen at 5 A.M., when no one else was present . . . Az patrolled the perimeter, knowing something was bound to go wrong, wondering when it would happen.

The sky was unsettled tonight, fingers of pink stretching

through the stars like a dawn that couldn't wait. And it was hot
– so hot that you could hear the fisher cats singing to each other,
and the heads of dandelions bursting into seed. Az turned the
corner at the north edge of the quarry, where the majority of the
charges had been wedged into drilled cores of the rock. There
were bags of ammonium nitrate explosive down there, sticks of
dynamite, blasting caps and non-electric priming cord. Delay
devices would be run by a computer to detonate the charges in
sequence, until seventeen thousand pounds of rock had been
moved. This was to be a two-step process – half the quarry would
blast at dawn tomorrow, the other half a few days from now, then
the miners would go in and harvest the slabs for commercial sale.
Az had dreamed of rubble, of smoke, of boils and scars;
Armageddon induced by the flip of a switch. He'd gone so far as
to tell his boss to wait a week, and the younger man had laughed.
'You stick to the night watch, Chief,' he'd said. 'And leave the
decisions to me.'

It came as no surprise, then, when Az spotted an intruder.
'Hey,' he yelled, but the man kept walking. Az jogged a little –
the best he could do, given the condition of his hips – and found
himself breathing hard a foot away from Comtosook's most notorious drunk.

Abbott Thule had outlived most of the people who'd made a
habit out of shaking their heads to find him passed out on the
porch of the Gas & Grocery, or on one memorable occasion,
sleeping buck naked under the only traffic light on Main Street.
He came from a long line of previous drunks, most of whom had
not been blessed with an ironclad liver like himself. A mixed-
blood Indian, he'd had four wives, two at one time, in a nasty
little episode that occurred around 1985. If Abbott had ever held
down a job, Az didn't know about it. 'For God's sake, Abbott,
you could have gotten yourself killed.' Az took the octogenarian
by the arm and turned him around.

'I come to talk to you. About some stuff I heard.'

Az didn't have time to baby-sit a drunk. 'Why don't you go on down to Winks and see if he'll give you a cot for the night, *henh*? I'm supposed to be working here.'

Abbott stopped walking. 'When I was a kid, my mom got put in a hospital. Not the one where your body was sick, but your head. There was a lady, I don't remember her name, but she came and said that there was something un-Christian about having two kids by two different fathers, and never getting hitched. So they took my mother off, and me and my sister, God rest her soul, we got sent off too, to different reform schools.' He took a deep breath. 'The thing is . . . the thing is, Az, I had myself four lady wives. But I got no kids, and it wasn't for want of trying, you know? And I wonder . . .' He looked up, his eyes swimming with tears. 'Did they do something to me there I can't remember?'

In Abbott's gaze, Az saw the steel flash of a knife. He felt hands pinning down his thighs; he bit down against the pressure of a hypodermic in his scrotum. Excavating the memory was like field surgery all over again – so much pain, and not nearly enough anesthetic.

'Abbott.' Az put his hand on the other man's shoulder. 'Let's get you a cup of coffee.'

They headed toward the quarry office, where a fresh pot of French roast was dripping. Az had been wrong, after all. This was the disruption he'd felt in the air, the devastation that was coming. Not with the blast of dynamite, but slowly, like those dried dandelions. In small waves, people would remember. In growing numbers, their sorrow would carpet the earth.

Meredith knew the moment that Ross's car crossed the city line into Comtosook, because suddenly the windshield was covered with gypsy moths, their wings beating in unison like a single heart. He swiped the wipers, scattering them, but not before Meredith caught Lucy hiding under her sweatshirt in the backseat.

Ruby had been left in the able hands of Tajmalla, who took it as a personal affront that Meredith had even hesitated to leave her grandmother – or whatever she was – in the health aide's care. For the most part, the ride north had been unremarkable, silence punctuated only by traffic updates on the radio.

Meredith did not speak to Ross. She used all the energy conversation would have taken and built a barrier instead, so that whatever he tossed at her in Vermont would bounce right back off and enable her to return to her home and her job. And like all good walls, with the fortification in place, she was concentrating so much on the enemy that she did not need to remember the moments she'd been a traitor to herself.

For one night, at that Starbucks, she had watched the smoke of his cigarette curl like the letters of the alphabet and believed it was a secret message. She had smelled vanilla on his skin and grown dizzy. She had drunk from his coffee cup when he'd gone to the bathroom, the spot where his lips had touched, so that when she finally tasted him for real – *when,* not *if* – her senses would remember.

She had made a fool of herself.

After all of the disastrous dates she'd been on, after all of the professional men she had met and judged to be as intriguing possibilities – it turned out that a guy she would never have noticed made her feel like no one else ever had. At first glance, Ross Wakeman was a nobody. Until you looked again and saw his humor, his charm, his vulnerability.

And his complete intoxication with another woman, a dead one at that.

'So,' Meredith said aloud. 'This is it?'

Ross nodded. 'Comtosook.'

As they drove, Meredith began to notice things. The trees, for example, seemed to play a tune like a harp when the wind sang through their branches. Children playing hopscotch hung a fraction of a second too long in midair. And Doubt, in the shape of a hitchhiker, crawled into her lap to ride shotgun.

They pulled off the main road and headed down a dirt path.

But instead of stopping at one of the few houses they passed, Ross drove to the end, a crossroads, and parked the car in front of absolutely nothing. 'Where are we?' she asked.

It was nearly dark by now, the sky looking like the shined skin of an eggplant and the loons coming out to call to their true loves. Meredith followed Ross into the woods.

She was a scientist, she told herself, and thus naturally curious.

With Lucy plastered to her side, Meredith stepped over roots and rocks and what seemed to be construction debris. Suddenly the forest opened up into a flat plane with wrecking tape cordoning off a wide, bald spot. 'This is where you live?'

Ross muttered something that sounded like *I wish*.

In that instant Meredith realized where she was. 'Oh, for God's sake,' she sighed, and she reached for Lucy's hand to tug her back to the waiting car.

She hadn't gone two steps before Ross spun her around. 'You,' he said, his eyes wild, 'will stay.'

Meredith had been wrong before. Until this, until now, she had not understood that Ross Wakeman truly was insane.

He was also bigger than she was, and stronger, and alone in the dark with her and Lucy. So Meredith folded her arms across her chest and tried to convey bravery. She waited for Casper or Jacob Marley's ghost or the moment that Ross grasped, like her, that there was nobody here to be seen.

Lucy's knees were knocking so hard Meredith could literally hear them. 'Ssh,' she soothed. 'This is all about nothing.'

Hearing her, Ross turned slowly. The stark desolation in his eyes made her mouth go dry. What if someone loved *her* as hard as that? 'I . . . I'm sorry,' she murmured.

Ross stormed out of the woods along the path they'd entered. Meredith reached for Lucy and followed. She reasoned that this should not have come as a surprise. *I'm not Lia*, Meredith told herself. *I'm not*.

* * *

Shelby was pulling her shirt over her head when all the hairs stood up on the back of her neck. She ran to the window just in time to see the headlights cut off on a car. 'Ross,' she whispered, and then she whooped with delight and raced down the stairs still in her pajama bottoms to welcome her brother.

On the driveway, she threw her arms around him. 'Thank God you're home.'

He smiled. 'I'm going to have to go away more often.'

Over his shoulder, Shelby noticed a woman getting out of the car. A little girl. 'Shel,' Ross said, stepping back, 'I want you to meet Lia Pike's granddaughter.'

'That remains to be seen,' said the woman, but she held out her hand for Shelby to shake. 'Meredith Oliver. And my daughter, Lucy. I'm very sorry to impose on you this late at night . . .'

'Oh, no. We're just getting up,' Shelby replied. 'Come on in, and I'll get you two settled.'

Ross walked in ahead of them, moving stiffly, like someone with a bum ankle or a bad hip – although Shelby knew it was nothing physical that pained him. She wondered if it was worse to have Ross pining for something he could not have, or to have him find it and realize it was not the panacea he'd imagined.

'I'm beat,' Ross muttered, and headed up the stairs.

It was difficult to say who was more stunned at this breach of hospitality, Shelby or Meredith. Recovering, Shelby bent down to Lucy. 'My son is out in the backyard, through that door. I think he's probably a year or two older than you, if you want to go say hi.'

Lucy cemented herself even closer to Meredith. 'Go on,' Meredith urged, peeling her daughter off.

The girl walked away like she was headed to an execution.

'Lucy has a hard time in new situations,' Meredith explained.

Shelby was left with a woman who clearly had about the same level of desire to be there as her child. 'Could I, um, interest you in a cup of coffee?' As she poured for both of them, Shelby studied

Meredith over the edge of the carafe. Honey-blond hair, chestnut eyes . . . she looked familiar, although for the life of her, Shelby couldn't say why.

Meredith stood in front of the kitchen window, watching her daughter acclimate. Relaxing by degrees, she took a seat. 'I take it you believe in ghosts, too?' she asked.

'I believe in my brother.'

Chagrined, Meredith looked away. 'It's just that Ross dropped out of nowhere, you understand, to tell me I had to come to Vermont.'

A flicker of lost opportunity crossed her face. Shelby heard too, how the word *Ross* slipped off her tongue, like a sweet butter-scotch candy passed between a kissing couple. She wondered if Meredith had noticed.

Shelby pushed a small pitcher of cream and another of sugar cubes toward her. 'Sometimes it's hard to be convinced of something until you see it right before your eyes.'

'Exactly,' Meredith agreed. 'A hundred years ago, no one would have held that something microscopic was responsible for the height or skin color or intelligence of a person – but now look at what we believe.'

Then maybe a hundred years from now, we will all be able to see ghosts, Shelby thought. But instead she said politely, 'Is that what you do? Work with DNA?'

'No, actually I do PGD. That's preimp—'

'I know what it stands for,' Shelby said. 'I actually once—'

She broke off, dropping the spoon she was holding so that it splattered in her coffee. She could see, in her photographic memory, the entry on her calendar, circled in red marker: *Dr Oliver, geneticist.* The appointment that had been canceled, because Dr Oliver had been having an abortion. Her head turned to the window, to the two small figures in the yard. 'You didn't get rid of the baby,' she whispered.

Meredith tilted her head. 'I'm sorry?'

'Don't be,' Shelby said, smiling widely, and she topped off Meredith's cup.

Lucy didn't want to be in this creepy backyard in the middle of the creepy night in this creepy town. Owls seemed to be at cross-corners and the night was a black bowl pressing down on her. Plus, whatever kid that lady had been talking about wasn't here; Lucy had the whole creepy place to herself.

She walked around the little yard, trailing her hands over the evidence that a child did exist, somewhere. A baseball bat, leaning against the fence. A Razor scooter folded neatly next to a gardening stool. The garden itself was covered with hawk moths that hovered like fairies over plants that bloomed in the dead of night. Lucy leaned closer to read some of the names on the stakes. Angel's Trumpet, Moonflower, Aquamarine. Just whispering them made her feel like she was walking underwater.

She took another step and her foot sent a skateboard flying. Lucy watched it skid across the driveway and crash into a pole with a hanging citronella lantern. A voice crawled inside her head. *Hey,* she heard. *What do you think you're doing?*

Spirits always talked that way to her, like there were radio speakers in her brain. So when she spun around, her heart racing, Lucy already expected the white face floating in front of her. She swallowed hard. 'Are you a ghost?' she asked.

What the hell kind of question was that? 'Not yet,' Ethan said, and he grabbed his skateboard from the little priss who had invaded his backyard. He proceeded to do the most bitchin' kick-flip he could, just to knock her socks off. *Ghost.* Like he needed reminding.

He circled back to her, breathing hard. She was maybe a year younger than he was, with hair in braids and eyes so black with fear he couldn't see their real color. He could tell she was dying to touch him, to see if her hand would go right through. 'Who are you?'

'Lucy.'

'And what are you doing in my backyard, Lucy?'

She shook her head. 'Someone told me to come here.'

Ethan stepped on the back of his board, so that it flew up into his hand. Another totally cool trick. He didn't get to show off to new people, very much. 'You looking for ghosts? Because I know how to find them. My uncle showed me.'

If anything, that terrified her even more. She opened her mouth to say something, but a strangled sound came out of it. She tapped at her chest and gulped. 'Get . . . in . . .'

Ethan froze. 'Inside? You want to go inside?'

'In . . . haler . . .'

He ran off as if flames were spreading on the soles of his feet, and threw open the kitchen door. 'She can't breathe,' Ethan panted.

A woman moved past him so fast he didn't even get a chance to see her face. By the time he got into the backyard she was leaning over Lucy, holding a little tube to her mouth. 'Relax, Lucy,' the woman said, as Ethan's mother put her arm around him.

'Asthma,' she murmured.

Ethan looked at Lucy's blue skin. He figured she didn't appear all that different from one of those ghosts she'd mentioned. 'Could she . . . could she, like, die?'

'If she doesn't take her medicine in time. Or get to a doctor.'

Ethan was floored. Here was a kid, normal by any other standard, who could have croaked just like that. Like him. There were thousands – millions – of normal kids who could step off a curb and get run over by a bus, who could get caught in a river current and not come up again. You just never knew.

Lucy's mother fussed over her a little while longer. 'Come inside,' she said. 'The humidity isn't doing you any good out here.'

Lucy followed like a sheep, passing by Ethan. 'They find *me*,' she said, as if their conversation had never been interrupted at all.

Az couldn't take his eyes off her. He found himself gazing at Meredith Oliver as they sat side-by-side on a Windsor bench at the state lab in Montpelier, two strangers with cotton balls in the crooks of their elbows, waiting endless hours for the results of a paternity test. 'I'm sorry,' Az said. 'It's rude of me.'

She opened her mouth like she was going to lace into him – but then shrugged. 'It must be as strange for you as it is for me.'

In many ways. First, she looked so much like Lia it was remarkable. Second, the private business of a paternity test was odd enough, but to be escorted into it by Ross Wakeman and Eli Rochert made it ever more bizarre.

Meredith seemed to know how he felt. She smiled to put him at ease – she had a dimple, but only in her left cheek, like him. 'So,' she joked. 'You come here often?'

'Once or twice a week.' Az grinned back at her, watched her eyes widen as they noticed his dimple, too. 'You can't beat the free juice and Oreos.' They settled back against the bench, a little more comfortable in their skins. 'You live in Maryland?' Az asked.

'Yes. With my daughter.'

'Daughter.' He spoke the title with reverence; he had not known about yet another descendant.

'Lucy. She's eight.'

'Does she look like you?'

Meredith shook her head slowly. 'She looks like my mother did. Dark hair, dark eyes.'

Like me, Az thought; and as an invisible wall fell between Meredith and himself, he knew that she was thinking it too.

'Eli tells me that you're a doctor there.'

'Mr Thompson.' She said his name kindly, but there was a steel in her that reminded him of his Lily's rebelliousness. 'With all due respect, there's a greater chance than not that we are going to leave here today strangers, just like we came in.'

'Ms Oliver, I didn't know my daughter very well. And I never knew my daughter's daughter. I would like to hope that – if you turn out to be more than a stranger, after all – you might help me improve my track record.'

Suddenly Eli and Ross stepped out of the lab, holding a few sheets of paper out of the reach of the researcher who was spitting mad and a few paces behind them. 'I really need more than eight hours to do this properly,' he argued.

'Relax,' Eli said over his shoulder, and he handed the papers to Az. For all Az knew, this might have been written in Navajo. The clumps of numbers, hooked together like the pairs on Noah's Ark, meant nothing to him. 'Maybe you better let him read it to us.'

But Meredith tugged it out of his grasp. 'Let me see.'

'You won't be able to—'

'She will, Az. She does this stuff for a living.'

'Does what?'

Meredith didn't look up from the column that her finger was tracing. 'Genetic diagnosis. I screen embryos so that clients can have healthier babies.'

Az remembered how, as a kid, he'd stood raw eggs on end during the autumn equinox, the one moment a year when day and night were of equal measure and time stood still. This felt the same; this was what happened when the past and the present collided. 'Just like your grandpa,' he murmured. He turned to Eli. 'Does Spencer Pike know?'

'How could he?' Meredith said. 'He's dead.'

Az laughed. 'I wish. Who told you that?'

He saw her turn, her eyes flashing fever. Ross and Eli suddenly became fascinated by the pattern of the linoleum floor. And Az realized that the issue was not what Ross had told Meredith, but what he hadn't.

*   *   *

'I haven't thanked you,' Eli said, 'for bringing Meredith here.'

He and Ross were standing on the steps outside the State Lab, waiting for Meredith to come out of the bathroom, where she'd retreated after finding out the double whammy that Az Thompson was, scientifically, her biological great-grandfather, and that her biological grandfather was still alive. Az being Az, he'd told Ross and Eli to give her some space, and he'd struck off in his old Pacer so that he wouldn't be late for work at the quarry.

'I didn't do it for you,' Ross answered.

'I know. But all the same.' Eli fanned himself with the DNA report. It was freaking hot out here; he hoped that Meredith Oliver, whoever she was, got her act together shortly. He glanced at Ross, who was crouched on a step drawing a tic-tac-toe grid with a rock. His hair fell into his face, shading his eyes. 'I also didn't thank you for bringing yourself home,' Eli said.

Ross glanced up. 'Did Shelby get you started on that? She's a drama queen. I mean, there was none of this *good-bye cruel world* stuff she seemed to read into the note—'

'I guess it's easy to make that mistake when you've already found your brother attempting suicide once.'

Ross rocked back, sitting down. He squinted up at Eli. 'She told you?'

'Yeah.' You could argue, Eli knew, that the love between a brother and sister, or mother and child, was a different strain – a lesser strain – than the sexual love between a man and a woman. And you could argue just as surely that it wasn't. Eli looked at his good blue dress pants, sighed, and sat down on the ground next to Ross. 'Do you have any idea how much she worries about you?'

'I can take care of myself.'

'Yeah,' Eli said. 'That's exactly what she's afraid of.' He rested his elbows on his knees. 'Look. I see a lot of shit going down, stuff that happens behind closed doors. I see people with problems that no one ought to have. Compared to that, you've got a great life ahead of you.'

'And you know this because you let me look at some autopsy photos with you?'

'I know that any guy who's got someone like Shelby waiting for him has no right to be thinking of killing himself.'

Ross tilted his head. 'You love her?'

Eli nodded. 'Yeah. I think so.'

'If she moved to Burlington, would you move?'

'Uh-huh.'

'How about if she moved to Seattle?'

Eli hesitated, and then felt something loosen in his chest. 'You know, I would.'

'How about if she moved somewhere even harder to get to?'

'Like New Zealand? Yeah,' Eli said. 'When someone loves you up one side and down the other like that, you make every effort to stick around.'

'Well, what if the place she moved to was even harder to get to than New Zealand? A place you couldn't get to by boat or by plane or even by fucking rocketship? What if she went somewhere and the only way you could follow was to put a bullet through your head or hang yourself from your closet rack or run your car in a closed garage? I did it *because* I loved someone up one side and down the other like that,' Ross said. 'Not in spite of it.'

He stood suddenly, and in the splash of sunlight Eli was temporarily blinded. 'I'm going to see what the hell is keeping her,' Ross muttered, and went inside.

Eli rested his head on his knees. Trained as a cop, he'd always thought of suicide as an escape – not something you might run toward. He thought of Shelby, and the way she'd stared at the autopsy photo of Lia Pike. *Is that what happens when you hang yourself?*

Eli's mouth went dry. He scrambled to his feet just as Ross burst through the doors. 'Meredith,' he said. 'She's gone.'

On the bus from Montpelier to Comtosook, Meredith had made up lives for the passengers. The teenager sleeping on the camel-hump of his backpack was a runaway setting off to find adventure in the veins of the mountains along the Appalachian Trail. The old man with a white handlebar mustache and a wrinkled seer-sucker suit was an alchemist who'd spent years seeing gold in everything his eyes lit upon. The twitchy young mother with an infant in her arms was not a mother at all, but a maid who'd stolen the baby out of her crib, and was spiriting her to Maryland.

Ruby was not her grandmother; her grandmother had died in 1932. Meredith's ancestors did not come from Acadia and France; they had been here all along. And her grandfather had not been some boy who'd broken Ruby's heart and left her pregnant – the lie she'd been told all these years. Her grandfather had been a scientist, studying the way substandard traits passed from gener-ation to generation, and trying to prevent it.

The apple doesn't fall far from the tree.

From the bus station in Comtosook, Meredith walked to Shelby's house. And there, Shelby had told her the truth – from the horri-fying results of her grandfather's eugenics movement to the fact that Spencer Pike was alive, if not well, in a nursing home ten miles away. She gave Meredith all the details that her brother had conveniently left out: Cecelia Pike's brutal death, Gray Wolf's dis-appearance, Az's confession just a week before. She knew now why the Abenaki were fighting so hard for that ragged piece of land. It was not about ancestry, and it was not about property. It was about trying to get back the essence of something that was irretrievably lost.

Once, a heartbroken couple had come to Meredith's office, asking her to help them conceive a daughter. They had three boys, but their baby daughter had died recently of SIDS. They wanted to know, before they went through with a pregnancy, that they'd be getting another little girl.

Meredith had refused to accept them as patients. Not because she wouldn't have been able to do what they asked, but because she didn't think they'd be satisfied with the results. They wanted a replica of the child who had died, and science couldn't offer that kind of miracle.

Yet.

Would her grandfather, in the same circumstance, have taken their case? Science was at the mercy of the people who created it. She was suddenly reminded of her conversation at the Starbucks with Ross. For all the greater good that genetic diagnosis and replacement therapy could do, there was still a line that had to be drawn – one which hadn't been, yet, by the government or any ethics organization: who got to choose which traits were worth keeping, and which should be eliminated from the human genome? A scientist, of course. But a scientist like Meredith . . . or one like Spencer Pike?

She looked down at the directions to the nursing home that Shelby had given her, along with the leave to borrow her car. Left at the light, another right, and she would be there. If Pike was alive, she didn't understand why Ross and his detective friend hadn't taken his blood for a paternity test – which, by definition, would have been scientifically simpler. Was it because they had wanted her to meet Az Thompson, whose sacrifice had been far greater than Meredith's could ever be? Or was it because no one even wanted to lay eyes on a man who'd done as much damage as Spencer Pike?

The nursing home was stately, an old winged Colonial flanked by oak trees and brick paths. Meredith walked up the stairs and into the lobby. Although the décor was pleasant and sunny, there was a stench in the room that seemed to seep from the cracks between the floor tiles. It was not the smell of death, but regret

– sweeter, more pungent. It caught in the folds of Meredith's clothes, and weeks from now, even after several washings, she would put on this blouse and pair of khakis and breathe it in.

A nurse wearing a stethoscope with a dinosaur clinging to its thick rubber vein sat at a desk. 'Can I help you?'

'I'm here to see someone.'

She smiled. 'You looked a little young to be checking in. Who is it?'

'Spencer Pike.'

The nurse furrowed her brow. 'He's not doing very well today . . .'

'I'm . . . I'm a relative,' Meredith said.

Nodding, the nurse gave her a pass to clip to her shirt and gave her directions down the hall. Spencer Pike's room looked no different from anyone else's – a row of hospital doors with cheery smile stickers pasted around the name of the resident inside. It reminded Meredith of nursery school, and for a moment she was grateful that her mother had not had to go through this regression before sliding into death. She pushed open the door.

The shades were drawn, the lights off. A respirator rasped somewhere to her left, and all she could see were the most amorphous shapes. Stepping gingerly around the largest one, which must have been the bed, Meredith walked to the other side of the room and opened the curtains just a slit.

Spencer Pike was frail and hairless, embryonic. A white sheet covering him only emphasized the bones of his spine. She walked toward the bed, expecting to feel resentment or outright hatred or even some sad kinship – but there was absolutely nothing. This man could have been a stranger.

What made a family wasn't blood, or genes, or what was passed down through either of them. You only had to look at Meredith and her mother and Ruby to see. You only had to look at Spencer Pike, dying alone, to know.

He rolled in his morphine sleep, catching his arm on some of the clear tubing that connected to his upper torso and face. *He'll strangle himself,* Meredith thought, and immediately on the heels of this: *Would that be a bad thing?* But she found herself reaching to untangle the lines.

His hand came up slowly, grabbing her wrist. When Meredith looked down, she realized that he was awake and crying. He tried to speak, but the oxygen feed over his mouth made it impossible to understand what he was trying to say. She hesitated, and then pulled the clear funnel away from his face.

'I'm sorry,' Spencer Pike said. 'I am so sorry.'

Meredith froze. 'It's all right,' she murmured, attempting to pull away.

'Don't go. Please don't go yet.'

She swallowed, then nodded. Drawing a chair closer to the bed, she sat down beside her grandfather.

His breathing grew more erratic, and a wash of pain crossed his face. 'Cissy,' Spencer Pike said, 'will you wait for me?'

Cissy. Cecelia. You look like someone I used to know. Meredith had forgotten the obvious – if she truly did look like her deceased grandmother, then this man would be the person most inclined to take notice.

'Yes, Spencer,' she replied evenly. 'For as long as it takes.'

He lay back after that, falling into an uneasy sleep. Meredith kept her promise. She sat with her grandfather as his lungs rattled and pumped. She sat until the symphony of machines that had been playing a swan song became a single note in her head. She sat until the nurses came to give Spencer Pike his next dose of morphine; until they convinced Meredith that it was all right for her to leave him now, because he'd passed away.

Tuck Boorhies was cranky, and deservedly so. He'd been paged from a golf game by Eli, and told to be at the Montpelier lab in an hour and a half. If he didn't show up, Eli promised to arrive with a warrant for his arrest for the obstruction of justice.

He was all bluster, Tuck knew that, but something in Eli's voice

– as though he were on the edge of the cliff and about to look over the rim – made him even more curious to know what was up than to find out if he'd finish his game under par. Eli had been pacing at the door when he arrived, and herded Tuck into his photography lab to enlarge another one of those prints from the murder. This one, though, zoomed in on the feet. Tuck had pumped up the contrast on Adobe Photoshop, and damn if there weren't footprints on the damp sawdust that seemed to match some of the other prints, a woman's. But even more interesting was the long drag mark through the shavings.

He looked up from the lab stool where he was sitting, at the ready with an instant camera. 'What are we doing again?' he asked Eli, who was rigging a Hefty trash bag to a hook in the ceiling of the borrowed room. Inside the bag was about three-quarters of a pint of water. On the ground was a load of sawdust Eli had secured from the nearest horse barn.

'According to Wesley Sneap, a human urinary tract system can hold about four hundred millileters of fluid, max,' Eli said.

'Which is important because . . .' Tuck raised one eyebrow.

'Just give me a hand here, will you?' He climbed onto a free stool, motioning to Tuck to shoulder the weight of the waterbag while he made a sturdy knot at the hook above. 'He said that at the moment of death, there's a loss of nerve stimulation to the anal and ureteral sphincters, causing incontinence.'

'Good to know.'

Eli kicked some of the shavings around under the garbage bag, then stepped back to observe. 'Okay, Tuck,' he said. 'Pop my bladder.'

'I beg your pardon?'

'My bladder.' Eli pointed overhead.

Tuck had learned that you didn't upset guys who got to carry a gun as part of their paycheck. 'Whatever,' he murmured, and he pierced the Hefty bag with his pen.

They both watched the trickle and stream of water, matting

down the sawdust. It covered their footprints, blurring the edges. When the bag was empty, the sawdust that had been stained wet beneath it was about the size of a manhole cover. 'Shoot that for me, will you, Tuck?' Eli asked, as he walked out the door of the lab.

Tuck glanced at Eli's holster, lying on its side on one of the examination tables, and then down at his Polaroid camera. Shrugging, he took a few photos.

As they rainbowed up, Eli came inside again, hauling a wooden crate. 'So?'

'So it looks like a puddle. What did you expect?'

Eli took the photograph out of Tuck's hand and stared at it, then placed it beside the print Tuck had just enlarged. 'Is it just me, or do those puddles not match?'

They didn't. The darkened spot of wet sawdust in the new Polaroid was nearly twice as small as the one in the black-and-white enhancement. Before Tuck could respond, however, Eli cracked open the wooden crate and grunted as he hoisted out a two-foot by one-foot block of ice. He carried this to the sawdust, tipped it so that it was vertical, and shoved it into the center of the puddle, creating a long, familiar drag mark in the sawdust. Then he pulled up a stool beside Tuck's, and took a folded *New York Times* crossword puzzle out of his back pocket.

'What are you doing?' Tuck asked.

'Four across.'

'No.' He waved at the setup in the middle of the room. 'Over there.'

Eli followed his gaze. 'I'm waiting,' he replied.

Ethan was tying his sneakers when he heard the scream. He ran down the hall, to the room where Lucy and her mother were staying, and pushed open the door.

She was sitting up on the cot, shaking like crazy. 'Lucy?' Ethan said, creeping closer. 'You okay?' He looked around the room.

Her mother was nowhere to be found. Well, it was only midnight. Maybe she hadn't gone to bed yet. 'Can you breathe?'

She nodded, and her hands relaxed their death grip on the blanket. 'Did I wake you?'

'Nah, I was getting up anyway.' Ethan scuffed his sneaker on the carpet. 'Where's your mom?'

She looked around, as if just noticing that her mother wasn't there. 'I don't know. *Your* mother tucked me in.'

Ethan grinned. 'You see one mother, you've seen them all.'

She smiled, but just a little. Ethan tried to remember what his mom did for him when he had nightmares. 'Milk,' he announced. 'You want me to get you some?'

'Why would I want milk?'

'I don't know. If you stick it in the microwave it's supposed to make you go back to sleep. That's what my mother says if I freak out when I'm sleeping.'

'I bet you never freak out.'

'Sure I do. Everyone has nightmares.'

'What are yours about?'

'Getting stuck in the sun,' Ethan said flatly. 'How about yours?'

'Ghosts,' Lucy whispered.

They stood in the still of the house for a moment, which suddenly seemed cavernous. All in all, Ethan knew, it felt better just then to be standing there with *someone*. 'Well, I'm not scared of ghosts.'

'I'm not scared of the sun,' Lucy answered.

He should have told her more. Ross beat himself up mentally once again, certain that he was responsible for Meredith's disappearance. She'd been gone now for hours, not even putting a call in to make sure Lucy was all right. Maybe she just needed time to think.

Maybe she didn't want to think at all.

He smacked his head lightly against the trunk of the tree on which he was leaning. What he would have liked, now, was five minutes in the past. Five minutes to talk to Meredith Oliver and make her see that he understood what it was like to wake up and realize your life had turned out different from the one you once imagined you'd be living.

Regret hung from the hem of everyone's lives, a rip cord reminder that what you want is not always what you get. Look at himself, outliving Aimee. Or Az, trying to find his daughter, only to have her wind up dead. Look at Shelby, with a child who was dying by degrees. Ethan, born into a body nobody deserves. At some time or another, everyone was failed by this world. Disappointment was the one thing humans had in common.

Taken this way, Ross didn't feel quite so alone. Trapped in the whirlpool of what might have been, you might not be able to drag yourself out – but you could be saved by someone else who reached in.

Maybe that was why he'd gone to find Meredith in Maryland.

Heroes didn't leap tall buildings or stop bullets with an outstretched hand; they didn't wear boots and capes. They bled, and they bruised, and their superpowers were as simple as listening, or loving. Heroes were ordinary people who knew that even if their own lives were impossibly knotted, they could untangle someone else's. And maybe that one act could lead someone to rescue you right back.

When Ross lifted his face, he was not surprised to find rose petals drifting down from the night sky. He closed his eyes, smiling, but became distracted by the cry of a baby. Maybe it was a bobcat in the hills, or an animal mating. But it came again: thin, wild, more human. Walking into the clearing, he found Meredith crouched down on the ground.

'What are you doing here?' he asked, and when she stood – her hands and nails dark with dirt – Ross realized that it was not Meredith at all.

*   *   *

Who's calling me? I look up, and around, worried that I have already been found out. But there is no one, only my own suspicion, which seems broad and barrel-armed as these old oaks. I bend down and pull aside more tangles and thicket, looking. Where has he hidden her; where can she be?

I heard a cry, I know I did. Once, the Klifa Club held a lecture with an African jungle zoologist, someone who had come to meet Spencer. The zoologist said that in nature, mothers know the sounds of their offspring. Put a clot of hippos in a wading pool, and a mama and baby will find each other. Stick a giraffe across a savannah and it will find its way home. The fetus hears a voice in the womb, and comes out able to pick its mother from a host of others.

My hands are bleeding. I have searched beneath every stone, behind every tree. Then I hear her again, silently calling to me.

This time all my senses narrow, and I find myself standing, turning, walking toward the icehouse. I push open the door, shuffle through the sawdust. And see her.

Her eyelashes are as long as my pinky nail. Her cheeks are milky blue.

Lily. Lily Delacour Pike.

Even after I put her back inside her crate, I can feel the still weight of her in my arms. There will always be something missing.

He will never listen to me; he will never understand. The only way to show him what he's done is to do the same to him. To take away what he wants most in this world.

There's one block of ice that's thinner than the others. I can tip it upright, I can drag it out. I tie the knot around my neck first. Then I balance on this makeshift stepstool, and I fix the other end to the beam. Wait for me, I think, and I jump after my baby.

It hurts more than I thought, the heaviness of my own life pulling me down along with gravity. My lungs reach the bursting point, the world begins to go black.

But then she cries. And cries. Through the window of the icehouse, as I turn on this rope like a crystal ornament, I see her tiny fist

*wave back and forth. She has come back to me, when I am already
gone.*

*Lily, I scream in my head, and I try to claw at the rope, to pull it
free from the beam. But I have done too good a job. Lily. I kick with
my feet at the posts, at anything. I scratch but only reach my chest;
my arms can't seem to make it any higher.*

Oh, God, I cannot lose her twice.

*She will hear my voice, even though I cannot speak aloud. She will
find me across a savannah; she will swim to me in the deepest pool.*

*I make my baby the promise my own father made to me, before he
had a chance to know me: I will find you.*

As she disappeared before his eyes again, Ross realized he had
been holding his breath. He let it out in a long, silent rush. Curtis
Warburton would have said that what he'd witnessed was a residual
haunting, a repetition of a significant event played over and over
like a video loop. Curtis would have said that the spirit wasn't
even there, just the energy that it had left behind. However, Ross,
who had watched firsthand, knew this was not the case. This had
been no imprint, no impression made in time. Lia's ghost had
come back again, trying to find something.

But she hadn't been searching for her baby, and she hadn't
been looking for Ross. It was not until after the vision dissipated
that he realized why she had returned: on the other side of the
clearing, her face striped with shock and disbelief, was Meredith
Oliver, who also had seen and heard everything Lia needed to
say.

12

For ten minutes, Meredith sat in silence, while the night closed like a fist around her. Her insides had gone to water, and Meredith knew she would not be capable of moving, thinking, breathing anytime soon. She was suddenly aware that this universe – big as it seemed – was still too small to contain possibilities beyond her own imagination.

Like a ghost.

Could insanity come on so quickly, like the flu . . . or a flipped circuit breaker? Her mind could not even process the vision. It was like being told that the sun would not appear in the morning: Meredith's balance of reality had been tipped over, a skyscraper that turned out to be only a house of cards.

Yet this had not been smoke and mirrors; this was not some lunatic's rant. Meredith had seen a ghost with her own eyes. A woman who had vanished just as quickly as she'd come. A woman who looked exactly like her.

Meredith thought of all the times she had told Lucy there were no such things as ghosts. Everything she had believed was now cast into doubt – if she had been mistaken about this, after all, what else had she gotten wrong? Maybe the sky was not really blue, maybe science did not hold all the answers, maybe she was not happy with her life. She could be certain of only one fact: the world she'd awakened in this morning was very different from the one she was living in now.

She found herself leaning down to touch the ground, certain

that it too might not be as solid as she expected. She shivered again, and felt something being draped over her shoulders. Until that moment, when Ross put his coat around her, she hadn't truly registered that someone was sitting beside her.

Turning, she tried to find her voice. 'Did that . . . did that happen?'

'I think so.' Ross seemed just as shaken as she was. Meredith looked at him carefully. She had not truly believed what he'd told her – about ghost hunting, about her grandmother. People who believed in that sort of thing were a little crazy . . . yet now she seemed to be standing squarely among their ranks. She tried to remember what other things Ross had said – comments she'd summarily dismissed that she now had to reevaluate.

'She looked like me,' Meredith stated the obvious.

'I know.'

'But . . . but . . .' There were no words in this new place.

She felt Ross's hand find her own, his long hair brush over her cheek as he leaned close. He was crying. 'I know,' he repeated, when what he was really saying was that he didn't.

She had not believed in ghosts, but she believed in pain. And she certainly understood what it felt like to be alone, when you didn't want to be. These emotions were so real that they transcended the impossible, gave her a hook to grab onto. Meredith's mind spiraled back to the frantic search, the fear, the suicide. 'Is that how it happened?' Meredith asked. 'Did she . . . kill herself?'

'I guess so.' His voice was raw with grief.

'Isn't there something we can do?'

'It already happened,' Ross said. 'She's already gone.'

The ghost had stared directly at Meredith. And it had been like gazing into a mirror – not just because of the physical resemblance, but because the expression in Lia Pike's eyes was something that Meredith saw when she looked at herself. Meredith might not have been able to grasp the concept that the line between life and death was drawn in invisible ink, but she understood what it was like to be a mother who wanted nothing more than to protect her child.

Motherhood was elemental, cellular. You could feel a child inside of you, even after you gave birth; share blood and tissue for that long and you become part of each other. And if that child died – as an embryo, as a newborn, as a thirteen-year-old with XP – a part of you would die too. All Lia had done, after looking into the still face of her baby, was hasten the process.

'She was following her daughter,' Meredith said.

Even if she knew that the human body disintegrated to become organic matter, on some level Meredith had hoped that her mother existed in some form, in some place with windows on the world where she could watch over Meredith and Ruby and Lucy. This had been Lia Pike's hope, too . . . but she'd never quite gotten there. If she made it to that place, after all these years, would her child even recognize her?

Meredith turned to Ross. 'Do you think in the end they'll find each other?'

He didn't answer; he couldn't. His face was buried in his hands, and he was sobbing hard. It was a sorrow that sprung as deep and black as a well; a sorrow that Meredith had seen minutes before on Lia Pike's face when she believed her daughter was truly gone.

'Ross,' she said, and in that moment she remembered something he had said to her once, something she had discounted that she now knew to be true: You could imagine yourself in love with someone who was not real. With great care she reached out to touch his arm, to let him know that this time, if he were falling, she would hold him upright. But he shook her off, and as he did, twisted his wrist enough for her to see a scar, a lightning bolt where his skin should have been smooth.

'They'll find each other,' he said, looking away from her. 'They will.'

* * *

'The baby wasn't dead,' Eli explained, 'but she thought it was, and that was reason enough to hang herself.' He moved around Shelby's kitchen, helping himself to a glass of water as he relayed what he'd discovered. 'She dragged a good-size block of ice through the sawdust and onto the porch, as a stepstool to reach the rafter. But by the time Pike found her in the morning, the ice had melted, and the hanging looked more like a murder than a suicide. After seventy years, I just officially signed off on the case.' He shook his head. 'Jesus. We might be a little on the slow side, but never let it be said that the Comtosook detective squad isn't on the ball.'

As he passed Shelby at the kitchen table, he touched her shoulder. 'And that isn't even the whole of it,' Eli said, sitting down across from her. 'Spencer Pike died last night.'

He kept talking, but Shelby did not hear a thing. She was concentrating on the way her shoulder felt when Eli's hand had drifted away, as if there were something missing.

In that moment a track switched in her mind, and Shelby could no longer imagine a time she had not known Eli Rochert. He had written himself onto every previous page of her life and only now in its edited version did she realize how great the ellipsis had been.

Oh, shit, she thought, *I love him.*

Shelby believed that love was like a solar eclipse – breathtakingly beautiful, absorbing, and capable of rendering you blind. She had not necessarily gone out of her way to avoid a relationship, but she hadn't wanted one either. It was called *falling* in love for a reason – because, inevitably, you crashed at the bottom.

She had been in love before, with her ex-husband – she knew what it was like to have your heart speed up at the sound of a man's voice on the phone, and to feel the world stop spinning when you kissed. But that relationship – which she'd been so sure of at first – had been doomed, just like every other one she knew. Love meant jumping off a cliff and trusting that a certain person would be there to catch you at the bottom. But for Shelby, that man had run away before she landed. And frankly, she wasn't so sure she wanted to leap again.

'. . . and if you look at it that way . . . Shelby, hey, are you all right?' Eli squeezed her hand to get her attention, and she flinched. Immediately, he drew away. 'What's wrong?'

A thousand answers to that question tangled in her mind. 'If I were dying, would you give me a kidney?'

Eli looked nonplussed. 'You mean one of mine?'

'How many others do you have access to?' She stared hard at him. 'Well?'

'I . . . I . . . yeah. I would.'

Groaning, Shelby buried her face in her hands.

'That wasn't the right answer?' Eli asked, bewildered.

She forced herself to meet his gaze. 'I want to love you, Eli. But at the same time, I *don't* want to. When I'm with you, I don't think I've ever felt anything so right in my life. But if I admit to that, then it's got nowhere to go but downhill. Look at what love did to my brother. Or to Gray Wolf. Or even to Lia Pike. Or . . . what's so funny?'

Across the table, Eli was grinning from ear to ear. He took her hand again, and this time when she would have pulled away he held her fast. '*Love*,' he repeated, all that he'd needed to hear. 'You said *love*.'

Lucy held the flashlight up to her palm so that it turned red. Ethan, balancing his own flashlight on his knees, could nearly see the tissue and bone. Their secret spot – beneath the plastic tarp that covered the outdoor furniture – was getting smoky, but it was worth it. This was Ethan's first pact, and he was planning to make the most of it.

He waved the blade of his Swiss Army knife through the candle flame. 'Is it ready?' Lucy asked.

It turned out that she was less than a year younger than him, but you'd never know it to talk to them both. Lucy jumped if a daddy-longlegs walked within a yard of her, and everyone knew that daddy-longlegs were about as scary as Puff the Magic Dragon. She was so quiet that sometimes Ethan forgot she was sitting right next to him. She couldn't even *stand* on his skateboard without falling.

On the other hand, however, she knew all the interesting body-part words in the dictionary without Ethan having to look them up, and said her *mother* had been the one to tell her about them. She smelled like sugar cookies. And because she'd been at day camp all summer, she had the most beautiful tan Ethan had ever seen.

She told Ethan what it felt like to swim out to a dock in a lake, and to fall asleep under the sun so that you woke up hot and dizzy and not sure of what day it was or how you'd gotten there. He told her how the hair stood up on the back of his neck when the ghost had followed his uncle out of that old haunted house. She admitted that sometimes, she hid under her covers to pretend she wasn't there when the spirits came. He told her how the liquid the dermatologist used to freeze a pre-cancerous growth off his skin actually burned like fire.

'Come on already, Ethan,' Lucy said. 'I'm choking to death.'

That was another thing – she said things like *I'm going to kill you,* or *I'll die if you don't hand over that bag of chips* – all the things his mother was so careful not to say to him, just in case he was stupid enough to take it the wrong way.

'All right.' Ethan held the flashlight over the knife, dropped the flashlight, and then the knife. 'Jeez. You hold this.' He handed Lucy the flashlight and wiped off the blade – no need to contract the bubonic plague – before waving it through the candle flame again. When he glanced up, Lucy seemed uncharacteristically pale. 'You're not gonna faint on me, are you?'

Scowling, she held out her wrist.

Ethan placed his right alongside hers. 'I'll help you find a ghost before it finds you,' he said.

She stared into his eyes. 'I'll take you to where the sun comes up.'

'To courage,' Ethan said, and he slashed the blade fast as a gasp across his wrist and hers. He pressed the open wounds together.

Lucy sucked in her breath. 'To courage.' She wrapped a strip ripped from Ethan's T-shirt around their arms as they both waited and hoped that bravery might be every bit as binding as blood.

Az woke abruptly at the sound of birds. On his cot, he lay still for a moment, trying to pick apart the threads of a junco's whine from the trill of a whippoorwill and the throaty contralto of the loon. It had been weeks since he'd heard this particular melody. It had stopped the same morning he had told the other Abenaki about the burial ground, and had helped carry a drum to the Pike property, to formally launch a protest.

He sat up slowly, feeling the creak and snap of each vertebra. Swinging his feet over the side of the cot, he toed off his slippers and put the sole of his foot right down on the packed earth that formed the floor of his tent.

It was warm, just like it should be in August. Not frozen, as it had been.

Az pushed back the flap of his tent and stepped outside.

The world seemed centered now, not off just a few degrees to the point where it would keep spinning just a little more lopsided each day until you could not help but notice. Az snapped a flower off the honeysuckle vine that grew beside his tent and watched the pearl of nectar bead at the base of its horn. He drew it onto his tongue and tasted sugar instead of tears.

Overhead, a plane cut the sky in two, and it did not fall. Az stood very still but did not feel yesterday pressing at the base of his skull like a hammer. He closed his eyes and knew, instantaneously, which way was true north.

Az poured water into his immersion heater for his coffee

and measured out the grounds. He washed his hands and his face and dressed carefully, because one missed button on a shirt can change your fortune for months at a time. He did not do anything differently in his morning routine than when Comtosook had been under a spell. After all, you couldn't mess with physics: just as Az had known what entropy was coming, he'd also known there would be a day when it all would fall to rights again.

Had he been a wizard, Ross would have left his sister strength. Not he-man brute force, but endurance, because that was the way to get through anything, and as someone without a shred of it, he ought to know. Instead, though, Ross found himself sorting through the meager possessions in his duffel. This softest shirt of his, he'd give Shelby, because it smelled like Ross and he knew she'd want to save that memory any way she could. His watch, that would be for Ethan, in lieu of the time Ross really wanted to give him instead. The pennies from 1932 he would take with him to lay a trail across eternity like Gretel's bread crumbs, so that Lia could find him, just in case.

Quiz: What kind of man spent thirty-five years on earth and accumulated only enough to fit in a single canvas bag?

Answer: One who'd never planned to stay for very long.

After seeing Lia's ghost, he had taken Meredith home. He'd heard her on the phone to Ruby – waking her, at 5 A.M., explaining what she'd seen in words filigreed with wonder. She'd said she would return to Maryland in a couple of days, after taking care of a few things here. Like the land, Ross imagined, and Spencer Pike's funeral. He didn't know if Meredith believed what he'd said about ghosts, now, and frankly, he didn't care. What mattered to him was Lia, and she wouldn't be back. He knew this the same way he knew that every breath was like drinking in tar, that every subsequent day cut like a knife. He was tired, so very fucking tired, and all he wanted to do was sleep.

Ross stuffed his hand into the duffel again. A razor that had been his father's; that was for Shelby. His EMF meter – Ethan, naturally. He pulled out the old spirit photograph he'd taken with Curtis – globules over a lake – and smiled. Maybe he'd give this to Meredith.

He wouldn't leave a note, that was for sure. Look at how his sister had read into it the last time, and he hadn't even been trying to leave one then. He deliberately shredded every last bit of paper in the desk into pieces and tossed them, confetti, into the trash.

Then he noticed Lucy Oliver standing in the doorway of his room. 'Hello,' he said. Truth be told, she made Ross uncomfortable. Her eyes were nearly silver, too light for the rest of her features, and she acted as if she'd known him for months instead of days. Tonight she was wearing jean shorts and a T-shirt that said madame president. She had a Shrek Band-Aid on her wrist. 'You fall down skateboarding?' Ross asked amiably.

'No,' Lucy answered, just no, and that was all. 'I'm supposed to tell you we're about to eat.'

Ross tried to answer – something like *All right,* or *I'll be right there*, but what came out instead surprised them both. 'Did Lia talk to you about me?'

Lucy nodded slowly. 'Sometimes.'

'What did she say?'

But instead of responding, Lucy looked around his room at the careful piles. 'What are you doing?'

'I'm getting ready to go,' Ross replied.

'Where?'

When he looked at her, he had the sense that Lucy knew the answer wasn't a place.

'Not yet though,' Lucy said, a confirmation.

He tilted his head. How much could she know? 'Why not?'

'Because it's time for breakfast.' Lucy took a step closer and held out her hand, the one with the Band-Aid at its base. 'So come on,' she said, and waited a long moment before Ross grabbed hold and put himself into her keeping.

It was not that Meredith expected a huge outpouring of mourners at Spencer Pike's funeral, but standing alone with Eli Rochert and a bloodhound as the Congregational minister did a hasty grave-side service was a little embarrassing. Then again, considering how the Abenaki picketed the development of his land, she supposed she should be grateful that there wasn't a drum banging on the other side of the fence. She hadn't brought Lucy, because Lucy didn't know the man from Adam, and the last place her impressionable daughter needed to be was a graveyard. Shelby would have come if Meredith had asked, but she needed someone to watch Lucy more than she needed moral support at the inter-ment of a man she barely knew. And Ross, well, who knew where he was. Meredith hadn't seen him since the night Lia had appeared, and didn't want to. Then she would have to find the correct words to say, and *I'm sorry* and *I'm here* didn't seem nearly as fitting as *Don't*.

'Would you?' the chaplain asked Meredith, although she'd missed the question the first time. She looked at Eli for help, and he nodded toward the earth on the ground.

Meredith picked up a handful, which she sprinkled over Pike's coffin. Eli discreetly slipped a check to the reverend, and Meredith flushed to think she hadn't even considered this part of the ritual. From whose bank account had that money come . . . Eli's? The town's? Neither, she hoped. Spencer Pike had bled Comtosook dry enough already.

The minister offered Meredith his condolences and walked solemnly to his VW Bug to drive off, leaving behind a faint trace of Simon and Garfunkel from the open windows. Eli's big hand touched her shoulder. 'You want a lift back?'

Meredith shrugged. 'I may just stay for a minute.'

'Sure,' Eli said. He started off with his dog, and then came back and unclipped his cell phone from his belt. 'Call me when you're ready, okay?'

Meredith thanked him and watched him drive off in his truck. She wondered if Shelby realized how lucky she was, to have a man like that who'd happened to cross into her life at just the right moment. A light breeze ruffled the bottom of the black dress she'd borrowed as she looked at the fresh grave. 'Good-bye,' she said quietly, because she felt that someone should.

'Good riddance,' she heard behind her.

Az Thompson stood a few feet away, dressed in an ill-fitting black suit with a white shirt and string tie. 'You're the last person I expected to see here,' Meredith said.

'I didn't come for him.' Az looked down at the raw mouth in the ground where the coffin lay. 'First time in a long time I'm happy to have outlived someone.' He glanced up at Meredith. 'You care to walk a ways?'

She slipped her heels off and padded along beside Az in her stockings. He climbed the hill, striding right across some of the graves. At some spots, she felt a tickling on the arches of her feet. He stopped at a weeping willow with a lopsided stone bench beside it. 'This is a poor excuse for a thinking spot,' he said, frowning.

'Where would you go instead?'

'A waterfall,' Az said immediately. 'Or flat on my back under the stars.' He looked at her, then stretched out on the ground. 'See what I mean?'

She only hesitated a second, and that was because this dress was not her own. Then she settled herself beside Az and stared up at the sky. 'What do you see?' she asked, the game she played with Lucy.

'Clouds,' Az answered, matter-of-fact.

Meredith hugged her knees. In the crook of her arm was a small bruise from the blood that had been drawn days ago. Az had one too. 'Can I ask you something?'

'Sure.'

'It's just . . . well, I don't know what I'm supposed to call you. Mr Thompson, or Az, or John.'

'I've always fancied being called Ted Williams by a whole stadium of fans, but I guess I could settle for one skinny girl calling me N'mahom.'

'What does that mean?'

'My grandfather.' He looked directly at Meredith. 'I suppose, then, you believe it all.'

She nodded. 'Not that it does anyone any good.'

'Why would you say that?'

Tears came to Meredith's eyes. Surprised, she told herself that it was the day, the heat, the lack of sleep. 'So much has already happened,' she said quietly. 'So many people hurt.' She was thinking of people like Az, like Lia, like the faceless Abenaki of this town, yet Ross's features came swimming up to the surface. 'This wasn't supposed to be about me, and somehow, it got that way.'

'People work too hard to figure out the meaning of their lives. Why *me,* why *now.* The truth is, sometimes things don't happen to you for a reason. Sometimes it's just about being in the right place at the right time for someone *else.*'

'That's it?' she said.

'That's quite a lot.' He turned and smiled. 'You going home today?'

Meredith had been planning to fly to Baltimore that afternoon. But she'd postponed her trip till tomorrow. She just didn't want to leave Comtosook with Pike's funeral as her last memory. 'Soon,' she hedged. 'Will you write me?'

'I'm not a big fan of the written word. Pike and his friends wrote down a lot of stuff that should never have been put to paper. And the Alnôbak prefer an oral history to a written one.'

'With one great big chapter left out,' Meredith murmured.

'Then that's the one you have to tell.'

When she realized he was serious, she shook her head. 'I wouldn't know what to say.'

'Doesn't matter. Just start somewhere.'

'To Lucy, you mean?'

'To anyone,' Az said, 'who will listen.'

She tucked her hair behind her ear. 'About that . . . I'm going to the reading of the will this afternoon. Eli arranged for a judge to write something up so that the property will revert back to me, because I was my mother's successor . . . and all these years, she was the one who really owned it. I'd like . . . I'd like you to have it.'

He laughed. 'What am I going to do with a great big piece of land like that?'

'I thought you might want to share it.' Meredith split a blade of grass with her thumbnail. 'Provided, of course, that Lucy and I have a place to stay when we come to see you. Will you take care of the details for me?'

'Look up a man named Winks Champigny. He's in the phone book. He'll know what to do. I would help you, but I may not be around for a while.'

'Story of my life. I meet a great guy, and find out he's sailing on the next ship.' Meredith smiled at him. 'You'll be here, when I come back to visit?'

'Count on it,' Az said.

'You're sure you don't mind?' Shelby asked for the tenth time. She looked at Meredith's reflection in the mirror as she fastened a locket around her neck.

'Why would I mind? The kids watch each other. I'll be sitting on the couch eating bonbons and watching soaps.'

It was a novelty for Shelby – she was being taken out on a real date, at a real time, for dinner. 'Well, I know you'll want to pack up for your flight tomorrow. So consider yourself off duty the minute Ross gets back.'

He had left to collect equipment he'd left at the Pike property. Why he'd chosen to do this in the dark, at 8:30 P.M., was beyond Meredith. 'Do you know where Eli's taking you?'

'Some five-star place in Burlington.' She fell backward onto the bed beside Meredith, smiling so hard that her face actually hurt. 'I've been out with him a dozen times,' Shelby murmured. 'To the store, to his place, for a drive. So why do I feel like this?'

'Because you're crazy about him,' Meredith said. 'Blame it on the dopamine being secreted by your brain.'

'Leave it to a geneticist to reduce love to a scientific reaction.'

'Those of us who don't have it readily available prefer to think of it that way.'

Shelby rolled onto her stomach. 'Who's Lucy's father?'

'A guy who shouldn't have been,' Meredith replied. 'How about Ethan's?'

'That guy's brother, apparently.' Shelby propped her chin on her hand. 'Did you love him?'

'To pieces.'

'Me too.' She looked at Meredith. 'Sometimes I pretend that I haven't met Eli. Or that he isn't the last thing I think about before I fall asleep. It's like a superstition, you know – if I don't put that much value on a relationship, maybe it won't get ripped out from under my feet.'

'No one's going to rip this out from under your feet,' Meredith said. 'Relationships succeed and fail because of the people in them . . . not some karmic plan.'

'You think? Don't you ever wonder if there's one person you're meant to be with?'

'God, no! To say that you've got one soul mate in the world, out of six billion people . . . well, mathematically that's setting yourself up for failure. What are the odds?'

Shelby shook her head. 'That's where fate comes in. If I hadn't had Ethan, I wouldn't have gotten divorced from Thomas. If Ethan hadn't had XP, I wouldn't have moved to a town like this one, where the houses are far apart so he can play at night. If Ross hadn't come to the end of his rope he wouldn't have been here to investigate the Pike property. All these things, which were awful at the time . . . maybe they were just leading up to my meeting Eli.'

'Did you think that you were destined to marry Thomas?'

'Well, sure, at first—'

'There you go. Fate,' Meredith argued, 'is what people invent to explain what they can't understand. If you think Eli's the one, you tell yourself it was meant to happen. And if he breaks your heart, you'll tell yourself it wasn't meant to be. I've spent ten years trying to find a man who knows where I am in a room the moment he steps inside, without even having to look. But it hasn't happened. I can admit the truth to myself – that I've got lousy luck at finding love – or I can tell myself that I haven't crossed paths with my soul mate yet. And it's always easier to be a victim than a failure.'

Shelby sat up. 'Then what's that *something* that draws you to one guy out of a crowd? Or that first strike of lightning between you? Or the realization that you've connected so deeply when you've only just met?'

'Love,' Meredith said. 'Love defies explanation. Destiny doesn't.' She thought of Lia, materializing in the clearing. 'There are things you can't explain, that happen anyway. Like the guy who takes a bullet meant for his wife, even though survival's a basic instinct. Or the little girl who writes in a diary a secret sentence that her true love will say to her, when they meet – and lo and behold, one day, he does.'

'That happened?'

'Well, no,' Meredith said quietly. 'But I haven't entirely given up hope. The thing is, if it does, it'll be because I went looking for him, and I found him. Not because it was *meant to be.*'

'Why, Meredith! You're a closet romantic!' Downstairs, the door-bell rang. Shelby leaped off the bed and shoved her feet into two different shoes. 'Which ones, the flats or the FMPs?'

'If it's destiny,' Meredith said, smiling, 'it shouldn't make a difference.'

Shelby grinned, and picked the heels. After one final look in the mirror, she hurried downstairs with Meredith trailing and opened the front door.

Eli stood holding a pink rose with a forked stem and a smaller rose growing from it. Like a mother and child. He was dressed in a dark gray suit with a crisp white shirt and cranberry tie. 'Well,' Shelby said. 'Don't you clean up well.'

'You look . . . you look . . .' Eli shook his head. 'I had all these words that I looked up for you, and I can't remember a single one.'

'It's the dopamine,' Shelby said sympathetically.

'Radiant?' Meredith offered. 'Resplendent? Bewitching?'

'No,' Eli said finally. *'Mine.'*

Az took another sip of the whiskey Ross had brought to the quarry. They sat side by side on folding chairs that Az had pilfered from a storeroom, drinking and watching the sky fall, a cauldron spilled of its stars. 'You know I'm supposed to tell you to leave,' he said.

'So tell me.'

'Leave,' Az said.

'You know I won't,' Ross pointed out.

Az shrugged. 'It's the dynamite. There are charges all over the quarry. The computers are gonna set them off in the morning, at dawn.' He glanced sidelong at Ross. 'Don't do anything stupid, all right?'

'Stupid,' Ross repeated, rolling the word around. 'Stupid. What would constitute stupid? Would that include pining after not one, but two dead women?'

'Hey,' Az pointed. 'Pass the whiskey, will you?'

Ross hefted the alcohol toward him, only to have Az toss the bottle into the quarry, where it shattered on broken rocks. 'What the hell did you do that for?'

'Your own good.' Az got up slowly from his folding chair, tucked it beneath his arm. 'Do me a favor, and keep an eye on this place for a few minutes, will you?'

'Where are you going?'

'Cigarette break,' Az said.

Ross watched him walk off along the perimeter of the quarry. 'You don't smoke!' he yelled after the old man, but by then Az couldn't hear, or didn't want to. He stood up, hands in his pockets, and looked down at the remains of his bottle of Bushmill's. The glass sparkled like mica. 'Shit,' Ross said, and he kicked at a rock, sending it caroming over the lip into the canyon. Because it felt good, he did it again. He glanced over his shoulder, saw Az was still missing, and then lit a cigarette. He tossed it into the quarry, where it landed six inches away from a dynamite plug and fizzled black.

He was tired of reliving his life, when he hadn't been so fond of it the first time around. Like Lia, he was trapped by his own past. The moment Aimee had died, so had Ross. And then when he found someone else to live for, it turned out she'd been dead for seventy years.

He imagined that cigarette landing on the dynamite, the bursting explosion that would shake the earth and send him tumbling into the quarry. He pictured his body being consumed by fire, flames that ate at his clothes and peeled away the pain. *Why me?* Why was he connected to the deaths of not one, but two women? Was he some kind of supernatural link? A cosmic pawn? A lightning rod for lost souls? Or maybe he was being punished. In the aftermath of Aimee's death, he'd been hailed as a hero, when Ross knew all along he was exactly the opposite.

As a child he'd read comic books, dazzled by the strength and the daring on pages cut into squares like a sidewalk, as if these superheroes were already walking a path toward greatness simply by appearing on the page. He had told Meredith he was invincible, but he was no Superman, no Captain Marvel. He was not

even the sort of man that good things happened to. Meeting the
girl of one's dreams, winning a scratch ticket, finding a ten-dollar
bill on the street – these were experiences in someone else's daily
existence. There was a point where the bad luck ended, and the
bad choices began, and Ross could not see the fine distinction.
He couldn't live a life worth saving, and he couldn't save a life
worth living.

Ross climbed onto the safety railing. He stood with his arms
akimbo, his legs spread, a messiah or a target or both. He was
swallowing glass with every breath; he was running on nails with
every step. *Jump,* he thought, *and you get to start over.*

He slipped, caught himself, and then laughed at his own
caution. He balanced like a chair on the nose of a circus clown
– something far too heavy and gravity-laden to defy the laws of
nature for very long.

Pitching forward, Ross managed to stop himself from falling
over the fence. His *Bogeyman Nights* baseball cap went spinning,
and landed on a stick of dynamite.

The clown might drop that chair, but he'd always snatch it
just before it smashed on the floor. After all, he had to come back
and do the same act night after night. Ross stepped away from
the fence, then took the prop that was his body and slouched
toward home.

Rod van Vleet had cashed his last paycheck at the only bar in
Comtosook, a place that had taken pity on him in spite of his
former association with the development property that had
caused so much unquiet. Oliver Redhook himself had called to
terminate his employment and to inform him that he expected
the company car and the company cell phone back at their
Massachusetts headquarters by Monday. 'I could have sent a
trained monkey to Vermont,' Redhook had said on speaker-
phone. 'But I made the grave mistake of sending *you.*'

In a truly Machiavellian twist of fate, the bartender was one of the Indians who had been banging a drum outside his company trailer for three weeks. Gracious winner, he'd given Rod three shots on the house before he started taking his money. Now on his eighth, Rod could barely get the nerve endings in his hand firing well enough to lift the drink, which seemed so small and slippery that he was about to ask the bartender for a magnifying glass to help locate it.

'One more,' he said, or he thought he said, he didn't quite think it was English.

The bartender shook his head. 'Can't, Mr van Vleet. Not unless you call yourself a taxi.'

'I'm a taxi,' Rod said.

The bartender exchanged a glance with a woman beside Rod. She had long black hair and the shoulders of a linebacker, and at closer glance turned out to be a man. Rod downed the last of his drink. 'Fine, then,' he slurred. 'I'll just take myself up and over to Burlington. Crash a frat party.'

'You do that,' the bartender said. 'But you might just crash your car first.'

Rod fished in his pocket and held up a set of keys on the first try. He stumbled and landed hard against the polished bar. 'Would serve 'em right.'

The police lights whipped across the truck's windshield, casting Shelby's skin with a faint blue tinge. She pulled Eli's jacket closer around her shoulders, shivering although she wasn't cold. He'd taken care to park off to the side, so that she would not have to stare at the wreckage and the body that had been tossed onto the street, but her head kept turning and her eyes kept straining to make out the details of the catastrophe.

'I'm sorry,' he had said to her, when the radio went off in his truck en route to the restaurant. 'I have to go.'

She understood, which was why she got out of the passenger door, now, her high heels slipping on the damp pavement. Outside the cocoon of the truck there was a rally of noise, from sirens to shouting cops to the subtle clicks of the crime-scene photographer. She edged closer to the circle of activity, fully expecting to look down and see Ross.

She had not been present at his car accident, the one in which Aimee had been killed. But he had been the mission of rescuers like these; there had been a car overturned like that; the EMTs had strapped him to a gurney like the one whining over the pavement toward the victim right now.

When the phone call came about her brother, she'd been breastfeeding Ethan. She'd almost let the machine pick it up, because it was so much trouble to juggle a drowsy baby and a telephone. Even now, she could not remember whether the officer who told her had been male or female. Only a few words remained, stuck like cement in her memory, blocks that she still tripped over every now and then: *Ross, accident, serious, passenger, dead.*

Time stopped, and Ethan had rolled from her lap onto the cushions of the couch. Shelby had tried to picture Ross, battered and bleeding, but could only see him as a skinny fifth-grader with fire in his eyes, taking it upon himself to beat up the eleventh-grade soccer star who had broken Shelby's heart.

Now, she pushed two uniformed policemen out of the way so that she could see better. The clothes were ripped, the face mangled, but Shelby could still make out the features of the businessman who'd been trying to develop the Pike property.

A hand tugged at her elbow and yanked her backward. Eli stared at her, upset. 'What are you doing out here?'

'I . . . I had to see.'

'No one should have to see this. Rod van Vleet totaled his car. The only mystery is whether it burst into flames on impact, or if it was the alcohol fumes coming from the driver.'

'Is he going to be okay?'

'Yeah, but he's got some bad breaks and burns.' Eli had led

her to the truck without Shelby even realizing it. He opened the door and tucked her inside. 'Stay.'

'I'm not Watson.'

His eyes softened. 'I know. Watson's used to this. You're not.'

As he turned to finish whatever it was he had to do, Shelby blurted out his name. Immediately, he turned. Even with the sentence on her lips, she did not know why she felt the need to tell Eli what was tunneling through her mind. 'Ross almost died in a car crash,' she said finally.

Eli looked over his shoulder at the debris, the rising smoke. 'Almost doesn't count,' he said.

Ethan had stolen his uncle's EMF meter from his bedroom and after some thought had chosen a short-sleeved T-shirt – one he was only allowed to wear inside the house – as the uniform for his escape. A soft knock on his door told him Lucy was ready. She slipped inside his room, her eyes so big and nervous that it made Ethan laugh. 'We haven't even left yet. Chill out.'

'Right.' Lucy started talking to herself under her breath. 'What's the worst that could happen?'

For Lucy, the worst was that she'd get scared. Uncle Ross had said that a human spirit couldn't actually hurt you. For Ethan, the worst was, well, a lot worse. He had told Lucy that he got sick if he stayed out in the sun, but he hadn't explained the ultimate cost – the skin cancers, the lesions, death. She never would have agreed to this plan, then. But Ethan had thought this through, and if he was going to die young, he wanted to do it on his own terms. He didn't want to get stuck in some Pedi ward, with stupid purple dinosaurs painted on the windows as if that was supposed to make any kid think he was anywhere but there.

Maybe hoping hard enough could redirect fate – it was possible that the blood vow he and Lucy had made the night before had changed them a little, so that Lucy was a little bit braver and he was a little bit stronger. 'Okay,' Ethan said, tucking the EMF into the loop of his jeans and opening his bedroom window. 'We'll slide off the gable onto the roof of the porch, and then jump.'

'We will?'

'Well, it's that or walk right past your mother in the living room.' He set one foot over the sill. 'I'll go first.'

'Wait.'

Ethan turned. 'Lucy. We talked about this, remember? You were born a chicken, and I have this weirdo disease. So what? Only losers would stay that way forever.'

'What if it's how we're supposed to be, and that's why we're like this?'

'That's crap,' Ethan said. 'I'll tell you what it was – it was God taking a coffee break and some dumbhead filling in for him when it came to handing out all the cool genes.' He stared at her. 'If you couldn't change things, ever, what would be the point of growing up?'

She nodded, convincing herself. 'Where are we going, exactly?'

'To the only place in Comtosook where you can find a ghost *and* watch the sun come up,' he answered. 'Trust me.' He held out his hand, milky and white, and waited until Lucy put hers into it, a sealed deal. Then they scrambled through the window and into the darkness, determined to turn themselves into what they were not.

On the banks of Lake Champlain, Az Thompson thought back to the moment his daughter, Lia, had visited with a social worker and he had given her a language to speak. He'd been too scared at that moment to tell her who he was, or that he knew her. Instead he'd fed her words, Abenaki; let her swallow them whole so that they took root in her belly, a bashful garden for the grand-baby she was carrying.

Words, for all they were flimsy and invisible, had great strength. They could be as fortified as a castle wall and as sharp as a foil. They could bite, slap, shock, wound. But unlike deeds, words couldn't really help you. No promise ever rescued a person; it was the carrying-through of it that brought about salvation.

It seemed fitting to Az, after all that had happened, that it all still came down to what was written and what had been said. He looked at the box of files and pedigree charts that sat on the banks of the river where his bucket of muskies once had been. It hadn't been difficult to get into the municipal building's basement – did anyone in Vermont think to lock cellar windows? – and to haul out the remaining evidence of the Vermont eugenics project, which Ross Wakeman's sister had brought back to the town's keeping.

Az knew that the only way to strip words of their power was to erase them. Of course, once one had been released into the world you couldn't call it back, but you could certainly keep it from being sent out again and listened to and digested. He picked up the roll of duct tape he'd gotten at the Gas & Grocery and unraveled the end, taping it to his shirt just beneath the armpit. Picking up the first of Spencer Pike's extensive files, he held it to his chest and ran the adhesive around his body to secure it.

As he continued to fasten the files and papers and unwieldy genealogy charts to his thin body, Az remembered his daughter: the way her eyes lit up when she saw him coming, the movement of her hands across her abdomen, the way she stood out at the Gypsy camp like an orchid in a field of daisies. But you could transplant an orchid to that soil, and get it to grow. You just needed someone with the time and hunger to make it survive.

His mind wandered further back, to the moment he had noticed his beautiful Lily, the first afternoon he'd been working for her father. He'd come in from the fields to get another basket for the berries, and saw her – silver-haired and white-skinned, dancing on the porch to a song she was humming under her breath. She held her arms in place around an imaginary mate, waltzing. She didn't know anyone was watching, and that alone took Az's breath away. *She needs a partner,* Az thought, and that was the beginning.

He wondered if Meredith had talked to Winks yet about the land. He wondered if she'd come back to Comtosook, like she said. He didn't know her well enough to read her. Sometimes in the fluid moments before he dropped off to sleep he confused her in his mind with Lia. They looked alike, certainly, but it went deeper than that. He would not speak for his daughter, but he thought Lia would be proud.

When he had strapped the last of the files to himself and used up all of the silver tape, Az walked into the water. Cold even in August, it numbed his ankles. He felt the files at his hips starting to soak. The papers were sponges, anchoring him to the muddy bottom.

Az took a deep breath just before his head went under. He moved along the floor of the lake, kicking up snails and stones and forgotten treasure. He let the air bubble out of his lungs and lay down on his back, sunken by the weight of the history he had strapped to himself, and he waited for the morning to come.

'I'm sorry,' Eli said to Shelby for the thirtieth time, as he opened the door of his house and greeted a lonely Watson.

'It's not your fault.'

They had not only missed their dinner reservation in the aftermath of the car crash, they had completely missed serving hours at the restaurant. Now 2 A.M., there wasn't even a McDonald's that was open for a bite to eat. Eli tossed his keys into a bowl on the kitchen counter that held three molting bananas. 'I'm a pretty awful date,' he muttered, opening the fridge. 'I can't even cook you something. Unless you like bread and mustard.' He scrutinized the loaf. 'Make that penicillin and mustard.'

Suddenly Shelby's arms circled him from behind. 'Eli,' she said, 'I'm not even all that hungry.'

'No?' He straightened, turned toward her.

She tugged loose his tie. Then she stepped out of her high

heels. Barefoot like that, she seemed so small and delicate that it reminded Eli of a snowflake; one blink and it might melt away into nothing. 'No,' she said. 'But I am a little hot.'

You're telling me, Eli thought, and then she turned around and lifted her hair off her neck. 'Unzip me?'

He inched the little metal tag down, and with every opened tooth Eli could feel his nerves fray. Shelby's skin was the whitest, smoothest expanse he'd ever seen. A little farther, and the hooks of her black bra came into view.

He stepped away. There was just so much a guy could take. 'Maybe, uh, you should go find something to change into,' he suggested.

'Oh, damn,' Shelby said, not contrite at all. 'I didn't bring anything.' She reached up behind her, finished unraveling the last six inches of zipper, and let the dress fall to the floor so that she stood before him like a mirage of flesh and blood and lace. With a smile, she turned and headed up the stairs, Watson at her heels.

Eli did not have to think twice. He pulled his pager and cell phone from his belt and turned them off, took the receiver of his home phone off the hook. This was all against departmental procedure, but one tragedy a night was enough. And to be honest, he didn't much care if the world was coming to end, as long as he was moving inside Shelby when it happened.

Meredith finished reading every catalog that had come to Shelby's house in the past month and realized something was very wrong – namely, that she'd finished reading every catalog that had come to Shelby's house in the past month. Her daughter, who seemed to have an internal radar that blipped whenever Meredith managed to sit down for a second, usually commandeered those smidgens of private time to ask questions that could not wait, like what made lips look pink or why they weren't allowed to have a dog. But Lucy hadn't bothered her at all tonight. Neither had Ethan. And mathematically, it stood to reason that a household with two children under the age of ten should generate twice the interruptions.

She put aside the Pottery Barn catalog and called upstairs. No answer, but they had been playing a computer game with the door closed. Meredith jogged up the stairs and rattled the locked doorknob. 'Ethan?' she called out. 'How are you guys doing in there?'

When there was still no answer, she felt the first wave of alarm. She grabbed a wire coat hanger from her own bedroom closet and straightened the neck, poking it into the simple lock device on the doorknob. It swung unlatched and Meredith stepped inside Ethan's room to find a typical messy boy's haven – nothing missing, except two children.

The window was open.

She raced downstairs to the list of emergency numbers beside the phone, the ones that Meredith had told Shelby she'd never need.

As Ross walked into the kitchen, Meredith slammed down the telephone and turned, tears running down her face. 'The restaurant's closed and Eli's pager and his cell phone, they're supposed to be on but they aren't, and the police won't tell me anything even though his number's unlisted and—'

The blue funk he'd ridden in on dissipated immediately. 'What happened?'

'The kids,' Meredith said. 'They're missing.'

'For how long?'

'I don't know. I don't know. I went upstairs just now and they weren't there.'

'And you can't reach Shelby and Eli?' She shook her head. 'Okay. I'll go find them.'

'You can't. You don't know where they are.'

'Yes I do. Stay here, in case they call, or Shelby comes home.'

But he knew as he headed out the door that Meredith was only a step behind him.

Who knew there were so many shades of black? Being under the moonless sky was no different from hiding beneath a blanket, and the bowl of the quarry, a big circle of nothing just past the toes of Lucy's sneakers, was a little bit darker than the night itself. One step, one mistake, and you'd go falling. Only by squinting could she see Ethan, who suddenly let go of the guardrail and disappeared before her eyes.

Her breath solidified, a block in her throat. She would have screamed, but what would Ethan think if she was afraid of simply getting to the ghosts, not just the ghosts themselves? Then his head popped up near her ankles. 'Are you waiting for an invitation?' he asked, and she realized he was holding fast to a ladder that led into the pit of the quarry.

Ethan said there was a ghost here, a quarry supervisor who'd been killed by some crazy guy. He said seeing the spirit was a sure thing. He'd told her they might have to avoid a guard, but she and Ethan seemed to be the only ones around. Maybe that was luck, maybe it meant it was okay to be there. At any rate, Lucy started to climb down. Huge pillars of stone reared up around her, seeming to move in the lack of light. The soles of her sneakers skidded down a slope of granite, and she wound up in a heap on a pile of rubble. 'You okay?' Ethan called. He probably turned around too, but it was too dark to see him.

She realized that this was what life was like for Ethan all the time.

They crawled through crevasses so narrow Lucy had to hold her breath, up columns of rock where their only foothold was hope, underneath listing piers and over great craggy tablets. They balanced on thin needles of stone, toppled like a giant's game of pick-up sticks. Every now and then their forward motion would dislodge some careful equilibrium, and the granite would crumble with a roar and a flurry of dust. 'You all right?' Ethan's voice would float back to her, and then they would keep going.

Lucy's hands and shins were scraped over and over, and she had one really bad cut that she was afraid to even look at. She smacked into Ethan's back and realized that they had reached the other side of the quarry, across from the ladder. 'We'll hang out there,' Ethan said, and pointed to two fallen slabs of granite that had haphazardly formed an A-frame and a ledge.

He climbed first. Then Lucy grabbed onto his hand so that he could pull her up, but their fingers, dusty, slipped away from each other and with a tiny shriek Lucy landed on a crumbled bed of rock. 'Jeez, Lucy, are you okay?' Ethan called.

Tears came to her eyes, but she made herself get up. 'Yeah,' Lucy said, and she made her way up to the ledge with great care, firmly jamming her feet between cracks in the granite before she released her handhold to climb again. On the ledge, she collapsed on her back and closed her eyes while Ethan set up his ghost-hunting equipment. When she'd caught her breath, she sat up and flicked on a flashlight, swinging its beam across the expanse they'd just traveled.

Lucy's eyes went wide at the spires and jagged edges, the sheer distance. The ladder they'd climbed down was so far away it might have been forever since they'd started.

She had *already* been braver than she thought she was.

'So what do we do?' Lucy asked.

'Nothing. Now's the part where we wait.' They sat with their shoulders touching, shivering from the cold and the awareness of what they had done. 'You know what a star is?' Ethan asked after a moment, and Lucy shook her head. 'An explosion that happened, like, hundreds of years ago, but that we're only just seeing now.'

'Why?'

'Because that's how long it takes light to travel.'

Maybe, Lucy thought, it was the same for ghosts. Maybe sadness moved at a different speed than real life, which is why they showed up years after they'd died. She squinted up at the cloudy sky, trying to find a single star. When it happened – the explosion – it had to have been loud and bright and terrifying. But what she saw, now, was beautiful.

Maybe everything looked better, with some distance.

Even before that radio thing that Ethan held in his hand began to beep, Lucy knew something was coming. She felt it in the weight of the air on her skin, in the hollow echo that came into her ears. The fine hairs on her arm stood up, and her stomach did a slow roll. 'Is it me,' Ethan whispered, 'or did it just get about a hundred degrees colder?'

The little radio began to twitch like crazy. 'Lucy,' Ethan whispered. 'Stand up.'

She did. She walked all the way out to the edge of their ledge and she thought as hard as she could in her head, *You can't scare me.*

Ethan had told her that ghosts couldn't materialize without energy. Fear was a type of energy, the kind you wrapped tight into a ball. So Lucy summoned all the terror she'd tucked into the creases of her bedsheets and behind the wall of clothes in her closet. She thought of all the asthma attacks she'd had when a spirit got right into her face. She squinched her eyes shut and focused and a moment later, when she peeked, she saw a man walking toward her.

It was a man, but it wasn't a man. This one was transparent, like the lady who came to her bedroom, and Lucy could see the jagged edges of rocks right through his shoulders and spine. He was dressed weird, too, in a striped shirt that looked like an old mattress and a pair of pants with no loops for the belt, and a vest with a shiny gold pocketwatch. He had a mustache that twirled at the ends like a circus strong-man's, and his hair was plastered down to his head. *Get to work,* he said, right in the middle of her mind.

Lucy felt her knees shaking so hard they knocked into each other. *Get lost,* she thought right back at him.

To her surprise, the ghost did exactly as she'd asked. He took two steps forward, one of which brought him directly through her, icing her bones and her blood so thoroughly that for a second she was still as these rocks surrounding her, and then he vanished.

Lucy smiled. She even laughed a little. She looked around, but there was nobody else haunting this pit. And sure enough, the tightness in her belly was gone. Slipping into their cave again, she sat down beside Ethan, who was banging the side of the EMF meter into the slab of granite. 'Well,' he said, 'this is a piece of crap.'

Lucy stared at him. 'You didn't see anything?'

'Nah, it was a false alarm.' He glanced up. 'Why? Did *you?*'

'Yeah,' Lucy said with wonder, and she sat down to tell Ethan all about it.

Shelby had been saving up words for this: *velutinous, sybaritic, hedonic, effulgent.* She had imagined them painted across the ceiling – *paroxysm, tumult, fillip, whet.* Yet as Eli's hands skimmed over her skin, as her nails dug into his back and urged him closer, Shelby found that she could not think at all.

His body was long and lean and sculpted, his touch as light as the promises he whispered. She followed his lead through the moment when she was certain she would not recall what to do or how to do it right, and by the time their limbs were tangled together, Shelby could not remember ever having doubts.

He kissed his way from her ankles up, calves and knees and thighs, until she was shaking for him to settle. When he did, when his mouth came over her, she arched into him and closed her eyes to see vistas of gold, glowing emeralds, scatters of rubies. They burned hotter, smaller, into quasars and novas and filled a universe. Eli moved as if he had all the time in the world. Then, just as she could not hold on any longer, he was suddenly above her, forcing her to look at him so that she would know exactly what road her life was heading down. 'Where have you been?' Eli murmured, and he filled her.

Their bodies rocked at a fulcrum; their rhythm told a story. And at the moment they both let go, Shelby lost every word she'd ever learned except for one: *Us*.

When Eli fell asleep heavily in her arms, Shelby slipped out from beneath his weight and curled up against him. She tried to memorize the constellations of his freckles and the crooked line of the part in his hair. She smelled herself on his skin.

Something bit into the soft side of her thigh, and she shifted, trying to get comfortable. But whatever it was moved with her, and Shelby reached down between herself and Eli to grab a small, sharp item. She held it up to the pink sliver of daylight that fell diagonally across the covers and frowned. This particular setting, this combination of stones, was all too familiar.

'Hey.' Eli reached for her.

'Hey yourself,' Shelby said against his lips, forgetting every-thing but Eli as she dropped the diamond solitaire Ross had once given to Aimee, and then lost months ago in a room at her own house.

It was the prettiest thing Ethan had ever seen – the thin pinks and creeping salmons, the rosy flush that swallowed the stars, the line where the night became the day. Ethan wanted the dawn to happen all over again, right now, even if it meant that he would be another day older and closer to dying.

Lucy had still been asleep when Ethan crept onto the ledge. He sat cross-legged, his arms held out in front of him, each degree that the sun hiked in the sky causing another blister to rise on his skin.

But, God, it was worth it. To witness the arrival of the morning, without a pane of glass between him and it. To feel a sunrise, instead of just to see it.

His left arm was an angry red now, itching like crazy. Lucy came up beside him, yawning, and then looked down at his arm. 'Ethan!'

'It's no big deal.' Yet it was. Anyone could see. Suddenly something glinting on the bottom of the quarry caught his eye. A silver button – or buckle, maybe. It was a baseball cap, and when Ethan leaned over the edge of the granite ledge he could make out the writing on it. 'That's weird,' he said. But before he could point out to Lucy what he believed to be his uncle's cap, it exploded before his eyes.

Like every other morning when Angel Quarry blasted for granite, the computers set off the first explosion of dynamite, pausing to let the rock settle for minutes before the next charge was detonated. Boulders flew and fine particles rose in a mushroom cloud; rock dust blanketed the roof of Ross's car. In the wake of the first blast, the second one rang out. One spike of granite smashed into the windshield, shattering it. 'Oh, God,' Meredith cried, and she opened the car door while Ross was still driving, stumbling out and breaking into a dead run toward the quarry where her daughter might be.

Great slabs of granite fell like dominoes, knocking other pillars of stone from their pedestals and sending up such a thick cloud of silver grit that Meredith couldn't see two feet in front of her, much less into the base of the quarry. Ross came running up to her. 'I can't find Az,' he said. 'I don't know how to stop it.'

She was breathing in rock; she was covered with residue. Meredith hooked her fingers into the chain-link fence. 'Lucy!' she yelled. *'Lucy!'*

The only answer was another round of bombardment, a one-sided war. The roar of rending stone was even louder than the blasts of dynamite, and rang in Meredith's ears. Then there seemed to be a détente, several long seconds of absolute silence, punctuated by the gravel avalanche of shifting granite.

Another person might not have heard it – the small gasp that preceded a sob – but Meredith would have been able to pick that sound out in the middle of a holocaust. 'Lucy,' she whispered, and she strained to see some evidence that her ears had not deceived her. She found it, huddling on a stone ledge – the thinnest flash of color through the haze, a magenta stripe of Lucy's T-shirt that hadn't been covered with gray powder. Meredith leaped onto the fence and began to climb.

'Meredith!'

She heard Ross's voice, before he simply stopped in mid-sentence and started after her. There was every chance that the dynamite hadn't run its course yet, that this was a lull to let things settle. Meredith could have cared less. She set her sights on Ethan and Lucy, down in the pit and five hundred yards away, and started her descent down a ladder drilled into the quarry wall.

At the bottom, she hesitated, daunted by fallen stone obelisks six times taller than she was. Determined, she scaled the first one and began to chart a course, the shortest distance between herself and her daughter. The rock scraped up her palms, and her own blood made it harder to grab hold. She slid down hard on one ankle and cried out, and at that moment Lucy caught a glimpse of her. 'Mommy!' she heard, that and crying, and she forced herself another fifty feet forward.

A horn went off, three long blasts. 'Get back,' Meredith yelled, urging them into the hollow of the cave they'd found. She covered her head, as if that might make a difference, just as the charge went off on the other side of the pit. The explosion was far enough away from where she huddled, but reverberations made the ground shake beneath her hands and feet. She felt the stone slide beneath her, her slick fingers scrabble for purchase, and then she was falling and landing all wrong, her bad leg brittle as a twig, as it snapped beneath the weight of the granite plate that pinned her.

Not again.

Ross saw the dynamite burst in slow motion; he heard the scrape and drag of rubble reshifting and it echoed in his ears with his own racing pulse. He could not speed up time; he could not make his arms and legs move fast enough. The entire world was being blown to bits around him and he was hypersensitive – the blasts louder, the explosions more brilliant – yet even in this cataclysm, Ethan's cry for help rang clear above everything else.

Ross was not aware of the unstable ground, the oncoming detonations, the sheer odds of getting across safely to the other side of the quarry pit. All he knew was that he would not let someone he loved die, again. That Ross was the only person who could save him. That this was what had to be done.

That history was *not* going to repeat itself.

By the time he reached Meredith, his calves were shredded to ribbons from the jagged granite. Blood ran down the side of his face where one flying shard had cut his temple. She was trapped beneath a shelf of rock as large as a grown man. 'The kids,' she gasped, and he nodded at her.

He jammed his boot into a fissure between two stones, stretched out with his hands, and then hauled himself forward. Again, and again. Sometimes the rocks would move beneath his feet or his hand would slip; from the bottom of the rubble Ross got up and kept inching forward. He kept his eyes on Ethan and Lucy, standing on that ledge behind a screen of dust, waiting for him.

The two leaning blocks that had formed a shelter for Lucy and Ethan suddenly collapsed. Lucy screamed and stepped as far out onto the ledge as she could. 'Hurry,' she cried. 'Please!'

After a thousand years, or maybe a heartbeat, Ross reached the base of the crumbling hill. He stretched for a handhold, and wedged his boot against the rubble, and started to climb. One hand over the other. One foot at a time. When he lifted his head, he could see the toes of Ethan's black sneakers.

A blast thundered behind his back, and then Ross was falling along with the wall he'd been trying to scale. He rolled to the left, a guess, and covered his head as rocks rained down in five-foot square cubes. Lucy's sobbing was louder now, and he could hear both Ethan and Meredith yelling his name. He stood up, wildly looking around to see how much damage had been done.

The ledge where Ethan and Lucy had been was still standing. But between it and the rock where he now stood was a chasm. A space six feet across and fifteen feet deep ran the length of the quarry, isolating the children on an island of stone.

Ross looked in both directions, and then into the new, vaulted pit. Its steep walls had been cut along the grain of the granite, a sheer drop. The only other way around was to cross all the way along the fissure to the southern edge of the quarry, scale the walls to the guardrail, and climb back in on the far side of the gap. 'Listen to me,' Ross yelled across. 'You're going to have to jump.'

Meredith had seen the whole thing – Ross's amazing progress across the devastated wreckage, his careful climb up toward Lucy and Ethan, the terrifying moment when the very mountain he was on deteriorated under his feet. When he disappeared out of her line of sight, she screamed for him, trying to turn so that she could locate him and setting off a wave of pain in her leg that nearly rendered her unconscious. Fighting to stay alert, she'd watched the ripple effect as a canyon split the bottom of the quarry in half, with the children on the other side.

It would be impossible for Ross to get all the way to the quarry wall and climb out, not before another explosion hit. He was right – the only way to save Lucy and Ethan was to catch them, once they leaped. Ethan would do what his uncle had asked. But Lucy – well, Lucy wouldn't jump. That required a depth of bravery that her daughter had never possessed.

Tears came to Meredith's eyes. 'Lucy,' she yelled, 'do it!'

They would die here, she and Lucy, buried by the rubble. She wished for courage, something that she might wing to her daughter. And just as she was thinking about fearlessness and taking flight,

Meredith saw Lucy take a step back, run for all she was worth, and soar into the air.

She landed hard in Ross's arms, knocking them both down; and on the side of safety now, she did not seem capable of letting go of him. Delighted, amazed – he hadn't expected her to jump, not before seeing Ethan make it to the other side – Ross kissed her forehead. 'I've got you,' he whispered into her hair as she sobbed against his shoulder. 'You're all right now.' He peeled the little girl away from him. 'I need to get Ethan, okay?'

'Okay,' Lucy sniffed. She wrapped her arms around her knees and ducked her head, still shaking.

Ross stood up again, cupping his hands around his mouth. 'Ethan, I won't let you fall.' He watched his nephew nod, race as fast as he could to the edge, and jump.

Ethan was Superman, and he was flying, and nothing – *nothing* – could stop him from saving the world, or at least himself. With his eyes closed he didn't have to look at how far away it was where Uncle Ross was standing, or at the broken-toothed rocks that were just waiting at the bottom of the pit. He stretched the tips of his fingers as far forward as they could go, and he chanted silently in his mind: *I am a bird; I am a plane; I am already there*.

When his fingers brushed something solid, he blinked right away and found himself hurtling into his uncle's embrace. He grabbed on tight and that was when the tears came, so quick and thick he couldn't even speak. His feet slid down Ross's legs, planting themselves firmly on the ground.

'You,' Uncle Ross gasped, 'are punished.'

And that was when the ground disappeared beneath them.

Ross felt them skidding down the slope into the crevasse, and he turned his body at the bottom so that he would bear the brunt of the fall. Ethan landed hard on top of him, and rocks dug into his legs and back. 'Get up,' Ross said, hauling his nephew to his feet. 'Are you all right?'

Ethan couldn't find words, but he nodded. Ross looked up. 'Lucy!' he cried. 'Where are you?'

A tiny white face appeared at the edge of the cliff overhead. Tears striped through the dust on her cheeks. Ross looked at the precipitous wall of rock – there were some spots where he could find holds to climb up, but he would never make it carrying Ethan. And Lucy wasn't strong enough to haul them up together.

'Ethan, I'm going to need you to help me,' Ross said. 'I'm going to put you on my shoulders, and you're going to have to climb up to the top by yourself. Lucy!' he yelled. 'I need you to grab hold of Ethan when he gets close, all right?'

He waited for her to answer, but she didn't. From where he stood, he could no longer even see where Lucy was. But if they waited, another explosion might go off. Another opportunity to climb could be lost. 'Come on,' he said to Ethan, crouching down so that the boy could scramble onto his shoulders. 'By the time you get to the top, she'll be there.'

Lucy was shaking so hard she could not catch her breath. She had seen the world turn inside out – the dawn go gray, the solid ground vanish, her mother trapped. Ross and Ethan were stuck in the bottom of that hole, and she was up here, and nothing was the way it should be. She covered her head with her arms, wishing she could make it all go away. It had worked before, after all – when you didn't want to see what was before your eyes, you simply had to keep them shut.

'Lucy!' That was Ross's voice. He wanted her to help Ethan up. But that would mean moving to the edge of that cliff, the one whose last edge had collapsed. And Lucy could not bring herself to do it.

'Hey!' Ethan's hand popped up over the lip of the chasm. 'Hey, Lucy, where are you? Uncle Ross, she's not coming!'

'Lucy!'

Lucy held her hands up to her ears. They would go away, all this would go away, and when she woke up she would be in her bed at home and the sun would be streaming through the windows and she wouldn't have to worry about ghosts.

She didn't have to worry about ghosts, though, not anymore. Lucy looked up, brought her hands to her side. Being brave didn't mean that you weren't scared out of your wits. You were – the whole time – but you just kept on doing what you had to.

She started to crawl to the edge of the cliff again, stopping only once when a little chunk of pebbles slid from beneath her palm into the ravine. Swallowing hard, she peered over the rim and saw Ethan, just a few feet beneath her, clinging to the rock wall like a spider.

Lucy lay down on her belly and pressed her cheek against the rock. Then she stretched out her right hand, the one that was closest to Ethan. She felt his fingers brush against hers, and then grab tight, a key to a lock.

Because she couldn't lift his weight, she made herself an anchor. He inched his way up her arm, grasping onto her shoulder and then hitching himself over the edge.

They stared at each other, panting, breathing in each other's air. 'Lucy,' Ethan said, his voice so husky that it was easy to imagine the man he might never become.

She managed a tiny smile. 'What took you so long?' she whispered.

Ross carried Lucy on his back, and guided Ethan footstep by footstep, as he carefully picked a path through the wreckage to the ladder on the other side of the quarry. Several times, he had to change his course as another distant explosion led to a rearrangement of the rocky landscape. It never occurred to him that they would not make it, and that alone was enough to propel him forward.

At the rusty ladder, he set Lucy on the rungs and told her to climb. Ethan went up behind her. 'Call 911,' Ross instructed. 'Break into the office if you have to.'

Ethan nodded. 'Aren't you coming?'

Ross looked over his shoulder. 'Not yet,' he said, and he squeezed Ethan's calf. 'Go.'

Then he crawled back the way he had come, frantically searching for the large tablet that had pinned Meredith. He hadn't heard her screaming for some time – either because she hadn't been, or because he'd been too busy to listen. By now there were many broad plates of granite scattered in the quarry; it was difficult to remember exactly where she had been. He crested a small rise of stone and saw Meredith's arm.

'Meredith!' he called, and she shook herself awake.

'Lucy?'

'Is fine. She's out.'

She could not see it, but her leg was bent back at a grotesque angle from her body. The large slab that had her pinned at the thigh was twice as wide as Ross, and as thick as his arm. To free her, he would need a smaller rock to make a lever, lift the slab, and drag Meredith away before the makeshift jack collapsed. Then he would have to immobilize her leg enough to carry her on his back across the rubble, like he had done with Lucy. 'Go get help, Ross,' Meredith said, crying.

'I *am* help.' He searched for something – anything – that might help him budge the rock. 'I'm going to try to lift this.'

She was shivering, a combination of pain and panic. 'Go back.'

Ross tried to get his weight underneath the rock, but it wouldn't move. In the distance a sounding horn blared, the warning of another round of explosions. He looked around frantically, trying to locate the dynamite or blasting cap. His eyes landed on Meredith, and the truth that stretched between them.

He couldn't help her.

He leaned down and brushed her hair out of her eyes. 'Ssh,' he whispered, and a charge shuddered somewhere to the left.

'Ross, go. Please.' She began to cry harder. 'I need to know that you got out of here safe.'

He forced a crooked smile onto his face. 'How many times do I have to tell you? I can't die.'

She reached for his hand, and the small movement unsettled the rocks beneath them. Ross lost his footing, going down hard on one knee beside Meredith's head. At the same time, they both noticed the small red tube about three feet beyond them.

Ross leaped over the rock that pinned Meredith and reached the stick of dynamite. He grabbed it in his fist and started running, sprinting on serrated granite, on broken stone, deeper into the quarry. Nothing mattered in that moment except getting as far away from Meredith as possible before the computers lit it off.

The charge swelled in his palm. In the instant before he let go of it, before an explosion hotter than a hundred suns razed the very spot where he stood, Ross had one moment where everything was crystal clear. He had saved Meredith, he had saved everyone. Maybe now, he had even made up for the rest of his life. The force of the blast knocked him head over heels and his skull struck hard against a ragged rock. And just as he considered that he might finally have found something worth living for, Ross discovered that he was not invincible after all.

By the time Eli and Shelby arrived, the first ambulances had already left. The quarry was crawling with uniformed policemen borrowed from other towns, who were roping off the site. Another detective was interviewing the owners of Angel Quarry, who had arrived hastily, in the company of their corporate lawyer. No one knew where Az Thompson – the night watchman – had gone; his absence made him the easiest scapegoat for blame.

Eli hurried over to a paramedic. 'The kids. Where are the kids?'

'They're all right. Cuts, bruises. The ambulance already went off to the hospital.'

He felt Shelby sag beside him, and he put his arm around her to keep her upright. Leaning close, he murmured words into her ear, comments that made no sense at all but were meant to give her a lifeline to hold onto.

'Can we go?' Shelby said. 'Now? To the hospital?'

But before he could answer, a commotion at the guardrail drew his attention. Three rescue workers gently lifted a stretcher over the edge. Strapped onto it, battered and bloody, was Meredith.

'Oh my God,' Shelby breathed, as she watched an unconscious Meredith being loaded into a waiting ambulance. Shelby seemed to notice, for the first time, Ross's car. Shelby grabbed a paramedic by the jacket. 'Where's my brother. *Where* is my brother?' When the man didn't answer, she refused to let go. 'Ross Wakeman,' she demanded. 'He's here somewhere.'

A silence fell. No one would answer her, and that was response enough. 'No,' Shelby cried, falling to her knees, as Eli's arms came around her. 'No!'

'He's at the hospital,' Eli said firmly. Then he turned to one of the EMTs. '*Right?*'

'Yeah, he's at the hospital.'

'See?' Eli helped Shelby stand, and carefully walked her to the truck. 'We'll go and find Ethan. And Ross.'

'Okay.' Shelby nodded through her tears. 'Okay.'

Eli closed the door. The paramedic touched his shoulder as he walked around to the driver's side. 'Uh, Detective. About that guy . . .'

'He's at the hospital,' Eli repeated.

'Yeah, but that was only a formality,' the paramedic said. 'He was dead before we even got to him.'

Ross was driving, and Aimee was in the passenger seat. 'Denmark,' he said.

She thought for a moment. 'Kyrgyzstan.'

He couldn't take his eyes off her, as if he had not seen her in ages, although he knew this could not possibly be true . . . they never spent more than seventy-two hours apart, and that only when Aimee was pulling the graveyard shift at the hospital. Ross found himself cutting glances away from the road to look at the curve of her jaw, the color of her eyes, the spot where her French braid fell against her back. 'New York,' he murmured.

Aimee rolled her eyes. 'Oh, come on, Ross, another *K*?'

'You have fifteen years of education; you can play a round of Geography.'

'Kalamazoo, then.'

He grinned and looked out the windshield. The car was moving quickly, and it was pouring outside, but he could swear that he'd seen someone he recognized walking along the edge of the highway – his old kindergarten teacher. She was wearing a yellow jumper Ross still recalled and her hair was in tight white pincurls. He looked again in the rearview mirror, but she was gone. 'Oshkosh,' Ross replied.

Aimee crossed her legs on the seat. She had taken off her shoes – she never liked to travel with shoes on. 'Heaven.'

'Heaven isn't a place.'

'Of course it is,' Aimee argued.

Ross raised a brow. 'And you know this for a fact.' He looked into his side mirror and nearly swerved: behind him on the opposite side of the road was his mother. She was wearing a sweater with little pearls around the top, one he remembered because as a child he'd sit in her lap and roll them between his fingers. She smiled at him, and waved.

His mother had been dead since 1996. His kindergarten teacher had been dead even longer than that. And Kyrgyzstan had still been in the U.S.S.R. when Aimee had died.

Heaven isn't a place.

Suddenly they curved around a bend and saw a tractor-trailer coming at them, in their lane. 'Ross!' Aimee cried out, and he jerked the steering wheel to the left, into the oncoming lane, noticing too late that a tiny car that had been hidden by the bulk of the truck was speeding toward them.

There was glass exploding inward, and the horrible screech of tires on a wet road, and the sudden, shocking impact of steel striking steel. Ross found himself sprawled outside the overturned car. The tractor-trailer had wobbled off to the side of the road with its driver thrown onto the horn so that the wail would not let up. Ross ratcheted open the passenger door, reached inside, and unbuckled Aimee.

Her shoulder was cut and blood stained her shirt, but her face, it was heart-shaped and smooth-skinned and stunning. Her French braid had unraveled, the impact loosening whatever she'd used to secure the bottom. It fanned over her chest like a silk shawl. 'Aimee,' he murmured. 'God.'

He sat down and pulled her into his lap, crying as the full force of his memories hit him in the gut. He brushed her hair away from her face, as the rain matted it together. 'I won't let you go. I won't leave.'

Aimee blinked at him. 'Ross,' she said, looking past his shoulder. 'You *have* to.'

In all of these years he had not recalled those words, that directive from Aimee that freed him from the blame of not being by her side when she died. He closed his arms more tightly around her and bent forward, but suddenly there was someone standing behind him, trying to get him to stand up just as hard as he was trying to stay.

He turned, furious, and found himself staring at Lia.

With Aimee in his arms, and Lia behind him, Ross went absolutely still. This was hell, a nightmare played out in his mind. Both women needed him; each held a half of his heart. *Which one do I go to?* he thought. *And which one do I lose?*

Lia tugged him upright, toward the other passenger car that

had crashed and now lay sideways against a highway barrier. Ross tried to break away from her, to get back to Aimee, certain that this was a test, the one thing he had to get right.

But by then he couldn't even see Aimee, because the other car was between them. Frustrated, Ross tore away from Lia's firm hold and yanked open the door of the totaled green Honda. A body lay crumpled into a heap behind the steering wheel, canted onto its side. Ross smelled gas; he knew the vehicle was going to blow at any minute.

He fumbled for the seat belt, which was stuck. 'Aimee,' he yelled over his shoulder. 'I'm coming. You hang on.' Another push of the button, and this time it sprang free. Ross reached in at an awkward angle with both hands and hauled the unconscious driver from the wreckage. He dragged the body a distance away, to the lip of the woods. There was a burst of light and heat, and the car torched into flame.

A fleet of sirens approached, a spray of water from a fire hose showered the car. As a paramedic ran up, Ross grabbed him. 'There's a woman at the other car who needs help,' he cried.

'Someone's already taking care of her.' The EMT knelt down beside Ross. 'What's this one's name?'

Ross did not know; it was a stranger. He glanced down at the body before him illuminated by the blaze, as he had done nine years ago. Just like then, there was a gash across the driver's hairline, and blood covering her face and her black dress. But this time, he saw her face – *really* saw her face – and everything was different. *My God.* 'Her name,' Ross said hoarsely, 'is Meredith.'

F. Juniper Smugg had been a resident for exactly twenty-seven days at Fletcher Allen Hospital in Burlington. He was doing a rotation in emergency medicine, but he really wanted dermatology or plastic surgery, something that wasn't a life-or-death specialty where he could go into private practice and not have to deal with all the surprises of a county medical center. Still, he was perfectly willing to pay his dues, which was why he didn't mind taking the body down to the morgue. It beat what they'd been doing to the guy when he arrived – shocking him and intubating him when any premed could have told you he was dead as a doornail upon arrival.

He was alone in the elevator. He pushed the button, waited till the doors closed, and turned to the mirrored wall so that he could watch himself rock out as he sang Smash Mouth vocals. He'd just gotten to the chorus of 'All-Star' when a hand grabbed his arm.

The dead man on the stretcher sat up. 'Shut the hell up,' he said huskily.

When the doors opened into the morgue, the dead man was standing, and the medical resident was slumped over the narrow stretcher. 'Can someone help me?' Ross asked the shocked staff. 'This guy's out cold.'

Once Az Thompson's body washed up on the shore of Lake Champlain, it was readied for burial within twenty-four hours, in keeping with native traditions. Winks Champigny, acting as a spokesperson for the Abenaki, recommended laying Az Thompson's remains to rest on the newly acquired property at the junction of Otter Creek Pass and Montgomery Road. He was interred facing east, on his side, to better see the sunrise.

In the months that followed, a seasonless garden that had never been planted would bloom around the grave – blackberries that did not dry up in winter, calla lilies that kept their heads above the snow line, holly and ivy that thrived in July. The site became a trysting spot for lovers, who valued its privacy and the scent of roses even in December, and who would come to catch sight of the black-haired boy and the blond girl often spied chasing each other through the wildflowers, feeding each other berries until their lips and fingers were stained red as blood.

*   *   *

Eli almost didn't come home that night. It was a hell of paperwork and arbitration with the owners of the quarry, and all he
wanted was to collapse next to Shelby and not wake up for the
next millennium.

Except that he wasn't sure if Shelby was ready to see him, or
anyone right now.

He had held her while she cried at the hospital, until she hiked
up her chin and said she needed to go home to make arrange-
ments. For the funeral, Eli presumed, but he'd felt her putting
up that wall and refusing to let anyone take care of her, and it
annoyed the hell out of him. He was going to shower and head
over there, whether she liked it or not.

He went to set his key in the door and realized it was open.
As it swung forward, he mustered his defenses, ready for anything.
But there was no thief in his kitchen. Just Shelby, her hands buried
in a bowl of flour.

'I broke in,' she said, her voice shaking. 'To a cop's house.'

Eli wrapped her close, kissed the top of her head. 'I'm sorry.
I'm so goddamn sorry.'

She was crying, and when she wiped her face with her finger
she left a white streak behind. 'I couldn't be at my house. I couldn't
make any calls to . . . to funeral homes. Reporters, they kept calling,
and I couldn't even listen to their messages. The doctors at the
hospital gave Ethan and Lucy something to make them sleep, so I
gave it to them here and put them in your bed. I made soup. And
bread. The phone rang once, but I didn't . . . I fed the dog for you.'

She was making no sense whatsoever, and yet Eli understood
every word that came out of her mouth. He rocked her in his
embrace and imagined her small white handprints on the back
of his suit jacket, as ghostly as the ones that had risen in the
mirror at the old Pike place. Shelby wiped her nose on his shirt.
'I'll go if you want.'

'Don't,' he whispered. 'Ever.'

*   *   *

Meredith looked nothing like Lia. Ross didn't know how he had ever even seen a resemblance, now. Her eyes were set farther apart, her hair was a completely different texture. Her skin, it looked to be as soft, but he did not want to touch her to find out, in case he'd disturb her sleep.

She was in traction. Her leg had been pinned and hoisted and set. Her bloodstream was pumped full of painkillers. Ross had been allowed into her room only because no one at the hospital seemed prepared to deny a man who had been dead just hours earlier.

He had tried to find Shelby first, or Ethan, but they had been released. Lucy had gone with them. Yet when Ross tried to call her house, there had been no answer, and the message machine had been turned off. He would have called Eli, but he could not seem to remember his home phone number, if he'd ever known it in the first place. The neurologist who had examined Ross after his head contusions had been stitched up said his memory might be like that – full of gaps and spots that might or might not come back. For example, he had no recollection of what he'd been doing before he found Meredith frantically searching for the kids at Shelby's. He could not remember how he'd gotten the fine white spiderweb scars on his wrists.

What he did recall was Lia's face, something he would have died to see again – and *had,* apparently. He could conjure her, and Aimee, as if they were close enough to stand two feet in front of him. Ross knew that he could have stayed back there – wherever that had been, exactly. But even more than he had wanted to hold Aimee in his arms, to follow Lia wherever she led him . . . he wanted to be with his sister. His nephew. Maybe Meredith.

Ross had spent so many years searching for something, he'd never realized that what you found might not be as important as the act of trying to find it. A life wasn't defined by the moment you died, but all the others you'd spent living.

As he watched, a tear tracked down Meredith's cheek. Her eyes
opened just a crack, and she focused on Ross. 'Lucy,' she whispered.

'She's fine.'

As her surroundings dovetailed into her memories, Meredith
startled. She cried out at the pain in her leg and the touch of
Ross's hands to settle her. 'You're a ghost.'

He smiled at that. 'Not anymore.'

'The dynamite – it exploded in your hand. I saw you,' she
said. And then added, more softly: 'They told me . . . you'd died.'
She tried to struggle upright again, and as she jogged her leg, her
eyes rolled back in agony.

'Stay still.' He stared at her face, at the hairline scar he'd
never noticed. 'You broke the leg you broke before in your car
accident. In six places. The fibula and tibia were crushed; they
operated and put a pin in.' Ross assumed that Meredith would
think the doctors had told him of her condition, but she surprised
him with her acuity.

'I never told you,' she said warily, 'that I was in a car accident.'

He sat down on the edge of the bed. 'You were driving a green
Honda and wearing a black dress,' Ross said quietly. You cut yourself . . . here.' He touched the spot on her forehead. 'They never
found your shoes.'

'You're not going to tell me you're psychic, too,' Meredith said
weakly.

'No,' Ross replied. 'I'm going to tell you I was there.'

He stared at her, unblinking, until the part of memory buried
so deep it's never more than a flicker fanned a flame, until her
eyes widened just a fraction. 'Twice,' she said, her voice groggy,
as she reached for his hand. Her lids drifted shut. 'Superman.'

He waited until Meredith's breathing evened out, and then his
fingers tightened around hers. 'Maybe,' he conceded.

Ethan swung his legs on the bench outside the hospital, waiting
for Lucy to get caught. She was walking in the drizzling rain

along the top edge of a five-foot brick wall behind the range of vision of a security guard. When she reached the end she did a little hop, like one of those gymnastics wizards on a balance beam, and then leaped off to land behind the guard and scare ten years off the poor guy's life.

He whipped around, and Lucy gave him that sweet Shirley Temple smile that cleared her every time.

In the past month, she'd become a daredevil. She was forever climbing onto roofs and hanging her head out of the windows of moving cars and renting the biggest chain-saw gore-fests from the video store. Ethan knew it was his fault; he'd created a monster. The shrink that they both had to go to, for something called post-traumatic-stress-disorder therapy, said it was a reaction to a near death experience. Ethan, of course, knew better.

He pulled down the sleeves of his long-sleeved shirt and tugged the brim of his baseball cap lower. He didn't feel like a mutant in front of the hospital, because other people came and went with all kinds of tubes and bags attached. Besides, he wasn't even the biggest freak in his household anymore. That honor belonged to Uncle Ross, who had been declared clinically dead and lived to tell about it.

He was fine, or so he'd told everyone from Oprah to Larry King to the Reverend Billy Graham, via a live feed to his hospital room. He was being released today after a month's observation – not for his sake, really, but for all the doctors who came to poke at him and try to figure out what had made him come back to life. Meredith was being released too. His mom and Eli had gone inside to wheel them out.

Ethan had visited his uncle a bunch of times while he was in the hospital. He'd coached him to the point where he could almost win one poker hand out of five. And he'd spent a lot of time just talking to him, because even if Ethan didn't want to let himself get his hopes up, you couldn't help but wonder if that kind of luck was a once-in-a-lifetime thing, or something that might be passed down to, say, other generations.

The last time he'd come to visit, his uncle had let him eat all the green Jell-O and noodle soup, and had brought him to Meredith's room. She told Ethan that even though his DNA couldn't repair itself, some scientist in New York had invented a cream that could repair the DNA damage already done. And people in her own lab were working on gene replacement therapy, which might cure XP permanently.

Who was Ethan to say a miracle couldn't strike twice? It ran in the family, after all.

'Hey, check that out.' Lucy dug an elbow into his side and pointed. 'That's weird.'

It was a double rainbow, one tucked beneath the bend of the other. But you could only see the left half of it, curving to the midpoint of the sky before melting into muddy blue.

The right side of the rainbow wasn't missing, Ethan knew, even if he and Lucy couldn't see it. It wasn't wishful thinking, or magic, but a simple law of nature. After all, once you know that part of something exists, it stands to reason that the rest of it is somewhere out there, too.

AUTHOR'S NOTE

This book is a work of fiction. However, the Vermont Eugenics Project in the 1920s and 1930s is not. It is a chapter of history that has only recently been rediscovered and that still causes great pain and shame to Vermonters of many different cultural backgrounds. The archives of the Eugenics Survey are housed today in the Public Records Office in Middlesex, Vermont – many examples of which serve as epigraphs in the middle section of this book.

Spencer and Cissy Pike, Gray Wolf, Harry Beaumont, and Abigail Alcott are characters I created, but Henry F. Perkins *did* exist. As pointed out by Nancy Gallagher on her Web site 'Vermont Eugenics: A Documentary History' (www.uvm.edu/~eugenics), he was a professor of zoology at the University of Vermont who organized the Eugenics Survey of Vermont in conjunction with his course on heredity. He believed that through research, public education, and support for legislation, the growing population of Vermont's most problematic citizens might be reduced. His leadership was instrumental in bringing about the passage of Vermont's Sterilization Law in 1931, and he continued to teach genetics and eugenics until his retirement from UVM in 1945.

Although it was titled a Law for Human Betterment by Voluntary Sterilization, there are doubts about just how voluntary a procedure it truly was. Evidence suggests that a person could be sterilized simply if two doctors signed off on it. Thirty-three states enacted a sterilization law. During the war crimes trials after World War II, Nazi scientists cited American eugenics programs as the foundation for their own plans for racial hygiene.

In the 1960s and 1970s, the ACLU targeted sterilization laws, leading to the successful repeal of many. Others were stripped of eugenic language and reworded to protect the rights of the indi-

vidual. Several states have passed resolutions officially censuring
the American eugenics movement and expressing regret for their
role in it. Vermont has not.

Henry Perkins died in 1956, just when the structure of DNA
had been discovered. Reproductive technology and genetic diagnosis are the new face of eugenics. And in a strange case of history
repeating itself, Human Genome Project research continues to be
done in Cold Spring Harbor, New York – the site, in 1910, of
America's newly formed Eugenics Record Office at the Station for
Experimental Evolution.

For those interested in finding out more about eugenics, I have
enclosed a bibliography of books and documents that were instrumental to me during the writing of this book. I would also like
to thank Fred Wiseman, Charlie Delaney, and Marge Bruchac for
enlightening me from the Abenaki point of view; Mike Hankard
and Brent Reader for initial Abenaki translations, and Joseph Alfred
Elie Joubert from Odonak Indian Reservation, P. Que., Canada,
for making corrections to the Abenaki phrases in the text, as well
as teaching me proper pronunciation. I am also indebted to Kevin
Dann, who in 1986 recovered the ESV documents, made sure
the world stood up and took note, and then let me explore his
files and his own imaginings in order to create a structure upon
which I could then build my own. And finally, I am grateful to
Nancy L. Gallagher, who graciously taught me what she knew
from her research for *Breeding Better Vermonters: The Eugenics
Project in the Green Mountain State,* and whose command of the
facts was invaluable. Readers interested in exploring this topic
further should read that book or visit her Web site, 'Vermont
Eugenics: A Documentary History' (www.uvm.edu/~eugenics).
I made liberal use of her insights and documents, which provided
the historical materials for my novel.

Without the work of these people, I never could have completed
my own.

Jodi Picoult

BIBLIOGRAPHY

Anderson, Elin. *We Americans: A Study of Cleavage in an American City*. Cambridge, MA: Harvard University Press, 1937.

Bandler, James. 'The Perkins Solution.' Vermont Sunday Magazine, *Rutland Herald,* April 9, 1995.

Dann, Kevin. 'Playing Indian: Pageantry Portrayals of the Abenaki in the Early Twentieth Century.' From a talk presented at a UVM conference, Burlington, Vermont, November 1999.

Dolan DNA Learning Center, Cold Spring Harbor Laboratory, New York. 'Image Archive on the American Eugenics Movement.' Online resource, www.eugenicsarchive.org.

Eugenics Survey of Vermont and the Vermont Commission on Country Life. Papers, Public Records Office, Middlesex, VT.

Gallagher, Nancy L. *Breeding Better Vermonters: The Eugenics Project in the Green Mountain State*. Hanover, NH: University Press of New England, 1999.

Gallagher, Nancy L. 'Vermont Eugenics: A Documentary History.' Online resource, www.uvm.edu/~eugenics.

Kincheloe, Marsha R. and Herbert G. Hunt, Jr. *Empty Beds: A History of Vermont State Hospital*. Barre, VT: Northlight Studio Press, 1988.

Laws of Vermont. 31st Biennial session (1931): 194–96. No. 174 – An Act for Human Betterment by Voluntary Sterilization.

Oatman, Michael. 'Long Shadows: Henry Perkins and the Eugenics Survey of Vermont.' Exhibit at Mass MOCA, Spring 2001.

Wiseman, Fred. *The Voice of the Dawn: An Autohistory of the Abenaki Nation*. Hanover, NH: University Press of New England, 2001.